for Donna

Enjoy

Patrick Fanning

# Infidels Abroad

## A Novel
### of Mark Twain &
### John Singer Sargent
### in an Alternate California

Written & Illustrated by

# Patrick Fanning

# ArtWorks Press

ArtWorks Press
9155 Grey Street
Graton, CA 95444
www.fanningartworks.com

MANUFACTURED IN THE UNITED STATES OF AMERICA

LIBRARY OF CONGRESS
CATALOGING-IN-PUBLICATION DATA
FANNING, PATRICK
INFIDELS ABROAD: A NOVEL OF MARK TWAIN
& JOHN SINGER SARGENT IN AN ALTERNATE CALIFORNIA

ISBN 978-1-300-19873-4

## Acknowledgments

I would like to thank my wife Nancy Kesselring for her patience, love, and support; Donna Yonash, Marylu Downing, Guy Biederman, Matt McKay for critiquing early drafts; my colleagues in Guy's fiction seminar for their feedback and examples of persistence; Jo-Anne Rosen and Marko Fong of Wordrunner eChapbooks for publishing an early excerpt; Evelyn McClure of the Western Sonoma County Historical Society for letting me raid the archives; Katherine Rinehart of the Sonoma County Library for her help in locating photos; and finally, Daniel Celidore for letting me steal his jokes.

## To Art Lovers:

You can see full color versions of the watercolors
and oil paintings that illustrate this book
at www.fanningartworks.com

## 1. I Meet Mark Twain

The steamship from the Sandwich Islands to San Francisco carried mostly cargo, with only a dozen passengers: myself, a Catholic priest with wife and five children, a retired colonel in an unspecified army, a sugar plantation manager, and Mark Twain.

At first I had no idea Mr. Twain was on the boat, since I spent the first half of the voyage in my tiny cabin or at the rail, in the throes of *mal de mer,* too sick for company. When I finally found my sea legs and ventured into society, it was late in the evening of our fourth day at sea. I entered the cramped "saloon" in search of food. The bar was deserted, and only one table was occupied, by three boisterous men playing cards. Oil lamps swung gently from the overhead beams, bathing the men with an ochre light and casting ultramarine violet shadows on the wall that moved with the undulations of the ship. I took some deep breaths, cautiously ate a cracker from a jar on the bar, and watched the game.

Mr. Twain was stacking coins and shuffling cards, looking and talking like a character from one of his books. He was a tall, thin, but vigorous older man of 44 years, with a fierce mustache and a corona of flaming red hair. A long crooked cigar was clamped in his teeth as he dealt cards, wobbled in his lips as he talked, or waved about in his hand as he used it like a conductor's baton to punctuate his drawling speech. His dark eyes seemed to smolder and then spark as he glanced my way, and I felt he could see more of one's character than one might choose to reveal.

"Pull up a pew," he said to me, gesturing at a chair that was screwed to the deck. "We need a fourth to dilute the odds and swell the congregation. I'm Mark Twain, this is the Sugar Plum Fairy, and that reprobate is Colonel Sutherland."

"Pleased to meet you," I said, sliding into the chair, "I'm John Sargent."

"Welcome to the fold. Are you familiar with a little game called Molokai Scratch?"

He had just published *The Adventures of Tom Sawyer* in 1878, a year before, when I was studying painting with Carolus in Paris. Even though we expatriate art orphans were buried to our eyebrows in chiaroscuro and perspective, we knew his name. Mark Twain was the great American rustic, casting his irreverent eye over our decadent age and deflating pomposity wherever he found it. I was 23 at the time and stood in awe of his accomplishments.

I said, "Sorry, I'm not familiar with Molokai Scratch. Is it anything like Whist?"

"Very much like, except you deal only three cards at a time, black sevens and nines are wild for face cards, and there are no rubbers, no dummy, and no trump suit. Here, I'll deal a hand for practice and you can be the Itch first. After you master Itching we'll make you an expert Scratcher."

I never learned all the rules, but it soon became obvious that Molokai Scratch was similar to Whist in only one way: a team of two players could communicate in code and distort the odds in their favor. Mr. Twain and Colonel Sutherland across from him were engaged in a lively exchange of blinks, coughs, sneezes, throat-clearings, and knuckle-crackings that soon won all the loose coins in my pocket.

"Oh, I forgot to tell you," Mr. Twain said at one point, raking in my last centavo, "In the third round, black sevens are only wild for black queens."

I excused myself and retired to a chair where I could sketch the card players surreptitiously. I made Mark Twain the focal point of the composition, placing his companions in silhouette and casting them in shadow. He had large hands with long tapering fingers that dipped and hovered over the cards and coins like gliding birds. He was wearing a burnt sienna suit of clothes over a cadmium scarlet vest, but I would paint him in banker's broadcloth to show his prosperity as a popular author, with a slouch hat and bent cheroot to show his frontier roots.

I calculated that he was or would soon be part of the *nouveau riche* class who can afford to have their portraits painted, at least by a cut-rate *nouveau artiste* such as myself. The gift of a charcoal study would be a good investment in future patronage. Perhaps his publisher would be in need of an accurate likeness in conté, on which to base a frontispiece engraving?

## 2. *Parvenu*

Mary Sargent, c/o Sanderson
Apartments Genessee
10 Clarastrasse
Berne, Switzerland
May 21, 1879

Dear Mother:

I trust this finds you and Father both well and well-settled into the Sandersons' apartments. I am sorry to hear that the Swiss winter has lingered beyond its welcome, and hope that *le printemps* comes soon to Berne.

We dock tomorrow in San Francisco after a long voyage. The days in the Sandwich Islands were glorious for sketching and painting. I have considerable material for exotic backgrounds, and one sketch of a native that might make a stunning oil in the style of Millais, but with more intense, saturated color.

This trip has exposed me to a much wider variety of images than I could have experienced in Paris or on a more conventional grand tour. I am very grateful for the support you and Father have given me and predict that it will be returned many times over when my portraits start gracing the salons of Europe.

Please excuse my hubris, but I am excited because I have become acquainted with my fellow passenger Mark Twain—

yes, *that* Mark Twain, the author of *The Innocents Abroad,* the book with the cerulean cover that you found so inaccurate but amusing last fall in Vienna.

If ever a *parvenu* required a portrait to announce his fresh-minted status to the world, Mr. Twain is that gentleman. His lean features and rustic state of *deshabille* would be delightful in paint, perhaps in contrast to an otherwise bland and derivative pose.

I plan to present to Mr. Twain a sketch I made of him playing bridge, hoping to plant a seed that will ultimately flower as a commission for a full-length portrait in oils. Given the popularity of his books, I do not think that 800 or 900 suisse francs would be out of the question. And he is just the sort of *outré* subject that might stand out among the usual *coterie* of coal merchants and minor nobles that one found so enervating in the portrait room of last year's *Salon de Paris.* A Mark Twain portrait coupled with an exotic tropical scene from the islands might be a winning combination for my entry in next year's show.

The purser wants all mail in the bag by midnight for delivery upon docking tomorrow, so I must make this a very brief note. Promising to write later at length, I remain…

Your loving son,

John

### 3. I Meet John Sargent

In May of 1879 *The Adventures of Tom Sawyer* was selling tolerably well, making my peculiar blend of tragedy and frivolity welcome on the lecture circuit. I voyaged from my home in the Sandwich Islands to San Francisco to deliver another round of travel lectures in the Republic of Alta California. That winter I had changed my name legally to Mark Twain and was resolved to leave that dour old humbug Sam Clemens behind me in the wake.

I was traveling with my new Submarine Super Camera, a tiny, cunning instrument, with which I made several photographs of our vessel, the steamer *Jupiter.* When I developed the negatives later, I found that the still images failed to capture the vessel's essential meaness. The ship was of the tramp variety: too small for sugar, too large for coffee, too Spartan for passengers, and so she specialized in a little of each. She was about as long as two streetcars and about as wide as one. I could reach the water when she lay over sideways in the swells, which she did constantly, to the detriment of one's digestion. Turned to meet the mountainous peaks of the Pacific head-on, the *Jupiter* pitched like a see-saw. At one moment the bowsprit was taking a deadly aim at the sun in midheaven, and at the next it was trying to harpoon a shark in the bottom of the ocean.

I spent most of my time in the saloon, waiting for the bar to open, playing euchre, draughts, and dominoes with my fellow passengers. There I first met John Singer Sargent, three days out from Honolulu, when he emerged from his cabin, green as spring grass, and staggered into the saloon in search of sustenance and entertainment. He was pale as any ghost, and in fact reminded me strongly of my own personal ghost, the shade of my brother Henry. Sargent had the same clear brow, the same open, innocent, quizzical expression.

He was a polished, charming young man of about 25 years of age, earnest, poised, and confident; but I am always prepared to forgive that in a tenderfoot. There was something energetic and engaging about the sprout that made it hard to get shut of him. As to character, he was a raw nerve, an empty vessel, a swelling bud, and my old pal Colonel Sutherland and I took pity on him. We resolved to soothe his nerves, fill his emptiness, and tap the swelling bud of his purse with a friendly game of Molokai Scratch.

At our invitation he demurred with the usual tenderfoot's protestations, as easily overcome as the average Sunday school teacher's claims of ignorance of drink, dice, or damsels of uneasy virtue.

"You would do us great honor if you would agree to complete our circle," I insisted.

"The honor is mine, Mr. Twain." He took his seat in surrender, running up the white flag and spiking all his guns.

Scratch is the preferred game of Honolulu's card sharks because it is Episcopal in its complexity, Presbyterian in its flexibility, and Quakerish in the silent, covert cooperation that is possible between two experienced devotees. Scratch is the bastard son of Euchre out of Stud Poker while Whist wasn't watching. Compared to Scratch, all other card games are like dancing with your sister. Colonel Sutherland and I were confirmed Scratchers and young Sargent was the perfect Itch.

"I beg your pardon, Mr. Twain," John asked, "But did you say that fives and sevens are wild?"

"Only black fives and sevens, and only for face cards."

"Then I believe I have four Kings," he said, laying down his hand.

"Normally that would be true, but this is the third rubber, in which wild cards apply only to black queens. In this instance you have two fives and two kings, and the Colonel takes the pot with three queens."

"I see. Thank you for the clarification."

He was wonderfully polite, reminding me again of my poor late brother Henry. Someone, probably his maternal relative, had trained him well, but with application he would soon learn to overcome his limited upbringing. When we had cleaned him out he retired with good grace to his sketchbook. The next morning he presented me with a wonderfully detailed drawing of myself dealing three-handed Whist. I accepted it with thanks and admiration, and thus I first introduced the camel's nose of trust into my tent of native caution.

## 4. Still Your Sammy Boy

Mary Clemens
17 Thatcher Street
Davis, Missouri
U.S.A.
May 21, 1879

Dear Mother:

Thank you for your letter of the 29th, and for the capital red
mittens. I marvel that your poor hands, after all these many
years of caring for our family, can still knit such clever
contraptions. I was the toast of Honolulu when I wore them at
home, and they were even more useful upon the frigid Pacific
waters approaching San Francisco.

We have steamed into San Francisco Bay through the
narrow opening called *La Porta Dorada*, or "Golden Gate."
I have made a photograph of it with my new portable
camera. Sometime tomorrow I will start touring about in
Alta California, lecturing on the Islands and reading from the
Spanish edition of *Innocents Abroad.* I am eager to catalogue
the differences between the twice-removed Spaniards of the
New World and their originals in Spain. Although my visa to
visit Rossland, north of Alta California, was not approved,
I still have hopes of visiting that country as well. Since so
few journalists have described Rossland, it would make a
compelling chapter or two in my next travel book.

One of my fellow passengers on this voyage is Father Juan
O'Toole, a Catholic priest of the Western variety, traveling
with his wife and five children. I think it very perspicacious
of the local Pope to allow his clergy to marry. Matrimony
brings a man of God down closer to the common level, and
can serve as spiritual galoshes on feet of clay. Father Juan is
returning to California after sixteen years of missionary work
in the Sandwiches. He assured me that the Baptists and other

Protestant denominations have sufficient toehold in California to provide me with spiritual succor during my travels, so you need not worry on that account.

As regards my recent change in name, please do not think I mean any disrespect whatsoever to you or to Father. In the beginning, signing my works "Mark Twain" was a purely commercial stratagem, intended to create in the minds of readers a rustic persona whose books they would habitually buy. Putting the same name on my passport and hotel registers merely clears up silly confusions while traveling. In all other areas and at all other times, I am still your Sammy boy, so you need not bullyrag me so. In addition, did not some of the greatest heroes in history change their names? To wit, Zeus became Jupiter, and Poseidon became Neptune. I'm sure their mothers adjusted to the change gracefully, and Providence has vouchsafed me the most gracious of mothers.

Thank you for inquiring so delicately about my diet and the condition of my digestion. I am in excellent health, sleeping the night through soundly, and my commitment to Temperance is firm as ever. Barley water and lemonade are my preferred beverages, and I do not like them too strong.

You will note that I have reached the end of the page without employing a single contraction, neologism, rusticity, or any other usage requiring the dread apostrophe. I wanted to prove to you that I am capable of dignified discourse, although writing this way feels to me like talking through an excessively tight collar. I cain't hardly stan' it nomores.

Your Loving Son,

Sam

## 5. A Humorist, Not a Politician

William Dean Howells
Atlantic Weekly
Boston, Massachusetts, USA
May 22, 1879

Dear William:

Thank you for your warning, however belatedly received. Your letter arrived just as I was embarking on my voyage to Alta California—soon enough to take heed and have ample fodder for worry; too late to do anything about it. Actually, I never worry. I cannot fret myself over the future because I have so much in my past to regret that it occupies my mind entirely.

Yours was not the only rumor of war I have heard, but I discount them. I am a humorist, not a politician. I doubt strongly that the powerful and greedy of Alta California and Rossland will even notice my sojourn there. And at the first sign of trouble, I plan to cut and run. However, if any political morsels fall my way, I will duly report them to you, and you may pass them on to your friends in Washington.

If I can find a suitable dark room somewhere, I will send you photographic specimens of my travels. I have just made an exposure of the dock on *Isla de los Angeles*, using my new

plaything, a tiny Submarine Super Camera from Japan that
fits in the palm of my hand and uses high grade 2x3 inch dry
glass plates, of which I have a ridiculously large supply in a
cunningly fitted case that is lined in plush and proofed against
light and moisture. Perhaps I will make a portrait of myself
in some wonderfully exotic locale, to use as the basis for an
engraved frontispiece in my next travel book.

I am doomed to lecture yet again on the Sandwich Islands,
Europe, the Holy Lands, etc. etc. I have translated some of
my best stories and jokes into Spanish, Esperanto, and even
Russian, in the hopes that I can get a visa to Rossland. The
Spanish I find most humorous and commodious, with room
for even the occasional pun. Esperanto is a little stiff and
awkward, like dancing with your granny. Being a recently
and rationally constructed language, it lacks idiomatic
expressions, regional accent, or literary history. One can tell a

joke in Esperanto, but it is rough sledding. As for Russian, it is suitable for only the most scatological or physical humor.

Although I have reservations about the lecturing part of this trip, I am glad of the opportunity to pen some travel letters for you. I would relish including a visit to you in this trip, however I reckon finances will not permit. The train fare from California to Boston is shamefully dear, more of a tariff than a toll. I would encourage you to come west to meet me, if I did not know how you are shackled to the grind of weekly publication. The trip would take a week out here and a week back, and without two issues of the Atlantic, the poor old U. S. of A. might perish. And anyhow, the Californians are unlikely to issue a visa to a ruffian like yourself. You really should concentrate more on the literary side of things and take less interest in politics—then you could drop your news coverage, put out a monthly literary rag, and become an impoverished man of letters and leisure like the rest of us.

Your obedient etc.,

Mark Twain


## 6. Isla de los Angeles

I found Mr. Twain on deck the next morning, smoking and playing shuffleboard by himself. He pointed at the empty court opposite him.

"Keep an eye on my opponent," he said. "I think he's cheating. I can't abide a cheat at horse billiards."

I presented him with my sketch of him playing cards the night before.

"By Jove, what a remarkable likeness," he said. "I look just like my Uncle Sowberry Finn that was hung for card sharking." He held the paper at arm's length and squinted at it through a haze of cigar smoke. "You haven't finished these other two gents," he said.

"That is intentional," I explained, "you are the center of interest, and so are rendered in more detail. For the other figures and the setting, I draw just the impression of the thing, not every detail of the thing itself."

"Well, I reckon I can't complain about being the center of interest, but in my experience, I'd rather smoke a real cigar than an impression of one."

We conversed genially at the rail as the boat entered the Bahia de San Francisco, a vast expanse of choppy gray water with scarcely a reflection or horizon line. In between lengthy stories about his steamboat days, Mr. Twain told me about the lecture and writing tour he was beginning. He invited me to his first lecture in Petalumo, a small town to the north, where he would address the local intelligentsia on his travels and adventures.

I said, "I'm surprised that you do not start your tour in San Francisco. It is the capital, after all."

"Oh no, it is never done that way. My lecture agent has booked me into the smaller country towns first. I'll work my way up the coast, polishing my Spanish and spying out the local gossip. Then I'll swing inland to the east, and circle back to San Francisco in about four weeks. I need to sharpen my wits on the rural strop before trying to skin the city folks."

"I don't see how your wits could get much sharper."

"Aw, shucks." He shook his head, a pretty blush revealing coppery freckles across his generous nose. "Sharpening the wits is a matter of timing, mostly. Every region has a preferred pace, a rate at which they can best follow a story or a joke."

"Like a horse?" I asked, forcing myself to stop staring at his complexion. He was one of the most compelling men I had ever met.

"Yes, an audience is much like a horse. You dasn't lecture at a gallop to a critter that was born to canter."

Then it was time to get our luggage on deck to clear customs on Isla de los Angeles, a small island in the bay. The customs official was curious as usual that I carry an American passport but have never been to the United States of America. I had to explain that I was born in England to American parents, reared in Switzerland, and educated in France and Spain. My parents did not return to America during my childhood, since the country was wracked by civil war and unrest. They say it is mostly peaceful now, but still economically depressed—not the sort of place an aspiring portrait artist longs to visit.

The customs man was very swarthy, burnt umber with a touch of scarlet and chromium yellow, perhaps a mixed blood with Spanish and Indio combined. His high cheekbones were almost Moroccan. On the crowded docks I saw complexions from peaches and cream to pure Negro. There were lots of soldiers standing around, and some rushing to and fro in small groups. The immigration officials took a long time to check our papers, checking our names against long printed lists and conferring with each other in whispers. We had to sign six different papers and get three stamps on our passports.

When we were finally approved and admitted to the country, I stuck close to Mr. Twain, following him to the booking office. There he was met by a short Spaniard in a yellow ochre suit and a mismatched sap green overcoat with a seal collar. The man introduced himself to Twain as Hilario Amado, the local lecture agent.

"And this is Marina Milanova," the agent said, "who will be your guide and translator." He pushed forward a slim girl not much older than I. She was taller and more slender than most Mexican women, with sharp features, pale complexion, and very dark, arched eyebrows.

"Mucho gusto," she said to Twain, and gave him a lingering handshake.

From that moment, I ceased to exist for Mark Twain. He transferred the sunshine of his regard immediately to *la femme*, and I was cast into her shade.

I trailed behind the happy couple, and I bought passage on

the same small stern wheel launch that would take us up the Rio Petalumo. The trip took nearly two hours, and Twain and his translator chatted as bright as two sparrows at the rail the whole time, addressing perhaps three words to me. I leaned on the rail and took in the landscape as the narrow, winding river revealed scene after scene.

Trumpeter swans and egrets dotted the reedy wetlands like little flecks of titanium white flake. The river twisted and turned like a lazy snake, pewter, silver, and white under leaden skies backlit with a barely golden light—just one short shade beyond silver gray. Mr. Twain brought out a very small camera and photographed nearly every boat we passed, entirely ignoring the natural scenery.

The sun came out in true gold as we glided into the grand canal of Petalumo, which Mr. Twain immediately dubbed the "Venice of the West," with good reason. I began to ache for my paints. Like the real Venice, this is a paradise for the watercolorist. Where most cities have streets of dead dark cobbles, Petalumo and Venice have streets of water. Alternating wide and narrow canals reflect and multiply the light. Arching bridges cast velvety shadows enlivened with gleams of dark, pure cobalt blue and cadmium orange.

Petalumo differs from the original in several ways. Where Venice is all marble and plaster, Petalumo is timber frames of curly-cued redwood and oak, or thick adobe atop native sandstone foundations. The Steam Age is more prominent here, with railroad bridges across the canals, steam dredges dragging channels for steam launches to thread, and the gondoliers cursing them both. Both cities share tile roofs, but in Venice church spires dominate, whereas Petalumo boasts overtopping grain elevators, shot towers, and a Moorish minaret.

### 7. Any Hue I Desire

Violet Paget
17 Rue Des Jardins
Montparnasse
Paris, France
May 22, 1879

My Dear Violet:

Greetings to you and all the poor starving inmates of les Beaux Arts. I enjoyed your "Vernon Lee" review of the student show. It served as an *aide-mémoire* of the life-and-death value we put on our student works, and how much they all look alike despite our efforts to distinguish ourselves. I wonder if I shall ever scrape all trace of the B.A. house style off my canvases?

Would you prefer me to address these letters to Vernon Lee? I still think it a shame your critical pieces cannot appear to be written by a woman. Genius should be qualification enough for publication, regardless of the sex of its owner. It remains difficult for me to think of you as Vernon, although you look quite fetching in trousers.

You will be astonished to hear that I am currently traveling with Mark Twain! I met him on the boat to San Francisco and he invited me to accompany him on the lecture circuit. *Naturellement,* I intend to secure a commission, either from himself, his family, or his publishers, to paint his portrait. But I do not want to appear too eager. I will strive to insinuate myself as a fellow traveler first. I would like to be his translator, but he is already equipped with one, a young lady called Marina, part Russian and part Indian, very exotic. She seems to have set her cap for me, never mind that mine is set more toward Mark Twain.

Mr. Twain and I are getting along famously so far, when I can get his attention. He is quite good looking, and still unmarried at 44 years old, which makes me wonder a bit about his predilections. However, he is not at all flirtatious with me, and is quite attentive to la Marina, alas. I put this in merely to satisfy your perverse curiosity—I know you will ask about this, and you know I shall remain the soul of discretion myself.

I am not sure that Twain really needs a translator. He spent this afternoon and all the evening prowling the waterfront bistros, sampling the harsh local wine and ale, swapping stories with the *demimonde,* and soaking up the local atmosphere. Although his Spanish is quite rudimentary, I admire how he is able to draw out anyone, of any class, at any time.

I spent this afternoon sketching and painting a view of the grand turning basin of the Rio Petalumo. Here two major canals intersect the natural course of the river, and the summer *palacios* of the Mexican Dons from San Francisco abut grain elevators and feed mills built to an Egyptian scale.

Towards sunset a fine, oblique gold light gave a jewel-like quality to the scene, like a wash of dilute raw sienna suspended in walnut oil. The rough and ready nature of the frontier architecture gives a more vigorous aspect to the waterscape than one finds in the original Venice. The scene combines elegant Venetian luxury with the odiferous necessities of the Valencia stockyards. What this land lacks in history it makes up in energy and aromas.

Over the course of this trip I have settled on a *plein aire* watercolor outfit that works well for me. I have in my pallette

three primary and three secondary colors, from which I can mix any hue I desire. With the addition of Chinese white, I can render any scene. I still have the enameled tin watercolor set I bought in Paris, but the original cakes of color are all gone, and I don't miss them. I fill the eight wells with fresh paint from tubes. These new tube watercolors are stronger and less waxy than the cakes. Some colors dry to a leathery consistency that keeps indefinitely in the palette, needing only to be refreshed with water occasionally. Others such as viridian dry hard as stone, and I must replace them frequently. Some stay liquid and runny forever, and must be cleaned up after every painting session. But I have finally made friends with each, and I know their nature.

The rough paper I have from Waterman's has held up well. I clip it to a varnished board without stretching it, which saves time. I have left nearly all of my small brushes behind, most of them lost in the grass in four different countries. I find that I can do almost anything I wish with a big 40mm flat brush, rarely reaching for anything smaller until the very end. A canteen for water, two tin cups, my sketch book, and a couple of rags complete the basic kit. I have an umbrella and a collapsible easel with me, but most often I leave them in the hotel room. I keep the sun and rain off with my wide-brimmed hat and use a tree or a stone for an easel.

My sketches and paintings on this trip have been largely narrative, full of detail, faithfully rendered, with little artistic interpretation. Carolus would laugh to see some of my "literal daubs." The artistry will have to wait until I am comfortable in the *Montmartre* studio again. Are Claude and Oscar still in residence there? Make sure they pay the rent on time. Although I hope to set up in a more stylish *arrondissement* some day, I will have need of our old digs when I return.

Your dearest friend,

John


## 8. The Fair Marina

I first took Miss Marina, she of the sable tresses and honey complexion, to be a ravishing Spanish beauty; but on the way to the welcoming banquet in Petalumo she reminded me that her patronomic name was Milanova.

"So that would make you Russian," I remarked.

"Well, Rosslandic, originally. By half. My other half is Pomo and Mexican. My mother's people come from one of the local tribes."

"Would the proper term be Mexi-Pomoan Rosslandic? Rosslandish Pomomexic?"

She smiled wanly and murmured, "nechistokrovna,"

"I beg your pardon? Did you say 'naked crocodile?'"

"It means—how to put it politely? Mongrel." Her smile faded.

I had been trying all afternoon to get a genuine laugh out of her, without much luck. She had too much reserve by half, or perhaps merely high standards for humor.

For the mayor's dinner party, she was dressed in threadbare red velvet and black lace, with her hair pulled up in back, piled on top, and fixed with an abalone pin. She was of majestic form and stature, her attitudes were imposing and statuesque, and her gestures and movements distinguished by a noble and stately grace. Her dark eyes flashed as she introduced me to the mayor of Petalumo, a distinguished looking gent whose name I didn't quite catch.

"Señor Twain, many welcomes to you," he said, working my arm like a pump handle, taking me in tow, and setting a course for the main banquet table. Miss Miranova followed me and John Sargent followed her. He had attached himself to our party like a limpet.

There was a glittering crowd of finely-dressed ladies and gentlemen in the municipal meeting hall, a vast, barn-like space full of tables and chairs, bunting, conversational jabber, smoke, music, and some very promising aromas of roast meat and garlic.

We sat with the mayor at the head table, with about a dozen Dons and Doñas whom he introduced in flowery Spanish and wilted English. Everyone smiled and bowed agreeably. The gentry of Petalumo are a convivial lot, hungry for occasions to gather and dine and palaver together. Miss Miranova kept me delightfully informed with the name, rank, and station of everyone I met.

The grub was ample and spicy, the musicians loud and enthusiastic, and the oratory predictably long-winded and boring. As my official translator, Miss Milanova sat at my off elbow where she could make a running summary of the Spanish speeches in English. There was a spice of deviltry in the girl's nature, and it cropped out every now and then when she was translating the speeches of slow old Dons who did not understand English. Without departing from the spirit of a distinguished gentleman's remarks, she would, with apparent unconsciousness, drop in a little voluntary contribution occasionally, in the way of a word or two that made the gravest speech utterly ridiculous.

"The tradition of English literature" became "the transgression of English lingering," with a sly glance across the table at young John. "We extend our hospitality" became "We extend our hostility." "A famous writer" became "famished rider." She was careful not to venture upon such experiments, though, with the remarks of persons able to detect her. I loved her for it, but wished she would direct her sly glances my way.

In time I was asked to make a few remarks in self-defense, and I did so cautiously, with a bouquet of Spanish phrases I had prepared beforehand. In English I told a couple of brief jokes and the fair Marina translated them into Spanish for the crowd. I will wonder to my dying day whether the laughter I drew forth was due to my unadulterated native wit or thanks to the annotations of my translator.

The mayor kindly presented me with a gift from the municipality, a beautiful abalone shell fountain pen in a redwood box. I was quite moved and thanked them effusively.

"I'm sure this is what my writing has required all these years," I said, holding up the pen and letting the lamplight flash on its abalone inlay. "I have always wanted a writing implement worthy of the language I butcher. I'm sure this pen will improve the quality of my hand, my grammar, and my garments."

Over brandy and cigars, the mayor drew me a map in my notebook with my new pen, giving me the lay of the land and suggesting how I might visit every little hamlet and pueblo in between my lecturing engagements. If Napoleon had enjoyed the mayor's services as tour director and booking agent, his winter jaunt through Russia would have been a much more enjoyable and rewarding trip.

It was late after the meal. I offered to hire a gondola to take Miss Marina back to our hotel, but she declined.

"Tonight I am staying with a friend on the other side of town. I will meet you tomorrow evening for your lecture, seven o'clock at the theater."

"What if I need some translating tomorrow during the day?"

"I'm sure Mr. Sargent here can help out until I return."

With that she shook our hands in the vigorous Alta Californian manner, turned and strode away alone, soon lost in the misty darkness.

"I'll take you up on that gondola ride, Mr. Twain," Sargent said.

"Sorry son. If it's just you and me, we'll walk." And so we did walk, back to our lonely bachelor rooms in the Alta Mira hotel.

## 9. A Candide Character

William Dean Howells
Atlantic Weekly
Boston, Massachusetts, USA
May 23, 1879

Dear William:

I write you from Petalumo, at my hotel room window, overlooking a canal that could easily be in Venice, if'n it warn't for the smell of cow flop. Tomorrow night is my first lecture here, but during the day I aim to scout out this town and get to work on the first of my travel letters for you.

I saw no fewer than twelve warships in San Francisco Bay, and quite a few military men at the Isla de los Angeles entry pier. So perhaps the rumors of war are true. But rumors of war are always true, eventually.

My lecture agent this time is called Hilario Amado, and I suspicion he is not "a gent" at all. He met me briefly when we docked, introduced me to my translator, then skedaddled back to San Francisco with a cheery *hasta luego*, leaving me to storm the provinces on my own.

On the other hand, the translator is a comely wench,

much more *simpatica* than Señor Amado, despite his amorous patronomic. I've never had a woman translator before. I reckon it's a specimen of Alta California's vaunted freedoms. Tonight she piloted me through the shoals and sandbars of a testimonial dinner in my honor. We put on the feedbag with a quorum of Petalumo's finest society: the conniving politicos, debauched clergy, crooked lawyers, guilty philanthropists, and drunken newspapermen without whom no thriving Republic can be run on a paying basis. I think I'm going to like this place.

Also in the party was a young artist named John Sargent, an expatriate Yankee painter, educated in Europe, whom I first met on the steamer from Honolulu to San Francisco. He has followed me to Petalumo and I gave him a complementary ticket to tomorrow night's lecture. He seems inclined to tag along, and I aim to encourage that, so I can observe his untutored reactions to California—I reckon he could function as a Candide, a naïve observer that will underline the humor and irony—like the Brown character in some of the *Innocents Abroad* pieces.

Your erstwhile correspondent,

Mark Twain

## 10. A Swan Among Geese

Our host for Mr. Twain's welcoming dinner was Alejandro Natalio Vargas i Diamante, the *Alcalde* of Petalumo. In Spain, *alcalde* means "mayor," but in California it seems to have acquired overtones of "innkeeper" and "procurer." Mayor Diamante was a short, rotund, overly jolly man, all convex greasy curves, with large drooping mustachios and well-oiled hair. He held one's hand too long and stood an inch too close, so you could smell his *eau de cologne* and the garlic he had for breakfast.

In painfully broken English he welcomed Mr. Twain, Miss Miranova, and me to the banquet and seated us at a long table on a modest dais at the head of the room. He would have made a good waiter, but as a mayor he was a disappointment. He did, however, make an interesting subject for a caricature, which I sketched in my book surreptitiously during the speeches.

Already seated at our table were various city council members and civic functionaries, with names like Vega and Santiago indicating their blood ties to Old Spain. But one man and one woman had guttural native names and earthy complexions that marked them as Indians. I tried to follow the introductions and remember the names and stations of my tablemates, but they were mostly lost in the tumult. Everyone was talking at once, in Spanish and Esperanto and various debased versions of English, with the result that nobody listened to anybody. I felt like a swan in a flock of honking geese.

The hall was decorated with atrocious murals of an historical nature. There were wooded landscapes with helmeted figures on poorly drawn horses, jabbing crosses and Spanish flags into an unconvincing riverbank. Dredges scooped up river muck, with adobe churches under construction in the background. Indians were baptized while doves and *putti* fluttered above their heads. A few painted medallions in the corners held murky portraits of bearded gentlemen who all looked alike, undoubtedly Petalumo's founding fathers. If this was the best the local painters could offer, I felt confident I might arrange a portrait commission or two.

The food was common and over-spiced, but no one cared. They shoveled it into their mouths like coal into a boiler, damping the fires with schooners of ale and raw red wine. The faces around me took on an overstoked glow, and I amused myself imagining how many tubes of burnt umber and crimson lake it would take to paint all the flushed complexions.

The manners of the Dons were boorish. They ate everything with their knives and sopped up sauce with wads of *tortilla*. They brayed and cackled at each other, screaming idiomatic and ungrammatical Spanish with their mouths full of half-chewed food, spraying beans and flecks of rice all about. Half a dozen musicians added to the din, strumming guitars, sawing violins, and tooting on trumpets. It was not subtle or even musical, but it was loud and lively and made primary colors explode in my mind's eye.

Every few minutes one of the dignitaries in attendance would be overcome with emotion and stand up, signaling the trumpet player for a shrill fanfare that mostly silenced the room. He would make a little speech about Señor Twain and propose a toast. The speeches were drunken and wandering, without flair or style. Miss Miranova translated the speeches for Mr. Twain and myself into better English than they deserved. She would occasionally mistranslate a word for comic effect, which mostly went right over the heads of the audience, although I saw Mr. Twain catch her eye a time or two and grin.

Mark Twain was amazing in his ability to communicate, considering his lack of facility for any language other than English. He could construct whole speeches out of the ten words of Spanish and twelve of Esperanto that he had by heart. He held his audience's attention with his magnetic glare, a comic smirk, or imperious gesture—while he dived into his right coat pocket for his Esperanto dictionary, or the left for his Spanish one. He pushed his chair quite close to Miss Miranova's and frequently turned to whisper in her ear, using her as his third dictionary.

Near the end of the dinner, the Alcalde caught sight of me drawing under the edge of the table. He came around to my place and looked at the caricature of himself in my sketchbook. Fortunately for me, he did not recognize himself or the satirical nature of caricature.

"Señor Sargent," He said, leaning over me, "Please, you must to make a picture of my daughter Constanza. In fall she will have ten and five years and we make a grand party for her."

The prospect of a portrait commission immediately raised the mayor in my estimation, and I forgave him the wine fumes he breathed in my face.

31

"Of course, your honor," I replied, "I am at your service."

On the way back to our hotel, I told Mr. Twain about the possibility of a portrait commission from the *alcalde,* hoping to plant the idea of portraiture in his mind. But he seemed tired and uninterested. We walked the rest of the way in silence, and parted to go to our separate rooms without another word.

## 11. So Much?

Violet Paget
17 Rue Des Jardins
Montparnasse
Paris, France
May 23, 1879

My dear Violet:

I must write you about my first adventure as a *portraitiste* in the New World. The mayor of Petalumo invited me to his *palacio* this morning to discuss painting a portrait of his daughter for her fifteenth birthday. I was so excited I could hardly sleep last night. I spent two hours dressing and checking and rechecking my appearance and my sketchbook. I marked several pages to show the mayor and his wife as samples of my work.

His home was not the grand palace I expected. Apparently, any dwelling facing on the grand canal, however commonplace and shabby, is called a *palacio*. The old man and his even older wife hovered around me like vultures, while I made a preliminary sketch of their daughter. She was a plump child with a high crimson complexion, as if she had a fever. She posed like a sack of turnips upon a divan, holding a puppy that squirmed and squealed the entire time I was there. I included the puppy in my sketch, but the mayor said, "No, not the dog. She must look like an old woman, with dignity."

By this I think he meant that he wanted a stiff, formal pose, along the lines of the portraits I had seen in the municipal hall the night before. I crosshatched over the puppy, making it part of a dark background.

Then the mayor added, "And the pearls. Make them more big."

"Like goose eggs?" I asked.

"*¿Que?*"

I pretended not to hear him.

"How much it costs?" he asked, "a picture in paints of oil color?"

"How large a painting do you want?"

He held his arms wide to indicate a canvas over a meter square.

I said, "750 pesos," and he immediately reduced his gestures to indicate a much more modest size canvas.

"I said, "650 pesos," and his eyebrows shot up.

"So much?" he said. "Why so much?"

I told him that a small painting takes almost as much time as a large painting. "You are paying mostly for my time, not the paint and canvas."

He said, "I have to think about it." He took the sketch from my left hand and started shaking my right hand. He stood up and hauled me to my feet as well, spraying me with rapidfire Spanish: "Thank you so much for coming to our home. It is my pleasure. *Mucho gusto, mucho gusto.*" He steered me out the door so quickly that I left without my stick of charcoal and eraser.

I turned toward my hotel and started walking. I could have hailed a gondola, but they are very expensive here, and the hotel was only a mile or two away. As I walked, I reviewed the currency conversion in my head, thinking that perhaps I had made a mistake and quoted the mayor a ridiculously high price. But no, all was correct.

The high and mighty mayor of Petalumo is just a cheapskate. For his daughter's *quinceanera* he will have to make do with his stolen sketch. It was a good one, too. I hope the puppy bites him where it hurts.

So far, Alta California is not paradise for an *artiste*.


Your disillusioned chum,

John

## 12. Gabino's Cantina

During my morning stroll my first impressions of Petalumo were confirmed: it suffered from a marked lack of handbills announcing my lecture series. I made a note to consult with the delectable Marina about Hilario Amado's advance man. Or advance woman, if that were the case, although I could not feature a woman posting handbills, carrying the heavy glue pot and brush, and fighting off the local dogs and merchants who so vigorously defend their territory.

When I am sizing up a new country that I aim to write about, I prefer to do my research not in the halls of power, but in the haunts of the common people. In the drawing rooms and ballrooms of the world I often feel like a performing monkey, aping the mannerisms of my betters but knowing that my cunning little britches lack the proper credentials. In the cafes and bodegas and cantinas of the underworld, the company is more congenial, the atmosphere more salubrious, and the liquor cheaper. My favorite laboratory in Petalumo was a canal-side saloon that functioned as the hiring hall for ox drovers and mule skinners.

The furnishings were mostly made of unlikely materials, evidence of a rich imagination and the devil finding work for idle hands. The chairs and chandeliers were made out of antlers and horns, the spittoons were of glass, mercifully tinted. Beer was served in a horn or hide tankard, and anything that could be fashioned out of leather instead of a more suitable material, was.

The saloon, or *cantina* as I learned to call it, served me as a classroom where various highly-qualified professors of Spanish taught me the spicier words I needed to lend color and emphasis to my conversation. On my first visit, I trotted out a conventional ice-breaker that I had laboriously prepared ahead of time with the help of my pocket English/Esperanto dictionary: Kiel vi povas? min estas Usona ĵurnalisto vizit via lando. Mia nomo estas *Mark Twain*, meaning "How do you do? I am an American journalist visiting your beautiful country. My name is Mark Twain." The drovers in the cantina thought this was hilarious. To a man, they could understand a good deal of Esperanto, but refused to speak it. As a made-up language, shorn of history and poetry, it was no good at all for cursing, and cursing made up fully 80 percent of their discourse.

My new best friend, Gabino the oxcart drover, was my particular tutor. From him I learned several new ways to discuss another's parentage, unsanitary habits, amatory deficiencies, and contortionistic proclivities.

Gabino was not a tall man, and that were a middling good thing, too, since he was as wide as he was tall. Were he any taller, he wouldn't fit through the average door widthwise. Gabino introduced me to his *compañeros.* a pack of picturesque rascals who were named like the dogs of Southern American gentry, with long and glorious monikers that denoted their ancestry through the matrilineal branches of some dense family trees. My favorite was Juan Carlos Geronimo Dos Santos de las Calabrese, whose name meant something like "Jack Chuck Jerry Two Saints from the Punkin." Fortunately, like the aforementioned dogs, they also had nicknames like *Gordo, Flacco,* and *Cabron.*

I have often noted the tendency for alcoholic refreshment to stretch the truth, but these rough Spaniards were some of the biggest liars I have ever met. I learned that Alta California enjoyed the prettiest women, the strongest men, the cleverest animals, and the dandiest climate in the world, most notably when compared to the Russian Empire of Rossland, thirty miles to the north, which had the ugliest females, weakest *hombres,* dumbest critters, and worst weather available anywhere.

*Mi amigo* Gabino invited me to a *fiesta* at *Bahia de Tomales.* At first I thought he was offering to bathe me in tamales, the fiery cornpone dumplings they served free on the bar. But no, he had in mind a Californian-style luau on the beach. I asked if I might bring a friend, and he said, *"Seguro."*

I immediately repaired to the telegraph office and wired Marina Miranova, reserving her services as translator for a business meeting in Tomales. To save expense, I did not go into great detail about the nature or location of the meeting.

## 13. Gibralter the Egg Mule

Reprinted from the *Atlantic Weekly*, June 6, 1879
Mark Twain
Petalumo
Republic of Alta California

Dear Reader:

This curious town is situated athwart and within the Rio Petalumo. By that I mean that she has never been content to emulate drier and less fanciful sisters such as St. Louis or New Orleans, who merely huddle around their rivers in a companionable conspiracy of transport and trade. No indeed—through profligate dredging and canal building, Petalumo has invited the river into her very streets, transforming what would otherwise be a commonplace river hamlet into the Venice of the West.

Please do not dismiss this as a fancy. If you could see the watercolor sketch completed the other day by my countryman and fellow traveler, John Sargent, you would think it done in Italy a hundred years ago by Canaletto, were it not for the grain elevators and steam launches. So taken was young Master John with the aqueous potentialities of the scene that he perched several hours atop a reeking tailings barge to record his view of the Grand Turning Basin. When he returned to the hotel to show me his masterpiece, he was so daubed with mud and muck from the barge that the doorman refused him entrance. I had to pay a bellman to hose him off. I used to have a spotted pup that would do the same thing: dig up a mole in the spring garden and proudly bring it to me in the drawing room, trailing dung and daffodils through the house.

Gondolas just like those in the original Venice ply the canals of Petalumo, and the young Mexican *vaqueros de agua* sing and shout in a perfect imitation of the Italian gondoliers, complete with maniacally insouciant airs and the obtuse arrogance of deposed dukes. I took passage on one of these gondolas late last night, bearing a sack of hard boiled eggs that were to be my breakfast. Observing the sloppy poling technique of the gondolier, I resolved to learn him a lesson in rivercraft. I placed an egg on the transom, grabbed the pole from the startled lad, and proceeded to show him how one could propel the boat so smoothly that the egg would never roll off into the water. Unfortunately my first few attempts were less than perfect, and I was soon out of eggs. The gentle reader will never know what a consummate ass he can become until he goes abroad.

And so this morning I sit writing to you, hungry and wishing I had an egg. The egg is King here. From Petalumo to the coast stretch vast egg ranches. These *huevos rancheros* supply all the omelets and pickled bar eggs for San Francisco, Sacramento, and points east. Eggs are packed in straw and cooled with wet sacking, floated down the Rio Petalumo to San Francisco Bay, then up the Sacramento River, where they are off-loaded and packed into the Sierra Nevada gold fields by mule train.

These famous egg mules have backs as steady as a gyroscope. Their "skinners" equip them with pack frames in gimbals, and claim they could bring their fragile cargo safely through Armageddon. A sober and honest mule-skinner I met in a canal-side tavern told me a story about one such fabulous mule, a jug-headed specimen named "Gibralter," for its stability.

Gibralter once carried fifty dozen eggs over the spine of the Sierras into the Mexican state of Nevada. At the height of the pass, an earthquake opened a chasm into which the hapless beast pitched headlong. Two days later the mule was spit out of a mineshaft in the eastern foothills, one hundred and forty-nine miles away. Nary an egg was broken, although Gibralter was skinned of more than half his hide and in fact became known as "Baldy" ever afterwards.

At first hearing about Baldy *née* Gibralter, I reckoned I had been sold a preposterous yarn, but I now believe it to be no more than the unvarnished truth, since its teller swore to me on the weeping eyes of the Virgin of Guadelupe, an infallible guarantor of veracity in these parts.

Your Servant in Truth,

Mark Twain

## 14. An American Vandal Abroad

I had from Mr. Twain a handbill in Spanish and Esperanto announcing his lecture, "Our Fellow Savages of the Sandwich Islands and the Holy Lands," with hand-written details of time and place. In the foyer of the lecture hall Twain had scrawled on the notice board: "Hear the American Vandal Abroad. . . Doors open at 7 o'clock, the trouble to begin at 8."

# MARK TWAIN

| Célebre Autor de | Famo Autoro de |
|---|---|
| "Innocentes en el Extrajero" | "Senkulpas Eksterlande" |

—————————— dará una ——————————

## CONFERENCIA PAROLI

—————— sobre — de ——————

| "Nuestros compañeros | "Nias Amikos de las |
|---|---|
| Salvajes de las | Sovagas de los |
| Islas Sandwich | Insulos Sandwich |
| y la Tierra Santa" | & los Sanktos Landos" |

| Fecha Dato |
|---|
| **25 Mayo '79** |
| Hora Tempo |
| **8,00 P** |
| Lugar Loko |
| **AQuI** |
| Asientos Segos |
| **25 ₵** |

I arrived at the lecture hall very soon after seven o'clock to be sure of a good seat. At first the hall seemed dank and dreary, the stone floor cold, the walls, benches, and balcony of dark native redwood soaking up the dull ochre light from smoky seal oil chandeliers. But people arrived, the air warmed, and my eye delighted in the ruddy complexions of the men and the colorful gowns of the women. The dull ochre light became golden and gleamed in myriad highlights.

Mark Twain spoke in a drawling, twangy Spanish, referring frequently to a thick sheaf of notes in Spanish, translated from one of his London lectures, and reading passages from the Spanish edition of *The Innocents Abroad*. Marina Miranova was on hand at the side of the stage, to translate questions from the audience and the offhand remarks Mr. Twain made in English.

He did passably well on his own. He threw in many English and Esperanto words, even a few Russian and French terms. Some of his jokes fell flat, victims of translation and his Confederate accent. But his enthusiasm and warm, lively delivery carried him and the audience over the rough spots. Mr. Twain had been kind enough to loan me the English text of his talk to read beforehand, so I was well prepared to understand the jokes and lead the laughter and applause for what was a very clever text. The best received portion of the lecture concerned the Sandwich Islands:

"The Sandwich Islands comprise the loveliest fleet of islands that lies anchored in any ocean. I first landed on the largest island of Hawaii, after a short, warm, pleasant sail across the gentle, stormless Pacific, as described by that infatuated old ass, Balboa. In the days before regular steamer service, the crossing to the Sandwich Islands by sailing ship was a long, cold, miserable voyage, beset by a constant northwest swell, squalls, head winds, stern winds, winds on the quarter, and winds that blow straight up from the bottom. It is anything but "Pacific," whatever you have heard from that shameless humbug Balboa.

"I was to be met on the dock by King Kamehameha V. I staggered down the gangplank and was greeted by a stately gentleman, resplendent in a royal blue military uniform with red striped trousers, gold epaulets, and a dented top hat adorned with a peacock feather. After I performed an elaborate curtsey of obeisance, and he placed a wreath of flowers around my neck, I learned that this potentate was the king's chauffeur. The king was perched on a barrel at the other end of the dock, fishing. King Kamehameha became my good friend. If every king was as unassuming, natural, levelheaded, and unimpressed with himself as this one, I would consider revising my opinion of monarchy. Forget your King Arthur and chivalry—give me Kamehameha and the spirit of *aloha* any day.

"Oahu is the capital island, and whenever I hear its name I suffer a spasm of painful memory. The most miserable six months of my life was the week I rode around Oahu on the back of a spavined mare of the same name. Oahu the horse had a head as shapely as a sack of doorknobs, ribs as broad as a barge, and a gait like a spastic kangaroo. She was so slow she took an eternity to get anywhere, and so uncomfortable it seemed somewhat longer. I had saddle boils on top of my saddle boils. I shall never be able to erase the horror of Oahu's memory from my brain, nor the imprint of her left hind hoof from my backside. But rest assured she shall remember me just as fondly. I added to her limited vocabulary of Hawaiian words a rich stock of Anglo Saxon and Teutonic terms of emphasis, heavy on the guttural and explosive consonants that the Hawaiian language so sadly lacks. I never struck on such a poor tongue for cursing.

"Not all island horses are of Oahu's stripe, and the islands do boast of a few extraordinary riders, more accomplished than even myself. Many of the best riders are young island women. They ride bareback and astraddle, naked heels kicking their mounts into a wild gallop, dense black hair and voluminous robes blowing in the wind of their progress. And yet, when these prodigious horsewomen dismount, they instantly become shy, giggling schoolgirls. Then as soon as you have let down your guard and begun to breathe normally, they leap back aboard their stallions and tear off like Polynesian Valkyries.

"The islands are not an unalloyed paradise. Ice water is unattainable. You cannot get an edible apple at any price, but must make do with oranges, bananas, pineapples, mangos, strawberries, papayas, guavas, and such truck. The islands are infested with insects, especially mosquitoes and missionaries. In the jungle at twilight, the mosquitoes will suck you dry as a life preserver. In church on Sunday morning the missionaries will make you wish you were back with the mosquitoes. There are more missionaries and more row about saving 60,000 islanders than would take to convert hell itself.

"Excuse me a moment while I light this excellent cigar. I must compliment you on the quality of your cigars. The only cigars smoked in the islands are trifling, insipid, tasteless, flavorless things called "Manilas"— ten for twenty-five cents; and it would take a thousand to be worth half the money. After you have smoked about thirty-five dollars worth of them in a forenoon you feel nothing but a desperate yearning to go out somewhere and take a smoke. Which I advise you to do now, during the fifteen minute intermission that is about to begin. For those of you who thought they were coming to the opera, this is your chance to rush off and catch the second act, leaving your seats free for those who arrived late, thinking this was a temperance meeting."

The applause for Mr. Twain was sustained and sincere. However, on the landing in front of the hall during the interval, I talked to two Serran clerics who took issue with his remarks about missionaries.

"He judges all missionaries by the Protestants," priest number one complained to me. He had large bushy eyebrows that caught the light from the torches lining the jetty and cast ever-changing shadows over his cheeks.

Priest number two had a prominent nose with a rat-like hump in the middle. He pointed to the entablature above the door to the lecture hall. "This hall is named after Junipero Serra," he explained. "He was the founder of our order and the greatest missionary of all time."

"Didn't he become pope?" I asked

"Eventually, yes," the priest with the eyebrows replied, "But at first he was a humble Franciscan friar. Father Serra came to Mexico City in 1750, just another Spanish refugee like all the other religious dissidents, free thinkers, *conversos* Jews, and Moors fleeing the Inquisition in Spain."

"He was washing the floor in a chapel in Mexico city," Father Ratnose chimed in, "When he had a vision. A voice told him to travel north and bring the good news to the Indians."

"Is it a vision," I had to ask, "If you don't see anything? If you just hear a voice?"

They looked at me with pity, as if I had inadvertently made a scatological reference in an unfamiliar tongue.

"Serra was a different kind of missionary," Father Eyebrows continued. "He considered the Indians people, just like white men. His idea of the good news included making sure the Indians had arable land, tools, and the time to use them. He fought the Viceroy's friends who wanted to reserve the best land for themselves."

Ratnose laughed. "Mexico City was very upset. The better he treated the Indians, the more he fell behind his superiors' timetable. They wanted him to claim all of California for Spain, before Russia could grab it. Serra wanted to create heaven on earth. So naturally he was defrocked, excommunicated, and ordered back to Mexico City. And just as naturally, he declared himself Innocent the First, the first Western Pope."

They cackled gleefully, savoring the joke.

I asked, "But how could he get away with that? Why didn't they arrest him and drag him back?"

"You have to realize," Eyebrows explained, "this was when Mexico was fighting for independence from Spain. Most of the

Spanish soldiers in Alta California had been recalled to Mexico and replaced with native militia, who were loyal to Serra above all."

"A detachment was sent from Mexico City to arrest Serra," said Ratnose, "But they mysteriously disappeared. While Mexico was busy breaking away from Spain, Serra quietly walked off with Alta California, proclaiming it a Republic. His militias seized the large ranchos and broke them up. Serra instituted land reforms and some canny ex-Jesuits set up our courts. Now anyone can own land or hold office—Indians, merchants, blackamoors, Jews, cowboys, miners, whoever. There are even some white Protestant Americans farming the marshes down in San Rafael."

"By the time Mexico City could spare troops to object," Eyebrows concluded, "It was too late. They had been outflanked by the greatest missionary of all time."

### 15. Daisy and Oscar

Henry James
Lamb House, the Willows
Rye, East Sussex
England
May 24, 1879

Dear Hank:

Thank you for your epistle of the 18th. You have no idea how your subtle wit and affirmations of affection buoy me up as I drift around this cold and lonely world. The more manly arts of love and comradeship seem almost unknown in the New World. The people I meet here are uniformly too coarse and insensitive to sustain for long the kind of refined discourse that I find so effortless and gratifying with you.

I met Mark Twain, the American humorist, on the boat from the Sandwich Islands. Last night I attended his South

Sea Island Lecture, a pastiche of rustic humor, mockery, and
sly wit that induced occasional paroxysms of mirth in the
local Philistines. Twain spoke, or rather read, in barbarous
Spanish, about the Sandwich Islands—their beauty, fecundity,
and hilarity. He follows a simple but effective comic recipe
consisting of equal parts exaggeration, misapprehension,
vulgarity, foiled expectation, and animal antics.

His remarks about the similarities between missionaries
and mosquitoes were coolly received. Alta Californians revere
their missionary past. The Franciscan missionary Junipero
Serra was not only the Saint Paul but also the Saint Peter
of New Spain. As the founder of the Western Papacy and
the architect of much of the Californian social experiment,
he was the kind of rebel I find so fascinating, and you find
so alarming—an Oscar Wilde of religion, if that is not too
sacrilegious.

Has Auntie Oscar committed any interesting atrocities
lately? I find his flamboyance and flaunting of convention
shocking, but fascinating. Sometimes I almost applaud him for
his bravery and daring. I think to myself, in the privacy and
safety of my apartment, "Why should he hide away like some
timid lavender aunt in Belgravia?" But other times, having
observed the blatancy of the Parisian chestnut gatherers in
the Champs-Élysées, I reflect on my own circumstances and
ambitions, and I shudder at the prospect of carrying on with
such wanton disregard for decency. I think it has something
to do with being a painter rather than a writer. The need
for portrait commissions precludes blatancy and requires
circumspection.

Here in Alta California they talk much about equality and
tolerance, but I suspect their tolerance does not extend very far
in the direction of sexual inversion. I am not very impressed by
the many political freedoms they have won, because they have
paid a high price, artistically. In rejecting control by Mexico
and Spain and the Church, they have also rejected their artistic
and cultural heritage. To my knowledge, the last decent

painter they had was Francisco Goya, and he was actually a displaced Spaniard. He did not immigrate to California until 1776 or 77, I think. The Californian painters whose work I have seen are little more than folk artists, decorating bull carts for farmers and painting murals in cantinas. The churches and public buildings such as last night's lecture hall are plain and uninspired. Basket weaving is more respected as an art than oil painting.

During our voyage from the islands, I re-read your novel and enjoyed it even more the second time. I especially admire the way you allow your reader to eavesdrop on Daisy's thoughts, as if one were inside her head. One comes to know her deeply and intimately, without exactly loving her, for she reveals more to the reader about her own foibles and failings than she knows herself. You are such a clever imp.

I strive to accomplish the same trick in portraiture, presenting my subject in a pose and setting and light so characteristic that he recognizes, approves of, and delights in the likeness. At the same time, the perceptive viewer can see beyond the surface, to the vanity, insecurity, and social pretensions that prompted the sitter to commission his portrait; or to the nobility and dignity of a genuinely great man; or to the affection or lack thereof that I myself feel for the subject. Heady stuff to be contained in a thin layer of pigment on canvas...


My letter to Henry was interrupted by Mr. Twain, who pounded on my door, saying something about oysters in a loud voice.

"I'm writing a letter," I protested, opening the door a crack.

"She can wait," he said, elbowing his way into my room.

"It's a he," I explained. "You might even know of him— Henry James."

"The story writer?" He craned his neck around to read my papers.

"and novelist," I insisted, blotting the letter and sliding it under a sketchbook.

"Didn't he write a story about an American gal in Europe? Maisie Dullard?"

"Daisy Miller."

"Ah, yes," he said dismissively. "It's hard to keep those magazine writers straight." He slumped onto my bed and began flipping through one of my sketchbooks.

"Henry is a serious writer," I said.

"As opposed to myself?" he shot back.

"Oh no, I didn't mean that."

He turned the sketches around and around, as if not sure which way was right-side-up. He glanced up. "Let me tell you, there is nothing more serious than writing humor. It's one short step away from obituaries. Nothing scares the Brahmins like laughter."

"The Brahmins?"

"You know, my stylistic betters, the Brahmin aesthetes: Ralph Waldo Emerson, Oliver Wendell Holmes, Henry Wadsworth Longfellow."

"Henry James?"

"Oh no," he protested, "Henry James will never ascend to that pantheon."

"And why is that?"

"He lacks a middle name," he said, "And it is too late for him to start using one."

"Very droll," I said, smiling politely.

"I swear it's true, else my name is not Marcus Beauregard Twain."

I had to laugh. He tossed me the sketchbook and said, "You should grab your paints and come along with me. A feller from the drovers' hiring hall has offered us a wagon ride out to Tomales Bay for a luau—a picnic to you. They roast clams and oysters and crabs and fish and whatnot in a big fire pit. I reckon the local color will be meat and drink to you."

"All right." I said, starting to gather my things.

"Bring a warm coat. I aim to pick up that Marina lassie on the way and make a night of it."

"Does one need a translator to eat oysters?"

He grinned. "I do. I'm like the walrus in Wonderland. I want conversation with my dinner."

## 16. Too Drunk to Dance

Young Sargent and I traveled from Petalumo to Tamales Bay in a beer wagon, a most congenial form of transportation that carries its own lubrication wherever it goes. I invited Master Sargent along for several reasons. To wit, to serve as a sort of chaperone for Marina Miranova and myself, to observe his reactions to Alta California in hopes of garnering some comic fodder for my next book, to have some English-speaking company on the first half of the journey, and to rescue him from his sycophantic courting of that stuffed shirt Henry James.

"This is real life," I said, spreading straw for us to sit on in the rear of the wagon. "You'd never catch a blue blood like Henry James riding in a beer wagon."

"Hank could afford to hire a carriage," he said.

"So could I," I lied, "but this is more fun."

Sargent eyed the wagon dubiously while I spread the straw. A pyramid of beer barrels towered above our nest, chocked and kept from rolling by oaken wedges, lashed tight with hempen lines to the scarred sideboard rails. A Conestoga-type canvas covering shaded the precious cargo. Two span of dusty oxen dozed in the traces. Gabino hopped up onto the driver's seat and waved us aboard. We climbed up into the rear of the wagon and settled into the straw, our backs against the bottom row of kegs, our legs stretched out over the open tailgate like a foot stool, and our gaze firmly fixed like the more reflective half of Janus, backwards on where we had been.

Gabino's whip cracked, the oxen strained, the wagon and all its barrels creaked in protest, and we began to move, almost imperceptibly at first, then picking up speed. Well, not "speed" precisely, but a less immobile form of slowness that took us sure as Destiny out of Petalumo and into the west. Warehouses and stockyards slowly gave way to scattered ranchos, each with its small adobe hacienda, large pole barn, extensive chicken coops, garden plot, windmill, and outlying pastures and fields of maize fenced against bears and bulls. The landholdings were small and many, thanks to Padre Serra's land reforms that constituted the foundation of this young Republic, and guaranteed a different dog every quarter mile to challenge passersby.

The sun warmed our legs, the canvas shaded our heads, and a pleasant breeze made us content as civil servants on pension. From under the straw I pulled a gallon pail of Gabino's lager and a greased paper sack full of tamales. Señor Sargent's alert posture and anxious frown eased gradually as we made our luncheon on the spicy comestibles and passed the pail back and forth to put out the fires.

"You know," I said, feeling more charitable towards the Jamesian sort, "Your friend Hank's problem is that he writes a book like he intends it to become a classic. That is suicide. A classic is something that everyone wants to *have* read, and nobody wants to *read*. However, I do admire Lord James' punctuation. He knows his periods and his commas, and he is a dab hand at the semicolon."

"You are too kind, sir" John protested, peering at me owlishy.

"My quarrel," I continued, "is with the words he packs in between the punctuation. A paragraph of James' prose lies on the page like a tombstone, heavy and unmoving and…and constipated. That's it! He writes like a Mayfair matron on a diet of *bon bons*, cream cakes and laudanum."

John snorted, beer erupting genteelly from his nose.

"And your own words?" he asked sweetly, pointing to a steaming pile of ox dung that had just appeared on the road unreeling beyond our toes, "do they drop more freely on the page?"

He let his hand drop to my knee with a suggestive "plop" and gave it a familiar squeeze. Shocked at his indelicacy and presumption, I removed his hand disdainfully and retreated into dignified silence. You just can't learn some people literature.

After a long upward grade which taxed the oxen sorely, Gabino pulled up at the crest of the hill to rest his team. We jumped down to stretch our legs and deliver the beer to its final resting place. I got out my camera to make a photograph of the oxen. Being a more placid species, they stand stiller than humans and can be trusted not to twitch or blink in the second required to expose a negative plate in bright sunlight. And no ox ever expressed to me disappointment in its likeness.

Gabino was waving and mugging from the springboard seat, eager to have his photo made. I resorted to my old trick of the empty camera portrait. I despise photographing people. It is always a disaster, a lie, or both. If Jesus Christ himself were to travel forward in time to the finest photography studio this modern day can boast, his picture would entirely undo his reputation.

No photograph of a person ever was good. Hunger and thirst and utter wretchedness overtake the outlaw who first pointed a camera at another person. Better to point a pistol and pull the trigger. Photography transforms the meekest of men into desperadoes; depicts ruffians as sinless innocents; gives the wise man the stupid leer of a fool, and a fool an expression of more than earthly wisdom. If a man tries to look merely serious when he sits for his picture, the photograph makes him as pompous as an owl; if he smiles, the photograph smirks repulsively; if he tries to look pleasant, the photograph looks silly; if he makes the fatal mistake of attempting to seem pensive, the camera will surely write him down an ass.

The sun never looks through the photographic instrument that it does not print a lie. The piece of glass it prints on is well named a "negative"—a contradiction, a misrepresentation, a falsehood. I feel strongly about this matter from bitter personal experience, because by turns the instrument has represented me to be a lunatic, a Solomon, a missionary, a burglar, and an abject idiot, and I am neither.

John Sargent was no help in this matter. He encouraged our driver's antics, climbing up to pose with Gabino, arm around his shoulder to give him a two-finger set of horns behind his head. One would think that a serious painter of portraits would disdain photography, but that was not the case with John. He was very taken with my camera.

When we were back in our seats and under weigh once more, he held up the Submarine Box Camera admiringly. "It is so small," he said, "I could take a camera like this with me everywhere, to make reference photographs for paintings."

"Aren't you afraid that photography will put you out of business?" I asked. "The camera can make dozens of photographic portraits in the time it takes you to paint one."

"And my painting will be worth a hundred of your photographs."

"You flatter yourself."

"Not at all," he said. "For one thing, or rather two things, the painting will be larger and in color."

I protested, "But, surely it is only a matter of time before photographs can be made in color, and as large."

"No matter," he said, "the painting will still be superior. A color photograph the size of a boxcar would still be no more than one frozen slice of reality; whereas the painted portrait, even a miniature hung around a lady's neck, will always be a work of the imagination, created over time out of many observations and insights into the sitter's character."

"In other words," I said, "the painting is a fiction."

"How so?"

"The painting is, at best, a fiction in that it picks and chooses which aspects of the subject to depict, and how much or how little to distort them. At best it is flattering fiction, and at worst a fraud, a lie."

He shot me a sharp look and almost barked, "No, the photograph is a lie. A lie by omission."

"Perhaps," I said, "but isn't the painting a lie by inclusion, by selection?"

John pouted and pondered a while, leaning back against his cask, staring at the rolling grasslands and shimmering waters of the Estero Americano.

Finally he said, "When a painting succeeds, it reveals a truth greater than reality, beneath and beyond mere appearances. If that is a lie, so be it. If painting is a lie, then life is a lie and there's no hope for it."

This philosophy was too deep for me, and too close to my own views to make for satisfying argument, so I laid off and took another pull from the pail of lager.

Presently we pulled into Dos Piedras, and there on the steps of a country store, to my great delight, stood Marina Miranova under a parasol, in a grey dress with its collar open and sleeves rolled up against the heat.

"Señor Twain," she said, "What has become of your carriage?"

"Alas madam, my fairy godmother has turned it into a pumpkin."

"I am very sorry to hear that," she said, stepping down into the dust of the road and gathering her skirts to climb aboard.

"No need to be sorry," I said, helping her up to sit between myself and Sargent. "because the pumpkin is full of beer."

I offered her the pail of lager and held my breath. She took a dainty sip, no snobbish blueblood she, and I let out my breath. She was my kind of woman.

"Miss Marina Miranova," I said, "I believe you have met Mr. John Sargent?"

We performed the usual polite re-introductions, the solemnity of the occasion marred only slightly by our environment. Marina wriggled to settle herself between us. It was a snug fit, and I halfway hoped Sargent would take the hint and go sit up front with Gabino on the drover's bench. But only halfway, since the enforced contact and pressure, hip to hip, was a delightful inducement to inertia.

Marina took another pull at the beer, then turned to me and asked, "Now, Mr. Twain, what is the business that takes us to the coast? What business is in such urgent need of translation?"

"The chief business of man: to wit, having fun and gratifying the senses."

"I am confused. The *padres* tell us the chief business of man is salvation."

"If that were true of today's business, I would have no need of translation. I have it on good authority that the Deity speaks English, leastwise he does in my Bible."

"I think that today the chief business of man is woman."

"That's right, funny business."

In this pleasant wise we wended our way westward, waxing witty. We arrived at Tomales Bay in the late afternoon. The bay was long and narrow and calm, not at all like part of the turbulent Pacific Ocean. It put me in mind of the lower Mississippi, seen from the Missouri shore below Hannibal, looking across at the Illinois woods, the sun coming up behind them in the early morning. The escaping tide even minted a convincing counterfeit of a current.

Women and children dug for clams on the mudflats. Men stood in the cool sea breeze, warming themselves around pits of embers where fish and clams and abalones and whatnot were steaming under blankets of seaweed. They were passing around bottles of mescal and pails of beer, chewing tobacco and spitting into the coals. John Sargent went into some kind of artistic trance, muttering, "the light, the light." He ripped out his sketchbook and sat cross-legged on the damp sand, soaking his pantaloons, drawing and scribbling furiously.

The sun sank slowly, as we were far enough north to enjoy a prolonged sunset. The pits were opened in clouds of fragrant steam, and succulent morsels of shellfish were passed around. After supper three guitars and a trumpet played dance music and young bucks kicked up their heels on the sand. I felt frisky as a pup myself. Marina and I ate and drank and sang Spanish songs and pirouetted trippingly in the sand until it was too dark to see, too full to move, and too drunk to dance.

### 17. Mismatched Triangle

(Letter to Henry James, continued)

...Henry, between the previous sentence and this one there is a gap of two days, full of incident. I have traveled via ox wagon to Bahia de Tomales to attend a bacchanal on the beach with Mr. Twain (Is it still a bacchanal if you drink mostly beer? If not, who is the ancient god of beer? I'm sure you know).

On the way, in an unguarded moment of too much beer and sunshine, I confess that I actually placed my hand on Twain's thigh. Fortunately, he shrugged my hand aside and seemed oblivious to the gesture. But I felt ashamed nevertheless. You are right, the Wilde style is not for me. Better to concentrate on my work and redirect my affections into my art.

To that end, I had a wonderful time sketching on the beach. The bay is a long, shallow body of water running north to south, with backlit hills to the west and vast shimmering

mudflats and rivulets of water at low tide. I am always amazed
how the simplest elements combine to create the most sublime
effects, and how the worst weather makes the best pictures. It
was a cold, blustery day, with clouds scudding through the sky
on a diagonal bias to the landmasses. Dappled sunlight allowed
me to place any object in light or shadow as needed. With
scarcely a tree or shrub to catch the eye, there was nothing to
look at but gray-green water and gray-brown mud dotted with
brown-gray jetsam. But the light! The light turned it all to
delicately chased gold and silver.

Against this simple, glorious background I sketched six
figures of women and children gathering clams. Yesterday
I worked my sketches up into a small oil that is the freshest
thing I have done in months. The cadmium yellow sunlight
edges the clouds, is reflected by puddles on the sand, warms
the highlights on the women's white blouses, and caresses
the bare legs of a little boy like honey. To the central figure
I imparted some of Miss Miranova's high color and willowy
grace, but used another woman's short light hair topped with a
sort of Breton bonnet.

Marina Miranova is Twain's "translator," a local functionary whom he duped into accompanying us. She is a clever linguist, and attractive in an obvious and common way, to judge by the attention Twain pays her. He pursues her persistently, with a rustic charm that seems entirely wasted on her. What a mismatched triangle we make! I am trying to charm my way into Mr. Twain's regard, while he is courting Miss Miranova, and she seems determined to befriend me. She bombards me with questions, compliments on my drawing, and sends me meaningful looks that I stupidly ignore. She is very forward and outspoken in a vulgar way that would restrict her to the lowest rungs of the Parisian social ladder. But Twain assures me she is a typical Republican free spirit. My friend Violet/Vernon would be at home in this situation, *tres amusant* by my *contretemps,* but I am not.

I look on what I wrote you two days ago, about the layers upon layers of meaning in a portrait. Then I look on the little canvas I have just completed, and I see nothing but common folk at their common pastimes, beatified by a celebration of light. Sometimes I think that I think too much. I am confused. There is so much here to admire, and so much to deplore, and what difference does it make in the end?

Your befuddled chum,

John

## 18. A Chance Encounter

In addition to the chance of securing a portrait commission from Mr. Twain, I had two other reasons to follow him to Petalumo: I wanted to see some important murals by Velàsquez, and I hoped to meet Goya's grandson, who still lived in Petalumo and was his ancestor's artistic executor.

Velàsquez fled the Spanish Inquisition in 1638 and came to Alta California, where he spent 22 years as the premiere painter of the New World Renaissance. The altarpiece in the chapel of the municipal palacio in Petalumo is a mural of 6 panels, larger than life, painted in oil on linen attached to plaster walls, ranged in a semicircle around the apse.

No one was in the chapel on the day I went to see the murals. The sky was mostly overcast, but a chance ray of sunshine through a leaded glass dome illuminated a corner of one of the panels, spotlighting the head of a peasant boy. I opened my sketchbook and copied the head while the light was good. Velàsquez had painted him in the foreground, looking back toward the virgin Mary, in an almost three-quarter rear view. I captured the essence of the pose before the sun went behind the clouds and the light dimmed.

I put my sketchbook away and began a close examination of the brushwork on the panels. I borrowed a votive candle from a stand near the altar rail and held it close to the surface of the wall. The finish was very fine, with highlights laid on creamy, smooth, and slightly translucent. The shadows seemed nearly a foot deep, thanks to a generous, almost reckless amount of medium—walnut oil, I'm sure—and a well-laid coat of varnish with very little cracking or surface dirt.

"Last year you would not have seen half the detail," a voice remarked in the crisply articulated Spanish of Alta California. I turned to see a stooped man in a stained smock, leaning on a cane.

"The paintings do seem very fresh and bright," I replied, in my more slurred, Castilian version of the same language.

"We have just finished cleaning them, freeing the master's work from over 200 years of dirt, dust, and candle smoke." He glanced at my candle and I moved it away from the painting.

"They are magnificent. I have wanted to see them since I was a boy. I am a painter myself, and I have come from Paris to learn from these walls."

"What can they teach you?"

"Oh, to my eyes they are like a text book. Look here how Velàsquez has created the highlight on Cortes' forehead with

one perfect stroke."

The old peasant leaned forward, squinting at the surface.

"It is only paint."

"That's my point," I explained. "With one daub of paint smeared on a flat canvas, he creates the illusion of round form, of a real human head, lightly perspiring on a sunny day. More than that, the shape of the edge somehow informs us that Cortes is noble, intelligent, brave, and passionate."

"He was the father of the New World. This painting is called *Discovery*. It is 1518 and Cortes is claiming New Spain for the Spanish king. However, in later pictures he is of a different mind."

The panel shows Cortes planting the Spanish flag in the sand of a stylized tropical beach. He is surrounded by brutish *conquistadors* in silver helms, their poses echoed and slyly mocked by three amused Indians in the background.

"This is so clever, so simple." I pointed to the lower part of the panel. "Velàsquez uses the noon shadows of the figures to tie them all together with one strong horizontal dark shape, like a solid border on a lace mantilla."

I spent more than two hours examining Velàsquez' work in detail, and the old gentleman stuck with me the whole time. He became my personal tour guide, as we worked our way around the apse with votive candles, like monks of art performing the stations of the brush. I was amazed at how much he knew of history, and how quickly he grasped the finer points of my explanations of composition, color, and brushwork. The old man pointed out that in *Conquest*, the second panel, the same three Indians reappear as the chiefs of the Aztecs, Zapotecs, and Mixtecs, surrendering to Cortes in 1522. Cortes' silver helm is now trimmed with quetzal feathers and he receives a symbolic golden mace from the conquered chieftains.

The third panel is *Repentance*. It shows Cortes bent over a stone altar, stripped to the waist, his helmet lying in the dust, being lashed by a tonsured monk in a coarse brown robe.

"Why is a lowly monk beating the Emperor?" I asked.

"Here it is 1524, and Cortes is not yet emperor. After the conquest he asked the bishops of Old Spain to send him priests from the Franciscan and other mendicant orders—priests who took a vow of poverty and ministry to the common people. Cortes feared that the corrupt secular clergy of Spain would enslave and murder the Indians. He wanted priests who might help him to include the Indians in a new society. Cortes had himself lashed in public to show the natives that even he was a sinner and not above the rule of the Church."

"The composition is wonderful, but the subject matter is not to my taste."

We moved on to the *Apparition,* the most famous panel and the one my teacher Carolus Duran raved about as the perfect depiction of ethereal light. It shows the Virgin of Guadalupe appearing to Juan Diego in 1531. The Indian peasant boy and the dusky Virgin are bathed in shimmering light that surrounds their heads with soft-edged, not-quite-halos.

"Look how Velàsquez blends his colors from white to yellow to brown. From a distance you would swear he had used gold leaf and not simple oil paints."

"The apparition," my guide explained, "was confirmed as a genuine miracle by Bishop Zumarraga of New Spain, in defiance of Rome. This miracle is considered the founding event of the Western Church, the slender edge of the wedge that eventually split the Catholic Church into the Western, Roman, and Eastern rites we know today."

"This painting is the miracle." I was spellbound, consumed with envy, almost inarticulate. "The spiraling, interlocking shapes of dark and light...the lost and found edges...it takes your breath away."

My guide just smiled. I could not tell if he approved of my enthusiasm or was merely amused.

The least successful panel is the *Cleansing.* Cortes appears again on another beach, banishing the Papal Nuncio to a deserted offshore island, along with seven of his own more vicious lieutenants guilty of murdering Indians. Burning in a bonfire are all of New Spain's copies of the 1545 Index of Forbidden Works issued by Pope Paul III. Even Velàsquez' compositional genius was foiled by the necessity of including such a large cast of characters and their stage props.

In *Coronation,* the sixth and final panel, Cortes crowns himself Emperor of the New World and protector of the faith in

1546. He sits on a throne-like chair and smiles triumphantly, but seems pale and thin. At his elbow is a sheet of parchment.

"That is the letter he wrote to Pope Paul III," my guide explained. "Cortes demanded that the Pope make Juan Diego a saint and Bishop Zumarraga a cardinal. Naturally, the Pope excommunicated him for his arrogance. Cortes was sick and died soon after. He didn't live to see New Spain become an independent empire, but his vision inspired later reformers."

The old conservator showed me where serious water damage had been repaired. As he explained how the linen had been removed, the roof and wall rebuilt, and the linen replaced and artfully retouched, I finally realized that he had done the repainting himself. It dawned on my poor, stupid brain that I had been lecturing someone who probably knew more about technical painting matters than myself.

I apologized for my single-mindedness and at last took the time for formal introductions.

I said, "My name is John Singer Sargent," including my mother's family name in the middle, so it sounded more like a Spanish name.

"Pleased to meet you." He bowed slightly over his cane. "My name is Francisco Goya y Sanchez de Goya y Lucientes."

As I deciphered his name, my mouth gaped wide open. "Then you are . . ."

"Yes, I am. Francisco Jose de Goya was my grandfather."

Here was the second object of my pilgrimage to Petalumo, the grandson of the great painter Goya. I apologized again and told him how much I admired his grandfather's early work that I had seen in Spain.

"I feel such a fool, to have come halfway around the world to visit you, then act like a know-it-all and actually explain your countryman Velàsquez to you, like a boarding school drawing master. I am exceedingly embarrassed."

He laughed. "Not at all. I was charmed by your enthusiasm. And you actually know quite a lot about the master's painting, for a boarding school drawing master."

"You are too kind. This is wonderful. I was hoping for the chance to meet you and talk with you about your grandfather's work."

"If you like, I would be pleased to receive you in my studio. I have some works of my grandfather's that you might find interesting, and I'd like to hear more of your observations of the state of art in the Old World."

Later that same afternoon Señor Francisco showed me his grandfather's old studio, the sky-lit upper floor of an enormous adobe palacio on Canal Hildalgo. It was full of my host's own work, mostly oil portraits, plus a few still lifes and landscapes. I admired them dutifully, but they were barely competent, with boring compositions, crude color, and numerous subtle drawing errors. It was apparent that the younger Francisco had not inherited the Goya genius.

That genius survived on the walls. Grandfather Goya had painted the walls with dark, fantastic scenes: a Greek Colossus towering over a tranquil California pueblo; an Iberian Saturn devouring his children; conquistadors drawing and quartering a peon farmer; heraldic pumas attacking Spanish imperial eagles; a carnival of infants; a jury of baboons. Some were allegories in which Vice triumphs over Virtue. Others recast mythological creatures as characters in the history of New Spain. All were unique and vastly different from the bravura portraits that I had seen in Europe. Goya's *alla prima* strokes and dynamic compositions were present, but in service of a darker vision, one more individual, more tragic, more insane than I would ever have imagined possible. The more one looked at these fantastic murals, the more peculiar and upsetting they seemed.

Señor Francisco confided in me, leaning close with his hand on my arm, as if it were our dirty secret, "I never receive the *Alcalde* or council members up here. Them I entertain downstairs."

"I can see why," I said.

"Alta California has become a nation of miserly merchants.

Cowards and dunces. No one wants a real painting. They just want their boring, excremental lives illustrated in gilt and aquamarine."

He pulled six canvases out of a rack in the corner and leaned them against the wall.

"These are the only easel paintings of my grandfather's I have left."

They were studies actually, not finished pictures. The figures and forms were roughly blocked-in, lacking detail and refinement.

The most complete was a half-size reclining figure.

"Grandfather called her 'The Maja Reformed.' She was mistress of a grand rancho to the east. Here you see her fully clothed like a Hellenic maiden. Her first portrait was a nude, same pose, but life-sized. One of the best things grandfather ever did, but he was nearly hung for it. You see, it wasn't Athena or Diana or some other classical slut. It was a real, contemporary slut and the local *jefes* could not tolerate that. Grandfather repainted her clothed, and this is the study for that painting. The nude he hid away for years. After he died, my Papa retitled it 'Helen Reclining During the Sack of Troy,' and sold it for pocket change to the Tsar's bastard third cousin across the river."

We had a good laugh over that, and I studied the study for "The Maja Reformed." Even though it was a rough study, it had been varnished, and on top of the varnish were traces of another layer of oil paint.

"It looks like he varnished it and then started to over-paint it."

"Oh, that is my fault. Years ago I thought I might finish it enough to sell it. But I am not the painter my grandfather was. My "improvements" looked terrible, so I wiped them off. I am a better restorer than forger."

"It's fortunate you protected the original with varnish."

"Yes, of course. It would never do to permanently alter his work."

"Yes, of course." I could understand the temptation. A

little refinement here and there, adding a darker background, some softening of edges, enhancing of lighting, and it would be a charming, fresh study by a master painter. It was beyond Francisco's skills, but I could do it. I pulled out my book and made a quick sketch to show him where I thought the darks should be massed, and where a few lost edges might be introduced to unify the composition.

"It is a pity," I said, "that Goya did not take it a little further and sign it. Small easel paintings by 18th century masters are scarce and in great demand. They bring good prices in Paris these days." I turned the painting over and examined the stretchers and tacks on the back.

"Is there much interest in these kinds of studies, unfinished and unsigned?"

"A little, surely." The back of the painting looked genuinely old and undisturbed. "There are dealers in Paris who would strip the varnish off a painting like this, get somebody to finish it off with some "authentic" touches, forge a signature, give it a new coat of varnish, cook it a little over the fire to age it, then sell it for thirty thousand francs."

"I don't suppose you've done any of that sort of work yourself?"

"No, not exactly." He raised his eyebrow, but said nothing.

I shrugged, "When I was in school in Paris, I copied a couple of the Dutch masters in the Louvre. A dealer bought one of them for a few francs, and I heard that he later passed it off to an English collector. As students, we weren't supposed to do that sort of thing, so I never looked into it too deeply."

"Interesting." He began putting the paintings back in the rack and said no more, but a seed had been planted.

I thought that perhaps I had been too forthcoming about my possible forgeries, so I changed the subject. I told him about traveling with Mark Twain, who hoped to visit Rossland to the north.

"Go with him if you possibly can," He said, "Don't waste your time in this country. In Rossland they still commission portraits worth painting, and they're aristocratic enough to like what they like, not what the peons or the church tell them to like."

"I'm tempted to take your advice. Alta California is a charming, colorful place, but I don't sense much of a market for portraits here."

"You are correct. In our so-called classless society, no one cares a fig about art. In Rossland you might have a chance. I know their Minister of Culture, Krepotsky is his name. He has the power to commission paintings, sculpture, and monuments for the crown. Here in California that job is performed pueblo by pueblo, by committees of cretins."

Before I left, he set me a task, as if he were Carolus assigning homework at *l'Ecole des Beaux Arts*: "You have an interest in forgeries. While you are here, go see the mantle of Juan Diego. It is on display this month in the cathedral. Examine it closely and tell me what you think."

### 19. Goya's "Relics"

Violet Paget
17 Rue Des Jardins
Montparnasse
Paris, France
May 25, 1879

My Dear Violet/Vernon:

I have met Goya's grandson and passed yesterday afternoon in the master's studio! It is covered with amazing murals that would surprise and shock you! They are much more *fantastique* and symbolic than any we have seen in Europe. Goya's grandson reminds me of Carolus Duran: the same age, mid-fifties somewhere, knowledgeable about art, especially *Grand-père's*, but not such a good painter as Carolus. He has a few tatty canvases from his Grandfather, all worthless but one, possibly. Have you seen the dealer Alain Moreau around town lately? I'd like to know, discreetly, if he is still out of jail and in the art business.

Goya's grandson especially reminds me of Carolus in his manner of assigning homework. He insisted that I go to the cathedral and examine the Cloak of St. John, so this morning Mr. Twain and I did exactly that. The cathedral is dark and heavy in the mission style. A long line of peasants was inching toward the altar rail, where a friar and two bored looking acolytes presided over an easel draped with cloth of some kind. I joined the line so that I could get close to the relic. Twain sauntered about with his hands in his pockets, murmuring satiric asides about the Catholic Church to himself, and looking decidedly too casual for the setting.

Supposedly, Juan Diego Cuauhtlatoatzin (Indian for "Talking Eagle") saw a vision of the Virgin Mary, who told him to build a chapel out in the desert. The local bishop didn't believe him. Then the Virgin told Juan to gather some roses and take them to the bishop, even though it was winter and no roses were in bloom. He found some miraculous out-of-season roses and wrapped them in his mantle, an apron of sorts, and took them to the bishop. When he dumped the roses out, they found an icon of the Virgin imprinted on the mantle.

The peasants were lining up to kiss the grime-blackened hem of the alleged mantle. When I got to the head of the queue I pretended to kiss it so I could lean in for a good look and a deep sniff. The image was dim in the poorly lit church, but I could catch a hint of turpentine and linseed oil. The fabric was a fine weave of linen, like *toile*, not the cactus fiber cloth that tradition says Juan Diego wore. And if the icon was of divine origin, then the Almighty used the same palette and iconographic conventions as the students of Velàsquez. I worked very assiduously to present a reverential demeanor on the outside, because I was chuckling heartily on the inside, along with Goya.

Twain was with me, and attempted a photographic exposure of the mantle. He left the lens open for fully ten seconds, but I think it was probably too dark for photography.

If you and I and the other hopefuls of Beaux Arts cannot find employment flattering our social betters with portraits, perhaps we can cobble together "relics" for the lords of the church.

With one blasphemous foot in brimstone, I remain,

Forever yours,

Juan

## 20. Homer's Watch

Reprinted from the *Atlantic Weekly,* June 13, 1879
Mark Twain
Petalumo
Republic of Alta California

Esteemed Reader:

My erstwhile traveling companion John Sargent and I have been initiated into the mysteries of the Catholic Faith, Western Division. Our guide was an amiable Jesuit named Carlos Gustavo Enrique Jose de los Santos y Maria, and proud of it. He greeted us at the door of the local cathedral and invited us in to view the relics on display. As a quondam practicing Protestant, I offered to apply for a visa, supply references, and post a bond, but diplomatic protocol was graciously waived.

Young Mr. Sargent dragged us up to the marble hitching rail at the front of the church to get a close view of the principle sacred object on display: the Mantle of Saint John Diego, bearing a self-portrait of the Virgin Mary, Mother of God. I do not know much about art, but I do know what I don't like, and in my opinion, it was a tolerable likeness. I doubt my own mother could have painted one half as good with her full paint box, and the Virgin was working in the hot sun, without a mirror, without a real canvas, without even a brush or paints. It is indeed a miracle.

Father Carlos Gustavo Enrique etc. bragged that the Virgin had painted herself on the back of Saint John's ragged cactus fiber cloak, which struck me as a callous and cavalier confiscation of a poor man's wardrobe. However, he pointed out that Catholics, especially native Aztec Catholics, are famous for their self-sacrifice and this is just another example of that virtue.

To my astonishment, John knelt before the graven image and kissed the hem of the cloak, already black and damp with the admiration of previous art lovers. Now, I'm not certain, but at the moment of John's kiss, I thought I detected a nimbus of light around his head, a genuine halo. I admit it was dim in the cathedral, filled with the gloom of the Holy Spirit, and my eyes were watering a bit, since the cloak emitted what I believe is called the odor of sanctity. I was deeply moved, reminded of when I attended my parents' wedding and witnessed my pap's cousin Elderberry Pope toast their union with a spittoon.

Padre Carlos ushered us from one relic to another. John seemed to float in a state of mystical transport, moving as if on tiny wheels. He crossed himself, bowed his head, and periodically genuflected to the cardinal directions. We saw wonder after wonder: one of Saint Sebastian's arrows, the right forefinger of Saint Junipero Serra, and the donkey's jaw bone Sampson used in the old testament battle, showing remarkable little wear after slaying a thousand Philistines. I was minded of cousin Elderberry's prize possession, the axe George Washington used on the cherry tree, kept in good repair over the years by replacing the head twice and the handle thrice. I noticed several other icons of the Virgin by lesser artists, each with a different complexion, from whitest Castilian to brownest Indio, beauty being notoriously in the race of the beholder. I have noticed this tendency before; painters make Christ a Spaniard in Spain and Irish in Ireland.

To me, the prize of the collection was a minute speck of sawdust from the true cross of Jesus. Papa Chuck assured me that Holy Mother Church has preserved enough pieces of the True Cross to build the Pope a steamboat. I was not blasphemous enough to inquire whether he referred to the pope in Monterey, the pope in Rome, the pope in Constantinople, or Elderberry Pope, who since he runs a tannery in Hannibal, Missouri is the only one of the quartet who possesses any real need of a steamboat, or has a river at hand to float it.

Knowing the Roman Church, I suspect their steamboat will never be launched. Rather, it will be encased in glass, surrounded by a Carrara colonnade, and touted three hundred years from now as the private launch of Saint John Singer Sargent.

Despite my native skepticism, I returned to my hotel room a changed man. Before retiring I created a literary shrine on my nightstand, arranging in a mystic triangle one of Shakespeare's fingernail trimmings, a lock of Dante's hair, and a pocket watch that once belonged to Homer. In my prayers I asked the Presbyterian God to bless me with a tenth of the pure storytelling imagination bestowed on the Catholics. I fell into blissful sleep, knowing that if my prayer were answered, my stories would be chiseled into stone, pilgrims would line up to kiss the ink stains on my fingers, and my publisher would scurry to reply to my correspondence within a year of receipt.

Devoutly yours,

Mark Twain

## 21. Clam Chowder Capital of the World

Hilario Amado had not answered my telegram lamenting the paucity of handbills posted in Petalumo, so I secured a quantity of blank bills from Miss Miranova and took them with me on the train to Bahia de Bodega, early on the day before I was to lecture there. John Sargent was kind enough to accompany me and lend his hand.

The *bahia* is a shallow bay kept open to deep water vessels by dint of ceaseless dredging. It is the shipbuilding center of Alta California, its northernmost port of call, an important railhead, and the clam chowder capital of the world, one of several I have visited in coastal regions. We disembarked on the eastern shore in a bustling seaport village boasting a sandstone town hall, a clapboard opera house, half a dozen adobe churches with their bells all ringing constantly, and a restaurant every twelve paces to fulfill our clam chowder needs.

As I suspected, outside the boardings of the town hall itself, where I was due to speak, there was not a single handbill posted to advertise my lecture. Sargent and I stumped from one end of town to another, for a good three hours, pasting bills to every fence, lamppost, piling, and snoozing dog we could find, writing in the date and time on each one.

"It's a disgrace," Sargent said, "that an author of your reputation should have to do this kind of work."

"You're right in principle," I replied, smoothing a corner around the curve of a telegraph pole, "but this is how one acquires a reputation—by leaving nothing to chance, by doing one's own begging for attention."

"Still, it must be extremely annoying."

"Oh yes. But much more annoying to talk to an empty house."

"Do you think it will be like this in all the other little towns?"

"I reckon it might be, till I can straighten out Señor Amado."

By the time we returned to the town hall, we were footsore, spotted with paste, and blown as two nags pulling a four-horse wagon. A great clamor was coming from the open doors of the town hall. I pulled Sargent into the foyer to give a listen. He hung back and I had to persuade him further. Finally we snuck in and pasted ourselves to the back wall of the meeting chamber. I was eager to witness Alta California's famous Republican Democracy at first hand.

The city council was in session. Between us we translated enough of the rapid-fire Spanish to understand that they were debating the claims of a local carpenter. Two years previous he had hauled a derelict oyster ketch up a slough to rebuild it. In the meantime, the slough silted over, the town leased the newfound land to the railroad for tie storage, and the railroad ran a spur line between the carpenter's workshop and the bay. Now the carpenter, having lovingly restored his boat to prime condition, would like the town council (two of whom are on the board of directors of the railroad) to direct the railroad to move 20 tons of ties and rip out their rails so that his boat can be shifted on rollers back to its element. He was to my mind the most hapless carpenter since Saint Joseph built his son's coffin.

To give the Republican system its due, everyone was allowed to weigh in on the subject. Farmers, townsfolk, the railroad interest, shipbuilders, merchants, Indians, and common drunks all put in their two bits worth, simultaneously and at great volume. At one point a shipyard navvy threw a train conductor's cap on the floor and stomped it. Two Franciscan padres shrieked at each other, face to face, spewing relevant bible verses and fragments of their luncheon. A spotted sow delivered herself of a litter of piglets, and the matter was tabled for further discussion next week.

If all the energy squandered on this debate had been directed to the actual task in hand, the assembled multitude could have picked up the boat, carried it to the bay, and sailed it to San Diego. But I would not have it any other way. I love Democracy. It is the most equitable system ever devised whereby every citizen is vouchsafed the opportunity to share the blame for bad government.

Contrast this lively give-and-take to the tradition-bound muddle that monarchy would make. Your average king would have despoiled the railroad, dug out the slough, moved the ketch to the waterline, then impounded it as tribute, and imprisoned the carpenter for shipbuilding without royal charter. Saint Joseph would have been lucky to keep his head.

After all this excitement, I wanted nothing more than to check into our hotel, have a smoke and a nap, then a leisurely supper. But no. John insisted on touring the waterfront with his sketchbook, dragging me along to deal with the natives. So off we tramped, down to the shipyards. Sargent was a husky lad, with a taste for the rougher side of town, but he was shy of its usual inhabitants. He liked me to come along to hobnob with the locals, distracting them so that he was free to sketch the decay and disorder he so admires.

## 22. Careened

I was glad to help Mr. Twain post advertisements in Bahia de Bodega. Anything that made me more useful to him was welcome to me. But I was eager to sketch the scene around us, and so very glad to finish the job. But then he dragged me into the town hall, and I was embarrassed about our dusty, sweaty, paste-stained condition. We listened to a confusing debate about boats and railroads. He kept asking me the meanings of words and drawing attention to us.

"*Navida*, what's that?" he asked.

"*Naviga*...sails, goes by boat."

"What does? The oysters?"

"No, commerce in general, I think. Why don't they say what they mean?"

"They're politicians, it's against the code." People were looking at us, two foreigners whispering in the corner, and I was embarrassed. But I suppose an author must study his subject and collect material as much as any painter.

I was more interested in the plaster on the wall. It was the same smooth, hard, almost glassy plaster as that in Goya's studio, with a sandy tooth that made it a bit too absorbent in its wet stage, as evidenced by some blurring in Goya senior's frescoes. But it took the paint very well after it was dry, and Goya had made great capital of that quality. I had noticed all this the other day, when I spent some time sketching his depiction of Saturn Eating His Son, a gruesome subject, exquisitely rendered.

The debate in the chamber ended apparently, and Mr. Twain pulled me away from my communion with the wall. The rest of our tour of Bahia de Bodega was glorious. We took a ferry across to the headlands, where I was able to indulge my fondness for drawing boats. The scene had everything—a steam boat towing a schooner, rocks and sand and water, a fort, a light house, three figures on the strand, and cannons for good measure!

A native woman was pounding nutmeats on a stone near the breakwater, but she fled when she realized I was sketching her labors. I made a quick thumbnail outline of her pose, thinking that I might use her in a painting later. I did quick studies of two soldiers sitting near the cannon. My hand felt stiff and awkward. I tended to draw the outlines of things, like an amateur, depending on my knowledge of structure, rather than recreating the actual appearance of form modeled by light. I had become rusty. I resolved to devote at least two hours a day to drawing, preferably from the figure. I yearned to draw the local Indians, however shy and disinclined to pose.

Twain clambered over the rocks and looked about with his telescope. Most of the buildings and roads were crude, raw, and recently built. Unlike Europe, there is nothing manmade here that is truly old. White people have lived here in numbers less than a hundred years. I was quite taken with the rawness and vitality of the new world. I felt sure that in California I would discover images and emotions of such power that they would take the *Salon de Paris* by storm.

We walked the shore road back to our hotel. It was a long walk, past sand dunes, trash dumps, warehouses, boat yards, chandlers, derelict hulls, piles of lumber, and other charming maritime *accoutrements*. We stopped to rest at the northeast arc of the bay, where the water was shallow and a boat was lying on its side in the mud.

"Look," I said, "that boat has run aground."

"No, she's careened. They laid her over on purpose."

"How did they do that?"

"They bring the boat in on a monstrous high tide, and ground her keel on the bottom, parallel with the shore. They winch her masts down to some trees on shore, and when the tide goes out, she lays over like that."

"But why?"

"So they can work on the bottom, scrape all the weeds and barnacles off, caulk and paint and whatnot." He pointed to some men on a raft who were doing something to the exposed bottom of the boat.

"How do they do the other side?"

"Wait for another monstrous high tide, and turn her around. They have to work like the devil, before a storm blows up and pushes her too far inland."

I was intrigued by the enormous diagonal line of the masts. It was as if I had never seen a mast before, so accustomed are we to their relentlessly vertical lines against the sky. The yardarms were sagging just a bit off square, creating counter-diagonals. Some of the slacker ropes were sagging with gravity into long, lovely *parabolae*. With an abandoned ship's skeleton in the foreground and the long horizontal of the railroad pier in the background, it was a ready-made composition of opposing lines.

I settled down to make a comprehensive sketch. The setting sun raked the forms from the left, and the right hand sky filled up with dark clouds, threatening to overcome the linear composition with interesting tonal possibilities.

I forgot about time. I forgot about myself.

I forgot about Mr. Twain, who apparently said goodbye several times without any reply from me, and continued on to the hotel. I caught up with him there, several hours later, when darkness had finally chased me from my *plein aire* studio.

## 23. Reconnoitering

William Dean Howells
c/o Atlantic Monthly
New York, NY
May 27, 1879

Dear William:

Thank you for your telegram. I am gratified to hear that my first two pieces were well received. I think the naïve Sargent character will work well, although the original is a mighty serious young man, and wants some stirring up to act properly silly.

We are in Bahia de Bodega today. "Bodega" in Spanish means "storehouse" and the bay by that name is certainly the storehouse for the northern coast of Alta California. Shipping is nearly as brisk as in my home port of Honolulu. Two trains per day discharge lumber, vegetables, hides and salt meat at the busy waterfront. The lumber trains come right out onto a pier that extends a quarter mile into the anchorage Large cranes can load cargo direct from railcars into the ships, anchored in two fathoms at low water. Hundreds of two-masted sailing schooners converted to steam ply up and down the coast like squirrels on a burning tree trunk.

The lecture tour is off to a sorry start. My local agent has left it up to local literary societies and civic improvement committees to place advertisements and post handbills, so the advance work so far is deplorable, excepting what I have done myself, stumping around town, chatting up strangers with bills and paste pot in hand. Tonight is my second engagement, and I fear I shall be lonely in the hall. Adding injury to insult, the business manager of the Bodega Hall informed me that the full rental on the hall has not been paid in advance, as per contract. I tried to have it billed to Amado in San Francisco, but was forced to pay it myself. But I shall have my revenge—I convinced him that I was authorized to collect the gate receipts myself, saving him the bother of sending a draft to Sr. Amado in San Francisco. That'll learn him.

Yesterday Sargent and I went to the mouth of the bay to inspect the shore gun emplacement and take a gander at the entrance to the harbor. Sargent sat down to sketch the brig *Invierno* under tow by the steam schooner *Maria Luz*. He was entranced by his art for nearly two hours, which I put to good use, snooping around.

The Russian border is only 18 miles to the north, so the Californian defenses here are extensive. The bayshore guns are six in number, on trucks of new lumber. They look to be well situated and well supplied with large stacks of balls near each gun, looking fresh and free of rust or trash. Locked stone sheds nearby undoubtedly hold much wadding and powder, making this side of the harbor entrance look to be in a good state of readiness. Four armed guards were posted, but they were less than vigilant—three playing cards and one asleep.

Through my glass I studied the fort on the headlands that is the main defense of the harbor. Three men were on the rocks below the fort, but there was no other sign of life. No smoke, no movement save the California flag stirring limply in the light sea breeze. The day was so quiet I could heard a seal barking fearlessly from a rock outcropping offshore, in serious danger of becoming a European's high hat or an Indian's rain cape. They say that the beleaguered mammals are seldom spotted near shore these days. The marine fur trade on this coast collapsed a generation ago, and has never come back. That collapse may have threatened the economy of this area back then, but there is no sign of a slump now. I would say that business is booming.

An Indian with a skiff saw me spying on the fort, and offered to row me across for a closer look, at bargain rates. It was slack tide and the narrow estuary was glassy as a millpond, so it took mere minutes to pull across to the headlands, where I landed unopposed and took the fort by storm. Well, no, actually I was turned away by a polite but firm sergeant who was just as suspicious of me as the many American and Confederate military men by whom I have been warned away from forts, bunkers, officers' messes, and other areas of journalistic interest.

The fort itself was tidy, clean, and in good repair. I asked the sergeant how many men were stationed there, and he just shrugged. "More inside," he said, but not how many. He indicated in broken English, with many hand gestures, that most of the army was to the east, in *las montanas*, keeping order in the gold fields. Since the discovery of gold in '54, all commerce in the region has turned one eye at least to *El Dorado Sierra*, the foothills to the east that supply the Republic of Alta California and Rossland with their lifeblood of dust and nuggets.

I'd say these people are prepared for war, but not perhaps today, and not perhaps in this neighborhood. Scanning the local newspapers, I do sense signs of hostility on the horizon: outrage over minor border incidents, speculation as to the geographic ambitions of the Russians, indications of distrust of resident aliens, jingoistic appeals to patriotism. At least, that is my best understanding, with my imperfect Spanish. I have been reading, or attempting to read, several Spanish papers from the surrounding towns. They are uniformly excellent: full of the outrageous claptrap, gossip and scandal I require in a paper. But they unfortunately all share the French fashion of telling a perfectly straight story till you get to the 'nub" of it, and then a word drops in that no man can translate, and that story is ruined.

In one of these newspapers, published in Santa Rosa, several miles to the east, I have found a wonder I am eager to explore: The front page is lavishly illustrated with no fewer than *five* large pictures, and they look very like photographic prints, not woodcuts or steel engravings. Close examination reveals that the images are made up of tiny dots of ink, some larger, some smaller, that combine in one's eye to form all shades of gray between black and white. I do not think that the dots are formed by the crosshatching of the engraver's tools—they are too regular and miniscule for that. I intend to solve this mystery when I am in Santa Rosa next week for my lecture there.

I shall write as soon as I have more of import to relate. Until then I remain…

Your Obedient Servant,

Mark Twain

## 24 TN Semi-Sinisterians

Reprinted from the *Atlantic Weekly*, June 13, 1879
Mark Twain
Occidental
Republic of Alta California

Dear Reader:

John Sargent and I took the local train to the town of Occidental in the mountains. Our little locomotive labored mightily, blowing and snorting like a grampus up the steep grade leading into town. Upon reaching the summit, where the track flattened to something less than vertical, the engineer kept the steam up full and high balled into town at full speed like a flaming meteorite, throwing on the brakes in a shower of sparks and blasting the whistle, as if to say, "I know we're twenty minutes late, but look how hard we're trying." I have seen a steamboat pilot do the same, loafing along at half speed all morning, only to pile on the firewood just before rounding the bend in sight of his landing. It cheered me to see a railroad run with some of the old steamboating style.

Dense forests crowded the hills surrounding the tiny pueblo, whose name means "western" in several languages, and lies in all; this place is by no means the farthest west of the Alta California towns. I have noticed this many times—people will name things capriciously, with no thought to the consternation their impulses cause their descendants. The founding fathers of places like Great Neck, Pahrump, and Askew have much for which they should atone.

We were late for our supper, but I told Master Sargent he dasn't fret, since Occidental is deep in the country, and time is an hour and a half slower in the country than in town. We dined at a restaurant called Gonaditas Negras, which gave me pause at first, since the literal translation seemed to be "Little Black Gonads." I opened the menu fearing I would find the special of the day to be prairie oysters purloined from the small black cattle that dotted the surrounding hills.

Fortunately I was mistaken. The menu ran more to spaghetti and ravioli and such exotic Italian truck. We settled on the five-course "family supper," looking forward to a change from the more usual Californian fare of beans and rice enlivened occasionally by rice and beans. Our order was taken by the owner, Allejandro Gonaditas. He was built like a barrel, squat and perfectly symmetrical from toe to crown, with a bulge in the middle, such that his pantaloons would have plummeted earthwards without the support of his staves, I mean his galluses. I addressed him in my cast iron Spanish, and he replied in quite supple and flexible English, after which we gave Spanish a permanent rest.

The rotund restaurateur hollered our order back to the kitchen, where his equally round wife labored in a cloud of steam that escaped through a porthole in a swinging door. He explained that his restaurant's name derived from the two most prominent families in the area, the Gonaditas and the Negras. They were traditional rivals on the scale of the Capulets and the Montagues, until twenty years ago, when a fortuitous marriage between their scions put paid to the feud forever. The restaurant was named by his father to commemorate the accord. Señor Gonaditas actually talked like that, as if he had learned his English from historical placards put up by the higher classes for the edification of the lower.

The good Señora bustled out from the kitchen with our first course, placed before us plates of brook trout with spaghetti in clam sauce, and retreated to her domain without a word. Because of my overindulgence at the Bahia de Tomales clambake, the sight of clams nearly gave me the fantods; but I steeled myself and dug in. John gazed at his plate adoringly and stuffed a checkered napkin down his vest top in preparation for a long siege.

As we ate, our host hovered over our table, pouring wine and sprinkling grated cheese on our noodles and sleeves. He explained that the Gonaditas and Negras were originally from Naples, whence they immigrated in the early 1700s, as part of the Sinisterian Diaspora.

Mrs. Gonaditas replaced my empty plate with a second course of veal and round noodles in red meat sauce. It was at this point I made my fatal mistake, and asked our host what on earth was the Sinisterian Diaspora?

He beamed like a missionary asked "Who was Jesus?" It being past the normal luncheon hour and the establishment empty save ourselves, he pulled out a chair and sat with us.

"My people were chased out of Italy by the Inquisition," he began. "The Pope declared the Gonaditas heretics because they were Sinisterians."

Having learned most of my Latin from American coinage, I asked, "Does that mean they worshipped evil?"

"No, no. It means they crossed themselves with their left hands."

"Why did they do that?"

"Tradition. My great great great grandfather was left-handed, and he made the whole family do it that way."

I thought about this for a moment, leaning back so that Señora Gonaditas could supply me with my third course of chicken with square noodles in green sauce.

"Wait a minute," I said, "That accounts for the Gonaditas, but what about the Negras? Were they Sinisterians too? Did they have a great great great lefty in the family?"

He looked at me like I was an ignorant boob, as if no one had ever learned me any history.

"The Negras were not Sinisterians. They hated Sinisterians. But they got lumped into the same heresy as us, because they crossed themselves backwards, with their right hands, only starting at the right shoulder and going right-left-stomach-head." He demonstrated this awkward ritual.

"So they were anti-Sinisterians," I quipped.

"No, no, no." He cast another of those looks at me. "Anti-Sinisterians are the backwards *and left-handed* sect. They were all burned at the stake in 1709. None of them made it out of Italy. The correct term for the Negras is 'Semi-Sinisterian."

"You must be joking," I said.

"Swear to God," he said, crossing himself with his left hand.

At this point I should have capitulated. It was too many for me. "So..." I said, stumped for words as has rarely happened to me in this life. "Excellent..." I continued, stalling for time, trying to get up a new head of conversational steam. Finally I squeezed out: "And... your family came to California early in the last century."

"Not directly," he said. He pulled my plate away so that his wife could serve me course number four, tripe with summer squash and tubular noodles in brown sauce. Sargent held onto his plate, mopping up the last of his green sauce with a crust of bread, then realigning his artillery to attack the tripe. Allejandro smiled in great good humor to see the boy eat.

"First the Gonaditas and the Negras went to France," he continued, "then England, then Spain. Everywhere they tried to settle, anti-Sinisterianistic and anti-Semi-Sinisterianistic sentiment forced them to move onward. Finally, hounded by hatred, hating each other, but bound together in their heretical misery, they found refuge in California, or New Spain as it was called then."

"And when was that?" I asked, picking at my squash.

"In 1750, the same year Father Serra arrived in Mexico City. New Spain was full of all the groups the Inquisition had been chasing out of the Old World for a hundred years: radical Catholic mystics, Albigensian revivalists, half-breed Moorish jihadis, social realist painters, *conversos* Jews, political dissidents, outspoken poets and playwrights, free-thinkers of all types."

I said, "I've heard that the Western Church only ever gave lip service to the Inquisition."

"That is correct," he said. "The Italian Pope accused them of using rubber thumbscrews and a Paper Maiden. New Spain was paradise for heretics, so the Sinisterian Diaspora finally came to rest on these hospitable shores."

I glanced over at young Sargent to see how he was taking this claptrap. He was shoveling the last of the tubular noodles down his gullet, listening to us with a glazed expression of satisfied appetite, with no more use for the topic than a rooster has for a hatband. He brightened as the Missus approached with our fifth and last course of lettuce salad with cold semi-ovoid noodles in pale yellow sauce.

I asked, "What was it like in these parts, back then?"

"Wilderness mostly. Indians mostly. The two families followed Serra northward, reaching San Francisco in 1760. They rented two adjoining haciendas from the brother of one of

Serra's mistresses. Then in 1763 there was a big building boom, and they got into the lumber business up here in Occidental. It started as a lumber camp, and gradually grew into a town."

I interjected, "With Sinisterian and Semi-Sinisterian ghettos?"

"No," he explained, "They learned their lesson finally. They used their lumber money wisely, buying up all the land around the town as it was logged off. To this day, the Gonaditas own everything west of the main road and the Negras own everything to the East. We meet in the middle and squeeze everyone else into the ghettos."

I left Allejandro Gonaditas a handsome tip when we paid our bill, in tribute to his ability to spin a yarn. He and his wife waved us farewell from the doorway as we waddled out.

I turned and said, "Goodbye and God bless," crossing myself with my left hand. He smiled and did the same. She used her right hand and did it backwards. Thus do feuds refuse to die.

We navigated down the street towards the station, slow and careful, with our swollen bellies before us like overladden barges. We tied up to a bench on the platform and settled into a doze to await the next train out of Occidental. When I awoke, I discovered that the wretched Sinisterian had told me such monstrous lies that they swelled my left ear up, and spread it so that I was actually not able to see out around it. It remained so for months, and people came miles to see me fan myself with it.

Your gullible correspondent,

Mark Twain

## 25. Haunting Gratonia

Mr. Twain hired me to post handbills in the village of Gratonia, at the peon's rate of five centavos each. Marina was helping me, trying to make up for the shortcomings of Twain's lecture agent. But she was not happy about it.

"I am a professional translator, not a peon," she said

"It's only temporary."

"Ah, no. This happens to me all the time. I am asked to fetch coffee and set up chairs and clean up after men, because I am a woman."

"Well, I appreciate your assistance."

"It is my pleasure. You are a gentleman and do not take advantage of your sex."

I had no answer for this. I just smoothed another bill onto the fence we were wallpapering. I liked the effect of the same image in a growing grid, filling space. Marina met me in the middle of the fence and playfully daubed my wrist with paste.

"Careful," I said.

"Careful yourself," she said, reaching to daub the other wrist. I skipped away, down the road to the next stretch of wall. She went the other direction and I felt I had snubbed her. But I never know what to do with flirtatious females. If one responds in kind, they become even more persistent, and if one rebuffs them, it seems such an insult. I knew that at my age I should be looking for someone with whom to settle down and share domestic life, but the prospect filled me with dismay.

We met Twain back in the center of town, where a small market was in progress in the square. He took the remaining bills from me and Marina, then pulled me aside.

"I've figured out how you can sketch the natives without them knowing," he said.

"Yes? How?"

"Come over here." He took me across the street where a hearse was parked in front of a funeral parlor.

"Climb inside," he said, "you can stretch out and look

through the smoked glass. Nobody will know you're looking."

He was correct. Sitting cross-legged, leaning back against an empty pine coffin, with my sketchbook in my lap, I could look out through smoked glass windows to a clear view of the street vendors, citizens, loafers, and many passersby. I watched Twain and Marina stroll away and wander through the market.

The smoked glass not only prevented people from noticing me, it also moderated the glare of the sunlight, dulled colors and made value differences easier to apprehend and appreciate. I used a sketching strategy that has served me well in the past on the busy canals of Venice. I very lightly drew horizontal lines to indicate my eye level, the horizon, and the foundations lines of the major buildings. Then I picked out one person at a time, observing him or her closely in terms of the characteristic

outline and motion of the figure. I sketched them lightly onto my pad, larger or smaller, higher or lower in relation to my eye line, so that they would properly inhabit the perspective of a composition that evolved over time.

When possible, I combined pairs and groups of people, having them overlap and interact in various ways. Thus, figure by figure, I created a lively crowd of individuals: A woman nursing a baby, another carrying bread from the *panaderia,* a Chinaman throwing dice with a figure in a *sombrero* looking on, a dandy leaning on a wall, and so on. The idealized scene was peopled by figures that were in fact not contemporaneous in my view. However, by adding one here and another there, in various poses and scales, I created an agreeable impression of a market day in a rural village.

When my figures were roughed in to my satisfaction, I added the suggestions of the paving, walls, and distant storefronts, placing them behind and among the figures as needed to reinforce scale and a sense of true proportion. This is more like theatrical set design than it is like drawing a portrait of the actual scene, which is too various, changing, and chaotic for anything short of the camera's lens to capture. Even the camera would fail here, however, since it cannot reliably stop fast motion, cannot select and combine, cannot adjust values, and cannot focus both near and far as I can with my artist's eye.

My sketching was finally ended when Mr. Twain warned me that the undertaker's boys were coming to move the hearse. I was crawling out of the rear door when two young fellows came around the corner. They looked quite startled to see a living occupant emerge from the back of a hearse.

One pointed at me and said, *"Mira, la fantasma,"* and we all laughed.

Mr. Twain, Marina, and I passed an agreeable hour at a local café, eating black bean soup and garlic bread. I put the finishing touches on my sketch, and he made amusing comments on the passing scene.

## 26. Mountebank on the Catafalque

Reprinted from the *Atlantic Weekly, June 20,* 1879

Mark Twain
Gratonia
Republic of Alta California

Dear Reader:

Let me tell you the story of the mountebank on the catafalque. My companion John Sargent and I stopped over in Gratonia, a pueblo on the main rail line between Petalumo and the *Rio Russo*. It was market day and John yearned to sketch the colorful but shy natives. I convinced him to hide in the back of a fancy hearse carriage in front of Panaderos Undertakers. Leaning against an empty coffin and peering through the smoked glass, he could draw unobserved, as invisible and all-seeing as the Creator.

I took a stroll about the town, a loafer's paradise where all the genteel vices of civilization may be had in convenient propinquity. I indulged myself in black bean soup and gingerbread at a small eatery, local ale at a tavern, and a fine cheroot offered to me by a boy with a bucket of mussels. The cheroot was laced with local hemp, which grows hereabouts in great abundance. It produced in me a profound languor and such pangs of hunger that I went back for another round of soup, gingerbread, ale, etc.

Somewhat bloated but still cheerful, I ambled back to Panaderos' stable yard, where I heard a man order two small boys to fetch the hearse from out front. I beat them back to the main street and, seized by some hemp devil, hissed to John, "Quick, hide in the coffin, someone's coming." I slammed the rear doors and locked him in, just as the stable boys came out of the alley and grabbed aholt of the singletree. They dragged the hearse down the alley and into the yard, with yours truly following, head cast down, bellowing and blubbering. The boys came round to the back of the wagon to see what was the hullabaloo, and there I was, all full of tears and flapdoodle, the picture of grief.

"Please," I begged them in my pidgin Spanish, "open the doors and let me see him one more time."

They opened the doors and John reared up out of the coffin, white as sheet, hair disheveled, eyes wild, a smear of charcoal across his brow—a perfect Lazarus. He could not have played his part better with rehearsal. The boys gasped, shrieked, levitated a full foot off the ground, shook the reefs out of their heels and took off like scalded cats.

I fell to the ground, helpless with laughter. Seldom has a simple jest filled me with such glee. Lazarus himself was somewhat less amused. In fact, he was decided cool toward me the rest of the day. I feel sorry for the younger generation, so full of desperate ambition and a sense of their future that they have lost all sense of humor.

Your misunderstood reporter,

Mark Twain

### 28. Imprudent Gentleman

Henry James
Lamb House, the Willows
Rye, East Sussex, England
June 1, 1879

Dear Hank:

I encountered this week one of the imprudent gentlemen you have warned me about. Francisco Goya is the grandson of the famous Spanish painter of the same name. I have made his acquaintance and believe he aspires to friendship as well, if not something closer.

He invited me to his studio to discuss the possible sale of one of his grandfather's studies. Since brokering that sort of transaction might be a source of ready cash for me, I was keen to explore the project, although the "cleaning and restoration" the shabby canvas requires will border on forgery. You writers are more fortunate in that regard than painters. When you write in the same vein as dead geniuses like Milton or Shakespeare, people consider it *homage* rather than plagiarism. Painters seem much more vulnerable to charges of forgery, or to having their honest studies "in the style of" later passed off by unscrupulous dealers as the *bona fide* goods.

Never mind that. I really want to tell you about his unwelcome advances. At one point in our conversation, he put his hand on my shoulder for emphasis, and left it there until emphasis became insistence, and insistence became proposal. I moved aside, as naturally as I could, and continued to speak as if nothing had happened. He pursued me and tried the same gambit with my elbow. Again I moved away. Some time later he was back at my shoulder, fixing me with a calculating stare. Finally I cut my visit short and left, ungracefully.

I'm sure I offended Francisco, but that was not my intent. I wish I had your tact and diplomacy in dealing with unwelcome attentions. You know so many sensitive, aesthetic men who are your friends and colleagues, and somehow you remain aloof from and above the petty squabbles that afflict that crowd. How do you do it?

I left Francisco with the impression that I wanted no more to do with him or his grandfather's canvas, and that is only half true. I wish you were here to advise me. You are so much wiser in these things than I. Should I make amends, or is all lost? Alas, I know by the time your reply arrives here, I will have moved on to three more dilemmas. Time moves so quickly.

Your perplexed friend,

John

## 28. Patrons of Art

Mary Sargent, c/o Sanderson
Apartments Genessee
10 Clarastrasse
Berne, Switzerland
June 1, 1879


Dear Mother:


Since I wrote you last month, much has happened here in
the New World. Mr. Twain and I have become *inséparables,*
traveling together, seeing the sights, and enjoying interesting
discussions about painting and writing. I am waiting for just
the right time to propose painting his portrait, and I feel pretty
confident that he will be agreeable.

I have also spent some time with another of my heroes,
or at least his descendant: Francisco Goya, grandson of the
famous Californian painter of the same name. He is a charming
older *caballero* who has many of his father's later murals in
his *hacienda*. They are astounding works of great depth and
allegorical meaning, although a little old fashioned and odd.

Señor Goya III reminds me of my teacher Carolus, in
the way he likes to set me an assignment and see if I come
to his same conclusion. At his behest I examined a holy
"relic" hereabouts, the mantle of San Juan Diego, which was
actually painted by someone of the Velàsquez school, 100
years after its supposed provenance. Francisco and I had a *très
amusant* giggle about it in his studio, where he showed me
his own portraits and contemporary work. He is a competent
technician, but I fear he is his father's son in name only—the
talent has not survived into the third generation.

Francisco finds his countrymen dull and uninspiring. He says of them what I have heard you and father say about Americans—that they are a nation of peasants and mechanics, hard working and energetic, but at heart Philistines who neither appreciate nor support their artists. He has much kinder things to say about Rossland to the north. He says the upper class there are active patrons of art, and that I should ply my trade there, if I can find a way in. I asked him why he did not move to Rossland himself, and he just shrugged and said, "I am too old and settled."

I said, "I will go there if I can. I want to go everywhere and see everything."

He laughed at me just like you do, Mother.

"Travel while you are young," he said, "while you have the energy and your eyes are fresh." He told me that he is acquainted with the minister of culture in Rossland, and I hinted that I would appreciate a letter of introduction. I think I am making valuable contacts on this trip.

So far my travels have been very interesting and educational. I have filled my sketchbook with novel scenes and ideas for future paintings. I have applied for a visa to Rossland, but do not know if it will be granted. Mr. Twain would also like to lecture in Rossland, but apparently travel there is very restricted right now. There is some tension between AC and the Russians over the gold fields and matters of trade. It is very inconvenient for travelers.

I must not complain. Or as Mr. Twain says, "One dasn't fret." There is much to see here in Alta California, in this border region where the Spanish and Russian influences meet and mingle. I am seeing and learning a lot, and I will tell you all about it when I return.

Your loving son,

John

## 29. Some Notes on Public Speaking

Sargent and Miss Miranova and I took the horse coach to Santa Rosa from Gratonia, a distance of perhaps 15 miles. The coach road paralleled the train tracks, and we were soon passed by the train. The coach line owner was making a good peso by providing timely transportation that the railroad could not match, thanks to the fact that train passengers had to disembark midway and wait for a wider gauge train to take them into Santa Rosa proper. Indeed, we soon saw the narrow gauge train returning back the way we had come, and later passed the way station where passengers were waiting for the wider gauge train.

This multiplicity of track widths near the border is a great impediment to north/south commerce by land. One of the few advantages enjoyed by steamboats is that a river has no gauge and acknowledges few man-made interruptions to its flow. In California and Rossland, commerce moved freely along the coast, and up and down the eastern valley thanks to the Sacramento River. But commerce north and south in the middle valleys was choked by the shallows of the Rio Russo and the lack of planning on the part of the railroads of both countries.

At a stop to water the horses, I observed a gang of Indians plowing a large field of many hectares, using a steam traction engine to pull the plow on a steel cable. The traction engine was clearly designed to travel about on its own wheels, but here it was staked to the ground with guy wires. By means of a winch and a wire rope it pulled the huge plow toward itself two or three hundred yards across the field. The thing cut down into the black mould a foot and a half deep. The plow looked like a fore-and-aft brace of a Hudson River steamer, inverted. When the Indian steersman sat on one end of it, that end tilted down near the ground, while the other stuck up high in the air. This great seesaw went rolling and pitching like a ship at sea, and it is not every circus-rider that could stay on it. I made a photographic exposure of the traction engine, and would have also captured the plow, but the coach's horn sounded the end of the rest stop, and I was obliged to turn back before my object was accomplished.

We rolled down the main thoroughfare of Santa Rosa at siesta time, weaving around sleeping dogs and hogs. I wouldn't say Santa Rosa was a one-horse town; that would be unfair to the horse. The streets bore an empty Sunday aspect, with not a human soul in sight, and I began to despair of attendance at my lecture. I sent my minions, John and Marina, off to poster the town. Or perhaps they were a retinue, or hangers-on. At the rate I could afford to pay them, I hesitated to call them employees. All morning Marina had proved by her conversation to be as astute as she is comely, but she kept me firmly at arms length, and a long arm at that. I reckoned it was pretty decent dramatic irony, the way I yearned for Marina, but she prefered the company of my younger companion, Master John, who is more interested in his art than romance. If this was one of my yarns, I could throw in an earthquake or a villain or a long-lost uncle and force a realignment of affections. But in real life, it ain't so easy.

I decided to go on the offensive in my campaign against my lazy, parsimonious agent Hilario Amado. Flanked by infantry in the form of John Sargent and elite light horse in the form of Marina Miranova, I stormed the opera house in which I was scheduled to lecture in the evening. As usual, the boardings between the lobby windows were noticeably bare of my handbills. I set my infantry to attack on that front, while the light horse and I charged through a side door propped open with a bucket, in search of the house manager.

The opera house in Santa Rosa would have made a tolerable dog house for the one in Honolulu. There were at the most 250 hard wooden seats, no balcony, a splintery stage more like to a loading dock, with a row of antique gas footlights backed by battered tin shades. The manager's office was by comparison the mouse hole in the dog house: tiny, of an odd shape, with a musty rodent smell. The three of us filled the space and then some.

The mouse was a twitchy gent with sparse whiskers who told me a by-now-familiar tale:

"I have billed Señor Amado for the balance of the rental, but his payment has not yet arrived." He handed me a statement of account. My Spanish vocabulary of commercial terms was improving day by day in Alta California. I hardly needed Marina's translation.

"I apologize for that," I said. "Señor Amado is very sick. He asked me to pay the balance, and I will collect the gate receipts on his behalf."

"That is irregular," the mouse twittered. "I will require a signed receipt."

"Very well," I said. "And also, cash is preferred to a bank draft."

"That is very irregular."

"Yes, but that is the wish of Señor Amado, as a special

favor." I started counting out bank notes while Marina relayed this reassurance to him.

He shrugged and counted the money. I reckoned he would be happy as long as his bill was paid, and not bother with the extra overhead of a telegram to Amado. And as long as he had a signed receipt for the ticket money, he was on legally firm ground. My agent's commission was not his concern, and I would settle with that skunk Amado when and if he showed his face.

We went outside to find John Sargent pasting handbills in a strange pattern on the boardings.

"What in Perdition are you up to?" I asked.

"Step back and squint your eyes. I'm using the bills to sketch out a giant portrait of your face. See, these two are the eyes, these five are your nose, and these six are your moustache."

"But some of them are sideways; you can't read them without breaking your neck."

"Well yes, but the pattern requires it. There are plenty right side up for reading."

"I think it's a charming idea," Marina said.

I shook my head. "Please," I begged him, "Just post a few bills in the normal manner. We don't have enough for you to paper the great wall of China. I'm going to have to print more soon enough."

Marina grabbed my arm, "You should print them here, in Santa Rosa. They have one of the best printers."

"Is he cheap? And fast?"

"I don't know, but he's good."

"With printers, you never get cheap, fast *and* good. Two out of three is the best odds on offer."

"I'll take you there tomorrow."

That night the dusty curtains parted, and I stood on the stage, pretending as usual not to notice the audience, although from the corner of my eye I scanned the seats and saw nearly a third empty. Whatever possessed me to harangue a country whose native tongue was not English? Marina was seated stage right, prepared to render everything I might say in English into Spanish, and to translate the crowd's questions for me. I was seized by the imp of the perverse, and decided to depart from my book and my prepared remarks about life in the islands.

"Oh," I said, noticing the audience as if for the first time and performing the double take I had stolen from Artemis Ward. They laughed, predictably, but not uproariously.

"Sorry," I continued, taking a slow step forward until I felt the heat of the footlights under my chin. "I was …lost in thought … contemplating my sins. By way of introduction, I must beg you to hear my confession: I am an American. It is an accident of birth for which I do not apologize, since no apology could ever be sufficient to erase that stain."

A few nervous titters flitted across the room like startled chickens, but most of the audience waited until Marina at stage left could mangle my remarks into Spanish. The laugh then was more robust, but not universal by any means. Although the delayed action of translation played havoc with my comic timing, I was relieved to have a translator. I could lope along in English at my natural pace, and the pauses allowed me to assemble my next sentences in leisure. Speaking thus was like laying bricks on a firm foundation, in pleasant weather and good health. Speaking in Spanish or Esperanto was, for me, more like building a stone wall in the middle of a raging river at night while racked with chills and fever.

I continued: "However, to my credit, I have been trying to get into your fair country for some time. A couple of years ago my brother Orrin served a term in the American embassy in San Francisco as a cultural attaché and spittoon polisher. Wishing to visit him and perhaps stroll through the Sierra gold fields picking up stray nuggets, I applied for a visa to enter Alta California. Wisely, you folks turned me down, an example of sound judgment that rendered me only more eager to breach the Golden Curtain, if I had to walk across Nuevo Mexico and Nevada to do it."

The crowd was warming up. The small flock of chickens was joined by several chuckling turkeys and a hee-hawing mule in the back row. If you just give them an excuse, people want to laugh, especially at another man's expense. But I was about to turn the tables.

"Please don't think that we Americans resent your presence in North America. It bothers us not one bit that you swindled France out of the western half of the continent, with its mountains of gold, leaving us the exorbitantly-priced and cholera-riddled swamps of Louisiana. We know that the territorial possessions of all the political establishments in the earth—including the USA, of course—consist of pilferings from other people's wash. No tribe, however insignificant, and no nation, howsoever mighty, occupies a foot of land that was not stolen. When the Spaniards, the French, and the English reached America, the Indian tribes had been raiding each other's territorial clotheslines for ages, and every acre of ground in the continent had been stolen and restolen 500 times."

The laughter had been steadily thinning as they realized that I was asking them to pick up the tab of humor with some of their own funds. I decided to abandon the deep historical vein and start mining more recent events:

"The USA has only recently settled a small family disagreement over the laundry baskets of the north and south. This bloody squabble between the states has darkened an entire decade, pitting brother against brother, slaughtering thousands, ruining our fortune, and so thoroughly soiling the white shirt of our Democracy that it may never come clean again."

Stunned silence. Too much real feeling to be contained in an over-extended metaphor. I fell back on lampooning myself.

"I myself was on the Confederate side early in the war, for about a week. I started as a corporal rabidly defending states' rights, and ended as a colonel devoted to abolitionism, without ever receiving the proper insignia or a pair of boots that fit. My war career convinced me to give over such dangerous notions as patriotism. It is too large an idea for me. You've got to admire men that deal in ideas of that size and can tote them around without a wheelbarrow."

A few brave laughs, but lonely ones. I have always maintained that a discriminating irreverence is the creator and protector of human liberty, but apparently they disagreed in Santa Rosa. I headed for safer territory.

"At week's end, terrified, demoralized, and completely fatigued by persistent retreating, I resigned my commission and made my way by torturous stages to the Sandwich Islands. I arrived in the Islands with straitened means and a weakened courage. To wit: I had six bits in my pocket and my opinion of my prospects had shrunk down to nearly the size of an ordinary mortal's.

"At first I went to ground in the jungle paradise of Hilo, living for days on six bits worth of pineapples, bananas, guavas and such truck. At first I was heartily glad to escape civilization. The blessings of civilization are all right, and a good commercial property; there could not be a better, in a dim light…and at a proper distance, with the goods a little out of focus. Eventually I began to tire of a diet of fruit and spring water exclusively. I longed for a good smoke, a dram of spirits, and enough beefsteak to slow the alarming pace of my digestion."

At last I had the whole barnyard back, cackling and hooting. I continued along my usual line, bored but basking in approval. Toward the end I touched upon my impressions of Santa Rosa.

"Ye weary souls who are sick of the labor and care of metropolitan streets, who yearn for respite from the clamor of modern affairs, who dream of a land where ye may lay your fretful heads in long and uninterrupted slumber—come to Santa Rosa. A week here will cure the dolefulest of you."

This went down smooth enough, so I continued in the same vein.

"I trust the observation will not be considered in the light of an insinuation, but if you send a damned fool to Santa Rosa and don't tell them he's a damned fool, *they'll* never find out. If you've got a damned fool and don't know what to do with him, ship him to Santa Rosa. It's the noblest market in the world for that kind of property."

I was losing them again. People will agree that their home town is dull, but not that its inhabitants are foolish.

I switched to Spanish, finishing the evening primarily in that tongue, falling back on my prepared digs at the jolly old Sandy Witches, and resolving to avoid extemporaneous departures

from my script henceforth.

Afterwards I compared notes with John Sargent. He and I had both counted the house and came up with 105 souls, of which 13 or 14 were under 15 years of age and eligible for free admission. This jibed well with the house manager's reckoning, and I walked out with a small but pleasant wad of AC cash in my britches.

On the way out, John showed me a sketch he had made during the show, of me in a characteristic pose and expression. It was quite clever, but I thought the lighting from the footlights made me look dead, or at least very old and good as dead.

"If you like," he said, "I can render this as a steel engraving for your new handbill. It would only take me two or three hours."

"Thanks," I said, "but I'm not sure I could afford it. I'll have to see how cheap Miss Miranova's printer is."

### 30. *Petit Vaniteux*

Violet Paget
17 Rue Des Jardins
Montparnasse
Paris, France
June 2, 1879

My dear Violet:

My dream is about to come true. Last night I sketched Mr. Twain lecturing in Santa Rosa, dramatically underlit by gas footlights. I offered to turn the sketch into a steel engraving for a handbill, and he was thrilled by the idea. Assuming the local printer has a decent setup for graving, I shall be on my way. First a handbill, then a frontispiece for his next book, then a full length portrait in oils to win me a blue ribbon at the Salon and grace his parlor in Honolulu, where there are plenty of plantation owners and government officials in need of portraiture.

Forgive me my *petit vaniteux,* but I am excited. I can feel the touch of the graver in my hand, the drag as it scribes a fine line in the steel, I can even smell the ink. This development makes all the grubby posting of his handbills worthwhile. I hate it—trudging around in the hot sun and dust, daubing smelly paste on anything that doesn't move, suffering the abuse of merchants and property owners. It would be more tolerable if Twain were truly appreciative, but he treats me and Marina like servants, and pays us like slaves.

No, that is not right. He treats me like a servant, but he treats Marina more like a shop girl, teasing and flirting with her as if she were some brainless hussy selling ribbons and cufflinks. It is ironic how Twain pursues Marina, she pursues me, and I pursue Twain. It is like the plot of a drawing room farce, with characters running in circles.

Tomorrow I plan to work on the engraving. We have a free day before our gypsy band decamps for Pueblo Forestal, the next stop on Twain's lecture circuit. I always thought that writers had it easy, being able to create their art with simple pen and paper, and having it distributed worldwide by the printing press. But following Twain around, I see that writers also have to scrape and bow and connive and flatter and strive to push themselves forward. Art in any form is not an easy life.

You know that as well as anyone. Although you love your trousers and your cigars and your gruff ways among the *demimonde,* I imagine you find the criticism and rejection of ignorant people tiresome and painful nevertheless. You can take heart from knowing the great Mark Twain also struggles as much as you and I.

But now the struggle is about to pay off. I can hardly wait for tomorrow.

Sleeplessly, Your Friend,


John

### 31. All I Need to Change the World

William Dean Howells
Atlantic Weekly
Boston, Massachusetts, USA
June 3, 1879

Dear William:

From my last letter, you know that I am impressed with the Californians' military readiness, but I am even more impressed by their inventiveness and their willingness to try anything to further the progress of industry. I suspect the Californians are much more advanced than we previously thought.

Marina took me to the headquarters of *La Prensa Democratica,* the lavishly illustrated newspaper I have mentioned to you before. It occupied a two-story adobe building between a livery stable and a swampy slough. The scents of horses, muddy water, paper and ink formed an agreeable miasma, and I felt quite at home. I entered the open door and peered around the dim, deserted interior. The ground floor was one large room, nearly filled with a hulking iron form—a steam press big as an elephant.

"Hay alguien aqui?" I shouted.

"Upstairs," a voice replied, drifting down a staircase at the side of the room. The Dons are always doing that to me—answering my Spanish with English instantly, upon first hearing, despite my authentic pronunciation and total lack of a Yanqui accent. They must have psychic powers, or else my Spanish is a sight more peccable than I presume.

Upstairs I found the only Santa Rosan awake and upright on his own pins. A wiry, mustachioed gent of middle years advanced on me, crossing well within the border of my personal territory and establishing a close beachhead from which to pump my hand vigorously.

"I am Jaime Rodolfo," he said, "How may I be of service?"

He wore a cap of folded newsprint, a dark brown apron over a collarless shirtwaist and besmirched linen pantaloons that ended leagues north of his foxy shoes, which were themselves run down at heel and bespotted with greasy ink. Slight regional variations aside, he was the spit and image of myself a few years back, when I set type and wrote lies for the New Orleans *Intelligencer.*

I fought the urge to take a half step back, and said, "Mark Twain, pleased to meet you."

"Senior Twain, what an honor you give to me." He dropped my hand like I had just said I had scarlet fever, and retreated to a bookcase in the corner. Before I could take offense, he returned with a copy of *Innocents Abroad.* "I will be attending your lecture tonight," he said, "But let me be the first right now to ask you to sign my copy of your excellent book."

He handed me a markup pencil and I magnanimously deigned to craft him one of my more flowery inscriptions. What a fine fellow he was.

"You know," he said, "there are several typographical errors your editor should correct before the next printing." He hung his head over my shoulder and began flipping pages.

He proceeded to take me through the book, page by page, pointing out misspellings, repetitions, faulty hyphenation, transpositions, and broken letters—many I had never noticed myself. I did not tell him that I did my own copy editing, nor that a new printing was not contemplated any time soon. I felt like a school boy who has carelessly blotted his copybook. What an irritating fellow he was. On the sly, I quickly proofread the inscription I had just written.

Jaime Rodolfo worked himself back into my good graces by showing me around his shop and demonstrating his recent advances in what he called photo-chemical engraving. He showed me a glass photographic negative, almost identical to those produced from the dry gelatin plates I used in my own camera. In a tiny darkroom off his upstairs office, he laid out a blank zinc printing plate, coated with a layer of silver nitrate and other secret chemicals. Over that he placed a glass "screen," whose darkly smoked coating had been finely crosshatched with a razor so that light could pass through it in a nearly microscopic grid pattern. On top he put the negative, and taped the stack around the edges. He carried this sandwich of zinc and glass downstairs and exposed it to sunlight for six minutes, after which we pounded back upstairs to the darkroom.

He donned heavy India rubber gloves, removed the zinc plate and placed it face down in a tray with a shallow layer of nitric acid and soapy oil on the bottom. He agitated the tray, tilting and shaking it to splash the acid/oil mixture against the zinc. Periodically he pulled the plate out and examined it under a magnifying glass. When he was satisfied, he rinsed the plate with fresh water and showed it to me. The oil had stuck to the zinc in the now-familiar dotted pattern, protecting it from the acid. The acid had etched away around each dot, creating an engraving that perfectly matched the original photograph, in finer detail than the most skilled steel engraver could achieve by hand, if he worked on it all day. The entire process consumed 30 minutes.

"Thus begins a new era in the history of journalism," Jaime said.

"It is so fast," I agreed.

"No, I do not refer to the speed of my techniques, but to the truth of the image. The camera is the only witness in history that tyranny cannot bribe. A printed photograph is worth a thousand lying words or a hundred flattering, distorting engravings."

"I hope you are right," I said, not mentioning that I had seen convincing photographs of mermaids and a donkey with a head at each end. But the sheer technical accomplishment astonished me.

"If you can ever figure how to do this in color," I said, "it will put painters like my pal Sargent out of business for good."

Jaime shrugged. "Color chromos are for holy cards and

calendars. Honest black ink and white paper are all I need to change the world."

In the end, I struck an excellent bargain with Jaime. I will write him three or four columns of copy about my travels in Europe and life in the Sandwich Islands to run in his paper. In return, he would take my photograph and print it on my new handbills. I reckon the novelty of the photo-chemical engraving will help attract attention better than the all-type handbill I have been using. Feeling magnanimous, I ordered a series of advertisements for my lectures to be published in the next three weeks, cost to be billed to my agent Amado in San Francisco.

We shouldered Jaime's equipment and hoofed it over to the opera house this very afternoon, so that he could make a long exposure while the house was empty. He set up the camera and I convinced the house manager to light the footlights. I climbed up onstage and struck a declamatory pose.

"The Sandy Witch Islands" I began, gesturing gracefully, "are the scabbiest handful of rocks, the most treacherous hazards to navigation, the foulest sinkholes of pestilence ever to blight the blue waters of…"

"Hold still," Jaime said. "And you must not talk. If you keep talking, your mouth will be a blur. It will look like your lips are made of cotton."

I froze into position like a statue, allowing my countenance to settle into a dignified, intelligent expression.

"Try not to look like your stomach hurts," he said.

I was beginning to remember why I hate photographing people, particularly myself.

"Just a little longer…hold still…nearly finished."

My neck and back began to hurt like the devil. An infuriating itch started on the tip of my nose and I was convinced a spider was crawling down my neck. The pose that had seemed so relaxed and natural two minutes ago was now tantamount to torture.

"All done," Jaime said, releasing me from the rack and slacking the thumbscrews. I scratched my nose hard enough to make it bleed, and my wrists and elbows popped like they were made of pipe stems.

Until some other novelty arises to delight me, I remain,

Your devoted interlocutor,

Mark Twain


## 32. Devastated

Marina took my hand and said, "I'm sure Mr. Twain did not mean to insult you. He is just thoughtless. He acts without thinking."

"Exactly—for such a great brain, he hardly thinks at all." I gave her hand back, a little annoyed at her touching me in public, although there was no one else in the hotel lobby at the moment.

She said, "I am sorry we went off without you. He was up early and in a great hurry."

"When I woke and found you both gone, I ran all over town trying to find that printer."

"His shop is down an unmarked alley, you would never find it."

"Then I came back here to the hotel, and I've just spent all morning refining my sketch, getting it perfect."

"I know." She tried to take my hand again, but I was having none of it.

"And he just decides to use a photograph, after he as much as promised me he would use my engraving?"

"As I said, he acts without thinking." She could not console me. I was too angry and disappointed. She picked up my sketch and held it at arm's length to admire it.

"Another thing," I said, "Mark Twain swaggers through the world as if he owns it. He gives off a kind of golden glow or energy that attracts people to him and makes them want to listen to him and buy his damned books and court his favor. But when you actually spend any time with him, you see that the glow is fool's gold. He's really rather short, and his boots want shining, and his cuffs are frayed, and frankly he could stand to bathe more often." I pointed at the sketch. "And he is nowhere near as handsome as that makes him look."

Marina was stifling a smile, which only made me madder.

"It is not funny." I took the sketch from her. "You know I'm right. He bosses us around like servants, especially me. He compliments you sometimes, but does he really respect you? with his leering looks and sly talk? He's arrogant and pompous and he tells the same stories over and over and he is so... so..."

"Fascinating?"

"Irritating."

"Exciting?"

"Infuriating."

She sat silently then, looking into my eyes, until I felt she saw a little too deeply, and I looked away.

"What are you going to do?" she asked.

"I quit. I give up."

"What do you mean?"

"I'm going to check out of the hotel and go back to what I was doing before. I'm going to stop following Twain around like a pet dog. I got along fine before I ran into him."

"Will you not come with me to Soto de los Piños this afternoon? He wants us to use up the rest of the old handbills there."

"I'm sorry, it's just not worth my time. What little I've earned posting his handbills I've wasted on the fancy hotels and restaurants he chooses. I can travel faster and cheaper on my own. I have my own work to do, and it has nothing to do with Mark Twain and his shabby little road show."

I went upstairs to pack my things. By the time I returned to the lobby Marina was gone. I was almost hoping Twain would be there, since I had thought of several clever things to say to him. But the lobby was still deserted, save for the desk clerk dozing over his papers.

I checked out of the hotel and turned west, heading out of Santa Rosa on the River Road. I was too full of feeling to sit still on the train or the stage coach. I was ready for a long tramp under the sky, just myself and my sketchbook and my paints and Nature.

It was a day of hard bright chrome yellow sunshine and high fast-moving flake white clouds. It was warm in the sun, but cool with a breeze in the shade. Once out of town, the road ran through broad stretches of flat marshy grasslands dotted with oaks, cows, egrets, and geese. Stone bridges crossed creeks and canals lined with willows and rushes. The Rio Russo was a line of trees far to my right. I saw few houses or barns.

The road became narrower and ruder, little more than a rutted wagon track, overgrown with brush. The sun dropped steadily in the sky before me as I trudged along. I stopped a couple of times to sketch a picturesque tree or bridge, but nothing really caught my eye. I thought of setting up my paints and spending some time on a watercolor, but the unsettled landscape lacked a figure or a structure to give it human interest and scale.

Eventually I arrived at Soto de los Piños—"Pine Grove" in English. It was the next stop on Twain's circuit, and he would be speaking there later that night. But I cared nothing for that. It was just another town to me, a place on the way to someplace else. Known locally for making wagons and farming equipment, Soto de los Piños was a noisy, cluttered, untidy place full of rubble heaps, half-finished buildings, old machinery, and the bustle of commerce. It was just the sort of place I love to sketch, where the smooth complexion of civilization is marred with grease on its cheek, and the corpulent gloss of propriety is sweated off to show the bones underneath.

The low sun raked every shed and fence post with pale burnt

umber light on its west side, and the whole scene was overlaid with an amber wash of light like maple syrup. I was attracted by a billowing cloud of steam emerging from a blacksmith's shed. Just inside the doorway, a burly man stripped to the waist was pounding red hot iron on an anvil, quenching it in a barrel of water, and pulling another piece of iron from his forge to pound some more. I pulled out my sketchbook.

Steam is an artist's friend. Like fog and clouds, steam exaggerates distance, neutralizes color, softens edges, and allows one to compose pictures with large, blank areas devoid of detail. Steam can reduce forms to their silhouettes. The younger *plein aire* artists in Paris have begun to paint portraits of steam engines in the stations and train yards, producing wonderful canvases of daring design.

I sat on a woodpile and sketched the man lit by the glowing metal, up to his waist in steam. Nearly half the composition was steam, rendered in very light shading, mostly white paper. It looked like the early block-in stage of an oil painting, when one's idea is still fresh and nothing has yet gone wrong.

Next to the barn a tower had been constructed by connecting four living redwood trees. The structure was seven stories tall, with each story an open platform surrounded by a railing. Some boys were racing up and down the stairways, so I felt encouraged to climb up myself. Pausing at each level, I looked out over the town on one side and rolling pastures and fields on the other. It was a lesson in perspective, going up one flight at a time, and seeing how the horizon receded, how flat-looking structures slowly became three-dimensional, how trees foreshortened and fences became lines.

Looking toward town, I spied Mark Twain and Marina in the distance, walking toward the edge of town and my tower. I sped down the stairs and ran up a side street, out of their line of sight. They didn't see me, and I liked it that way. I avoided their probable route and continued my walk downtown in a wide arc that would not bring me face to face with them.

As the light faded, I searched for a cheap rooming house for

the night. Here and there I saw handbills Marina had posted, advertising Twain's talk here tonight and tomorrow in nearby Pueblo Forestal. I was pleased to know that I would never have to hear him bluster and rant again.

## 33. And Yet…

Marina Miranova and I were strolling in Soto de los Piños, pasting up the last of the Amado handbills and generally killing time before the appointed hour of my evening talk. It was a small farming and manufacturing center, full of bustle and self-importance. There was traffic in the streets, dust in the air, and trash in the corners. Marina took my arm to lead me around a pile of wood shavings and trimmings outside a cooper's.

She said, "John left because you did not use his drawing on the new handbill."

"That's mighty presumptuous of him."

"He claims you promised to use it."

"I never said anything of the kind." I squeezed her hand in aggrieved earnestness, but she withdrew that precious article from my custody.

"I don't think you realize how much he admires you."

"Admiration don't signify," I said, "I can't adopt every stray pup that wanders in."

"I think he adopted you."

"Well that's cheeky, is all. I reckon to John I'm no more than an opportunity to pick up a few coins and some tips about surviving in the art game."

"No, he worships you. You're his hero."

"Rot."

"No, really. He follows you around like a puppy in love."

"That's hunger, or maybe envy, not love."

"Oh, you're impossible."

"Whatever do you mean?"

"I mean, how can such a smart man act so dumb?"

I stopped talking at this point, and stopped listening too. She continued to fret me like a mandolin, picking out each note of my misbehavior in regard to John Sargent. I did not care for the tune.

We walked out of town a ways, toward a curious tower in the distance. While Marina went on telling over the rosary beads of her grievances, I made a photograph of the structure, steadying my camera on a stump. Some eccentric local farmer had notched beams into four perfectly straight and equidistant redwood trees, hung joists and flooring and railings therefrom,

built stairs up another ten feet high, and done it all over again. The result was a living tower seven stories high, commanding a view over miles of the local countryside.

The treehouse tower adjoined a campground for transient grape and hop pickers, who were wont to climb up drunk and fall off. Local fraternal organizations draped it with bunting and held picnics in the campground on holidays. Neighbor children used it as a fort, a castle, a refuge, and an opportunity to break their precious necks. It was a famous local curiosity and attractive nuisance.

Marina waited below while I climbed to the top, blown as a racehorse by the third floor. The view was capital. I could see the many small holdings that gave Alta California its Republican flavor, every man a landowner, every woman a homesteader. The terrain was agreeably quilted with pastures, woods, farmyards, and fields of corn, wheat, hay, grapes, and hops. I could see wagons moving in and out of cover a good mile away. What a post it would make for a fire lookout, a shot-dropper, a suicide, or a sniper! There is something inspiring about a high vantage point that makes me feel like writing a story.

Back on the ground, Marina continued saying the rosary of her grievances, telling over each bead of her disappointment in me *in re* Señor Sargent.

"He wasn't helping me with the handbills for the money," she said, "Everything he earned and more he spent on hotels and train tickets, following you around."

"I never asked him to attach himself to me."

"You captured him."

"How so?"

"Like the earth captures the moon."

"Or the ship captures the barnacle."

This time it was she who lapsed into silence, punctuated with disgusted sniffs. It was curious how she had so quickly taken on the role of my nagging harridan wife, without ever moving through the more usual and pleasant stages of paramour, fiancé, newlywed and so on. As much as I admired and desired this *señorita*, I resented her appointing herself my conscience. I have very little use for such an item as a conscience. It is a great bother. Even if I required a conscience, I'd druther pick out my own on the open market, in the form of a mongrel yaller dog, and then shoot the dog.

My lecture that evening was a grim affair: barely enough audience to cover expenses, and a translator who seemed to be draining every ounce of humor out of my jokes. I concentrated on my Spanish material, got offstage as soon as I decently could, and retired to my room with a bottle.

In the morning there was still no sign of John Sargent. We took the train to Pueblo Forestal, a sprawling settlement where swamp meets river in an expanse of mud. There was a supply of mud sufficient to insure the town against a famine in that article for a hundred years, and a middling portion of it was on my boots. Marina left me to post bills, and I went for a slog along the river, where the more marginal and interesting business establishments were located: tannery, dyeworks, a small factory making fireworks. I perused their wares and laid in a supply of firecrackers in honor of my late brother Henry, who loved to blow things up.

I was in a melancholy frame of mind—would have been anyway, even without Miss Miranova's disapproval. It was the anniversary of my brother Henry's death. He died in the explosion of the steamboat *Pennsylvania* on this very date, nine years ago.

As I leaned against a post, scraping fruitlessly at the mud on my sole, I spied an omen: the remains of a wreck out in the river. A burst boiler and part of a smokestack were stuck in the mud. It reminded me most vividly of the *Pennsylvania* and my brother. I missed being on that boat myself by only the most unlikely circumstances, and have always harbored the guilty conviction that, had I been present, I might have saved Henry. Or I could have died instead of my brother, who was a better man than I in every way. That would have been much more convincing evidence of the existence of a benevolent Deity than my survival has so far proved to be.

I walked on and soon entered a dark forest of redwood trees. They are much admired as the oldest living residents of the earth, but I was not impressed. My aunt Sally is the oldest living resident of my family, and she is anything but admirable. I walked under a trestle with a logging train stopped on it, and made a photograph, but my heart was not in it.

As I continued deeper into the forest, I found the redwoods to be incorruptible sentinels against the sunshine, creating a

cold and gloomy atmosphere that perfectly matched my mood, haunted as I was by my dead brother. His specter seemed to float just out of view, hiding behind the shaggy and repetitious tree trunks.

The faint path I was following led to a shack that had been added onto a truly enormous redwood tree whose trunk was hollowed out by fire. Seated at a table in front of the shack was an old, old woman. Arrayed before her on the table were charms and amulets made of shells and feathers. She was some kind of gypsy/Indian/African woman, her heritage composed of the darker and spicier human strains. She was older than Methuselah's nanny, with wrinkled skin stretched tight around her skull and bulging yellow eyes that caught mine and held them. She reminded me of my aunt Sally, but I was drawn to her nonetheless.

She pointed her claw at me and said something in Spanish, then something in Russian, then in English, "Tell me about your brother."

My blood ran cold in my veins. I steadied myself against the counter.

"He died," I said.

She shook her head and said, "But he does not rest easy."

I have consulted and been defrauded by some of the best mediums on the Pacific Rim, but I never learn my lesson. Inside of ten minutes she had me in the charred darkness of her shack, breathing God knows what kind of homemade incense, drinking a lovely cup of dirt tea, and holding her bony hand while she attempted to contact Henry beyond the grave.

"Close eyes and call your brother," the crone intoned, "Call Henry to here."

She squeezed my hand with surprising force and began humming or chanting in a jerky, decidedly unmusical way.

"Henry!" she cried hoarsely, "Stop that!"

I peeked under my eyelids and she caught me looking.

"He is here," she whispered. "He holds my foot, not let go."

She kicked the table leg a couple of times. Despite my skepticism, the hairs on my forearms rose up.

"Henry, be good boy! Speak to me. Speak to you brother." More humming and chanting. Her bare foot began rubbing up and down my shin. It was annoying. Just as annoying as when Henry used to do it, in our bed together when we were boys.

I should know better, but the mystery of death confounds me. I am a legislature of conflicting views, endorsing the orthodox Christian geography of heaven and hell, flirting with the attractions of reincarnation, utterly convinced at times I have seen ghosts, and trying without consciously thinking about it to suppress my atheistic suspicions.

"He sad. Got trouble. Got no peace."

According to Methuselah's nanny, Henry is uneasy in death because of unfinished business in life. I have heard that before. It plays on common regret over deeds left undone, things left unsaid. And yet she knew that he was the younger, that he loved dogs, that he was left handed.

"He need silver on the water," the medium intoned. "Sacrifice."

She grabbed my hand and led me out of the tent. We stumbled down to the creek, over rocks, through mud, to the swiftly flowing water. From her apron she pulled a small, soggy loaf of bread and had me push a silver five-peso coin deep into the center. She bowed her head and mumbled over it, lifted it high in four directions, and threw it into the stream.

We watched it float out of sight. She dusted crumbs from her hand and smiled at me.

"Good," she said. "You sacrifice. You buy Henry peace."

Had she palmed the silver before throwing the bread? Probably. Would I ever check her apron pocket to retrieve my coin? Never. Somehow that would be flying in the face of Providence. False or true, she had earned her silver. I did feel, for a few murky moments, that I was once again in my brother's presence, that he was not completely gone from me. For that I was grateful. For that I wept, and gave the woman what she asked and more.

And yet, earlier, I had also felt Henry present in the trees, and in the wreck on the river. Do I merely succumb to the past, become an enraptured slave to memory from time to time? Do I pay these humbugs to add their illusions to the fabric of my own fantasies?

I don't know. And sometimes I don't know I don't know.

And yet…

## 34. A Letter to Alta California

Reprinted from *La Prensa Democratica*, June 5, 1879

Mark Twain
Santa Rosa
Republic of Alta California

Dear Reader:

I am writing to you in English, and you are reading something, hopefully similar in sense to what I wrote, in Spanish, thanks to the kind translation of our editor, Señor Jaime Rodolpho. He invited me to address you on the topic of Republicanism in general and my impressions of your country in particular—a very broad, a very generous, a very foolhardy offer, but let that go.

Let me start with just that one word: Country. What is "the Country," really? Is it the Government which is for the moment in the saddle? Why, the Government is merely a servant, and a temporary servant at that. It cannot be its prerogative to determine what is right and what is wrong, and decide who is a patriot and who isn't. Its function is to obey orders, not originate them. Who, then, is "the Country?" Is it the newspaper? Is it the pulpit? Is it the school superintendent? Why, these are mere parts of the country, not the whole of it; they have not command, they have only their little share in the command. They are but one in a thousand.

In a republic, it is the thousand who are the Country. It is in the thousand that command is lodged; they must determine what is right and what is wrong; they must decide who is a patriot and who isn't. They are the voice of the country. In a monarchy such as Rossland to your north, the Tsar and his family are the voice of the country, and that is an abomination. In a republic it is the common voice of the people. Each of you, for himself, by himself, and on his own responsibility, must speak from conscience.

The thousand do not speak in a single voice, nor should they. To speak against your own true convictions is to be an unqualified and inexcusable traitor, both to yourself and to your country. If you alone of all the nation shall decide one way, and that way be the right way according to your convictions of the right, you have done your duty by yourself and by your country—hold up your head. You have nothing to be ashamed of, let men call you what they may. This creates a certain cacophony of competing voices, the harmony of which, sometimes difficult to hear, comprises the republican voice.

I have heard that voice in the Republic of Alta California. I have heard it in the lecture halls, in the newspapers, in the schools and bars and taverns, in the offices of government. I have contributed my own small voice, as I shall tomorrow night in Pueblo Forestal (8pm, Teatro Amigos). That is my chief impression of your great Republic—that it has room and tolerance for more than one opinion, that it has ears aplenty for all the patriotic voices in the air. This newspaper is one such ear, and I am grateful for the opportunity to fill it with my foreign voice.

Your Admiring Visitor,

Mark Twain


### 35. Mushroom Wine

Henry James
Lamb House, the Willows
Rye, East Sussex
England
June 6, 1879

Dear Hank:

I am in Pueblo Forestal. Mark Twain is due to speak here tonight, but I shan't be present. I am shut of him and mean to stay shut. My plan to paint his portrait was ill-conceived and foolish. He is not really a subject of such stature that I need to waste my time courting his favor. All my efforts to befriend him have been ignored or rebuffed, so that is that.

If you detect a certain pique in my tone, you are correct. Let me describe some typically boorish Twain behavior. This afternoon I was in a local cantina, sampling a sweet fortified wine similar to Spanish Porto, to which was added a tincture of a local mushroom that I believe to be mildly hallucinogenic. It left me in a most unusual state of inebriation. I suffered, or enjoyed, a persistent alteration of my vision that fascinated me. Everywhere I looked the surface texture of the world seemed to crawl with a barely seen motion. It was as if the world were one vast tuning fork sounding a perfect note, or as if each object were a transparent vessel filled with tiny writhing worms. I felt that my eyes themselves were vibrating. The most placid scene seethed with energy.

I sat at a table in the corner by myself, staring in fascination at my own hand, rotating it ever so slowly to observe the changing shadows caused by the play of light, and the universe of wrinkles and whorls that make up its complex form.

My enjoyment was cut short by one of the genius Twain's common jokes. At some point he entered the cantina, drunk already. I saw him before he saw me, and resolved not to be the first to make an approach. Rather than come over to me and try to make amends, he tried to get my attention with schoolboy antics. He actually tried to startle me by setting off a firecracker behind me. However, being drunk himself, his attempts at stealth were ludicrous, rather like being stalked by a hippopotamus.

I was tapping my wine glass, observing closely the coruscations of the lamplight reflections in the surface of the wine. I tensed every muscle of my body, so that when the firecracker exploded, I did not start up, but kept calmly tapping my wine glass.

Disappointed, the Bard of Louisiana tried rolling another firework toward me from a distance, but I feigned a stretch and kicked it back to him. At that point I left the bar and retreated to my bunk in a rooming house, where I am now writing you.

The effects of the mushroom wine have faded now. They remind me of my mother's descriptions of an oncoming migraine headache, without the inevitable pain. I am left with a passionate desire to recreate the sensation for viewers of my paintings, by manipulating the colors, values, and surface texture. I understand in a new way why certain complementary hues seem to "vibrate" when placed next to one another. I have a new way of describing to myself the impression that the white lace highlights in a Velàsquez portrait are about to boil off the surface of the canvas and hover in the air above it.

You see, Henry, the surface of an oil painting is not really a flat plane, in effect or fact. Lighter, brighter colors advance, appearing closer to the viewer, while darker, duller colors recede, appearing further away from the viewer. This much painters have known for centuries. It is the genius of the modern age to explore and celebrate the *actual, factual* texture of the painted surface, rather than striving for the perfectly flat, "fine" finish so prized by the older artists of the Academy.

A close approach to a truly modern canvas reveals swirls and whorls of paint no less complex than human fingerprints. The correct distance for viewing a painting, to my new way of thinking, is precisely the distance at which your eye most rapidly switches between seeing the painting's subject matter and seeing a writhing mass of brushstrokes. This ocular "vibration," if you will, is very similar to what I experienced under the influence of Pueblo Forestal's mushroom wine.

Mark Twain would have been the perfect subject for a portrait to demonstrate these effects, for he is a writhing mass of contradictions himself. In my mind's eye he vibrates between seeming a literary genius and a common lout. I would have painted him in a classic pose, but with colors, textures and details that belied the dignity of the composition. Maybe his shirttail untucked, his waistcoat mis-buttoned, or a tea cozy on his head—all details I have witnessed in actuality.

Perhaps the effects of the mushroom wine have not worn off as much as I believed at the start of this missive, and I should sign off.

Your fond friend and lonely traveler,

John

### 36. Spiritual Toothache

Mary Clemens
17 Thatcher Street
Davis, Missouri
U.S.A.
June 6, 1879

Dear Mother:

Please do not take me to task for it, but I have been thinking about Henry lately, yesterday being the anniversary of his passage to a better world. I was walking along the bank of the Rio Russo, a pint-sized Mississippi that the local Pomo injuns call "Shabaikai," meaning something like "Home of Spirits." They hold it to be inhabited by ghosts, and I suspect they are correct.

A wreck on a sandbar put me in mind of the accursed *Pennsylvania* that caused our Henry so much suffering and took his life. Soon after seeing the wreck I was in conversation with a local minister of sorts—a Lutheran I suspect—who suggested that Henry has gone ahead of us, to prepare a place

of rest and glory for me and thee, a comfort for which we
rightfully should be thankful. I know that is true, but Henry
was the best of us, and his untimely departure still seems too
great a sacrifice to bear. If this earthly circus really needs an
advance man for its booking with Providence, I would that it
had been me. I'm more suited to the task of posting Heaven's
walls with gaudy advertisement.

Forgive me, I mean no blasphemy. This spell comes over
me from time to time, when Henry's spirit visits me. He is my
guardian angel, my guilty conscience, my spiritual toothache
that still throbs.

My fellow traveler John Sargent puts me in mind of
Henry sometimes. He is near Henry's age when he died, and
has much of Henry's innocence and appetite for life. But he
is more bullheaded and self-righteous and ungrateful. I have
been employing him as part of my advance team, and using
my influence hereabouts to advance his artistic aspirations, but
he does not appreciate my patronage. I reckon it comes from
the same sort of stubborn pride that made Henry standoffish
and prickly sometimes. Like Henry, John insists on hewing
his own path through this world, instead of taking the broad
road before him. In that humor he is entirely without a sense of
humor, which provokes in me a contrary frivolity and tendency
towards jokes and japes.

I believe I will close this letter, before I discourage myself
any further. I can hear your voice in my ears as I write: "Say
you're sorry, Sammy, and be more patient next time."

I'm sorry.

Your loving son,

Sam

## 37. Dancing the *Jaleo*

The day after the mushroom wine incident I took the train west
to the next town, a border settlement with the unlikely name of

*Aserraderos de Duncanov el Russo* – the Sawmills of the son of Duncan the Russian. The mill burned down years ago, Duncan was long dead, and the Russians were are a despised minority, but never mind that. A mongrel population of Spaniards, Indians, Russians, Moors, and Gypsies had created a vigorous marketplace where one could buy faux Faberge eggs, dud fireworks, limp piñatas and crooked guitars. All these dubious wares and more are offered for sale in booths and shacks and hovels spotted along a shady path that wound through a grove of magnificent redwood trees.

I tried sketching the redwoods, but found them difficult to capture. When I was among the trees, they seemed like columns in a vast and dimly lit cathedral, whose roof soared far overhead. However, on paper the trunks became an uninteresting collection of vertical lines. When I drew the upward-looking angle to emphasize their height, the trees lost all their solidity and majesty. They could have been a bunch of straws seen from the bottom of a glass of weak tea. I would need several days to study the problem, to discover the graphic means by which to suggest the non-visual aspects of the scene, such as the silence, the crick in my neck from looking upwards, the smell and the spongy texture of the duff carpeting the ground, the feel of my eyes themselves focusing and refocusing near and far. I envied Henry James and other writers the materials of fiction that allow them to invoke all the senses in describing a landscape.

I spent the afternoon perusing the market. Russian *émigrés* from across the river ran a miniature Faberge egg factory, crafting an improbable New World version of those imperial confections out of emu and ostrich eggs, Sierra gold, and local semiprecious stones. I imagined that the eggs are much coveted as wedding gifts, for which purpose they would be the ideal choice: expensive, fragile, impressive, beautiful, and utterly useless. At least some artisans had found a way to make money from their art.

I dined in a large cantina run by a Spaniard from Old Spain. The food was more European in its refinement, and the red wine was excellent. It was crowded, so I had to share a table with another man. His name was Tomas, but I never heard his family name. He was about my age, perhaps a year or two younger, with lustrous, curly black hair and large brown eyes with long lashes. He said he was a guitar maker from the southern part of the country, visiting family in the north.

We got along well at first. Tomas spoke Spanish with some English and French, well complimented by my English with some French and Spanish, so we enjoyed a tri-lingual interchange that sometimes even rose—or fell—to the level of the pun. He told me about his work with guitars, pointing to some guitars hanging on the walls of the cantina. I never knew there was so much to consider in making a guitar: the choice of woods for various parts, the pattern of the internal bracing, the thickness of the soundboard, the type of strings, and so on. It is like composing a painting: the choice of medium, the color scheme, the balance of lights and darks, the placement of the center of interest, and so on.

We ordered another bottle of wine and lingered after dinner. Two guitarists and a tambourine player struck up a tune and a Gypsy woman danced. Her white skirt swirled and her pale arms flashed in the lamp light. I pulled out my sketchbook and worked up a decent sketch of the scene.

Tomas said that the dance was a *jaleo*, a new and wondrous word to me. In Spanish the "J" is pronounced like the English "H," so the word has a breathy quality, as though the speaker were excited or panting.

"*Jaleo* is an Andalusian dance," Tomas said. "The word means 'clapping and cheering.'" Indeed, the drinkers at the other tables were clapping and cheering, and the woman clapped her hands like castanets and whooped as she spun around.

"*Jaleo* also means come to the party, join the wild people for much fun."

"We would say it is a binge or a spree," I said.

"Yes," here his voice dropped. "Also it can refer to the excitement of courtship." With this he put his hand on my arm

and began playing with the hairs.

"*Jaleo* can mean you are excited about meeting someone new," he continued, touching my beard.

I pulled away and went back to my sketch. I found him too forward, and I was embarrassed. I felt flushed and rather sick.

"What is the matter?" he asked.

"Nothing. I feel sick. I've had too much to drink."

He continued to fuss over me for a while, but I kept all my attention on the dancers, and refused to respond. He soon excused himself and left. I felt confused and very sad. I consider myself an open and affectionate person. I have walked arm in arm and shared many confidences with dear friends like Henry James. But some fellows go too far, especially on first acquaintance. They make assumptions that are unwarranted—one might even call them advances.

I value the friendship and company of other men highly. Only a man can truly understand another man. But one must confine one's impulses and enthusiasms within the boundaries of good taste and propriety. If I dance the *jaleo* with boys met casually in bars, I will never gain entrée to the level of society where successful portrait painters ply their trade. Still, for a few moments the music was more intoxicating than the wine, and I had been clapping and cheering inside.

I staggered out into the night, heading unsteadily for the train station, with the drunken intention of taking the night train to the coast to sleep on the beach. As I passed a dark alley, a figure rushed out and pushed me into the gutter. I skinned my hands and knees and was violently sick all over the cobblestones. I was so shaken for a moment that I scarcely felt the fellow paw at my coat and remove my billfold. By the time I had recovered my wits, he was a small figure running away in the distance, turning a corner and gone. I thought it was Tomas, but I was not sure.

"Dios mio," a voice said, "Are you all right?" Another figure in a long overcoat helped me up to my feet."

"I'm all right," I said, looking around for my sketchbook. I found it in the gutter, only slightly soiled. "I'm fine."

"Is that you, Señor Sargent?" he asked.

My savior was Francisco Goya.

## 38. Hemp Dodgers

Reprinted from the *Atlantic Weekly,* June 27, 1879
Mark Twain
Pueblo Forestal
Republic of Alta California

Dear Reader:

Greetings from Pueblo Forestal in fabled Alta California. This is the home of a tribe I call the "Addendi," because they cannot leave their grub alone, but must "add" to every common food or drink something extra, to make it uniquely their own and keep visitors on their gustatory toes. Typical California cuisine adds mint to beans, prunes to lamb, and chilies to everything. They drink water with rose petals, coffee with licorice, and beer with lime juice.

The other night I was treacherously ambushed by the lowly corn dodger. Young Sargent and I were dining on the patio of our hotel. Children threaded their way among the tables, selling fireworks, paper flowers, kites, and local delicacies called *calle perritos,* or "hush puppies," the same term we used in the Greenville, Mississippi of my youth, or what soldiers in the war called corn dodgers: bite-sized morsels of cornmeal, fried a golden brown. At home we eat them with fatback and gravy. Here they are flavored with cinnamon and honey, and laced with finely powdered hemp that does nothing for the taste but wonders for the outlook. These appetizers were their own best advertising, because they made one careless of his purse and famished for more. After three or four I became so filled with the hemp of human kindness that I laid in a generous supply of firecrackers, ladyfingers, smoke bombs, squibs, pinwheels, kites, fake violets, and enough hush dodgers to supply Grant's army.

One urchin dealt with me so sharply I considered adopting him. The young Shylock performed a Yankee switch on my change that had me gasping in admiration and counting my eyeteeth. I had to ask Sargent to loan me more pesos. When he did not reply, I first thought he could not hear me over the noisy crowd in the restaurant. I asked again, louder, but he did not stir.

The poor dupe in his inexperience had been swilling the local port, which the Addendi had improved with a fungal extract much prized by the natives hereabouts for its spiritual properties. He was still as stone, staring at his wine glass with glazed eyes.

"Go easy on that," I shouted. "If you are going to drink so much, at least eat something. Have a corn puppy."

He continued to ignore me, too far gone in his cups to hear my voice. I was seized by the notion that the happy juice was turning him to stone, as if he'd had a gander at the Medusa.

"John," I said, "Are you all right?" Still he did not reply, but sat still as death, staring at his wine glass.

"Sargent," I yelled, "Your hair is on fire." But he turned a deaf and dumb ear and tongue. My most intriguing conversational sallies were thoroughly rebuffed, with an impervious demeanor that might have stymied a more defatigable feller. I ate another hemp dodger and marshaled my forces.

"Goya was a hack!" I cried, "I wouldn't let him paint my barn!" Even this heresy failed to rouse him, so sunk was he in Enervated Catatonia, a dangerous state that can only be cured by a large dose of Twain's Elixir—rapid and violent stimulation of the auditory nerves. I lit a small squib and tossed it under his chair. It exploded with a sharp "crack!" but he budged not an inch. Not a flinch, not a twitch, not the tenth part of a tic.

Fearing that his malady had progressed to rigor mortis, I rolled a cherry bomb under the table, but he kicked it away and it blew the heel off my boot. I dropped a fizzing pinwheel onto his plate, but he doused it absentmindedly with water. Sargent was immune to all my treatments, protected by the dumb luck and guardian angels of drunkards everywhere.

As I was contemplating my next move, he slowly levitated off his chair like a barrage balloon whose mooring ropes have been axed. He stared through me with a gaze so fixed I began to doubt my own opacity. Then he floated up the stairs toward his room, stiff and inflexible as a bust of Caesar being assumed into Heaven.

It was too many for me. I gave up my career as a missionary of sobriety, and ate another hesh pumper.

Sincerely yours,


Mark Twain

### 39. Casa Goya

Violet Paget
17 Rue Des Jardins
Montparnasse
Paris, France
June 7, 1879

My dear Violet:

How I wish you were here to comfort me and listen to my sad complaints. How I miss your *sympathie*! I was attacked and robbed on the street the other night. It left me feeling quite shaken and nervous—actually a little sick in my stomach. I was pushed down and relieved of my billfold so quickly that I did not even see my assailants clearly. Thankfully, I was not physically harmed, and they did not get my sketchbook. But I am very short of funds now.

I am writing you from Casa Goya. Francisco Goya has rescued me and given me a place to stay in his *hacienda*. I have a pallet on the floor of his grandfather's studio, and the atmosphere is most inspiring, with his fantastic murals constantly looking over my shoulder.

To repay Francisco's hospitality, I agreed to help him restore *grandpère* Goya's studies. I have started with the best of the lot, the study for "La Maja Reformada." It is a reclining figure of a local beauty, classical in its allusions, but very modern in its composition and paint handling. I've worked up the background in keeping with the master's bravura brushstrokes on the face and hands. I have refined the contours of some shapes, softened a few edges, and harmonized the color a little. It now shines as a stunning, fresh study that I believe is truly in keeping with the master's intentions. I've learned a lot in the few brief hours spent with this painting.

It is not signed, of course. According to Francisco, Goya seldom signed his studies. Even some of his larger, finished works are not signed, or are signed only on the back. But were this one signed "Goya," I flatter myself that no one would dispute it.

Francisco is a kindly gentleman, one of those older chestnut gatherers who wants to recruit everyone into the band of brothers. He told me that I should enjoy my youth, just give in to my impulses and celebrate my predilections. According to him, artists are true aristocrats and as such are not to be bound by the narrow moral strictures that bind common men. But his sexual inversion seems strangely theoretical. He seems more interested in converting me to his way of thinking that in any straightforward act. At the least, I am becoming more able to write about these things, if not yet talk about them.

I don't understand him. He really wants me to go to Rossland. He keeps mentioning this Krepotsky, the minister of culture who gives out official commissions. He has offered to write me a letter of introduction, if I can only get a visa.

I have a few more days of work to do restoring Goya's canvases, then I do not know what I will do. I can't stay here forever. I have barely enough for my passage home, so I fear my trip is coming to a premature close, and that I will have to start for home very soon. Francisco has offered me a generous commission on the sale of the studies, but he has no money to advance me against that future income. Perhaps I will see you in a few weeks.

Yours truly,

John

### 40. Command Performance

The telegram from my agent Hilario Amado was a big surprise:

*TSAR COMMANDS PERFORMANCE NEXT WEDNESDAY PM FORTRESS ROSS. ALTO. 3 VISAS YOU & 2 SERVANTS PETALUMO CONSULATE. ALTO*

With Marina's help, I deciphered this to mean that I would be allowed to enter Rossland, with two other people, to perform for the Tsar at a coastal town in less than a week. To my delight, the fair Marina agreed to accompany me as part of my gang of three.

On the train to Petalumo, she went to work on me.

"For the third person you should take John Sargent."

"I don't even know where he is. The scamp has disappeared."

"He is staying with Francisco Goya in Petalumo."

"How do you know that?"

"I hear things. I listen to people."

"Well, he ain't gonna want to take up with me again. His nose is all out of joint."

"He will tolerate you if it means he can get into Rossland."

"Oh goody, that's what I want most in the world, to traipse about with folks who *tolerate* me."

She narrowed her dark eyes and flashed them at me. "You hurt that boy's feelings, you owe him an apology. If you say you're sorry and ask him to come, he will accompany us and be glad he did. You'll be glad he did." She smiled, "And I'll be glad."

"I never could resist a beautiful woman," I said, taking her hand.

"Bother," she said, pulling it back.

"Tarnation. I'll do it then."

We tracked John Sargent to a shabby hacienda in Petalumo. He answered our knock dressed in a linsey-woolsey smock all daubed with paint, wiping a brush on a rag. He looked surprised to see us, and more than a little spooked. He stood in the doorway, not inviting us in, wiping the brush, staring at me for a longish moment.

"What are you doing here?" he asked.

"We just got in on the train," I said, "and came straight here."

"Yes, but what do you want?"

"For starters, I reckon we want to get out of the wind."

"Just a minute. I'll be right back." He started away, then turned back to the door, "I have a kettle on the stove, I need to set it off." He pushed the door almost closed and retreated into the depths of the hacienda. That boy never could lie worth a damn. I pushed the door open a bit and peered inside, but I couldn't see where he went. Two whistles and a shake later, he was back at the door, all breathless and polite.

"All right, please come in," he said, opening the door wide. He ushered us into a bright interior with lots of light from windows and skylights. The place was littered with painter's trash: canvases leaned up against walls and furniture, papers and rags scattered everywhere, all surfaces daubed with paint and holding pots of brushes, dried out mortars with crusty pestles, palettes and jars of paint and pigment. A canvas on an easel was covered with a cloth.

"I've been helping Señor Goya clean out his studio," he said.

I said, "You're doing a wonderful job," looking around at the hopeless mess. "And I hate to take you away from it. But I need your help as well."

"I'm awfully busy here."

"I can see that, but you see, I've been invited to perform for the Tsar in Rossland next Wednesday. They'll let me bring two others with me, and I know how much you'd like to go sketch the Russkies."

"I don't have a visa."

"That's the thing I came to tell you. I can get you a visa right now, this very afternoon. They have three waiting for me and my *entourage*."

He grimaced at my pronunciation of the French, a language he liked to reserve for his own use. Marina came up behind me and nudged my arm.

"Wasn't there something else you meant to say?" she asked.

"Oh right." I said to John, "I'm, ah, rather, you know... sorry."

"Sorry?"

"About...you know, what happened." Marina snorted and John looked skeptical.

"Listen here," I went on, "I'm just no good at this apologizing guff. The plain fact is, I went off halfcocked with Jaime Rodolpho and had him make me the new handbill, and forgot entirely that you offered to do one with your sketch. That's what I'm sorry about."

John was still holding his brush, wiping it, and looking at his feet now, shaking his head slowly.

"I'm sorry too," he said, "but it doesn't really matter. I was robbed the other night, so I'm very short of funds. I have to start for home in a couple of days, or I will be stuck here."

"I'll pay all the expenses, or make the Russkies do it. If we have to, we can share hotel rooms and eat beans from a can. I'll smoke cheaper cigars."

"They don't come any cheaper," Marina said. John laughed at that.

"Oh, all right," he said. "But I have to have some time off for sketching and painting."

"Done," I said, and we shook hands.

### 41. Literary Secretary

Mary Sargent, c/o Sanderson
Apartments Genessee
10 Clarastrasse
Berne, Switzerland
June 8, 1879

Dear Mother:

Events are moving very quickly in my adventure here. I feel like I am inside one of my own watercolors, with the colors and shapes constantly changing. A few days ago I looked at a calendar and calculated the state of my funds, and decided that it was time for me to turn once again toward Paris, and start the trip back to civilization. I was looking forward to seeing you and father once again after such a long absence.

Then I was offered a position with Diego de la Goya, cataloging, cleaning, and restoring what remains here of his grandfather's *oeuvre*. I was only two days in his employ when Mark Twain put in his bid for my services. He burst into my room waiving a telegram from his agent in San Francisco. He was grinning like a boy. Here is a specimen of our conversation:

"I have been invited to palaver with the Tsar in Fortress Ross," he said. "I aim to take you along as part of my gang, all expenses paid. You can be my personal whatchamacallit."

"Portraiteur? Landscape artist?" I asked.

"More like literary secretary. You must hang on my every word and take the occasional note."

"Oh, I do that regardless" I said with considerable irony.

"I can spin the Emperor yarns about the royal family of Hawaii. He won't understand enough English or Esperanto to catch the real drift, and Miss Miranova will pretty it up for them. She's as fluent in Russian as she is in Spanish."

"Be careful," I warned, "Nicolai attended Oxford for a term, before the Crimean war called him home. He probably understands more English than he lets on."

Twain looked at me sideways. "How can you know all this? Next thing you'll tell me Romanovsky is your second cousin on your mother's side."

"My mother's side would be honored, but no. Diego de la Goya has briefed me about the Russians. He thinks they are more high class than the Californian Dons."

"I like the Dons. They're cantankerous as islanders, and practical as Yankees, but they cook better than both."

"That may be, but I'd rather be paid for my work in Russian bluebacks than in *chile verde.*"

We went on in this vein. Mr. Twain may disdain hereditary nobility, and he certainly waxes vitriolic about monarchy, but he purred like a kitten over his invitation to an audience with Nicolai Romanovsky, Tsar of Rossland.

With the Tsar's letter in hand, all obstacles melted away before us. The consulate officials who have been curt and dour were all smiles today. We were ushered to the head of three different queues and accorded every courtesy and mark of respect. As we walked out of the building with our freshly minted visas, Twain remarked that it almost made him feel respectable. For my part, I was delighted to have my expenses paid on a visit to exotic Rossland. It will be a relief to be in a country with a functioning aristocracy, who support the arts as they should be supported. Who knows, I may remain there for some time, if I can secure some portrait commissions.

I will write to you soon about the western Russian Empire.

Your loving son,

John

## 42. Quicksilver Sketches

Francisco was not pleased that I was leaving his place before finishing the restoration of the Maja painting.

"It will only take you a few hours to complete it," he said.

"No, there is still much to do, and I can't rush it. I will finish it when I return."

"How do I know you'll ever pass this way again?"

"I will return. The painting will be all the better for some natural drying time. Don't cook it over a fire or anything until I get back."

He retreated into a distant room and did not even say goodbye when I left. I was sorry to leave without finishing the job, but the sights of a new country beckoned me. I had every intention of returning in time.

Twain was as good as his word. That night I moved into his hotel room and took possession of the extra bed. His manner was all bluff good humor and charm as he stripped to his "skivvies" and climbed into his "bunk." I did the same and lay for several minutes awake, staring at the ceiling, very aware of his breathing as it slowed and turned to snores.

In the morning I was full of a familiar restlessness. It was an itching of my sketching fingers, a conviction deep in my soul that a scene was calling me, that somewhere out in the wide world a painting wanted me to paint it. A composition was hidden in the landscape somewhere and it was my destiny to discover it and coax it out onto paper or canvas.

Perhaps this is a self-important way of saying that I felt like drawing. Perhaps I am dramatizing myself, as my father sometimes accused me of doing. But it feels like more than a mere whim or mood or preference. It has the same visceral force and propulsion as physical hunger or amorous desire. My urge to paint is to mere preference as the sun is to the moon in luminance. At these times, I feel disoriented, almost drunk. Colors seem more intense, the edges of things vibrate, and my hand moves of its own impetus to draw the shapes I see.

Marina joined us for breakfast in the dining room. We were a merry trio, Mark and I working our way manfully through large plates of steak and eggs, while Marina sipped coffee and nibbled at tortillas and fruit.

"I reckon we can catch tomorrow's ferry," Twain said. "There's one from Roca de Cabra at noon. Then there's a train up to Fortress Ross at one thirty."

"What are your plans for today?" I asked.

"I've got a notion that is right down your alley. Now that we've got these visas, what do you say we nip across the river at Pueblo Forestal and take a look around. There's a cinnabar mine over there I'd like to see."

Cinnabar! A delicious word. It sounds like a stick of

cinnamon, my favorite spice.

I told him, "My mother used to give me cinnamon lozenges with horehound when I had a sore throat."

"Cinnabar lozenges would not be so tasty," he said. "Cinnabar is actually the ore from which quicksilver is refined. You know, mercury."

"Oh, I know that. In the refining process, a lovely pigment is produced—vermilion. It is a deep russet, more red than burnt umber, sometimes almost violet. It is very useful in under painting florid complexions or adding warmth and neutralizing cooler tones."

"I don't think that's what the Rosslanders use it for. They run more to thermometers and explosives and medicines."

"Regardless, I would love to see the mine."

"Leave all the details to me," he said, "I know a river rat who will rent us a canoe very cheap."

Marina folded her napkin and stood up. "I hope you river rats may have fun paddling your canoe today. I must pack my things and settle my affairs. I will meet you at the ferry tomorrow." She strode out of the dining room and Twain watched her go until she was out of sight.

The river rat actually did look like a rat, a noble Egyptian rat. He had a narrow head and a prominent nose, with little by way of a chin or brow to take away from his rodent-like expression. His skin was a ruddy gold, with high spots of crimson that I would paint with a cinnabar pigment. He sniffed repeatedly and wiped his runny nose on the sleeve of his filthy linsey-woolsey shirt, in a twitchy, rat-like gesture that only confirmed the comparison. My eyes itched to paint him, but there was no time or opportunity.

Sometimes I wish I could freeze time or step aside, outside of time. Everyone would be frozen except myself, and I would be free to walk around people like they were statues, seeking the perfect angle, setting up an easel and lights and taking all the time I needed to paint them. Then with a snap of my fingers, time would resume its flow and I would have a finished portrait, perfect in all its detail, and no one would know how long it took. No one would complain of backache or postpone their next appointment. No one would fidget and shift out of their pose and be unable to recall it no matter how much one tries to re-position them.

The canoe was actually a rowboat, short and wide and hard to steer. We each took an oar and started rowing, looking over our shoulders to aim at the crooked oak tree across the Slavyanka River where the river rat said we could land. For a riverman of his experience, Twain was very inconsistent in his rowing. I had to slow down and speed up my pace to keep us going straight.

After a wet walk up a creek, we came to a bridge where we caught a ride to the mine on a wagon full of lumber beams. The mules strained to pull the heavy load up a winding dirt road. Slowly the mine unfolded before me. It was the scene that had been calling to me all morning: like an Italian hill town built of raw lumber and tin sheeting.

I jumped off the wagon, shouting to Twain, "Pick me up later."

Rambling wooden sheds and chutes were stacked against the hillside like a child's blocks, their shapes accented by the sun slanting in from the right at a forty five degree angle, just where I would have put the light if I were setting the scene in miniature in the studio. I perched on a rail fence a few yards from the dust of the road, where I had a good view of the whole hillside and mine from a distance. My first sketch was loose and wild, running off the edge of the page like an excited beginner in figure class. My second was better composed, and my third began to capture what I was after.

The first impression of an Italian hill town was not quite right. The scene had greater size variety than that—many buildings were scaled by industrial necessity, not the average size of an Italian peasant. Although normal offices and bunkhouses and storehouses established a human scale, the need to contain and shelter vast machinery confounded that scale with truly

enormous structures requiring outsized foundations, beams and braces made of whole trees.

Everything had to conform to the slope of the steep mountain, which the vast agglomeration of buildings and machines was in the process of demolishing: boring into it, chopping it into terraces, spilling vast floods of earth and gravel and boulders, creating ponds of water at the base. The buildings seemed to grow out of the ground and to be melting into it—not in the calculated and diffident manner of formal architecture, but in a more organic and natural way that suggested growth and decay.

The colors were subtle but breathtaking. New lumber made bright notes of red, orange and yellow. Older buildings mellowed into browns and eventually silver gray, with water stains and shadows of purple black. New tin sheeting reflected dazzling white in the sun, pale blue sky in the shadows. Old tin was silver and gray and rusty shades of burnt umber and sienna. The earth was stained with yellow oxide and acid green, and ten shades of gray that harmonized with the muted greens of scrub brush and the few surviving trees, all coated with dust.

Here and there distant figures of men swarmed over the hillside like ants. It reminded me of the quarries outside Carrara in Italy, but more interesting because of the structures dominating and transforming the landscape.

After a while I moved up the road to get closer and made a sketch of some kind of crusher building atop a small mountain of dirt and gravel. Then I moved as far to the right as I could get for another angle. The sun was moving higher in the sky, going behind me, flattening the scene, but also revealing more detail as smaller structures came into the light.

It was late afternoon when I came back to ordinary consciousness. I had put away my sketchbook in my bag, and was massaging the kinks out of my back and neck. Twain came down the road, escorted by a policeman who was saying something rude in Russian. Evidently our fresh visas lacked proper entry stamps. We were taken back to the river, put into our rowboat, which had taken on about three inches of water, and watched suspiciously all the way back to the other side. I was glad that the policeman had not seen my sketches and tried to confiscate them.

## 43. A Spot of Espionage

William Dean Howells
Atlantic Weekly
Boston, Massachusetts, USA
June 9, 1879

Dear William:

Good News! Wednesday next the Tsar of Rossland in his Wisdom has scheduled a command performance by my unworthy self at his summer palace in Fortress Ross. Your readers can look forward to many amusing glimpses of the Western Russian Empire. I'm taking Miranova as translator and Sargent as secretary. We have visas in hand and leave tomorrow, even though it means canceling a couple of my lectures in A.C. I would much rather speechify in Rossland— you know how I love to skewer the nobles.

Meanwhile, I have engaged in a spot of espionage on your behalf, for whatever it may be worth. Under cover of a sketching expedition for Sargent, we slipped across the Rio Russo yesterday to spy on the Rtut Cinnabar Mine and Smelter northeast of the Russian village of Mercury.

Enclosed you will find photographic prints of several exposures I made with my handy Submarine Camera. You can see that the Rtut is a large operation, in full production. The mine itself consists of seven main galleries, some extending 2,000 yards into the mountain, and reaching a depth of 350 feet, where constant pumping is required to clear the shafts of seepage.

I was unable to determine exact tonnages, but from the traffic on the road and the size of the smelter, I think this operation alone must supply Rossland with all the quicksilver they need, with considerable left over for export.

The mining is largely a pick-and-shovel affair, carried out by Indian and Chinese laborers for the most part, with the encouragement of Russian overseers. Miners are a scruffy lot, but these seemed poorly turned-out even for miners—ragged clothes, skinny, limping, crude gear. A southern Confederate would be ashamed to treat his niggers so shabbily.

The crushing, milling, and smelting operations are more modern, under steam power with an extensive power train of belt and gear drives. A relatively small crew of men can process a lot of ore with this setup.

By looking open and cheerful, as if I belonged, no one challenged me for about three hours. A foreman came out several times from the ball mill to stare at me. He must have sent a message to the authorities, because eventually one of the local sheriffs arrived in a black buggy to see me off the property. I played the innocent tourist, bumbling and harmless, a persona that has saved my bacon many times. I fumbled with my Esperanto dictionary, showed the deputy my mother's picture and my passport, and generally made a fool of myself. The deputy didn't spot my camera, thankfully. Eventually he kicked us out with a stern warning not to trespass again.

Also enclosed is another letter for the paper, giving the more comic account of our trip across the river, and the front page of a local newspaper, *La Prensa Democratica*. Just look at the quality of the pictures! I have met it's owner, editor, and inventive genius, Jaime Rodolpho. As I suspected, his methods owe nothing to the engravers art, and everything to a shrewd combination of photographic chemistry and acidic metallurgy. Beyond that, I have promised to say no more. But between you and me, I urge you not to enter into any long term contracts with engravers or police sketch artists. Someday very soon, newspapers will be full of cheaply and easily produced photographs.

Señor Rodolpho has promised to publish any interesting photographs I might make in Rossland. He has also asked me to enquire about the possibility of importing bulk quantities of silver nitrate and nitric acid, which are scarce and dear in Alta California.

As you see, I am adding commercial espionage to my more political spying. Please remit my cloak and dagger by return post. Until then, I remain...

Your faithful conspirator,

Mark Twain

## 44. Cockleshell

Reprinted from the *Atlantic Weekly,* July 4, 1879
Mark Twain
Santa Rosa
Republic of Alto California

Dear Reader:

Many here admire the Russian River, the border between the Spanish Republic to the south, which likes to call it the Rio Russo, and the Russian Empire to the north, where they refer to the waterway as Slavyanka. As a border, it is a tributary of much historical interest and dispute over the last three hundred years. As a river among rivers such as the Mississippi or the Nile, it is a mere creek. It has about four feet in the channel and a few scows floating around on it. It would be a very plausible river if they pumped some water into it. They all call it a river, and they honestly think it is a river, these sunny and sanguine Spaniards and these dark and determined Russians. They even reinforce the delusion by building bridges across it. I do not see why they are too good to wade.

Sargent and I went punting on the stream last Tuesday in a cockleshell they call a rowboat. This vessel was so broad in the beam as to be nearly circular. Fortunately I am an experienced riverman and was able to deduce that the point on the circumference where the anchor rope was tied must be the bow. Oarlocks 90 degrees on either side confirmed my suspicions, so John and I jumped in and grabbed the oars.

For an old riverman, rowing with a landlubber is like a horse being hitched with a cow. First the landsman will pull with a will, driving the vessel hard a-port. Then he gets a stitch in his side and lays back so she falls off to larboard. He becomes so relaxed in his new regime that he falls asleep, then wakes with a jerk, and redoubles his efforts in embarrassment, overpowering the poor craft again to port. Every shift in the wind, every slap of the waves, every horsefly and mosquito so distracts and discomforts the landlubber cow that he changes the force and tempo of his rowing. It is up to me, the experienced plow horse of the waters, to anticipate and react immediately with enhancements and diminutions of my own output to balance the chaos on the other side of the boat in such a way that she tracks straight and true. The landlubber then disembarks at our destination and looks back at the ruler-straight wake, beaming with pride in his seamanship, while I am left in the bilges, shaking and panting with nervous exhaustion.

"It might have been faster to build a bridge," Sargent remarked, "Or wait for the river to dry up." He went on in this vein, pickaxing his way from the dull clay of incomprehension toward the humor-rich ore of levity, without ever striking pay dirt. For many years I have never lost my cheerfulness and wanted to lay me down in some secluded spot and die, and be at rest, until I heard him try to be funny today.

We picnicked on the Russian side and took a walk up the road to the famous Rtut Quicksilver Mine, where seven Chinamen with wheelbarrows were working ceaselessly to keep the thermometers of the world full of mercury. Our visit was cut short by a Russian cop—apparently the oak tree to which we tied our scow was not an official port of entry to the Slavic Empire. I remarked that this country must be paradise for smugglers, since you can throw contraband across the border without it getting wet. Fortunately the official did not understand my quip. He insisted on seeing a demonstration of our rowing prowess, and indeed he watched us all the way back across the creek.

Having narrowly avoided yet another international incident, I remain,


Your faithful servant and correspondent,

Mark Twain




## 45. Totems


Very early in the morning Twain and I caught the train to the mouth of the Slavyanka, an area called by the Californians Estero de las Cabras, after the many goats that are raised there. We planned to meet Marina there and continue by ferry into Rossland, then take the Russian train up the coast. But the ferry was not running, and there was no sign of Marina.

While Twain inquired about alternative transport, I wandered the shores of the estuary on a network of interlaced goat paths, through thickets of gorse and fern. The morning overcast and fog was slowly dissipating, and the sun cast long hazy beams the length of the valley. Had there been Parliament buildings or ships on fire, it would have been a perfect subject for Turner or Gainsborough.

But this was not the Thames. Rather, the water was spider-webbed with frail jetties that showed black against the misty mirrored surface as if drawn with a crow quill in India ink over a loose watercolor base. At least, that is how I would do it, had I the leisure. But my paints were in my bag back at the station, so I contented myself with a quick sketch in my little book.

As the visibility increased, Indians materialized like wraiths from the fog. They strolled out in twos and threes to the ends of the jetties with long poles and nets. One Indian would peer into the shallow water, hook up an enormous fish, and flip it backwards to another Indian, who clubbed the fish and laid it out on the dock. From time to time women dragged the accumulated fish ashore, where they skinned and filleted them, laying the long vermillion strips of meat out to dry on trellises overhead. The offal they threw to the dogs who scuffled for it in the sand.

I sketched the scene until the day warmed, the flies came out, and the smell of fish guts drove me inland, to higher ground where a breeze blew the stench and flies away. Along a low bluff I found a series of carved totem poles, oriented so that they looked out to sea. I stopped and made several sketches. They were different from the Polynesian tiki carvings I had seen in the Sandwich Islands. Instead of gods and kings, the California Indians seemed to prefer natural forms from the world around them—animals such as eagles, foxes, frogs, and fish, but stylized and idealized in a way that fascinated me. Also the poles were painted in black, white, russet, gray-green, and ochre—something the Hawaiian carvers seldom do.

The sculptors differed in their solutions to the problem of fitting a form to the cylindrical shape of a tree trunk. Some animals or people were posed in a vertical, stacked-up pose entirely within the cylinder. Others had pieces of wood added for wings, beaks and noses that stuck out of the cylinder. Structural necessity made heads the same diameter as bodies, so human forms for example had a big-headed charm like puppies or kittens. Human features were distorted, with wide gaping mouths and goggling eyes. I could not discern the impulse behind the creation of the sculptures. The aim of the artist could not be portraiture, due to the distortion. The humorous nature of some of the figures suggested parody or burlesque, but what kind of artist is moved to satirize a frog or a salmon? The hawkish birds that topped many poles had an innate nobility, suggesting a heraldic motive. But how could I know? This was an art entirely outside the European tradition, and I found it exciting, mysterious, and humbling. The poles hinted to me of a different way of seeing the world—a vision of reality that, to my profound regret and annoyance, was not open to me.

On my way back to the station I saw a man sketching the mouth of the river, and was surprised upon closer approach to see that it was Francisco Goya. I held back a moment, remembering our awkward parting in his studio two days earlier. Finally I screwed up my courage and approached him.

"Don Francisco," I said, "what are you doing in this backwater?"

"I am working on a commission," he said, "an historical mural for one of the Petalumo Civic organizations."

"The light was better earlier, when there was more moisture in the atmosphere."

"I am certain that is true, but this is sufficient for my needs. I wanted to remind myself of the lay of the land."

He opened a leather portfolio on the grass at his feet. "I have something for you," he said. "I have been carrying it with me in case I met you."

He handed me a small envelope sealed with viridian green wax.

"Take this with you to Rossland," he said. "it will introduce you to Gregor Krepotsky. He is their Minister of Cultural Affairs, and an important figure in the art world there."

"Thank you," I said, tucking the letter into my book, "But I may never get to Rossland. The ferry isn't running and there is talk of closing the border."

"Political games," he said. "It will all blow over by the end of the week. It always does."

"At any rate, thank you so much for the letter. I am much obliged."

"It is nothing," he said. "We artists must help one another however we can. You will find Minister Krepotsky at Fortress Ross this time of year, and he is quite approachable. You will have no trouble securing an appointment. But I must warn you that some of those surrounding Minister Krepotsky are jealous and scheming politicians, always suspicious of any special favors he might grant. It will be to your advantage to deliver this letter privately."

"Of course, whatever you say."

"Quien sabe? You may be invited to try your hand at an official portrait. That is what I have suggested to him."

"Thank you again, my friend."

We parted on excellent terms, me to the station to catch the coach to Bodega Bay, he to continue his sketching. He seemed entirely friendly and natural at the time, as if I had never left his grandfather's study unfinished on an easel.

## 46. Plans Knocked Galley-west

William Dean Howells
Atlantic Weekly
Boston, Massachusetts, USA
June 10, 1879

Dear William:

This morning afforded me the most convincing evidence yet of the bellicose nature of relations between the Dons and the Russians. My train ticket, purchased yesterday in good faith, promised me passage on a ferry into Rossland once I reached the terminus of the Californian rail line at the mouth of the Rio Russo. However, our plans have been knocked galley-west. When we arrived at the ferry dock, it was barricaded by soldiers. and we were informed that the ferry would not be running until further notice.

A skinny corporal in a baggy uniform told me that the Russians have closed their border. I could see myself that the road to Fortress Ross on the other bank had been blocked with a pile of logs. However, there were many Spanish soldiers on our side, guarding the ferry, so perhaps it was the Dons who initiated the border closing, and the corporal was merely blaming the Russians. *Quien sabe?*

On the ferry dock I ran into Francisco Goya, grandson of the famous Goya and a painter in his own right.

"Mucho gusto," he exclaimed, which is the local equivalent of the Shakespearean, "Well met." He grabbed my hand like a long-lost cousin and reminded me of our previous meeting in Petalumo.

"How is Señor Sargent?" he asked, peering at me keenly as if I were hiding John under my coat.

"He has gone to stretch his legs along the strand," I replied.

"I have a letter of introduction for Señor Sargent to the Minister of Culture of Rossland."

He showed me the letter. Goya claimed to be in Estero de las Cabras on business, but I don't know what he means by that. He is a painter, and the only business around here seems to be in goats and dried salmon. I had the impression that he was in the vicinity looking for John Sargent, else why would he be carrying a letter of introduction for him? Perhaps I am just suspicious by nature, but Goya seems shifty to me.

I told him about our problems getting into Rossland, and he recommended that we backtrack by coach to Bahia de Bodega and take a steamer up the coast. Apparently the Russians feel they have more control over this approach and have not closed that access to their hallowed ground. Having crossed the river myself by rowboat only yesterday, I was not impressed by Authority's attempt to seal the border.

The coach to Bodega Bay will not leave until well after noon, so I took a turn around the town, although that is too fine a term for it by a long stretch. I examined a partially completed trestle that will allow trains to cross the estuary some day, if it is ever completed. Rust stains on the weathered timbers and erosion around the footings told me that the trestle has been under construction for some time, and there was no sign of any contemporaneous work being done. To my eye it had all the signs of a pork barrel project in the USA.

I made a photograph of the ferry, anchored forlornly out of reach of either bank. Every time I take out my camera, I imagine what my picture would look like in a newspaper, engraved with Jaime Rodolfo's photogravure method. That man is a comer, and if I had any money, I would invest it in his enterprise in the blink of an eye.

Indians were shoveling salmon out of the river and drying fish along the shore. Their methods dated back to the Stone

Age. The size and number of the spawning fish would make this an inexhaustible fishery, if only white men would get it organized properly with seine nets and trawlers. But the Dons seem to prefer beefsteak, so the salmon goes mostly to Indians, Chinamen and dogs.

The Indians around here remind me of the Sandwich Islanders in their idolatrous affection for dogs. Although the animals are baseborn and spiritless yellow curs for the most part, they are loved and cared for by the Indians more fervently than their own children. They might carelessly forget a child or drop it overboard, but never a dog.

The coach leaves in an hour, and I see John returning from his walk. I should close this missive and look for Marina. She should be here by now. I will write again when I have a more commodious desk than the crate I am writing on now. Until then I remain,

Your Faithful Servant,

Mark Twain

## 47. Personae Gratae et Non Gratae

Twain and I arrived at the dock in Bahia de Bodega two hours before our boat was to sail. At short notice all we could get was deck passage, for which Twain had to part with a sizable bribe. We loitered near the ticket office as long as we could, waiting for Marina to arrive. Twain stared up the empty street, fidgeting from foot to foot, slapping our three tickets on his thigh and muttering to himself.

I stared out toward the bay. The mist reduced the scene to flat shapes stacked one behind another—the pier a black outline, the Fortress Ross steamer in dark grey, and each ship anchored in the bay a lighter shade of gray with distance, receding all the way out to Bodega Head, so pale gray it almost disappeared into the pearly atmosphere. The scene was too simple even for watercolor. One could paint it with diluted India ink.

Marina did not arrive by the time the last whistle blew for boarding. Twain left her ticket at the office, hoping she would catch the next boat, and we went on board.

All the cabins and even the saloon lounge were packed with passengers. Most of them were Rosslanders who had boarded in San Francisco, taller and more angular that the common run of folk in Petalumo. They huddled in small groups around tables, tapping the wood with glasses of vodka and tossing it down like water. They were all talking at once in Russian, some whispering, some muttering sideways and hardly moving their lips, and other shouting in shrill, belligerent tones.

"*Personae non gratae*," I said to Twain. "Getting out of town while they can. I'll bet the boats coming back are just as full of Californians."

"I wish they'd all stay put," Twain said. "And stop treading on my toes." We were sitting on the floor of the lounge, against a wall, by a drafty door, as close as we could get to a stove set in a box of sand with a brass rail around it. We had to pull in our feet every time somebody came through the door. When one of the Russians steadied himself on Twain's shoulder so he could lean over and spit in the sand, Twain sighed and stood up, staring out the door at the dock where men were preparing to cast off.

"Tarnation!" he said, and bolted out the door. I followed him out on deck, where I found him leaning over the rail, craning his neck to see ahead to the front gangplank. Two policemen were leading a woman in shackles aboard the boat. A man in a cobalt blue coat with gold braid around the cuffs met them.

"I think that's Marina," Twain said.

"Are you sure?"

"Yes, dammit, it's her."

The policemen removed the shackles and handed papers to the man in the blue coat. He signed a paper and handed it back.

"That's the captain, or maybe his first mate," Twain said. "What in perdition is going on here?"

The policemen walked down the gangplank to the dock. One of them strolled to the rear gangplank and stationed himself there, watching the Captain and Marina disappear up some stairs.

I said, "They want to make sure she sails on the boat. It looks like she's being deported. She's *persona non grata* too."

"Come on," Twain said. He led me forward to the middle of the boat, where we crossed over to the other side. He found some stairs leading upward and started climbing, despite a sign that read "Crew Members Only."

"You can't go up there," I said.

He laughed. "I'm Mark Twain, I can go anywhere I want on a steamboat."

He continued up the stairs and into the glassed cabin where they steer the boat. I waited a while below. When he didn't come out, I crept up the stairs and slipped quietly into the cabin. Twain was standing next to the ship's wheel, talking in a mixture of Spanish, Esperanto, and English to a portly gentleman in another blue coat, this one with three gold bands around the cuffs.

Twain was saying, "Si, si, 'mark twain' is que nosotros dicen when la agua es doce piedos profundos," by which I think he meant that his name means the water is twelve feet deep.

He went on and on about his days piloting a steamboat on the Missouri River, charming the captain by communicating more enthusiasm than actual information.

In the end, he got what he wanted: an invitation for us to ride in the little glassed cabin on top, the *casita de piloto*. This impressed me as a significant benefit of fame, for without the cachet of Mr. Twelve Feet's name, we would be back in the sandbox being spit upon by Russians.

All this time, Twain ignored the true object of his curiosity—Marina sat quietly on a stool, in a nook alongside a chart table, rubbing her wrists. Her head was down, but her eyes darted from side to side, looking up from under thick lashes. She gave no sign that she knew Twain.

We retired to the rear of the cabin on our own stools as the boat was cast off. The captain took the wheel, easing the craft out from the dock and threading his way through the anchorage, around the headlands, under the guns of the fort, and into the open sea. Twain inched his stool closer to Marina and whispered something. He questioned her about why she was being sent back to Rossland, but I could not hear much, since my stool was on the other side of the map table. She appeared to be crying, and Twain wiped her face with the end of his cravat.

I lost interest in their conversation entirely when we hit the open ocean. The boat started pitching and lurching in a most alarming fashion, and I got quite seasick. I flew down the stairs to the rail and was violently ill.

## 48. Maiden in Distress

Sargent and I were astounded and dismayed to observe Marina Miranova being delivered to the boat in chains. The first mate took her up to the pilot house, and we followed after in a roundabout way, running all the way to midship to find a stairway to the pilot house.

I was fairly confident I could bluff my way into this sanctorum, trusting that some crew member there would have read *Tom Sawyer*. Most steamships have a copy kicking around the officer's mess, since the paper and ink used by Broadwell Publishers make the pages superior for starting a fire in the stove.

The captain himself was a literate stove lighter and recognized my name straightaway. I stood talking to him by the wheel, casting glances sideways to where Marina was huddled on a stool, half hidden by the chart rack. Sargent dithered at the door, unsure of the social proprieties. Marina's thick black hair was lank and limp, hanging down over her fine dark eyes, which lit up upon seeing me. She waited patiently while the captain bent my ear.

We both watched the helmsman thread his way out of the bay. The captain told me that the *Maria Luz* was a wooden steam schooner of the type they call a *goletapor*. I later made a passable photograph of one called *Libertad* as it entered San Francisco Bay through the *Pórtico Dorado*. They are single-enders, what we call in the Islands stem-winders, with all the cabins and superstructure aft, and cargo hatches and booms forward. He told me the *Maria Luz* was built by a joint Russian and Spanish company in St. Olaf's Bay, about 150 miles up the coast. At the Russian end of the operation, where tall timber and sawmills abound, she was launched without an engine, stuffed with lumber, and towed to San Francisco. There the Spanish half of the operation sold the lumber to help finance the fitting of the engine. The captain says there are 250 such vessels whipping the coastal waters of the Pacific into a froth. He claims there will be no war, because the north needs the south's factories and the south needs the north's lumber. To my naïve ears, this marvel of international interdependence seemed almost as valid an argument for conquest as for peace, but I held mine.

The *Maria* was a trim vessel, but she was lightly freighted in the hold and top heavy with deck cargo. Consequently she bobbed like a cork when we reached the open ocean, skittering from swell to swell with a nasty, corkscrew motion that lost John Sargent his breakfast inside of ten minutes. He went below to pray to Neptune at the rail.

Finally the captain ceased boasting about his boat, and I was free to drift back to where Marina was sitting.

"My dear, what have they done to you?" I asked.

"I'm being sent back to Rossland."

"By whom?"

"The Federales," she said with a sniff.

"Why, what have you done?"

"Nothing. Nothing at all." she began crying silently. I blotted a fat teardrop with my handkerchief and touched her hand.

"Please, compose yourself," I said, "There must be some mistake."

"I was only doing my job, translating. But everyone is so suspicious these days. They tore up my work permit."

"I'm sure everything will be all right," I said.

"No, I don't think so. They said I was a spy."

"That's preposterous."

She shrugged and huddled deeper into herself.

"Try not to take this too personal," I said. "When people see war on the horizon, they abandon their wits. They go crazy. Think of this as a free vacation, a free trip to visit your homeland."

"There is nothing for me in Rossland."

"What do you mean?"

"I'm worse than a serf there. My father was a soldier. He died in a fire. My mother was Miwok. She died of small pox when I was sixteen. The Russians and the Indians hate half-breeds. I was starving, so when I was eighteen I swam the river and snuck into California. Back then AC didn't care so much about having the right parents. Now they do, so they're sending me back to Rossland."

"Surely, with your talent at languages…"

She interrupted me with a bitter laugh. "You don't understand. In Rossland nobody will hire a half-breed bastard, whatever her qualifications. Not for a real position. If I'm lucky I can get room and board on a farm, far out in the valley. I can work myself to death and try to keep the farmer and his sons out of my bed."

"Nonsense. You've got a job with me while I'm in the country. And before I leave, we'll get you set up properly."

She smiled at this and wiped her tears. "Maybe so. At any rate, I've got to calm myself. Perhaps things have changed in Rossland. And I'm not sixteen anymore. I'll get along somehow."

She was plucky, that girl. Whatever else you may say about her, and I came to say most of them in my time, she had more pluck than a mandolin orchestra.

Our voices had become audible to the captain at the wheel, and he said "Leave her be. You're better off not associating with her type."

Marina squeezed my hand and whispered, "Go now. I'll find you in Fortress Ross as soon as I can."

I joined the captain at the wheel, listening with half an ear to his tales of sailing the treacherous coast, ducking into dog hole ports to snake out lumber and avoid the wrath of the Pacific. But his yarns could not truly distract me from Marina and her plight.

When Sargent and I disembarked at Fortress Ross, the first port of call, we had to step lively. The boat stopped there only thirty minutes to offload passengers and mail. Fortunately, most of our fellow passengers were bound further north for Sevastopol, St. Olafsburg, or New Vladovostok; so we were among only a few souls fighting to the rail to abandon ship.

Calling Fortress Ross a "port" is an exaggeration and an undeserved courtesy. The tiny cove is more properly termed a "dog hole," a temporarily-calm eddy in the maelstrom of the Pacific, where one might safely anchor a canoe or a skiff long enough to light a cigar. Any longer stay is likely to be interrupted by a change in the prevailing wind that will blow your vessel onto the rocks and crack her like an egg.

Nevertheless, the Rosslanders had three sizable ships cheek by jowl in this hand basin. A vast spider web of ropes and steel cables criss-crossed the cove, connected to four donkey cranes on the headlands that snatched cargo off the decks and into the air, to be winched up to the cliff top with impressive speed. Bundles of lumber sizzled down an immensely long zip line into the hold of a lumber schooner. It was busy as a Jacquard loom and entertaining as God's own marionette show.

I later hiked out to the headlands to make a photograph of one of the donkey cranes supporting a lumber shoot. It shows the construction of the apparatus well, but that day it was not in operation, there being no ships in the cove on account of the weather being too fine.

As visiting dignitaries, we were accorded the privilege of riding up to the top of the cliff in a two-man bosun's chair decked out with gold braid and a red velvet cushion, rimed white with salt. We were whisked upwards faster than prayers to heaven. As we sailed through the air I saw Marina far below, ushered aboard a cargo lighter and rowed toward a small jetty. She would have to walk up the long switchback road from the beach to the top of the headland.

We disentangled ourselves from the bosun's throne on top, where we beheld the orderly confusion of dockyards everywhere. Horses, carts, and men carrying sacks wove in and out. Lumber, logs, casks and crates were strewn around like a careless child's toys. A squad of soldiers were levering a cannon barrel onto its caisson. A corporal with enough braid and piping for a general was standing by, holding the lead horse of a team of four to haul the cannon away. Another squad of soldiers was nailing boards to a new fence that bordered the switchback road and funneled all arriving passengers toward a customs and immigration shed.

Inside the shed we were met by four large men wearing thick woolen overcoats and red sashes. They introduced themselves as the Ministers of This and the Viceroys of That. I stuck out my hand and they bowed. I bowed and they offered their hands. John finally broke the stalemate by asking if we needed to present our passports.

"Yes, if it please you," the Chief of Protocol replied. "Is formality only."

The formality took over forty minutes, as the Immigration Tsar pawed our papers and asked us impertinent questions in broken English and fractured Esperanto. They did not seem very impressed with our visas and my telegram from the Tsar. They shrugged at my questions about what might be happening to Marina. Then the Customs Pashaw went through our bags looking for bombs, republican tracts, or loose gold sovereigns. He pounced on my camera like a jackal.

"What is this?" he asked, turning the tiny black box over and over, looking repeatedly at the "Super Camera" and "Made in Japan" labels.

"Super Submarine Box Camera," I replied. "Made in Japan." He had never seen such a small camera. I had to show him where the dry plates fit into the back, and finally charmed him by pretending to make a photograph of him, posing with his foot up on my portmanteau like a big game hunter with a dead lion.

After a long whispered confab, they allowed me to keep the camera. They graciously allowed us to pack up all our gear, and warned us to keep our passports and entry papers on our persons at all times. Either they were convinced I was not a spy, or they were planning to loan me enough rope to hang myself with.


## 49. Caviar and Intrigue

The trip to Fortress Ross was so rough that I arrived thoroughly nauseated. The crew dumped me into a tatty bosun's chair like a sack of meal. They winched Twain and me up the cliff in the chair on long cables, like a pair of Virgins ascending to heaven, although Twain's rumpled duster and my viridian green complexion would never grace anyone's altarpiece.

We were ushered out of the chair at the top by a brawny roustabout with a wind-reddened face and hooded black eyes. He pointed us up a path to Customs, through a chaotic whirl of cargo handlers and soldiers toiling on the cliff top like a village scene by Pieter Breugel the elder. Despite the noise and chaotic motion, I was so grateful to have solid ground beneath my feet that I felt like kissing the earth.

After interminable delays, I was at last shown to a handsome room in the Summer Palace, where I fell onto the bed for a much-needed rest. I still felt as if I were at sea, the mattress seeming to move like the heaving deck of the steamer. I closed my eyes and drifted into a shallow sleep, troubled by dreams of waves and wind and sailors lost at sea. Eventually the dreams faded, the mattress stilled, and I slept deeply.

When I awoke, I felt considerably better. I emerged from my room, and a servant showed me the way to a long, narrow drawing room brightly lit by three enormous electric chandeliers that cast a much whiter, more neutral light than candles or kerosene. I joined Twain and a crowd of notables assembled in our honor. A long table was laid with thick linen, crested with the double eagle of the Romanovskys. Heavy silver salvers, also crested, bore smoked salmon, caviar, pickled beets, and other Slavic delicacies. Our hosts were various ministers and bureaucrats, who presented themselves to me in strict accordance to their rank and title, which made it simple to keep track of them. It was a refreshing change from the casual mob scene of similar occasions in Alta California.

One of the ministers was introduced as Vladimir Krepotsky, head of State Security. My ears pricked up when I heard the name, because I had in my room the letter from Goya addressed to Gregor Krepotsky. This Vladimir was a tall, thin, aristocratic man. He told us in tolerable English that Tsar Nicolai had been called back to Nicholagrad on matters of state, and that Twain's command performance must be delayed. I was sharply disappointed to learn that.

My disappointment was blunted when we were next introduced to Vladimir's brother, Gregor Krepotsky, the Minister of Cultural Affairs. Gregor was a shorter, rounder version of Vladimir. He explained that he had arranged a series of lectures for Twain, ending in Nicholagrad, where the Tsar would ultimately entertain him. Twain beamed like a boy scholar who has won all the class ribbons.

Minister Krepotsky had dark eyes very close together, a low hairline and a very thick neck. He looked more like a wrestler than a Minister of Cultural Affairs. He asked me how I was feeling, and told me the best cure for seasickness was Black Sea sturgeon roe.

"We place sturgeon in Slavyanka River and in Sakrametska River here," he said, "but caviar from Mother Russia is still best." He arched his eyebrows and regarded me warily, as if I would dispute his taste in caviar.

"I'm sure that's true," I replied, trying the caviar to be agreeable. It was very salty and did not sit well on my tender stomach.

I set the rest of my portion aside. "I have a letter of introduction to you," I said, "From Francisco de la Goya in Alta California."

"Ah, I see," he said, tilting his head to one side and giving me a sharp glance.

I said, "I can deliver it to you whenever it is convenient. May I make an appointment?"

"Oh, not to be formal. You have letter with you now?"

"No, it is in my room."

"Very well, let us go."

I was astounded. I thought it would be difficult to track this man down and get him to pay attention to me, and here he was before me, willing to leave the reception and accompany me to my room. He nearly rushed me out into the hallway and back to my quarters.

"This way good," he said, "You have privacy to deliver your message."

I pulled Goya's letter out of my suitcase and handed it to him. He broke the wax seal on the envelope and pulled out the letter, unfolding and reading it on the spot.

"Very interesting," he said.

"Do you mean Señor Goya's proposal?"

"Proposal?"

"That I be commissioned to paint an official portrait"

"Portrait?"

"Purely on speculation, of course. To see if my style suits your needs."

"Ah, yes, of course. Very good idea. We must have one of your paintings." He snatched the envelope from me and stuffed it into his tunic. He opened the door and glanced up and down the hallway. Then he ushered me through the door, patting my back as I went by, gingerly, as if I were a dangerous dog.

"We will talk again, soon," he said.

Pleading official business, he took his leave and I saw no more of him that night. I was more certain than ever that Twain was correct, that Goya's letter concerned more than a straightforward proposal to paint state portraits. Otherwise why not simply send it by regular post? I wished I had taken Twain's advice, defeated the wax seal, steamed the envelope open and read the letter for myself.

Nevertheless, I was mildly thrilled to be a small part in the political intrigue of Rossland. I would do anything to get my foot in the door. I never figured they would eventually want to chop that foot off, rather high up, at the neck.

The next morning I ventured out on my own to explore Fortress Ross. I left Twain snoring in his room, sleeping off the effects of the vodka, cigars, and exotic Russian card games of the night before. The evening had markedly diminished my desire to mingle with the salt of the earth. I don't seem to have the necessary stamina or powers of recuperation.

About 10 o'clock the sky cleared, and I sat on the plinth of a strange one-legged statue to sketch the Tsar's palace. The grounds are part of the original fort of 1840 or thereabouts. The Russians have preserved a section of the original stockade and the Orthodox chapel, a quaint structure of weathered gray wood that is dwarfed by the newer cathedral and government buildings behind it.

A policeman in a dirty blue uniform came up to me and started talking loudly in Russian. At first I thought he did not want me to sit on the base of the statue. Finally I understood that he wanted to see my papers. I showed him my passport and entry papers, and he went away.

I was quite taken by the gilded onion domes. They provided a warm accent to a scene that was dominated by green and gray. On the outskirts of town were fields of early potatoes, onions, and beets. The fields were tended by men and women in rough, earthy smocks like those worn by peasants in Breton. They ignored me for the most part.

One old man with many missing teeth cackled at me as he walked by. Over one shoulder he had slung several wire traps and over the other shoulder a string of dead rodents. I tried to sketch him from memory after he had passed, but the result was dreadful.

I must train my eye to work more like a camera, recording in a second the exact pattern of light and dark in a scene. I must train my hand to accurately and faithfully reproduce these patterns as pure shapes, devoid of meaning. I must train my mind to stay out of the partnership of eye and hand, until it truly has something of value to offer. Too often the mind trumps the simple, straight connection of eye and hand with some easy but unsuitable knowledge.

With this in mind, I leaned on a pillar in the train station and made a series of quick sketches of people waiting for trains. For once, my hand and eye worked together with little interference from my mind, and I was happier with the results.

## 50. A Rich Cast of Characters

Henry James
Lamb House, the Willows
Rye, East Sussex
England
June 11, 1879

Dear Henry:

Do you think that clear distinctions between classes are
necessary for artists to thrive? So often a painting I admire has
for its subject matter the lowest classes and for its patrons the
highest. I am thinking of Millet's *Man with a Hoe*, purchased
for the nation by the *aristos* of the Salon; or Velàsquez's
dwarves and water-sellers, painted in the employ of royalty. It
seems to me that in highly stratified societies, artists depict the
various strata. In more egalitarian societies, we can only depict
the landscape.

Although I have only been one day in Rossland, I see
evidence for this everywhere. The division between upper and
lower classes is quite clear, with each rung on the social ladder
clearly marked in its neighborhood, its language and accent,
its costume, its pursuits and privileges. These distinctions the
democrat and the social reformer may deplore, but the artist
applauds and celebrates them. Everywhere I look, there is
a rich cast of characters to people my compositions. There
is so much more to paint here than there is among the drab
mob of republicans in California. This morning I dashed
off a watercolor of a man and woman in indigo robes. They
were camped outside of town in a tent—some kind of recent
nomadic immigrants from the steppes of Russia, I suppose.

I am drawn to this land for other, more obvious reasons.
Rossland seems more like Europe than does California. The
Rosslanders have never severed their ties with Mother Russia,
whereas the Californians are cut off from their roots in Spain
by two revolutions, the Mexican and the Serran. The Russians

who support the arts are mostly secular and imperial, whereas the Californian church is the mainstay of art in the south. The Russian Orthodox Church stays out of painting for the most part, seeming content with small, formulaic icons of saints. Portraiture is the business of the governing nobles and the military, who dominate the society and require frequent and sometimes massive paintings to dignify their position.

The officials I have met in California almost deny their power. Like Americans, they pretend that everyone is the same, that any peasant can be king: "We are all just plain folks here." This patent untruth affects how they act and dress—in a common, coarse manner that obscures class. For the painter, it is like attending a market day skit by school children in paper crowns and pasteboard swords. Rossland by contrast is a grand opera with a cast of hundreds, all properly kitted with sharp metal spears, dented helmets and real chain mail. Of course, one must see to one's own uniform. While I was out spying the landscape today, I was stopped twice by officious police and military men, suspicious of the foreign cut of my coat, and desirous of seeing my papers. Fortunately my visa was in order, and all was well.

Mark Twain says he despises Rossland, but I can see that he is in his element here. In California he found much to admire, and thus little to deride. Here in Rossland nearly everything offends or annoys him and his satiric darts never want for targets.

I am courting a man of power here, one Gregor Krepotsky, Minister of Culture. He is a gruff, enigmatic sort, but he holds the keys to my kingdom. All requests for state portraiture pass through his office, so he is in a position to pass out many commissions every year. I have given him my letter of introduction from Francisco Goya, and have high hopes of receiving a commission for a trial portrait while I am here. Nothing would please me more than to earn a little traveling money and add some Russian nobility to my *curriculum vitae* before I return to Paris. As much as Rossland resembles

Europe, I am a bit homesick for the genuine article, for your charming company, and for my place at your fireside as...

Your friend and fervent admirer,

John

## 51. Dyspeptic Gorillas

It is a commonplace to compare Russians to bears. I have done it myself, out of ignorance and laziness, when both the *bon mot* and the *mot juste* escape me and I make do with a middlin' *mot*. But no mo'. I resolve to belay the bear talk, because it is an inaccuracy, an injustice, and an inneccessary insult to the bears. No bear would stay up so late, swill so much vodka, swear so many oaths, or smash so much crockery.

My first morning in Rossland was a rumor of a suspicion of a blur. I was deep in mental fog, parched as the Sahara, guilty as a Pharisee, near blinded by headache. With each beat of my heart, my ears and lips and nose throbbed painfully, alternately swelling and deflating like the throat of a bullfrog.

I took a bearing on the door of my room, tacked handily into the hallway, and beat my way to the dining room, fighting a stiff headwind. From a steaming samovar I cut a slice of strong tea and gnawed at it, coming slowly and regretfully to consciousness like a condemned man waking to another day on death row. My fellow inmates lumbered along the sideboard collecting tea and dense black bread. They fell heavily into chairs around a massive wooden table. They grunted and growled and gestured for jugs of sour cream with their hairy paws, like...like sleepy animals newly awakened from a long winter's hibernation. But not like bears. No, not like bears. More like dyspeptic gorillas.

I was finishing my breakfast about one or two o'clock when Minister Krepotsky found me.

"Good, day, Mr. Twain," he said, leaning to shake my hand over the crumbs and puddles that surrounded me.

"Good day," I growled back at him, my voice still hoarse from last night's choruses of *Natalya Roll Over* and *Ivan the Large*.

"For you today, brother Gregor has ordered tour of city."

"You are too kind," I said, thinking wistfully of my bed and the nap I had planned.

"Yes, I desire only to be too kind, but there is problem. Mr. Sargent is lost.

"Pardon me?"

"Mr. Sargent is not in room, not in fort, not to be properly guided."

"Well, I wouldn't worry about that. He wanders off to sketch things. He's probably on docks, or in train yard—wherever you have much machinery and things are not to be properly tidy."

His eyes and lips narrowed suspiciously, lending an unpleasant and unwelcome emphasis to his moustache. Unlike my own gracefully curved facial adornment, his was an unruly tangle of bristles, as if he had unsuccessfully tried to force a bottle brush up each nostril.

Finally he said, "We will find Mr. Sargent. We will return him to proper place. He will join you in most good and proper tour of city." He spun on his heel and strolled away like a burglar leaving by the front door, very casual but covering ground fast as a trotting horse.

I fetched another slice of tea into the library, grabbed a book at random, and settled into a soft musty chair to wait for events to unfold. I was feeling uncommonly passive and content to do nothing. I must have fallen into a slight doze, because it was three thirty when John Sargent shook me awake.

"Mr. Twain, are you all right?"

"Of course I am," I said, clawing my way back to consciousness. My voice was still rusty as an iron hinge in the rain.

"Sorry, I wasn't sure you were breathing. You looked still as death, and you didn't move for the longest time when I shook you."

"I was deep in thought, that's all. It takes me that way sometimes, like death or something worse."

"Well, you should be careful. Someone might bury you."

"That's enough," I said. "You must leave the jokes to me and stop poaching in my pea patch."

He grinned like a wild cat, his hair windblown and his face flushed with wholesome, sober, innocent energy. In my admiration I decided on the spot to take the pledge and never drink again.

"What are you reading?" he asked.

I looked at the book in my lap and saw to my horror that it was a French translation of *Ivanhoe.* I showed it to him and set it on a side table.

"Please don't think I would ever read that trash."

"You don't care for Walter Scott?"

"Not one bit. Ivanhoe is a curious exemplification of the power of a single book for harm."

"Really?"

"Indeed. Consider the effects wrought by *Don Quixote* and those wrought by *Ivanhoe.* The first swept the world's admiration for the medieval chivalric silliness out of existence; and the other restored it."

At this point, Krepotsky trotted into the room and reined himself up before us.

"At last," he whinnied, "Mr. Sargent is found. It is not too late for the official Tsarist tour. Allow me to introduce to you official guide and translator, Miss Miranova."

He pranced aside and revealed Marina with a stage magician's flourish. She was dolled up in a fancy black dress, her raven tresses piled high to reveal perfect shell-like ears adorned with pearls, her bearing straight and proud, as if she had never been dragged along a gangplank in chains.

"Is perfect answer," Krepotsky enthused, "I desire provide translator for you. Alta California is so kind to send Miss Marina back to us. And already you know her."

He bustled about, pouring small glasses of vodka for all and prattling on in his broken and abbreviated English about Fortress Ross and the historically significant sights we were about to see. In my surprise and consternation I inadvertently downed a couple shots of the likker.

We bowed formally toward Marina as if meeting her for the first time. I resisted the impulse to kiss her hand and regretted the lost opportunity to give it a conspiratorial nip. It was a fortuitous turn of events. The Tsar would pay Marina, saving my wallet, and she would prove herself invaluable to the state apparatus, thus insuring her future. So taken was I with our good fortune that I failed to consider Krepotsky's deeper motives. As it turned out later, he was merely putting all his rotten eggs in one basket.

Krepotsky also laid out the details of my lecture tour, starting in Fortress Ross and ending up in the capital. He gave me a sheaf of documents that in the USA would have been sufficient to confer an ambassadorship, but here were merely travel passes to points east.

### 52. Island Hopping in the Bering Sea

William Dean Howells
Atlantic Weekly
Boston, Massachusetts, USA
June 12, 1879

Dear William:

I am sojourning in Rossland, having gone over to the darker side in hopes my literary star might shine contrastingly brighter. The Tsar and his minions have invited me to visit and lecture them, although the Tsar decamped from the coast to the interior the day I arrived by steamer. The invitation I lay to cultural MeTooism on the part of the minions, and the Tsar's exeunt to his perusal of my notices.

I know you advised me to steer clear of the Russians, but do not be alarmed on my account. I am resolved to keep my views on hereditary aristocracy and feudalism to myself, or at least fire only warning shots, aiming my salvos of sarcasm over the heads of the local gentry. I already have the impression that there's things here they don't want us to see. These Rosslanders make me nervous. I feel more like a fly in a spider's web than a writer on a lecture tour. I was much more comfortable in A.C. with the Dons.

But I have good reason to stay: ample fodder for my satiric nag, novel sights to decorate our new book, and the opportunity to help Marina Miranova. The drums of war have beat her out of AC—she was deported back to Rossland and needs my patronage here to establish her in her native but estranged land.

Sargent is also with me, and today Marina gave us a tour of the Fort with some historic background on Russia's uneasy affair with commerce in America. Fortress Ross is the tag end of 150 years of Russian Eastward expansion, started by the first Tsar, the appropriately and honestly named Ivan the Terrible. Cossacks and fur traders spread across the steppes to Kamchatka and sailed into the Bering Sea, snapping up islands for Mother Russia and the Russian American Company. By 1800 they reached the North American continent, founding New Archangel on a site the natives called Sitka. They spread quickly down the coast, claiming territory for Russia, collecting otter and seal pelts, setting up colonies, and fetching up here in Rossland or "New Albion," at their southern border with Alta California.

That border is being fortified and tightened, with sizable new canons and the most suspicious customs inspectors I have encountered since I tried to smuggle gin into the Holy Land.

Fortress Ross is a minor coastal town, but it boasts cobblestone streets, a cathedral in all but name, lively trade, daily train service to the interior, and many fine homes and estates. Looking at the riches here, I'm convinced that the Louisiana Purchase was Jefferson's biggest mistake. Back in '03 Napoleon was so desperate for money, Jefferson could have snapped up the entire Mississippi watershed. But no, he had to play Solomon and settle for New Orleans and the eastern bank. Half a river is of little more use than half a child. He let the bulk of the continent slip through his fingers, cutting us off from overland access to the west coast. I blame false economy and those east coast senators who wanted to limit the number of potential new states in the union.

Sorry for the diatribe. I know the sons and grandsons of those senators are your friends. And I know Jefferson thought Spain and Russia were biting off more than they could chew, and that we could pick up the rest at fire sale prices later. But who knew they would discover so damn much gold? Or that our own argument with the South would drag on so long? I see that president Grant has declared Reconstruction officially over and a success. If that is true, I wonder why cotton shirts still cost 8 dollars and just last month the Butternutters bagged themselves a carpet-bagging federal judge in Georgia? If the USA ever pulls out of her economic doldrums, I doubt she can catch up to Rossland, much less Alta California.

Tonight I give my lecture here, then tomorrow we take the train east toward Nicholagrad, eventually to meet the Tsar and tell some more tall tales. I'm sure I will have interesting sights to report back to you. Until then, I remain,


Your obedient, etc.,



Mark Twain

## 53. Noble Nabobs

Reprinted from the *Atlantic Weekly,* July 11, 1879
Mark Twain
Fortress Ross
Rossland

Dear Reader:

Last Tuesday Mr. Sargent and I were regally entertained by four hearty and hirsute sons of Mother Russia named Vladomir Kropotsky, Vladmirich Poptovsky, Vladopo Mirpovsky, and Vladimirov Toposovky, all known affectionately as Vasha, Sasha, Anya, Pasha and possibly Bushwa. I have never encountered a brace of noble nabobs half so rich in syllables, titles and nicknames yet so poor in distinguishing characteristics.

But I digress before I have even gressed. It all started with a lovely ride up the coast from Bahia de Bodega to Fortress Ross, southernmost port of Rossland. The mist was so light my hand almost found my pocket. The breeze blew barely hard enough to scour the paint off the deckhouse. The ripples on the Pacific were scarcely twelve or fourteen feet high. I swear the worst winter I ever spent is this summer on the north coast of California.

The chill of the air and *mal de mer* turned Mr. Sargent's face the colors of a dogwood flower in spring: pale green in the center fading to a light blue at the edges. To cheer the poor fellow and distract him from his stomach, I commenced to sing, but young John remonstrated with me, a dangerous calm in his voice: "Now look a-here, Mr. Twain—It ain't no time, and it ain't no place, for you to be going on in that way. I'm sick and tired and sore in the gut. If you was to start in on any more yowling like that, I'd shove you overboard—I would, by geeminy."

At Fortress Ross we were hoisted to the top of the cliff like sacks of grain, and were greeted by the aforementioned Bushwa brothers. These Russian giants wore identical bristly black beards, coarse woolen uniforms with an excess of braid, and enormous fur hats. After much bussing of cheek and swatting of back, they ushered us along a cobbled drive, over four sets of railroad tracks, and into the Tsar's summer palace. The Tsar having been called away for an urgent confabulation in Sakrametska with Alta California's Generalissimo Vallejo, these four Russian bears were to dance attendance on us until we could follow the Tsar inland.

My consternation turned to admiration when they set us down at a table furnished with smoked salmon, caviar, cigars, vodka, and fresh decks of cards in which the royalty were Tsars, Tartar chieftains and Kazakh princesses. John and I pitched in with a will, and soon we were smoking, eating, drinking, and learning the rudimentaries of a card game called Irkutsk Showdown, remarkably similar to Molokai Cutthroat.

By dawn I had grown quite fond of my new friends Sasha, Pasha, etc.—despite the fact that they had relieved me of my Californian reals, my grandfather's watch, and the deed to Diamond Head Harbor, to which I may not have had entirely clear title. Some things about the visit have escaped my recollection. For one, I suspect that Russian vodka may have considerably more alcoholic content than one might assume of a beverage made from potatoes. Secondly, I cannot quite recall how the Minister of Culture came to own my new boots and why I was wearing the Viceroy of Immigration's fur hat. No matter. These are mere details and cannot possibly diminish my fondness for the jolly Russians of Fortress Ross.


Your Befuddled Servant,



Mark Twain

## 54. SN One-Legged Man

Marina led Twain and myself from the Tsar's Summer Palace to the original chapel of 1802, now used as a baptistery. Like most of the buildings in Fortress Ross, it was constructed of the native redwood, which is typically left unpainted. The chapel has a unique circular cupola that I sketched later. The bare wood interior is dim and earthy in the shadows, bursting into radiance like beaten red gold where the sun shines through the cupola and hits the walls. The redwood has a smell like cedar incense.

Marina took Twain's hand and ran it over the rim of the baptismal font. "This fountain was carved from one piece of the red wood," she said, "from a giant root ball knot," by which I think she meant "burl." Unlike the soft trunk wood, the burl wood was very hard and dense, its tight grain swirling like crimson smoke patterns on the rim where it was polished. A stagnant pool of holy water in the center had turned the wood black and slimy, and I could see mosquito larvae dotting the surface, writhing in a shaft of sunlight.

"Come see the new church," she said, taking Mark's arm and pulling him toward the door. I trailed behind them, pleased that Marina was directing her feminine charms toward Twain for a change. We went back out into the sunshine and turned inland. She led us around a remnant of the original stockade, and into the newer part of town. There were few stone buildings, and the Rosslanders do not have the facility with adobe that the Californians enjoy, so most of the architecture, even the grander edifices, were constructed of the same unpainted redwood. It gave the town a rustic, frontier aspect that was charming. New construction showed fairly intense hues of crimson, gold, cadmium orange, and raw sienna. As the wood weathers it loses its intense color, shifting through the browns to a very subtle palette of warm and cool grays.

The new church was easily ten times the size of the chapel, with a huge gilded onion dome of stone-burnished stucco. It was a startling sight. Twain said it looked like a chunk of Saint Petersburg had flown across the Bering sea like Baba Yaga's fairy tale house and plunked itself down in the New World. The gold leaf on the dome shone in the sun, and I tipped my head back to drink it in.

"I know just how I'd paint that," I said, "with a dark violet-grey cloudbank behind it to bring out the yellow, and a chunk of pure titanium white the size of your thumb for a highlight."

In the cobblestone square in front of the church there was a bronze statue of a one-legged man, the same one I had seen earlier in the day. It crossed my mind that if one set out to sculpt a free-standing statue of a one-legged figure, without a cane or staff of some sort, one would have to render it in bronze. The unsymmetrical weight of the unsupported side would likely break a marble leg. So this gentleman's loss of a limb at least guaranteed him the nobler material for his memorial.

Marina said, "This is Kushov, Commandant of Fortress Ross for the Russian American Company. In 1820 when the sea otters disappeared and the fur trade declined, he saved the colony. They had no pelts to trade for food. Their gardens were stunted by the coastal fog and eaten by the gophers. Kushov forced his people to walk east through the mountains, to the interior valley where they could plant wheat and potatoes. He took over the village of Sacramento from the Mexicans and crowded them out. He told the Kodiak Islanders they no longer had jobs as seal hunters. They could become farmers or go home. Most went home. Kushov tamed the valley Indians and taught them to till the soil."

"I heard most of those Kodiaks and Aleuts starved to death," Twain said, with his usual tact.

Marina nodded, "Kushov was a hard man. The shark that ate his leg died of food poisoning."

"How precisely do you "tame" an Indian? The same way the Yankees tamed the niggers?"

"Niggers are slaves," she said. "Indians are serfs. The Rosslanders make a great deal of that distinction. According to them, serfs belong to the land, not to the lord, so they are not slaves."

"What's the difference to the serf?" Twain asked.

"Very little, as far as I can see. At any rate, Kushov did not enjoy his serfs very long. In 1830 the Russian American

182

Company went bankrupt and Kushov declared himself Tsar Petros of Rossland, stretching from the Russian River north to Sitka, and east all the way to the Rocky Mountains. He had never even seen the mountains, and had no idea of the actual size of the territory he was claiming. Three years later he was assassinated by agents of the real Tsar in Mother Russia. The Tsar sent his third son Alexander with 1,000 troops and a company of minor nobles to establish a colonial government. Alexander moved the capital from Fortress Ross to Sakrametska."

"Why did they do that?" I asked.

"It was easier to trade with San Francisco. Steamboats down the river were more reliable than schooners down the coast. Nowadays Alexander's son is Tsar and Sakrametska is even more important because it is closer to the gold fields."

We strolled through town, up the hill to the train station, where we turned to look back at the town. The new church, the palace, and various government buildings combined with the native cypress trees to make an interesting silhouette against the ocean beyond. Unfortunately, the weathered wood, grass, dirt, rocks, and trees were all very close in value, so the town as a whole was a mid-value shape you could have cut out of brown wrapping paper. I missed the contrasting lighter values of stone cities, like the limestone of Venice or even the adobe and stucco of Petalumo.

On the other hand, the clothing of the people thronging the station was much more paintable that the drab outfits of the Dons. The better classes of people wore high jackboots with blousy trousers or jodhpurs, embroidered vests, tall fur hats with earflaps, clerical robes with gold braid, high-collared tunics with epaulets, red sashes, gold and silver medallions. Even the poorer classes had more variety to their garb—different combinations of homemade linsey-woolsey shifts, felted wool over vests, knit caps, shell ornaments, moccasins, and wooden clogs. Down south the uniform was jeans, boots, shirt and sombrero, with maybe a serape here and there.

Marina told us that Fortress Ross is mostly owned by three

families of Russian nobles, who sent their younger sons to be adventurers in the new world. The Krepotsky family is the largest landowning clan. Rumor has it that their holdings were a reward for their membership in the cabal that assassinated Kushov fifty years ago.

## 55. On Second Thought

William Dean Howells
Atlantic Weekly
Boston, Massachusetts, USA
June 12, 1879

Dear William:

I enclose another letter for the magazine, but I have reservations about it. I know you admire my scathing humor, but this letter is more scathing and less humorous than usual. I will understand if you want me to temper my scorn, although it is as temperate as I can make it at the moment.

Rossland combines the mindless monarchy of the Old World with the mindless bureaucracy of the New in a way that truly astounds me. I am like a cat with its tail nailed to the floor—everywhere I turn, a new outrage. These people remind me of the Southern "Country Gentlemen" of my youth. Perhaps that is the source of my discomfort. They are walking contradictions, a mixture of high and low. They have lace at their throats and manure on their boots, china cups of tea in their hands and revolvers in their belts, a smile to your face and a dagger to your back.

The Russians appear to treat their Indians like niggers in the southern USA were treated before the war. I made a photograph of some tired Indian workers on a wagon this evening. Soon after my exposure, the driver shooed them all off and made them walk, so he wouldn't tire his horse, which proceeded to pull a load of empty baskets.

The common people, the serfs, are all right. By an irony of law and phrase, Rosslanders sometimes refer to serfs as "freemen." Seven-tenths of the free population of the country are of just this class and degree: small "independent" farmers, artisans, etc. To wit, they are the nation, the actual Nation; they are about all of it that is useful, or worth saving, or really respectworthy, and to subtract them would be to subtract the Nation and leave behind some dregs, some refuse, in the shape of an "emperor," nobility, and gentry—idle, unproductive, acquainted mainly with the arts of wasting and destroying, and of no sort of use or value in any rationally constructed world.

One minister, Krepotsky, is particularly two-faced. One minute he is filling my ear holes with enthusiasm for *Innocents*. The next minute he turns into Dostoevsky's Grand Inquisitor. He questioned me sharply about my previous relationship with Miss Marina, hinting lasciviously that she might be more than a translator to me. He treats me and John Sargent like visiting royalty in the morning and like spies for President Grant in the afternoon. The wretch Krepotsky had the effrontery to suggest that I might care to submit my articles to him for "fact-checking" before sending them off to you! I declined and he became decidedly cool.

Sargent and I have been asked for our papers almost every time we venture out into society. I would not put it past the Russians to search my rooms or have me followed while I am here; and so I have taken to keeping my papers on my person at all times. I give them up only when they are finished, and I have Miss Marina deliver them personally to the local Post Office. Since I will not be able to resist taking pot shots at monarchy and other hereditary social diseases while sojourning and writing here, I think it wise for you to delay publication of my Rossland letters until I am safely south of the border once more. I see no evidence that the Rosslander gentry are readers at all, but I would rather not take the chance of them coming across my pieces while I am within their boundaries.

Perhaps I can churn out a couple more retroactive Alta California letters to fill in the next couple of weeks. I know you plan to have one of my letters every week, and I do not want to disappoint your readers or lose their attention.

Thanking you for lending me your compassionate ear, I remain...

Yours truly,

Mark Twain


## 56. Fabulous Singing Ox

Reprinted from the *Atlantic Weekly*, July 18, 1879
Mark Twain
Fortress Ross
Rossland

Dear Reader:

I am recuperating from lecturing the Rosslanders on the Sandwich Islands, an endeavor as doomed as lecturing lions on lyric poetry—roars of laughter, but in all the wrong places, and the distinct impression that the audience wants to eat the speaker alive. To be fair, I reckon most of my yarning went tolerably well, but I was not easy in my mind. Something about this country makes me itch like the chicken pox.

The upper crust here all speak a kind of English, but their omission of definite or indefinite articles and other grammatical gingerbread makes them sound tetchy. A cozy tete-a-tete with a Russian is like sitting in a cast iron arm chair: A man can never get comfortable. I have better luck with those who speak Esperanto, a language designed from the start to make its speakers equally uncomfortable.

Much about Rossland is explained by noble inbreeding and the constitutional insecurity of younger sons. Most of the ruling families hereabouts are descended from second-, third-, or fourth-born sons who could get no show back home in Russia. Their fathers' farms and fortunes went to the eldest brothers, and so the young'uns went adventuring on the Steppes, across the Straits of Kamkatchka, and eventually down the coast of Rossland. Having been hove out of the nest themselves, they line their nest here with every cow and tree and boulder they can grab, with nary a pebble left over for the lower born or the original inhabitants of this land. I know they say Rossland is a Christian nation, but so is hell.

Rossland has all the faults of the feudal Russian system, with none of the virtues, which were thin on the ground of Mother Russia to start with. These third sons of second rate despots have all the land, money, and political pull. They grant the lowborn Russian serfs enough land and seed to eke out a poor living. But if you are an Indian, a Mexican, or a displaced Yankee, you are so low on the totem pole you have dirt up your nose.

Although the Rosslanders are inclined to despise Americans, they do admire authors. When they remember that I am a mere Yankee, I am treated like a yellow cur begging bones. But when they recall that I am a published writer, I am accorded a measure of respect that almost, but not quite, raises me to the status of a prize bird dog. To wit, I was speaking to the Minister of Culture, the honorable K——, who was comparing my efforts in *Innocents Abroad* favorably with *War and Peace*, that tedious potboiler. All was well until I asked about the state of native literature in Rossland—whether there were any notable Indian writers working in the rustic vein that has been so profitable for some lowborn Americans like myself.

He thought I was making a joke. He chuckled and assured me that, as much as he was dedicated to furthering the arts in Rossland, he did not have time to teach oxen to sing.

I replied, "Then let them play the banjo."

He gave me a look that was untranslatable in any language, although "askance" comes close. Soon after that we both retired from the field of combat, he to further art and I to practice my scales. And so I remain…

Your humble servant,

Mark Twain, The Fabulous Singing Ox

### 57. Colonel Sweetheart

After an interminable and unexplained delay, they fired up the little Shay engine and our four car train pulled out of Fortress Ross station like a child's toy leaving the parlor for the drawing room. It was a narrow gauge railroad, with tracks so diminutive and closely spaced I could straddle them like the Colossus of Rhodes. The narrow coaches swayed drunkenly around the bends of the Slavyanka River. Each of the cars had a name, which Marina translated for us. We were in a second class car called Siberia, directly behind the wood wagon where we could enjoy the invigorating smell of burning oak logs with the windows open, and our fellow passengers with the windows closed.

Behind us were two first class carriages named after Peter the Great and a type of porridge, followed by a battered third class car crammed with peasants as thick as niggers in a slave pen. For no reason I could fathom, the serf car was named Serenity. I assumed the naming of the coaches followed some aristocratic Russian logic that I was too common to grasp.

For the most part we followed the northern bank of the Slavyanka as it wound through heavily forested hills, clattering over occasional trestles spanning its tributary creeks. From time to time we would rattle through meadows of grass studded with oaks, and spy small settlements scratching out their sustenance on the narrow bottomlands.

I was sitting by a window, sharing a seat with Marina, to my delight. John was knee-to-knee with me in a facing seat, which he shared with a Rosslander in leather pants, a dingy collarless shirt, and a goatskin vest that undoubtedly had looked better on the goat. Thankfully the Rosslander slept most of the time, snoring with his mouth open. My writer's knack of close observation told me that he had skipped his bath this week and had a fondness for garlic sausage. The poor man's sleep was so troubled that I feared for his health and resolved that upon his wakening, I would champion to him the benefits of taking the waters and a more vegetarian diet. I do not as a regular practice intrude on my fellow man in a proselytizing way, but sometimes the desperate circumstances of others cry out to me.

Marina was chirping like a mocking bird, trying first this tune, then another, in an effort to charm us into an appreciation for her country.

"This is called 'Stump Town' in Russian," she said, "because of all the trees cut down."

A small valley opened up to the north, it's hillsides bare and dotted with stumps. Shacks and tents lined the river, logs were stacked in haphazard piles everywhere, trash dotted the right of way, and a dun cloud of dust filled the air.

John looked out the window. "It's beautiful," he said. He always did like disorder and decay. He was rubbing his eyes, irritated by the dust and the gritty smoke from our engine. Marina snagged a passing porter and asked him to bring John a glass of water to rinse his eyes. The porter hustled back towards the rear of the train.

Marina excused herself to seek the washroom at the front of our car. I leaned forward to speak to John.

"Don't forget to tip the porter," I said. "It's the custom here. His name is Kreski and he likes to be called Colonel."

"How do you know?" he asked.

"I heard his life story on the platform, back in the station, while we were waiting to leave."

"All right. Thank you."

I knew he would appreciate the information, since he always liked to behave with perfect propriety. What he didn't know was that I didn't know the porter from Adam. "Kreski" meant something like "sweetheart" or "darling," in Russian—I had heard it from a charming peasant girl with whom I had passed a pleasant hour the night before, comparing the practices of the Protestant theological union with that of the Greek Orthodox.

I sat back and bided my time, saying a brief prayer to Providence to provide me some entertainment. My prayers were answered when the porter brought John his water. John thanked him, tears in his eyes, and slipped him a coin.

"Thank you, Colonel Sweetheart," he said in his best Russian.

The porter sorely disappointed me, being much too reserved for my taste. He reared back slightly like someone who has inadvertently stepped in something malodorous. He looked at the coin in his hand, picked it up as if it were polluted, and dropped it into the glass of water in John's hand.

Then porter retreated quickly to the rear, revealing Marina standing in the aisle.

"What was that about?" she asked John.

John shrugged.

"What did you say to him?"

Slowly and delightfully the joke unfolded, and John began

blushing a lovely shade of pink. I laughed so hard I woke our sausage-eating seatmate. Marina failed to find anything funny in the situation, a problem with the untranslatable nature of my humor that has kept my works largely confined to the English language.

My companions were decidedly cool towards me for a while, but on balance I was grateful for the momentary relief from the tedium of the trip.

The next opportunity for fun was on the steep grade climbing out of a town whose name Marina translated as Hop Land. It was here the Shay steam engine came into its own. The narrow rails climbed a grade that appeared nearly vertical, around curves so sharp I could almost see my own backside. If we had been pulled by an ordinary locomotive, its rigid frame and huge driver wheels would have bounced us right off the track and into a ravine. But the Shay's independent trucks with their small wheels stuck to the track like limpets. We slowed to a crawl and I could hear the clashing and grinding of the beveled gears that powered each set of wheels.

The engineer blasted three notes on his whistle and peasants begin dropping off the rear platform and walking up the ties behind the train. They were lightening the load, but it was really no disadvantage to the peasants. The train was going slower than the slowest laggard in the group, so they had no trouble keeping up. Furthermore, it may have been easier for the walkers to climb the ladder of the ties than it was for us still on the train, lying as we were, almost prone on our backs in our seats, being covered over by soot and ashes from the roaring fires of the Shay's offset boiler.

The two hours we spent climbing to the top of the grade were the longest two weeks of my life. At last the good ship Siberia crested the wave and once more approached the horizontal. The train stopped. I assumed that the peasants were reboarding, and perhaps the engineer was cooling the boiler or taking on water. Time stretched out and relief turned to boredom. I got out to stretch my legs and reconnoiter. The blunt, flat face of the Shay engine was nose to nose with a huge stone, part of a massive rockslide that completely blocked the track. I retrieved my camera from my satchel to make a photograph of the situation.

I climbed up the pile of rubble to get a better look at the cliff above the tracks. It looked like a sizable chunk of mountain had been blasted out by dynamite. This was no natural landslide. I approached the engineer and conductor, who were talking to a man in uniform by the cab of the locomotive. The man in uniform grabbed my arm and escorted me back to my seat, ignoring my questions.

When he left, my garlic-loving seatmate muttered something in Esperanto, two words that I had to look up in my pocket dictionary: *sabotage* and *rebels.*

## 58. A Roundabout Admission

It took four days to repair the tracks over the mountain, a task that proved endlessly fascinating to Twain. He spent nearly every waking hour watching the work crews, barraging the superintendents with questions, and poking his reporter's nose in everywhere he found an opening. You would have thought he was writing a history of the railroad, or of ditch digging.

Marina used Krepotsky's influence to secure us lodging in the dacha of Duke Django, a local Tartar potentate who wielded considerable power in that mountainous area. It was his landsmen who were drafted to work on the roadbed repairs, and he told me that he would be dunning the Imperial government "ferociously" for their labor.

The duke gave me a corner bedroom, opening on a small terrace with wonderful north light, where I spent many happy hours painting. On my first night in the room I was lying awake on my bed, gazing out the window to the terrace, and I saw Marina leave her room across the way and come to knock softly on my door. I arose and opened the door a crack.

"May I come for a minute?"

"It is late."

"I know, but I think we should talk."

I let her in and she went straight to my bed and sat down.

"Don't worry," she said, "I have no designs on your virtue."

I sat across from her in a chair and assured her that I was not worried. I did think that she was picking up bad habits from Twain, mentioning the unmentionable, becoming careless of her actions and her tongue.

She leaned forward. "I want to apologize for Mark's joke on the train today, that "Colonel Sweetheart" nonsense. It was cruel and thoughtless."

I shrugged and gave her a small smile. "Can you tell me why someone so smart must make such stupid jokes?"

She had a charming, silvery laugh.

"He acts first and thinks later."

"If he thinks at all." We both laughed at that.

"But this time," she said, "you seemed particularly upset. More than when he's made you look silly before."

"This was different. He tricked me into giving offense to someone else."

"To the conductor?"

"Yes, I hate to be rude or insulting to people."

"Oh, don't worry. In Russian it was not really insulting. It was more…flirtatious, perhaps."

"Exactly. It was precisely the sort of remark that I am always careful *not* to make to other men."

"Because they might take it the wrong way?"

"Of course."

"Or the right way?" She looked at me with her eyebrows raised, calculating. I had no intention of revealing my true romantic inclinations to her, so I just shrugged. But it was too late.

"Oh," she said, looking down at her hands clenched in her lap, and then back up at me sharply. "I think I see now why you were so upset. You thought Mark's joke was some kind of accusation, that it was his way of letting you know that he sensed your interest in other men."

"Perhaps." I didn't know what to say. I felt the same way I did when I shared my true feelings with my friends Hank and Violet—scared and relieved and excited.

"I don't think you need worry about Mark Twain finding out. He is no detective. For a famous reporter, he can be remarkably unobservant. Look how he is running around asking questions about the train wreck, looking for rebels and saboteurs, despite everyone's efforts to shut him up."

"I hope you are right."

"I'm sure I am. I never guessed anything about you myself. I thought you were a perfect gentleman, prim and proper. You were so polite and distant in your manner, I thought you did not like me."

"I do like you."

"But you don't *want* me."

I sighed. "I'm afraid not."

"Fine then," she said, giving my arm a sisterly pat. "I don't want you either, so there. That's settled."

I smiled again and said, "In my experience, these things are never settled. I assume I can trust you to keep this conversation confidential?"

"Of course, it's just between us. This actually makes things easier. I have become very fond of Mark, but I did not want to slight you by going about with the older, more famous man. Unless you fancy him too?"

"God no. I do not fancy anyone, man or woman, dog or child. I'm a confirmed bachelor and intend to stay that way."

She giggled. "I'm sorry, it just sounds strange, a boy your age claiming to be a 'confirmed bachelor.'"

"Not at all. You are a beautiful woman, and I've grown fond of you, but I will never ask you or any girl to marry me, even for show. I really am a confirmed bachelor—I do not intend to court and marry any woman at all, ever. And while I prefer the company and conversation of men, that is as far as I go."

"That sounds so lonely, never falling in love, never… touching anyone."

"Painting a portrait is a way of touching someone."

"It would not be enough for me. I should like to be married some day."

"It will have to be enough for me. I am married already to my work and intend to stay that way."

"Very well." She reached over and touched my arm. It was somehow the opposite of her usual flirtatious touch, firmer and feeling very dry on my skin.

I said, "Now that we understand each other, tell me why you came to my room. Did you really have *no* designs on my virtue *at all*?"

"Well, perhaps the smallest of designs. But mostly I wanted to talk about Mark. I'm worried about him."

"Why?"

"He is asking too many questions, talking to too many people. That's not always a good idea in Rossland. You've got to help me rein him in."

"He's a reporter. Asking questions is his job."

"Not in this country. Here the newspapers all support the government, and reporters write the stories they are assigned to write. Mark's kind of writing could get him in trouble."

"What do you want me to do?"

"Help me keep an eye on him. Maybe you could get him to sit for a portrait, so he will stay in one place."

"Nothing would please me more. I've offered to paint him several times, but he always puts me off. He's too cheap, and restless as a cat."

"I know, and he is making people nervous. It is bad to make Russians nervous."

### 59. Tartar Enchantress

Violet Paget
17 Rue Des Jardins
Montparnasse, Paris, France
June 16, 1879

My dear Violet:

I am writing you by the light of Aladdin's whale oil lamp, the westering rays of the sun having grown too dim to paint, here in my studio on the flagstone terrace of a Tartar mountain stronghold in Rossland. Mark Twain and I are stranded here, awaiting repairs to the train tracks. We left Novo Grostok three days ago for a trip over the Grostok Grade that was supposed to take ten hours. The drafty, noisy Russian train crept up a nearly vertical slope for five hours, then jerked to a halt. A rockslide had completely blocked the tracks, which will not be cleared and repaired for several days.

Meanwhile, we are guests of the barbaric but dashing and very hospitable Duke Django. We are even invited to his daughter's wedding next week, if we are still marooned here, and I have been commissioned to paint her wedding portrait.

I am painting her in this commandeered terrace studio, wearing her ceremonial white linen wedding gown, a vast veil, and many pounds of bizarre silver jewelry. I posed her on a kind of pentangle pattern I chalked on the flagstones, holding her veil like an awning over her head to catch the magical vapors from an intricate silver censor, which emitted clouds of pungent *ambre gris* incense. The girl is a dusky beauty with silky eyebrows that nearly meet in the middle, with a sultry and diabolical cast to her features. She needs less perfume and more bathwater, but her clothes and the setting are magnificent.

The painting is an essay in white: white woman in white clothes and silver jewelry, against a white stucco wall. And yet there is scarcely a single brush stroke of pure white pigment. I am using both titanium and flake white, tinted with nearly every hue in my palette. The effect is *subtil* and *tres charmant*.

Twain is kept very busy supervising the railroad workers, telling me how to paint, and dragging our lady translator all over the mountain to quiz the locals about their quaint customs. He claims that he and I are alike—both artists depicting exotic people and lands for the entertainment and edification of folks back home. He is both correct and wildly wrong. I seek not the exotic subject but the moment of beauty, wherever I find it. This week it is a Tartar enchantress, but last week it was muddy water in a ditch. Beauty resides in my vision of the moment, not in the exoticism of the subject.

As for the folks back home, I wonder who they are and where home might be? You once said I am American by nationality, Spanish by temperament, French by taste, English by demeanor, and an artist by religion. True enough, and where is home in that? I love my parents, especially my dear mother, but I don't paint for them, and their borrowed home of the moment is not mine.

I suppose I paint for you and Hank and Carolus and the few like-minded souls with whom we are mated in spirit. I miss you here, in this New and Strange World. I wish this oil

lamp were the faintly hissing gas jet in your flat, and that this pen were your hand, and that I were stretched out on your divan with my head in your lap, telling you my troubles. And you would say, "Let us go out for some *absinthe* and more trouble."

Hoping you will go out for a drink and some trouble on my behalf, I remain,

Your wistful friend,

John

### 60. In the Key of White

Marina left to change for dinner, and I settled back in my chair to watch Sargent paint the Duke's daughter. Her pose required her to hold her veil up for long periods of time, so her hands were propped up on curtain rods like long canes, to ease her fatigue. She fancied herself a witch, conjuring up spirits within a mystic pentangle traced out in blood on the stone terrace. But she didn't have the stamina for witchcraft, apparently, since she was falling asleep on her feet, her head drooping repeatedly.

John was like a dancer, swooping forward to peer into her face and lift her chin by a cat's whisker. Then he glided back to his canvass and pirouetted in front of it, his head bobbing up and down, his brush moving in the air in grand circles as if conducting an unheard symphony. Then the brush arced toward the canvas, smeared a dab of paint in just the right spot, and flew away again, completing another grand circle.

He froze like a statue, hand on chin, staring at the brushstroke he had just executed, squinting his eyes, glancing up at his subject, and staring again at the canvas. Then he took up his palette knife and scraped off the brushstroke, reloaded his brush with fresh paint, and began the whole ballet over again—dancing forward, peering, gliding back, flailing his arms, slashing once more at the canvas, then freezing to evaluate.

"You look like you're dancing to music, or conducting it," I said.

"I am," he said. "Colors are like notes. I blend them to make chords. I lay them next to each other in sequence to make a melody. The brushstrokes beat out the rhythm—legato here in the background, more and more staccato as I approach the crescendo, the *finale*, the center of interest around the face."

"What's the title of your composition?"

"I don't know yet, but it's in the key of white." He dashed up to the girl again to adjust her pose.

I asked, "Would you mind if I made a photograph of this young lady tomorrow?"

"I'd like that. I could use it to show you how it is inferior to the painting."

"You're awfully sure about that."

"It's an item of my religion, part of my creed."

"Do all painters think that way?"

"No, sadly. Under the onslaught of photography, a lot of fellows are retreating into symbolism."

"You think that's a mistake?"

"Yep. I'd rather stick to realism, but allow the painting to look like paint."

He continued to peer at the girl, dance around, lay in brushstrokes and frequently scrape them off to try again.

I asked him, "Why do you scrape off and start over?"

"It's more 'painterly,' as the English say. One wants to paint the highlights at the end of a painting with fresh, clean strokes. In Italian it's *alla prima*, or in French *au premier coup*—at the first stroke. Make it look like you dashed it off, first time every time. Each stroke is a little sculpture. Each one must look like paint close up, but perfectly render the subject when you stand further back or squint your eyes."

"That's why you keep squinting"

"Exactly."

"I thought you needed spectacles."

He smiled thinly.

"Watch," he said, pushing his latest stroke of paint around on the canvas. "If I try to reshape an awkward stroke, it blends with the paint alongside it and gets muddy. See, it's less pure, less fresh."

The area he was working was a highlight on the girl's necklace. It became flatter and grayer, losing all contrast, going out of focus like a bad photograph. He scraped it off and reapplied a fresh bead of creamy white paint.

"It takes a lot of effort," he said, squinting at the new stroke, "to make painting look effortless."

"It's the same way with writing," I said. "Sometimes I have to wrangle a paragraph around for an hour. I have to break the damn thing like a wild bronco, until it finally trots out smooth and easy, with the funny part right at the end where it belongs."

"Indeed?" he replied, squinting and grinning.

"Yep. And then critics say 'Twain has no real style of his own. He transcribes low class discourse and tries to pass it off as literature.'"

"Art critics are the same," John said, wiping his brush and putting it down. "They call this kind of painting 'slapdash, artless daubing, with no refinement or finish.'"

"That sounds like one of the reviews of *Innocents Abroad.*"

John cleaned his hands on a rag and said, "I guess we are both just misunderstood artists, and will have to wait for history to vindicate us."

On that note we went in to dinner, arm-in-arm, with the girl swaying sleepily behind us.

## 61. The Devil's Gift

Mary Clemens
17 Thatcher Street
Davis, Missouri
U.S.A.
June 17, 1879

Dear Mother:

I am writing you from a Duke's palace (the guest wing, not the dungeon). Our trip to Sakrametska has been delayed by a rock slide across the train tracks, and we are the guests of Duke Ivan Django. He is a rough and ready despot who puts me in mind of Uncle Sowberry Finn in his wilder and more grandiose days. Thankfully there is a chapel adjoining our quarters and a Russian Orthodox priest on hand to minister to our spiritual needs, albeit in a Popish way.

I amuse myself in this enforced idleness by long walks in rugged mountains, by reading and re-reading the Duke's English library of two books, and by repairing my tardy correspondence. I have tried to do some writing, but it goes slowly. By contrast, my traveling companion, young John of whom I wrote you, is the soul of enterprise. He has made use of the layover to wangle a commission to paint the Duke's daughter's portrait. He is a whirlwind of creative energy and would put me to shame, did I not believe that creativity is a gift from God, industry from the devil. I have been more calmly polishing my creativity, praying to Providence to grant me inspiration, and laying out endless games of patience.

I have attended a wedding—the Duke's daughter, whose name sounds like "Shiftless," married the very young son of a neighboring Duke, one mountain to the east. I undertook to photograph the matrimonial pair, and they seemed shy and of short acquaintance to me. I suspect the union to be more a political or commercial transaction than a spiritual one: where the bride and groom are quite diffident and reserved, the two Dukes are merry and thick as thieves cutting up the swag. Nevertheless, it made me once again resolve to marry at my earliest convenience, as soon as I can find a trim Baptist woman of good family, breeding and humor. Unfortunately, that article is very thin on the ground hereabouts.

As I write it is about seven o'clock in the evening, and

Rasputin the Rooster is starting up. As uninvited guests, we are quartered rather near the kitchen garden and chicken yard. Rasputin is a coal black bird, very taut and trim, who usually takes his dinner at six o'clock; then, after an hour devoted to meditation, he mounts a barrel and crows a good part of the night. He gets hoarser and hoarser all the time, but he scorns to allow any personal consideration to interfere with his duty, and keeps up his labors in defiance of threatened diphtheria. He is a great inspiration to me on my lecture tour. Come to think of it, he may be the answer to my prayers for inspiration—how can people say Providence has no sense of humor?

I see I have wandered a step too near blasphemy again, and I can also see that dear wrinkle forming on your brow, and hear in my mind's ear your thimble tapping the table top; so I will apologize to you and the Power above and sign off,

Your naughty but devoted son,

Sam

## 62. Esperanto Etiquette

Reprinted from the *Atlantic Weekly, July 25*, 1879
Mark Twain
Fortress Ross
Rossland

Dear Reader:

If you enter into conversation with a well-dressed, purebred Russian in Rossland, address him in Esperanto as *Noblo* or "Lord" and watch his countenance carefully. Your chances are better than even that he will glow and bask in your assumption that he is landed gentry, a class that makes up over half the expatriate population and responds to *Noblo* like geese to grass.

If your victim frowns or shuffles his feet at your form of address, change your tack and call him *Konsilisto:* "Counselor." He is probably a cog in the bureaucratic machinery of Rossland—a prosecutor, bailiff, lawyer, inspector, minister with portfolio, deputy sheriff, dogcatcher, licensed undertaker, or other variety of official felon with a license to steal.

However, if your interlocutor arches an eyebrow at your presumption, immediately apologize and call him *Generalo*. He is a military man, and since the lowest rank they confer is lieutenant-colonel, you are safest in calling him a general.

At the train station I was asking directions of the serf behind the newsstand.

"Noblo," he said, mistaking me in my new otter skin hat for

a Russian, "How fare your estates?"

"No, no," I replied, "I am not a landowner here."

"Ah, I see, konsilisto," he said, "you are here on official business."

"Well, actually," I said, "nor am I in the government, thank the lord."

"I am terribly sorry, generalo," he replied, putting his purse away. "How may I assist you?"

"Wrong again" I said, "Although I am of European stock, and have the hat to prove it, I am not Russian at all."

"Well then, what the devil are you?" he queried.

"I'm just a private personage," I said, "An American originally, lately from the Sandwich Islands."

"Oh, bless you sir," the serf replied, grasping my hand reverently and bestowing the softest of kisses thereon. "I have longed all my life to meet a white man who is not a Russian. Not a lord, an official, or an officer. I shall treasure this moment all my days."

He continued to fawn over me, patting my clothes and tugging his forelock. Finally his grateful emotion overcame him and he swooned away entirely. I was deeply touched, moved to pity and wonder. I arranged his supine limbs, kissed him for his mother, relieved him of his small change, and "shoved" for points east.

Your unique servant,

Mark Twain

## 63. Boundary Values

In Nicholagrad, or Sakrametska as we came to call it, Marina dragged Twain and me from door to door, trying to find lodging of any kind. After fruitless inquiries at five hotels, all bursting at the seams, we settled into a "boarding house" at the end of a dusty street baked by the sun. The structure was wooden, with ugly black iron shutters on all the windows and even over the doors. Only two rooms were available, both small and expensive. Marina had a garret space up three flights of stairs, and Mr. Twain and I took the basement compartment, a dim cave smelling of damp, but blessedly cool. I did not relish sharing a room, but I welcomed the chance to save a little money. Even Twain was low on funds. Krepotsky's promised honorarium for a command performance would not be paid in full until Twain had finally sung his number for the emperor.

He and Miss Marina were in high spirits despite our long hot search for quarters. They jostled and mocked each other like siblings of an age, although he had to be over twenty years her senior. In the last few days, she had focused her teasing attention on Mr. Twain instead of me, much to my relief. I found her company exhausting, although she had proved to be an excellent model. She knew by instinct how to strike an interesting pose, relax into it, hold truly still, and return to the exact same position hours or even days later. I wondered what she would look like draped in cashmere, surrounded by ferns in some lush, bucolic setting out of a Wordsworth poem.

I stowed my belongings quickly and ran out to escape the confines of the horrible room. The street was thronged with wagons and horses and men afoot, stirring up a choking dust, even on the streets paved with cobble or macadam. I made my way down to the Embarcadero, by the river.

Shiny black carriages twinkled past with noble crests on the doors and curtains open to catch the breeze, giving me a glimpse of a silk hat, a bit of lace or braid on a sleeve. Burly drovers urged their teams forward against an almost impenetrable wall of traffic. Small boys and Chinese ducked and bobbed and weaved in and out of the traffic, darting like swallows through the smallest opening in the crowd.

Vendors sold roasted grain, parched corn, skewered meats, donuts, sorghum candies, and honey-sweetened barley water and lemonade. I had a berry turnover and a lemonade, sitting

on a pile of stone blocks, in the corner between a buttress and a levee wall, where I was out of the way and had a good view of the docks. When I finished my sweets, I wiped my fingers on my trousers and took out my sketchbook. I did a quick study of the scene, in black and white only, no shading.

Sometimes that is my favorite way to make sense of a complex subject. One arbitrarily chooses what my teacher Carolus calls a "boundary value"—a point on the value scale between the darkest and lightest colors of a scene. Everything that is the same or a lower value than the boundary value is rendered in pure black. Everything that is lighter than the boundary value is left alone, as pure white. Thus, a man's trousers, shoes and shadow on the street will form one large black shape, merging with other black shapes in the background, while his shirt and head and hat will be all white, merging with other white shapes in the background. I might include a few black marks for the shadows of his hat on his forehead, his nose on his upper lip, or his chin on his neck.

Sketching this way, in black only, is very good practice in

connecting all the darks into one powerful shape, intertwined with a large, powerful light shape. If I choose a very light boundary value, the scene looks flooded with light. Or I can choose a very dark boundary value, and the picture becomes very dark, brooding, and mysterious.

After an hour's sketching, I felt relaxed and calm, having completely forgotten Twain, Marina, our mean boarding house, and our tedious search for a place to stay. I looked up and discovered that I had collected a small crowd of children watching me. I smiled briefly at them, but did not say anything or maintain eye contact. I like children as a rule, but they can ruin my concentration with their endless questions. I've found it best not to give them an opening.

### 64. The Unholy Family

When I received the Tsar's invitation for a visit to Rossland and a command performance, I was as relieved as the woman whose baby came white. Travel letters from California and a subsequent book on the California experiment would have been all well and good, but the real jewel in my literary crown would be impressions of the Tsar and his tin pot empire. As a rule, journalists were as welcome in Rossland as typhoid fever, but my two book-length efforts had apparently elevated me to the status of a novelist. No more a Shklovsky, exiled to Siberia to write about the history of fishing in Minsk—I was now a Tolstoy, honored and admired and safe enough to be let into the capital city. I had felt very smug, two weeks ago, anticipating the solid blows I would land on the body politic of tyranny, bragging to Howells that against the assault of laughter, nothing can stand. I even thought I would do a bit of business in photographic chemicals for Jaime Rodolpho, cementing my association with the photo-engraving genius.

But Rossland had turned out to be largely a feudal swamp, mired in the past, inefficient and backwards. Now I was becalmed, tired, and dispirited. No commercial prospects, no fawning crowds at my lectures, apparently forgotten by the Tsar and his minions. No one to meet the train, no hotel reservation, no booking agent in sight. I was left on my own like a cub reporter fresh off the boat, forced to scrounge for a bunk and buy my own drinks. Like the unholy family, we slunk into town with humbled crest, knocking fruitlessly on every inn door, me as Joseph, Marina as Mary, and John a very premature and precocious Christ Child.

Marina was at a loss, embarrassed once again by her betters in this horrible country.

"I'm sure it is just a mistake," she said. "The hotel cancelled our reservations because the train was delayed. They must have thought we returned to Fortress Ross."

"We telegraphed ahead with all our particulars."

"I know, but sometimes the telegraph office is not entirely reliable."

"This place is a dump," I said, referring to the basement room she had rented, the street outside, greater Sakrametska, and the entire Northwest Empire. I dropped my satchel on one of the narrow beds, creating a jangle of springs and stirring up a musty smell. Sargent said something about mushrooms growing in the corner.

"At least it will be cooler here," Marina said with a sniff. She picked up her own bag and started up the stairs on the long climb to her garret.

Sargent and I unpacked, fighting for space between the beds and in the narrow cupboard that served as a wardrobe.

"There's barely room enough to swing a cat in here," I said, "but not vigorously, and not with entire security to the cat."

Sargent said nothing. Not even a chuckle. I believe he was practicing that virtue so many mothers teach their children: "If you can't say something nice, say nothing at all." He shoved his half-full bag under his bed, grabbed his sketchbook and a straw hat, and left without a word.

I was glad to be alone. I stretched out on the bed in socks

and shirtsleeves, closed my eyes, and set to work restoring my sunny disposition by meditating on my many excellent qualities, the failings of my enemies, and the hope of revenge in future.

I was asleep almost immediately. I dreamed I was in the pilot house of a Mississippi steamboat, pushing upstream in low water, beset on all sides by snags and sandbars, no clear path ahead and not the foggiest notion of the whereabouts of the channel. My mother was in the wheelhouse with me, saying, "Sammy, be careful. Slow down. You'll run us aground sure." She was distracting me, and I yelled at her to let me be, let me concentrate on the river. Then she poked me vigorously in the side.

"Mark? Wake up. You're having a bad dream." It was Marina, sitting on Sargent's bed, poking me, leaning over me so close I could see tiny beads of perspiration on her brow at the hairline. The top two buttons of her shift were undone and she was glowing with the heat of the day.

I was confused for a moment, still dreamy, and I took her hand. She brushed a lock of my hair off my brow, leaned over further, and kissed me. However many times this had happened in my imagination, I was still unprepared for the enormity of the act in reality. I rejoiced in my good fortune and kissed her back. Events unfolded in the usual way, given the weakness of the flesh, and I forgot all about the Tsar, his piddling empire, and my poor mother stuck on the steamboat.

## 65. Boom Town

Violet Paget
17 Rue Des Jardins
Montparnasse
Paris, France
June 21, 1879

My dear Violet:

Sakrametska is nothing like I imagined it would be. As the capital of a Russian Colony, I expected a miniature Moscow or Saint Petersburg. However, it is more like Nashville or Louisville, or one of those other Wild West boom towns, as described in the dime novels I used to find hidden under your sofa cushions. If only your editors knew your true taste and preferences in literature. They would be appalled!

Vernon would love it here. I saw two native women mucking out a stable today, wearing very manly canvas *pantalons*. Since the Gold Rush, when all of the able-bodied men ran away to pan for gold, women here have held down men's jobs, including wearing the pants as well.

I have included a black and white sketch of the dock area, done in a kind of woodcut style. I think it is a good example of the primacy of value in communicating your subject. It is the light and dark of things that the mind sees first, not the color. The portrait of the Duke's wife that I wrote you about last time is a possible exception. I wish you could see it. It is in such a high key that I do not think I progressed more than three fifths the way to black, even in the darkest details. And yet, perhaps the Duchess makes my point as well. When the value range is restricted, the more subtle differences between dark and light take on even more importance. I almost asked the Duke to loan me the painting for the Paris salon next year, but decided it is not quite the right thing.

Forgive me. I go on like this in my mind constantly, and I have inadvertently let you eavesdrop on my thoughts without filtering them or editing them for their significance or capacity to amuse you. Actually, this is why I treasure your friendship so highly—because I can relax with you and be myself, and not a carefully crafted version of some fellow I think you might like.

Mr. Twain has not taken any of my recent hints about painting his portrait, although he did watch me paint the Duchess several times, while we were waiting for the train tracks to be repaired. He and I were to share a basement room in a dreadful house here, but Marina asked me to trade rooms so that she could share with Twain. She is bold and cares nothing for convention. I must say, that sort of casual cohabitation seems unremarkable in this racy town.

For an older man of letters, Mark Twain sometimes acts younger than I. He is carrying on like Tom Sawyer himself, swaggering about in miner's boots, shirtsleeves, and a long tan duster. He is talking about buying a pair of "six shooters" like the sports in town have strapped on their hips. He loves their tall tales of panning for gold, claim jumping, gunplay, brawling, and wenching. To me it seems silly *braggadocio*. My artist's eye is drawn to the extremes of human behavior, but my practical burgher's soul likes things settled and civilized.

So I will remain,

Your *démodé* admirer,

John

### 66. New Dog, Old Tricks

William Dean Howells
Atlantic Weekly
Boston, Massachusetts, USA
June 22, 1879

Dear William:

I now understand the expression "a new lease on life," having become party to that figurative document myself this week, on terms that greatly favor me over the celestial Landlord. I am domiciled in the fair regard of Miss Marina, a paramour out of chivalry, a raven-haired, fiery-hearted damsel of legend. Pardon me, but I feel frisky as a pup, and it spurts out incontinently over this page. No doubt I am as deluded as Quixote, seeing my tryst with this half breed woman in a dank cellar in a dirty town the same way that Spanish lunatic saw his princess in a pigsty. But I don't care. After all, I am in the illusion business at work, and so may as well be in delusion at home.

Let me begin a more sober paragraph and try to get things in order. We have at last reached Nicholagrad, called with local perversity, Sakrametska after the old Mexican name, Sacramento. This is a city of contrasts: dogs and diamonds, swine and swells, mud and *mademoiselles.* The Embarcadero reminds me of Mississippi river towns like Vicksburg and Greenville in the old days. To wit, the sultry sun brooding in the white sky, the slow pulse of river traffic quickening with a big steamboat's arrival, the fine gentlemen and ladies mixing with louts and layabouts on the wharves. But Nicholasakrametska is a bigger concern altogether. Six story hotels and swank restaurants lie cheek by jowl with squalid vodka mills and bordellos. The opera house where I will lecture, albeit on a quiet night midweek, is grand as any cathedral. I made a photograph of the outside for you. Inside

it is too dim for photography, but just imagine to yourself the great show of gilt cupids and red plush wallpaper and crystal doodads on the lamp shades.

My own *mademoiselle* Marina has returned my affections and led me to such verbal excesses as marred my first paragraph. It pains me to see how patently she is disregarded on the streets here. Her mixed birth, which to my eye creates nothing but beauty, marks her here as less than human. She is ignored at best and routinely slighted by these rude Russians. Like the Mississippi river gentry of my youth, the Rosslandish upper "crust" refers in the main to the mud on their boots and the dried vomitus on their cravats. Life on the streets of Sakrametska is very like the American Wild West. A man of quality is not properly dressed without his six gun and spurs and a wide Panama sombrero. The *code duello*, although technically illegal, is alive and well. The soft nights ring with whoops and hollers and gunshots. Cattle may be driven down Main Street from midnight until six in the morning, and during those hours they are the most well-behaved citizens one will meet. It is intolerable and appalling, but still, I cannot deny the appeal of swaggering down main street at high noon with one's teeth clamped on a fine cigar, one's feet stamping regally through the pig droppings, the sun shining off a pair of deadly six-shooters, women and children and dogs scurrying out of one's way.

I have enclosed another piece for your Weakly, dealing chiefly in the elevation of the downtown streets. Since it is somewhat critical of the regime, you should probably save it for publication after I am safely back in California. Believe me, I could have given the rascals an even harsher scouring, had I chosen to speak of the laborers who are doing the work—they are little better than slaves. It seems to me that the Russians build nothing for themselves. The Summer Palace in Fortress Ross was built over decades by Aleuts from the Straits of Kamkatchka. When those died off, the onion domes of the cathedral there were completed by Pomo and Miwok Indians.

The Winter Palace here in Sakrametska is steeped in the blood of poor Chinese, Yankees, and yet more local Indians. Their descendants, no better off, no further up the ladder of society, are now raising the very streets to the level of the Tsar's driveway, without any hope of raising their own prospects.

Twenty-five years after the discovery of gold in the Sierras, you can still feel the bustle of the gold rush in this town. I have tried to limn that feeling in the enclosed piece, for the entertainment of your readers. But it is not a healthy excitement. It is like the final fever of typhus, when the patient seems to become more animated and alert, just before the last decline. I sense a fatal fervor in the tone of civic discourse here, that speaks to me of revolution and civil war. I think the Tsar's contemplated invasion of California is more desperate distraction than true ambition. You may pass that along to your Washington cronies, for whatever it may be worth.

Fiddling sweet love's refrain while New Rome burns, I remain…

Your earnest interrogator,

Mark Twain

## 67. A Thousand Grays and Browns

Mark and I walked out early in the morning to explore Sakrametska and observe the street life. The low sun cast long shadows, throwing the buildings in strong relief, while the misty air toward the river softened the edges of trees and buildings in the distance. I set up my easel by the docks and Mark watched me work for a while.

"It looks like St. Louis in summer," Mark said, waving his hand at the street choked with traffic and scaffolding and sawhorses.

"It's beautiful. Lots of grays and browns."

"But there's no real color. Everything's covered with dust."

"On the contrary, it's teeming with color."

"How so?"

"Grays and browns have many colors in them. Watch this." I laid a brush full of pure violet into the corner of a wet rectangle on my paper. The other corner I flooded with pure cadmium yellow.

"Those colors are too bright," he said. "they don't occur in nature, leastways not this nature."

"Just wait." The pigments met in the middle and started to blend. Encouraged by my brush and my tilting the paper this way and that, the violet and yellow merged in a smooth gradation, cool purple grey in one corner, changing subtly to a warm yellowish brown in the opposite corner.

"Amazing," Mark said, "now it's a thousand grays and browns."

"But it's violet and yellow too, right? Can't you still see the bright colors, lurking beneath the grays and browns?"

"I reckon. But that's a mite mystical for me."

"Color *is* mystical. It's pure feeling. It vibrates like the ether. It's God and all the angels."

Twain laughed. "Amen brother, whatever you say. Just don't

baptize anyone with the paint."

A small crowd of street urchins, vagrants, and the idly curious had gathered, as usual, to watch me paint. Mark chatted with them, one after another, asking questions and swapping stories, even though they shared barely a dozen words of any language together.

During a lull in his inquiries I asked him, "Where is Marina this morning?"

"She is seeing about permits to lecture and post bills. Apparently only the Tsar can grant the right to speak one's mind or paste paper on these pristine walls."

I laughed. I was scraping and torturing my paper, trying to recreate the worn, weather beaten texture of the buildings around us.

"That looks like a Winslow Homer building," Mark said, pointing to the wall surface I was distressing.

"Winslow Who?" I teased.

"Homer, like the Greek. He's the best painter in the states. You should see a painting called *Snap the Whip*. It's the spittin' image of Tom Sawyer."

"I think I've heard of Wilson Homer. Isn't he one of those regional *genre* painters? Bloodhounds on the cabin porch, kittens in an old slouch hat?"

Twain eyed me narrowly, "You're pulling my leg, ain't you? You shouldn't bullyrag your old pardner thataway."

"Sorry," I said, "us portrait painters just get jealous of real artists who make a living at it."

"I thought forging the old masters was more in your line."

"It's all the same line. Every portrait is a forgery, you know. Just like every forgery is a portrait of the forger." I wasn't sure if he was just "joshing" as usual, or if he had some inkling of what I was up to with Goya back in Alta California. I decided to change the subject.

"You and Marina are quite close now," I said, feeling devilish, "are you going to marry her some day?"

"And make an honest woman of her, you mean?"

I shrugged.

"She don't need me to make her an honest woman—she's honest enough for the both of us. You'd understand if you had a woman like Marina. That's what we need to do, find a woman for you."

"I'm not interested in any woman."

"How in perdition can you say that? Every man's mainly interested in women."

"Not me. I'm a confirmed bachelor and likely to remain so."

"It's a pity."

" I suppose it is, but that's the way it must be. I need all my power and energy for my work. I intend to succeed."

"You'll change your tune when you meet the right gal."

"If you say so." I let the subject drop, not wanting to protest too much.

Soon Mark lost interest in my painting and wandered off to "explore on his own," which I knew would involve cigars and beer and talk in some dark tavern.

### 68. Sakrametska Raises Her Streets

Reprinted from the *Atlantic Weekly*, August 1, 1879
Mark Twain
Sakramentska
Rossland

Dear Reader:

This bustling city was originally founded by Mexican friars, who named the modest pueblo and the river that is its life's blood *Sacramento*, referring to the Sacrament of the Eucharist. When Tsar Alexander conquered it for the Russians, he renamed it *Alexandergrad*. The next Tsar was Petros, who upon his ascension renamed the town *Petrograd*. The current Tsar, one Nicholai by name, came up with the novel notion of calling the town *Nicholagrad*; and you will hear it called that at court, in Nicholai's Winter Palace; but everybody on the street calls this city *Sakrametska*. The situation puts me in mind of my cousin, Jonathan Dingleberry Pope, who wanted to be called Jonathan but everybody called him Dink.

Sakrametska is rebuilding itself, on top of itself. After years of annual flooding, the Tsar has decreed that the entire downtown area must be raised by over two meters. This comprises fully ten square blocks south of the river, between the Winter Palace and the docks. The original ground floors of all the buildings are being turned into basements, their doors and windows boarded up, their outside walls bricked over and coated with bitumen. The streets are being built up with earth from a great excavation to the north, where the very course of the river is being straightened to eliminate a dangerous bend. The new streets are being paved with square cobbles, a vast improvement over the planking or soft Nicholson paving in the rest of town. Russ paving with granite blocks would be even better, but they haven't heard of that here, apparently.

Looking southwards, at the Winter Palace, this scheme is a marvel of order. The Tsar's driveway and front yard have been completed at the new level, flat and true as a billiard table. The trees lining the roadway were set with line and plummet, their uniform height determined with a spirit level, the pure white pavement jack-planed and sandpapered every morning.

Looking northwards toward the river, it becomes clear that only about half the job is done, and chaos reigns. Walking anywhere downtown necessitates trudging up stairs or ramps to the new street level, then down again for a few meters of the old street level, then up again, then down, and so on *ad infinitum,* like an ant traversing a washboard. Some poor shop-owners, having fallen behind in their renovations, must pay for temporary shoring, retaining walls, trenches, stairs and tunnels down to their old ground floors. Some blocks resemble prairie dog towns or open pit mines more than urban environs.

Civic improvement by decree is fascinating to watch. As the

official timetable for the project grinds forward, the townsfolk scurry and scramble like mice before an approaching steam roller. Business owners pool their resources, block by block, to bribe the earth-movers to stay away until they are ready. When they are ready, they must bribe the earth-movers to come back and fill up their block like a Brobdingnagian flower bed. Then they must bribe the pavers to lay cobbles before the earth turns to mud and washes away.

What the Republic of Alta California would accomplish by a rational and progressive system of taxation and public works, the Empire of Rossland achieves more slowly and ruinously by proclamation, confiscation, corruption and coercion. Concerned in the main with pure survival before the Juggernaut of Imperial Whim, citizens and tsarist flunkeys alike take no pride in doing good work. Poorly tamped streets settle and must be repaved. Sinkholes and cave-ins and labyrinthine detours are frequent. Everywhere it is dusty and dirty and noisy.

Not being a landowner or citizen here, free to leave at any time, I love it. The shortest stroll to the corner cigar stand is an adventure. The bustle and excitement appeal to me, but only because I am not subject to the fear and uncertainty of the average *Sacrametskavik.* I am a happy grasshopper frisking about an anthill overturned by the plow of monarchy.

Fiddling while tsardoms smolder, I remain,


Your humble servant,

Mark Twain


### 69. Anglophiles

On my second night in Sakrametska I lectured in the opera house, a grand pile of heroic proportions. The audience was tolerably large, well dressed, and well behaved in the main. To wit, they did not throw antique cabbages nor holler catcalls at me. They minded their own business and left me to mine. I nattered on about the Sandwich Islands and my adventures in the Holy Land, in a mixture of English, Esperanto, and a few prepared phrases of Russian. Marina stood downstage left in the heat and glare of buzzing electric footlights, offering a running translation of my remarks to the dozen or so audience members who were listening.

The rest of the crowd chatted amiably amongst themselves, sharing out their box dinners, drinking from silver flasks, paring their nails, catching up on sleep, dry-firing their revolvers, and pursuing the myriad homely pleasures of a pack of boors baying after spiritual enrichment. I found myself directing my remarks exclusively to the front two rows, occupied by a group of swells and their ladies who occasionally laid off their festivities to listen to me. They even laughed at some of the simpler English jokes, before Marina could render them fully into Russian.

These same swells came backstage to meet me after the talk. Baron Something, Lord Something Else, Madame Garble, and a half dozen others introduced themselves in highly accented English, interrupting each other to display their mastery of Anglic vocabulary and grammar. These were the Sakrametsniks that Marina and I came to call the Anglophiles—Rosslandish aristocrats who were infatuated with all things English and American, just as their Russian counterparts in Napoleonic days were infatuated with all things French. They bombarded me with questions:

"Have you ever to meet Queen Victoria?"

"Which is best writer, Shakespeare or Sir Walter Scott?"

"How is Mr. Disraeli really like?"

"Is U. S. President Grant reading you books?"

"Would you come to supper Tuesday week?"

"For you does Sakrametska River resemble Thames River in London?"

"Do you like kippered herring?"

"Will you come to luncheon?"

"Do you like orange marmalade?"

"Can you write for our journal in English?"

"Is true in England is nobody carrying a gun, and in America is everybody?"

"May you attend salon of English literature?"

That night I found these enthusiastic Anglophiles quite comic, but I eventually came to love them. They were the literati of the town. They had the best salons and the best conversation to be had in Sakrametska. More important, they treated me like visiting royalty. Thanks to the Anglophiles, I soon had a full social calendar of literary luncheons, testimonial dinners, and lecture bookings in outlying areas. They had an English language journal to which I cheerfully contributed a couple of letters, cribbed shamelessly from my *Atlantic Weekly* offerings.

At the back of the backstage crowd was a gray little fellow with a leather portfolio clutched in hand. When the crowd around me had finally thinned, he stepped forward and presented the portfolio to me. Inside, in lovely calligraphy, was an invitation to present myself in the Hall of Audience of the Winter Palace, for a palaver on the morrow with Tsar Nicholai hisself; this momentous occasion to be followed the next evening by a command performance in the Topaz Ballroom. Also in the portfolio, trumping everything, was a chit for room and board at the Imperial Hotel for myself and my *entourage*. Pinned to this meal ticket was Gregor Krepotsky's card, scrawled "With the emperor's compliments."

We wasted no time. Marina and I repaired directly to our mean boarding house, scooped up John Sargent and all our traps, and checked into the Imperial Hotel. The desk clerk told me that there was a carriage available at my command, and handed over a wad of 900 roubles, provided by the palace for "incidental expenses." We were shown to a suite of five rooms on the third floor, with a commanding view of the waterfront.

I settled into my private sitting room, refreshing myself with a nightcap of some capital Barbados rotgut, savoring the keen pleasure of luxurious surroundings paid for by others.

Although I reckoned Emperor Nicholai's largesse to be the tsarist equivalent of me buying a friend a drink, it was welcome nonetheless. Old Nick o' Lie's money did much to temper my disdain for monarchs. He almost convinced me not to steal his towels.

I had half a mind to acquire a pair of *pistolas*. Double action Nagants were the weapon of choice in Sakrametska, being manufactured just a few leagues north of town at the royal armory. According to an advertisement in the local newspaper, a pair of the gas-sealing cavalry model with 160 centimeter barrels could be had for only R500, price including cartridge belt, holsters, and long straps to keep the guns out of the mud if one drops them at a gallop. The local swells cut a fine figure on the street, their belts bristling with brass and their red leather horse thongs brushing their boot tops. In Sakrametska the proper revolvers were a more important male accoutrement than cufflinks or a repeater watch. It was a surprising fashion to find in the capital city of a governmental system so given to assassination.

Торговый Домъ **Я. Зимина вдова и С. Никифоровъ**, Москва, Тверская.

7-мизарядный боевой револьверъ Бельгійскаго образца, фабрики НАГАНА (L. Nagant à Liége).

Рис. № 420.

Цѣна **R500**

ƒ 7-мизарядный, фабрики Нагана, револьверъ облегченнаго образца соединяетъ въ себѣ всѣ качества, которыя желательны въ хорошемъ ручномъ оружіи: громадную силу и вѣрность боя, абсолютную прочность, практичность устройства (при разборкѣ всего пистолета отвинчивается только одинъ шурупъ) и минимальный вѣсъ.

**Дальнобойность** достигнута снарядами изъ новаго малодымнаго пороха и уничтоженіемъ прорыва газовъ въ щель между барабаномъ и казеннымъ срѣзомъ ствола (при подъемѣ курка барабанъ, подаваясь впередъ, надвигается на выступъ казеннаго срѣза, а рыльце очередной патронной гильзы входитъ въ самый стволъ); **практичность** устройства, равно какъ прекрасный фасонъ и правильный балансъ револьвера выработаны многолѣтней практикой, возможное же **облегченіе** произошло отъ выбора металла только наивысшаго качества и прочности.

Вѣсъ 1⁷⁄₈ фунта, длина съ ручкою—5¹⁄₄ вершковъ. Курокъ двойного дѣйствія. Прочіе вороненіе Патроны къ нему за 100 штукъ **8 руб.**

223

## 70. Head & Shoulders of Majesty

Henry James
Lamb House, the Willows
Rye, East Sussex
England
June 28, 1879

Dear Hank:

It has been too long since I last wrote you about the clear divisions of the class system here in Rossland. I appreciated your prompt reply, and your observations on the difference between royalty, aristocracy, and the commercial class. *Quelle drole*. I read that passage to Mark Twain, and I swear he went green with envy at your eloquence.

I am still in Rossland with Twain. We have reached Nicholagrad, the capital on the Sakrametska River, and tomorrow Twain is to be received in audience by Tsar Nicholai Romanovsky. The prospect of a Missourian Yankee in Emperor Nicholai's court is just too delicious. I will go along in the role of literary secretary, part of Mark's *entourage*, but I will be looking out for any chance to bring up the subject of painting and portraiture. Minister of Culture Krepotsky has all but promised me a royal commission for an official portrait, so why not start at the top? I've already painted a Baron's daughter and any number of serfs and soldiers on the street, so I don't see why my next *oeuvre* should not depict the head and shoulders of majesty.

I could certainly use the money. The modest commission I received from Baron Django is almost gone, so I subsist day to day and hand to mouth on Twain's payroll, which he himself describes as "a license to starve." Today he paid me 80 roubles against back salary, which he said brings us "up to Noah's back teeth." That is a typical rusticism, I suppose, but it makes no sense to me. Sometimes he just tries too hard to be funny.

I fill my days wandering, sketching, and painting *en plein air*. I am often observed by idle street youths, some of the boys quite comely and more than willing to pose for me, or indeed to follow me home. I remain discrete and chaste, but it is harder here in this licentious and permissive atmosphere. The

upper classes of Sakrametska are a free-wheeling bunch, and the lower classes follow suit. Excess and and indulgence are in the air all around me. Twain is freely cohabiting with Marina Miranova now, in open disregard of propriety, but no one save me seems to notice. Am I a prude, or the only man left with a natural sense of discretion, if not shame?

Perhaps I should not brag about my discretion. In a weak moment I recently revealed my predilections to Marina. So far she has kept my secret, but it makes me nervous to have my circle of confidants widened by even one. How long before she lets it slip past the boundaries I would set? I wish I had your *aplomb*, your ability to always appear calm and unruffled. You admit nothing, deny nothing, just hold a mirror up to shabby reality and smile in a knowing way.

I'm sorry for the fanciful images of you. They come from my nervousness about tomorrow's audience. I have actually been checking myself repeatedly in the three-inch mirror in my garret, making sure my appearance is up to imperial standards, whatever they may be. I must close now before I become entirely incoherent.

Your silly friend,

John

## 71. Bushwhacked

July 19, 1879
William Dean Howells
Atlantic Weekly
Boston, Massachusetts, USA

Dear William:

I find I have let myself down. I have succumbed to the flattery of monarchs, failing to extinguish in myself that instinctive awe that hereditary rulers evoke in the common-born. Despite my republican values, I approached my audience with Tsar Nicholai in a state of giddiness. I polished my boots, trimmed my moustache, and had Marina coach me in several phrases of well-turned Russian. Then I made one mistake: I brought Marina and Sargent along, in the guise of translator and secretary, to fill out my *entourage*.

To my disappointment, we were received by the Tsar in a large drawing-room, rather than in a genuine throne room. A few chairs around the walls were occupied by miscellaneous courtiers and hangers-on, whispering in the background. The Tsar is a tall, skinny sprout, with that poker-up-the-backside carriage I associate more with Prussians than Russians. He and I got on tolerably well, with a minimum of bowing and scraping. He seemed truly glad to receive the leather-bound copy of *Innocents Abroad* that you provided me—thank you for that, by the way.

I had just started to relax and enjoy myself, when Sargent bushwhacked me. The whelp stole my thunder! One moment I was trading Russian and Esperanto witticisms with the emperor, the perfect image of the visiting literary lion; and the next moment I was holding Master John's coat while he gossiped endlessly in French with *my* Tsar.

Sargent has taken to Sakrametska like a bear to honey. He scoops up the attention of all those around him and plays the Russians like a cello. He and Nicholai were chattering like a pair of schoolgirls at a tea party. The Tsar even offered him a commission for a portrait! I can just imagine the sort of flattering, sugary image that will result. In France and Italy I saw miles of such paintings by the old masters. Some of them were beautiful, no doubt, but their nauseous adulation of princely patrons was more prominent to me than the charm of color and expression which are claimed to be in the pictures. Gratitude for kindnesses is well, but some artists carry it so far that it ceases to be gratitude and becomes worship.

Sargent has been baldly hinting that I should allow him

to paint my portrait. To my shame, I have occasionally been attracted to the notion—he is undoubtedly talented in that line. But his fawning behavior with the Tsar has hardened my heart against that proposition.

My command performance for the court takes place Saturday night. The Tsar assured me that he would attend, but I will not count on him. I am resolved to make no special effort to please the Tsar. He can take me or leave me as I am, a free man speaking freely. I have earlier considered which of my stories might be most interesting and palatable to the court, but now I care not a fig. I shall please myself, hew to the heartwood of my theme, and let the chips fall where they may. I trust to Providence that the Tsar will then see which of us is the true artist, or if he lack such powers of discernment, to perdition with him.

Meanwhile, I remain…

Your faithful correspondent,

Mark Twain

## 72. Commission of a Lifetime

July 19, 1879
Mary Sargent, c/o Sanderson
Apartments Genessee
10 Clarastrasse
Berne, Switzerland
July 1, 1879

Dear Mother:

I am to paint the portrait of a Monarch! Tsar Nicholai himself! But wait, let me start at the beginning: This morning Mr. Twain and I were received in audience by His Excellency Nicholai Romanovsky, Tsar of Rossland and Lord Protector

of the Southeastern Realm. He is a tall, slender gentleman
of about thirty, very imperial in bearing, very good-looking,
with an erect, military carriage. Mr. Twain presented the Tsar
with a leather-bound copy of *The Innocents Abroad*, which he
received graciously.

His Excellency greeted us in heavily accented English,
then switched to Russian, speaking through Miss Miranova,
our translator. He asked Mr. Twain, "How are you finding your
visit to the Americas? Will you write a new book about us?"

Mr. Twain answered in English, "I reckon there are lots of
opportunities for my peculiar style of writing."

"How would you compare the Spanish and ourselves?" the
Tsar asked, getting right to the point.

"Unfavorably to both, of course. That is my style. For
example, in Alta California, half the people suspicion you
will attack them, and half that you will not, whereas in your
country, the situation is reversed."

The Tsar frowned at this. I could not tell if he had taken
offense at the allusion to impending hostilities, or if he was
merely confused by a quirk of Marina's translation from
Twain's frontier English into courtly Russian. I paraphrased
Twain's remarks in French, since I knew the Tsar was fluent in
that tongue. He smiled then and nodded.

"*Ah, quelle drôle*," he said, and we were off on a long
*détour* in French. At first, I translated Twain's remarks into
French for the Tsar. Later, Nicholai and I conversed in French
and Miss Miranova murmured English into Twain's ear.
Neither of my companions was pleased by my commandeering
the conversation, as they informed me later in no uncertain
terms. But I couldn't help myself—the Tsar and I hit it off
from the start. He asked me about my family, my education,
and my painting. He knew all about the wedding portrait of
Siska Django I had done for the Count of Hopland.

"I would like for you to paint my portrait," he said, staring
into my eyes in a very direct manner. I stammered that I would
be honored to paint him. He said, "Very good. My chamberlain

will make all the arrangements." And that was that: The commission of a lifetime, one that most painters labor all their lives to receive, granted to me at age 22, after twenty minutes of conversation.

At that point, the Tsar turned back to Twain and switched back to Russian, welcoming him again to Rossland and expressing his pleasure in the author's visit. But it was clear that the audience was drawing to a close, and I had taken up most of it chattering in French. Mr. Twain has been decidedly cool toward me since then.

But I do not care overmuch. I am floating along like my body is made of cloud. My feet scarcely touch the ground. Tomorrow I have an appointment with the Tsar's chamberlain at the palace to settle all the financial and practical details of the portrait. I must find a studio, procure the best canvas and paints. So much to do and it is night and all the shops are closed and I cannot sleep and must stay up all night writing to you and everyone I know.

Your Loving and Ecstatic Son,

John

### 73. A Modest Proposal

Reprinted from *English Life* (Английская жизнь), 7/2/79
Mark Twain, Nicholagrad, Rossland

My Dear Rosslandish Friends:

It is with great pleasure that I address you in these pages, the only ones to my knowledge being published in English in your fair country. I say "English" advisedly, because sometimes the spelling employed by the editors is not quite the same brand I learned in my American boyhood, nor yet is it the British standard spelling.

But do not think that by this observation I intend any criticism—none of we native speakers of English can spell it, either. English spelling is the most haphazard, ridiculous, confounded mess of a system ever devised. We should take what centuries of Angles and Saxons—and that New Englandish nincompoop Noah Webster—have devised, and toss it into the ashcan of history. We really should just start over.

To that end, I have a modest proposal for a reform of English spelling that could regularize it in a gradual, 20-year process. To wit:

**Year One** would drop the useless letter "c," to be replased either by "k" or "s." The only kase in which "c" would be retained would be the "ch" formation. Likewise "x" would sease to eksist.

**Year Two** would reform "w" spelling, so that "which" and "one" would take the same konsonant and bekome "wich" and "won."

**Year Three** will abolish "y" completli, replasing it with "i" or "ai."

**Iear Four** would fiks the "g/j" anomali wons and for all, solving a jiant problem.

**Iear Five** kontinues bai doing awai with the useless double consonants that are so anoiing.

**Iear Siks Thru Twelve** or so modifaiz vowlz and the rimeiniing voist and unvoist konsonants.

**Bai Iear Fifteen or Sou,** it wud fainali bi posibl tu meik ius ov thi ridandant letez "c", "y" and "x"— bai now jast a memori in the maindz ov ould doderez —tu riplais "ch", "sh", and "th" rispektivili.

**Fainali,** xen, aafte sam 20 iers ov orxogrefkl riform, wi wud hev a lojikl, kohirnt speling in ius xrewawt xe Ingliy-spiking werld.

Well, maybe not. Perhaps it is better that I do not have the power to trifle with the English language on a universal scale. Power, when lodged in the hands of man, means oppression, insures

231

oppression, guarantees oppression always. Give power to me, and I will turn a subtle vehicle of expression into a jumble of nonsense, all for a morning's amusement. Give power to an unassuming chap like the Emperor of Russia, and with a wave of his hand he will brush a multitude of young men, nursing mothers, gray headed patriarchs, gentle young girls, like so many unconsidered flies, into the unimaginable hells of his Siberia, and go blandly to his breakfast, unconscious that he has committed a barbarity.

Of course, your local reformers would never do that, Siberia being inconveniently far away, and so many provinces hereabouts requiring an eager workforce. No, on review, I thank Providence I was born a common man. There was a reason Providence sent Jesus to earth as a common man. Had he been born to power, Jesus might well have had the clean hands and Pontius Pilate might adorn our churches today.

Thank you for this opportunity, so graciously granted to one so undeserving of trust, to utter in your pages and charmingly Anglophile ears, my few words of praise for Rossland and the Rosslandish way of life.

Your visiting gadfly,

Mark Twane

## 74. Studio to Let

I could not sleep. I stayed up sketching portrait ideas, making lists, and writing letters. I wrote about the commission to paint the Tsar to my mother, Hank James, Vernon Lee, and Carolus Duran. I exhausted all my compositional ideas. I made lists of paints and canvas and turps and brushes enough for ten portraits. But still I could not sleep until nearly four in the morning. By seven I was up again, knocking on Marina's door to ask her to help me find a studio in this crowded city.

There was no answer at first. I heard a furtive, scrambling

sort of noise, and Twain's voice. Finally Marina opened the door, her dressing gown awry. I smelled cigar smoke, and saw the toe of Twain's boot sticking out under the bed, but I had no time for such trivialities.

"Will you help me today?" I asked. "I must buy art supplies and find a studio."

She smiled and nodded. "Meet me in the lobby in an hour."

I waited for her in the lobby, passing the hour by reviewing my lists. I must have slipped into sleep, because the next thing I knew, Marina was before me.

"I am ready for you to buy me breakfast," she said, "but first, you may want to comb your hair and tuck in your shirt." I repaired myself, and we repaired to the hotel dining room. Over *blinis* and tea she told me that Twain intended to spend the day scribbling in their room, so she was at my disposal.

I gulped my tea, wrapped some rolls in a napkin, and dragged her into the streets. She took me straight north, across the Tsar's new bridge, to the cheap side of the river. Here they were not raising the streets and buildings to prevent flooding. In fact, the district was called "The Lakes" in Russian, on account of the annual spring floods. Some buildings along the river were on stilts, but most were flimsy shacks with high water marks on their rotting wooden walls.

We were in the slums. A man with no legs sprawled in a doorway, begging for coins. A blind woman displayed her skinny baby and held out her hand. The people were thin and their clothes drab and dirty. I felt sorry for them, but I also yearned to sketch them, drawn by a hawklike profile, a rakish turban, the expression of crafty desperation on a swarthy face. Marina strode purposely by them, without a glance.

Marina wrote out the Russian letters for "To Let" in my sketchbook, and we looked for signs and notices for several blocks, to no avail. She began entering every business to ask about space to rent, but nothing was available. One chandler told us that the whole area was stuffed with goods from across the river, in storage until the construction of the Tsar's neighborhood was completed.

We had better luck when she began telling them that I held a commission from the Palace. Then the light of greed lit up several eyes. One boatwright in particular sounded promising. He had a boat house where he built skiffs and canoes and repaired boats for others. He had just finished a repair on a large blue boat. It was floating in the slip that made up the riverside end of the boat house. In a couple of days he would open the large doors at the end of the slip and deliver the boat to his customer. He had no repairs scheduled after that, and was willing to rent the building for what Marina considered an exorbitant fee.

The building was long and narrow, on the ground level at the street end, and built on stilts at the other end, extending out over the water, creating a covered slip where boats could be docked entirely within the structure. The landward end of the building was large enough for an easel and posing stand. The water made the interior somewhat damp, but it was cool. The ceiling was high and the north wall had two large skylight windows, high up so that they cast a good light for painting. Below the windows, the north wall was marked with long, swooping chalk lines, the lofting of many different craft.

It was not the elegant, drawing room-style studio I had envisioned, but I fell in love with the light. I imagined setting up a large easel under the windows and staying on in Sakrametska for a few months, painting happily in my studio on the river. I would make some money, buy the building from the boatwright, and fix it up with carpets and wallpaper and a velvet-draped posing stand. In the slip I'd keep a trim little skiff with white lap sides, mahogany rail, gleaming brass bits and a little flag on the bow. I'd row across the river for tea with the Tsar. Nobles would beat a path to my quaint studio in the slums, and the whole neighborhood would become a soggy Montmartre as other artists gathered around to bask in my shadow.

The landlord sensed my enthusiasm, and asked Marina for a deposit. She said we would have to think about it, and dragged me away. I was somewhat overexcited, and that always makes me hungry, so I pulled the napkin from my coat pocket and offered Marina a roll. She scorned it and insisted on buying us lunch in a dingy café. Marina was not one to picnic on the street when she could sit down in a restaurant, even if it meant paying for it herself.

We had borscht with sour cream in it. I crumpled my rolls into the soup to make a mush the exact shade of gentian violet.

"I like that boat shed," I said, chewing.

"Yes, but you could never have the Tsar there."

"I know, but the light is perfect."

"Everywhere has light."

"Of some kind, yes, but not the right kind. In this hemisphere you want North light, from a high angle like those windows on the back wall."

"I can't see what difference it makes."

"South windows let the sun in, which makes everything look too yellow and warm. East and West windows are too bright and warm half the day, and too dim and cool the other half. North windows give you a steady light all day long, not too warm, not too cool."

"Still, I don't see the Tsar posing in a boat shed."

I just sighed. I did not want to admit it, but she was right. Perhaps I would have to paint in my hotel room, dragging the canvas and paints and easel back and forth to the palace for the posing. That would be more practical, but hardly convenient.

I drew out my sketchbook and began drawing Marina's profile. Although she often mocked me and annoyed me, I found her a good model. She was not self-conscious and nervous like most people when they become aware that an artist is studying them. She merely glanced over at me, saw what I was doing, and calmly returned to her meal. In our travels together I had noticed that she had a wide range of expression. She could be voluptuous, coquettish, haughty, or cold—so changeable one could not easily discover the real woman underneath. As she finished her soup, I blocked in her hair, swept back in a *chignon*. It made her look like a haughty noblewoman, so I added a low-cut gown, one strap shamelessly fallen off a bare shoulder. When I showed it to her, her eyes widened and her nostrils flared, ever so slightly. But she studied the drawing for a long moment.

"Is my nose really that long?"

"A long nose is good. In Europe, long noses mean a long lineage. You could be a notorious Parisian socialite."

She smiled at that.

"You're good, Johnny. Maybe too good." She handed the book back to me. "Be careful how you flatter the Tsar. He's had lots of practice being flattered, and seeing through it."

In the afternoon we shopped for art supplies on the other side of the river. My travel kit was entirely inadequate for a royal portrait. I needed the finest canvas, best paints and mediums and solvents, a larger palette, and so on. Marina found the best shop, which had a good supply of the correct materials, but I bought little. Prices were high, and I was not sure what I would need. I itched to get started, to *do* something, but I was frustrated.

As the day grew dim, my agitated state abated. I passed from giddy excitement to irritable frustration, and thence into melancholy. When I left Marina at her hotel room door, I'm sure she was happy to be quit of me.

I was exceedingly keen to begin my new calling as a royal portrait artist, but try as I might, I could not make events unfold fast enough to please me. The real world plodded on, one dreary minute after another, the globe turned slowly through each hour of the day, and I could not find purchase to push it any faster. I fell asleep without dinner, dreaming of my appointment at the palace the next day.

### 75. A Minor Moon of a Minor Planet

Violet Paget
17 Rue Des Jardins
Montparnasse
Paris, France
July 2, 1879

My dear Violet:

Thank you for the news of the first round of submissions to the Paris Salon. I am not surprised that there are so many. Year after year Beaux Arts and the other schools churn out more and more graduates, and we all must compete for space on the same walls.

I do not think my portrait of the Tsar will ever grace those walls, however. It seems doomed from the start. Following hard on my last letter, you will find my mood in this one much deflated. As Mark Twain would say, I have at last been to see the elephant, and it was a disappointment. I should not have allowed my expectations to rise so high.

After wasting a day looking for a studio, I learned from the Tsar's Chamberlain that I will be required to paint in the Palace *atelier*, a large, crowded room he showed me this morning. It is a sort of gymnasium or factory for artists, with lockers, work stations, and a small staff of painters and sculptors turning out royal portraits and busts like carpenters hammering together tables and chairs. I have been assigned an easel, workbench, and a *taboret* in a corner, away from the best light. I have a locker to store my supplies, and one fellow painter told me to be sure to lock up all my paints and brushes or they will be stolen. He is a fat, nervous type with a persistent cough, which he blames on the sculptors' dust that gets into everything. Naturally, the sculptors blame the pervasive smell of turpentine. Are you experiencing *deja vue*? It is art school all over again, with the same bickering, the same maneuvering for advantage, and the same petty jealousies.

The Chamberlain showed me a portrait of Tsar Nicholai in oils on a large canvas, competently done, but nothing special. "This is what we want," he said, "Same size, same pose, but in this costume." He handed me a photograph of the Tsar in a turban, a shirt with billowing sleeves, and an elaborately embroidered vest or doublet—very middle eastern.

"This one will go to a Kazak Baron in Montana," the Chamberlain said.

"When will the Tsar pose for me?" I asked.

"Oh, not till the very end. Meanwhile, you have Ivan the Terrible."

Ivan is a dressmaker's dummy who will wear the Tsar's costume and pose for me. I am to work on the costume and the background first, bringing them to a high degree of finish. The hands will be my own in a mirror—the Chamberlain says they are close enough to Nicholais'. I am to block in the head from the photograph. Then the Tsar will come in for an hour at most, probably posing for several artists at once.

It is a dreadful way to work. I had imagined leisurely hours in a private studio, laboring at a masterpiece of sensitive, bravura brushwork while trading witticisms and state secrets with the Tsar, almost as equals. In reality, he is the sun and I am no more than a minor moon of a minor planet.

But all is not darkness. My fee for the portrait is 1,500 roubles, a very decent wage here. As an advance for materials, I have received a draft on the exchequer—don't you love the sound of that?—that any bank will honor with gold. And I have saved the best for last. As a hint that all may not be as cut and dried as the Chamberlain says, Tsar Nicholai himself paid a visit to the *atelier* while I was there. He made a special point of speaking to me.

"Ah, my dear friend John Sargent," he said, remembering my name and placing a hand on my shoulder, "I am looking forward to posing for you." He gave my arm a squeeze and laughed, indicating the Chamberlain with a nod of his head. "This man has many rules for artists, but do not be discouraged. You and I will make a beautiful picture together. Baron Druschek will hang it in his dining hall, and everyone will be happy." All this time retaining his hold on my arm, giving it a little massage.

The Tsar then told the Chamberlain to put me on the list for an invitation to a royal ball! I stammered my thanks. Maybe my expectations of intimate *têtes-à-têtes* with the Tsar are not pure fantasy. I think he fancies me! When Nicholai left the room, it was like the sun going behind a cloud—everything seemed a little darker and dimmer. That is the effect of true nobility.

The Chamberlain explained that the paintings and busts were an important part of government here. He said, "It is a mark of favor and distinction to receive an official portrait of

Tsar Nicholai. It sends a silent message of loyalty, support, and certain expectations. Your painting will help ensure that the Baron will not fall short of his full levy of wheat for the winter, mounts for the cavalry, and conscripts for the army."

So it seems that in my small, carpenter's way, I am helping to rule the empire.

Imperially yours,

John

## 76. Nicholai the All Powerful

Reprinted from the *Atlantic Weekly*, August 8, 1879
Mark Twain
Sakrametska
Rossland

Dear Reader:

Last Saturday night I could have been smoking in bed. I could have been paring my fingernails and performing the other delicate tasks of personal hygiene towards which my mother has urged me, lo these many years, in her efforts to support the perfection of my personality and the salvation of my soul. I could have got drunk. But no, instead of engaging in these virtuous, harmless endeavors, I frittered away the evening entertaining the Tsar with my tales of Tangiers, the Holy Lands, and the other circles of Hell I have visited.

It was a command performance, to begin at 8PM sharp, so I launched the good ship Mark Twain as commanded, promptly at 8:45. We were in a middling large hall in the Tsar's Winter Palace. The walls were hung with life-size portraits of various European monarchs, sent hither as tokens of that cousinly regard which exists between all kings, at least on paper. The event was well attended by various relatives, supplicants, and hangers on. They were seated not in rows, but in archipelagos of spindly Louis the Something chairs scattered over an acre of pink and white Wilton carpet as soft as mush. They reminded me of aristocratic Southern planters: wealthy, well-born, ignorant swells, tinseled with the usual harmless military and feudal titles, full of cheap shams and windy pretense.

I was ten minutes into my pitch when I noticed a disturbance in my audience, caused by the late arrival of the Tsar. All heads turned to the royal archipelago, where Tsar Nicholai the All Powerful was fussing with his cushions. I was nearly struck dumb by the fact that the man came in late, after the curtain! This is an offense that in a civilized Democracy would have had him cooling his heels in the lobby, flirting with the cigar stand girls and taking target practice on the cuspidors, waiting until the first interval to be seated. But here in Rossland I suppose they are accustomed to wandering in at any time they please, interrupting all manner of lectures, operas, and their mothers' weddings.

If I may speak freely, I think this all comes of elevating a weak, trivial-minded man to a position of rank and power—of making a tsar out of very inferior material—of trying to construct greatness out of constitutional insignificance. It is incredible to think that this slight figure, chatting like the most ordinary individual in the land, was a man who could open his lips and ships would fly through the waves, locomotives would speed over the plains, couriers would hurry from village to village, a hundred telegraphs would flash the word to the four corners of the globe. Here was a man who could do this wonderful thing, and yet if I chose I could knock him down. If I could have stolen his coat, I would have done it. When I meet a man like that, I want something to remember him by.

My estimate of Tsar Nicholai is not carelessly formed; there is evidence to back it. He gossips habitually; he lacks the common wisdom to keep still that deadly enemy of a man, his own tongue. "But Mark," I hear you say, "One should make allowances for monarchs, who were raised in castles by royalty and thus cannot be expected to behave as well as an American ribbon clerk or shop girl, who have had the benefit of a proper upbringing." But I say "no, standards must be upheld." I chided the Tsar gently with a remark to the effect that I hoped he did not enter the coming war with California twenty minutes late. However, I wisely phrased my quip in a sentence of so intricately intertwined Russian, Esperanto, and Cajun slang that he couldn't decipher it without three glossaries and a corkscrew.

Reviewing my first paragraph, I see I am in error, writing that I "entertained" the Tsar. Entertainment implies attention. I should have said that I occupied the same chamber with the Tsar, speaking eloquently to the air, while he drank champagne and held a shouting match with his courtiers, sycophants, and bumboys. I am used to rustic circumstances, having been raconteur to countless barbarians such as Mexican cowboys, Kentucky miners, and Washington senators, but I have never struck the like of these New World Russians. They are more cantankerous and ill-mannered than a badger with the toothache.

Previously I had bragged to the editor of this fine paper that the Tsar might take me or leave me as he finds me. Well, he scarcely found me at all, and left me without a qualm. This is my punishment for pandering to royalty—no one ever learned them how to behave. They do wear pretty clothes, though. The flunkeys were dressed like emperors and the Tsar was dressed like God Almighty. I almost yearned to be a flunkey myself, for the sake of the fine clothes.

I am itching to quit this city and head down the river for a breath of fresh air. I have arranged a couple of amusing excursions, which I shall share with you presently.


Your faithful correspondent,


Mark Twain

## 77. Pygmalion's Dilemma

Being newly arrived in town, I knew no one appropriate whom I could invite to accompany me to the ball. Were I in Paris, I might choose a well-behaved younger sister of a classmate. Or if I were feeling wicked, I might bring Violet Paget. Although she frequently went abroad in trousers and passed her writings off as the work of Vernon Lee, that literate man about town, she also took delight in dressing up and aping the airs of the more conventional members of her sex. We spent many happy hours at student openings, whispering our ironical comments on the scene behind our hands, the perfect picture of the proper young couple in evening dress and gown.

I was forced to choose between the only two women I knew in Sacramento: Marina and our old landlady, Mrs. Orloff. After careful consideration, I asked Marina if she would do me the honor. I doubted that she could comport herself with the requisite dignity, but the alternative was even more dubious. I was afraid Mrs. Orloff would bring the lard can into which she habitually spit her tobacco juice.

"Oh yes, yes, yes," Marina said. "I would love to go." Her eyes lit up alarmingly.

"There is just one condition—you must help me make a good impression on the other guests."

"What do you mean?"

"I mean that, for me, this is not a party. It is more like a business meeting, or like scouting the enemy in a war."

"Sounds like fun," she said, the light dimming in her eyes. "Just tell me what you want me to do."

"First of all, I think you should wear your black evening gown. A couple of the jet beads on the bodice are missing, and the hem in back is frayed, but we can trim the ragged edges and no one will notice. And it is awfully long-waisted and straight-lined compared to the styles around here, so you should wear your largest bustle and a tight corselet to give it some shape."

"If I understand you, I should present the same profile as the Hottentot Venus?"

"Not at all." Marina was so prickly and easily offended. "Merely the same profile as all the other ladies of quality."

"I see. And which of my many jewels should I take out of the vault?"

"The mother-of-pearl brooch, with a scarlet ribbon. Wear it in your hair, close to your eyes. They are by far your best feature."

"Why Mr. Sargent, I do believe you flatter me."

"Not at all. I merely make the best of the available resources."

"Then as your best available resource, I hope I will be adequate to your needs." Miss Marina could be just as ironical as Violet sometimes.

"You mustn't make ironical remarks like that at the ball," I warned.

"Then whatever shall I talk about?"

"My mother says a lady talks only about three things in company: the weather, the good fortune of others, and upcoming events of general interest."

"No gossip?"

"Never."

"No jokes?"

"Heaven forbid."

"Your mother must be the most boring person on earth."

I cringed. "That is exactly the kind of remark that you must avoid on Saturday."

"Oh, I'm only joshing you," she said. "I love that word, 'joshing.' Mark taught it to me yesterday. Who is he taking?"

"Krepotsky has fixed him up with the Marchesse du Fontaine."

"Don't you love how the Russians steal every other country's titles?"

"It adds variety to all the tsars and barons. Listen, I know you know all this," I lied, "but let us go over a few details of how we can fit in and charm these Russians of yours."

"I am your willing pupil."

"First of all, no yelling, no loud laughter, no touching or pointing at people." She nodded.

"When we are introduced, shake hands only with the women. Give the men a slow nod of the head and the barest suggestions of a curtsey. On the way back up, look them in the eyes through your eyelashes. That is to be the absolute limit of your flirting."

"For such a proper young man, you have made a deep study of flirting."

"I notice things. It is my gift."

"Go on. This is what my mother never told me, poor old squaw."

"Well, whatever food they have, do not eat anything. It is too dangerous. Take one glass of champagne and try to make it last an hour. No spirits. Tea might be safer, if they have it. But when you drink, raise the saucer along with the cup."

"Is that how your mother does it?"

"Always. And another thing: when we walk together, take my arm. Never take me by the hand except when we are dancing. You do dance?"

She pirouetted in place and gave me the merest hint of a curtsey, looking up at me through her eyelashes.

"Excellent. Do not touch any other man unless he asks you to dance, and then touch only his hand and upper arm."

"May I cough?"

"Discreetly."

"Giggle?"

"Frequently."

"Sigh?"

"Wistfully."

"Sneeze?"

"No."

"Spit?"

"Now you mock me."

She poked me in the ribs, one of her most annoying habits.

"Oh John, calm yourself. I really do know how to behave like a lady. It is just so boring most of the time, so I do as I please. But for this night, I promise to do what you please."

"I can ask no more," I said, and prayed to God to hold her to that promise.

### 78. A Confirmed Bachelor

Mary Sargent, c/o Sanderson
Apartments Genessee
10 Clarastrasse
Berne, Switzerland
July 13, 1879

Dear Mother:

Tonight I attended the Tsar's *fête*. The ballroom of the Winter Palace was lit with a hundred electric globes, more brilliant than a thousand gas lights, throbbing with a barely discernable pulse that gave one a headache and may cost some poor electrical engineer his head in the morning. Beyond the novelty of electric light indoors, the *décor* and *modes des habillés* were decidedly old fashioned. I felt I was back in 1874 rather that on the brink of the 80s. It is no longer a mystery where the excessive bustles of the *demimonde* emigrated after 1875. They are all here.

I made some excellent contacts on the dance floor and around the punch bowls. My patron Krepotsky, Minister of Cultural Affairs, made an appearance, and generously squired me about for a while. There were about 250 in attendance, and I managed to be introduced to at least a third of them. As Mark Twain would say, I "collared" the Tsar, six ministers of state, three counts, a Baroness, and a Marquis from the French Embassy.

We paid our respects to Tsar Nicholai, who called me warmly by name.

"Mr. Sargent," he said in French, "Very pleased to see you again."

"I am delighted to be here," I replied. With most of his guests, Nicholai exchanged those abbreviated Teutonic bows which involve a very slight, very precise inclination of one's head, but give the impression of a vigorous clicking of the heels. With me he shook hands in the English intimate fashion, his other hand on my elbow. He even murmured a few private pleasantries in my ear, too low for anyone else to hear, a signal honor.

In answer to your query, no, I have not met any young ladies of my generation, interesting or otherwise. They tend to be cosseted away from casual commerce, and anyway I am too busy with my painting to do any serious courting. To accompany me to the ball, I chose our translator and guide, Miss Miranova. She is a charming companion, of a good Rossland family, but she is six years older than I.

Thank you for suggesting that we dine with the Sandersons when I return. I promise to be cordial to Miss Betsy, but I would much prefer painting George Sanderson's portrait to marrying his daughter. That is where my true passion lies. I am probably too young to refer to myself as a confirmed bachelor, but I begin to suspect that I may be one. It is not that I do not appreciate the importance of the family. In fact, when one is a confirmed bachelor, family becomes extremely precious—whatever family one has: parents, brothers, sisters, nephews, nieces. They take the place of a wife and children of one's own. None of the girls we know in Paris or Berne are really a proper match for me. I cannot imagine settling down with any one of them. You might say I am already married—to Art. At this point in my life, I am so determined to further my career that a flesh-and-blood family would inevitably take second place. It seems to me that, were I successful as a painter, I would be a failure as a husband and father.

Besides, I travel too much to please any woman of a settled nature.

Please give my regards to *tout le monde,* and father too.


Your loving son,


John


## 79. Death on Two Legs

With more than a week to idle away in Sakrametska before my next lecture, I was eager to get out of town, to pass time alone with the charming Marina, to forget the Tsar, to be shut of John Sargent for a while, to lick my wounds, and to plot more ways to further my fortunes amongst the Rosslanders.

We booked a stateroom on the *St. Ludmila,* a packet steamboat headed south towards San Francisco, with numerous

stops along the way. She was a trim side-wheeler, with much polished brass and painted wood curlicues, a prime example of steamboat gothic at its best, fancier than the boats I piloted on the Mississippi in my youth. I made a rather fine photograph of her at one of the local stops. A mate told us that the local redwood forests provided a superior wood for fancywork: light in weight, easy to cut and carve, retentive of detail, tenacious of paint, and resistant to rot. I wondered why the Almighty had not made everything in the universe out of redwood.

Marina and I leaned on the rail as we eased out from the vast reach of plank wharfs encrusting the banks of the capital. In minutes the confusion of town was behind us and we were in open country. There is no better way to travel than on a river winding its way through the heart of a country, delivering a new vista around every bend. On this downstream leg we loafed along quietly, under just enough steam for headway, letting the current do most of the work. The boiler burbled below the deck, the lazy slap of the wheel sounded like distant hands clapping, and our forward progress created a welcome cool breeze. I made an excellent photograph of a sister boat steaming past us upstream. I broke my own rule of not photographing people and offered to make a photograph of Marina, but she declined. She was the perfect woman for me.

My piloting instincts asserted themselves, and I could not help noticing and mentally cataloging every snag and sandbar we passed. I pressed my elbow subtly against Marina's on the rail and remarked, "See that V-shaped ripple there, pointing upstream? That's a snag just under the surface."

"What's a snag?"

"Tree limb that the devil has wedged into the bottom, sticking up in hopes of poking a hole in your boat. And look there, do you see those little riffles?"

"Like tiny whirlpools?"

"Yes, exactly. That indicates a sandbar, or a mud bank, more likely. The water is only about six inches deep over there."

"You see so much that I would never notice."

She grasped my hand on the rail and raised it to her lips for a soft kiss that took my mind entirely off river lore. I decided it was time to inspect our stateroom. The boat's schedule allowed only 10 hours to reach San Francisco Bay, so a stateroom was not strictly necessary, not for sleeping at any rate. It is curious to me that the missionaries, in imagining the pleasures of Heaven, have left out sexual congress. It is as if a lost and perishing person in a roasting desert should be offered by a rescuer anything he might wish, and the thirsty wretch should elect to leave out water.

After refreshing ourselves in the stateroom we refreshed ourselves in the bar. Marina had for her rouble a glass of vodka the size of a lard bucket, and for mine I had a gill of brandy in a shot glass so small I needed my lorgnette to pick it out of the dust and pepper grains on the table. In Rossland any likker with color is dear.

We did not go all the way to San Francisco, but disembarked at a small border town called "Lock" in Russian, named with characteristic lack of imagination after the enormous double locks there. The locks were overlooked by a small stone fort armed with batteries of twelve- and thirty-two-pounders, which they thought quite impregnable; but if the Americans could ever get after it with one of their turreted monitors, it would be pounded to gravel over night.

Under the guns of the fort, we waited twenty minutes in line to tell the Russian border officials that we were not leaving the country—something we could have demonstrated in one minute by simply walking into town. Those few passengers desirous of escaping Rossland had a much longer wait in a kind of customs corral and immigration loading chute, constructed of log posts and barbed wire, reminding me of an American concentration camp from the war.

While we stood in line, I watched the nervous presentation of bills of lading and passengers' papers, glad that we were not attempting to leave the Rosslandish Utopia at this time. I tried to ask one of the officials about the rules governing exports of silver nitrate and nitric acid into AC, but he pretended not to understand my Russo-Esperanto. My impression was that the petty Rosslander bureaucrats in their comic opera uniforms were loath to let anyone or anything leave their country. By contrast, the Californians at the other end of the loading chute were more soberly dressed, as befits efficient civil servants, but they appeared equally loath to let anyone or anything enter their country. All was quiet and orderly, but the air was vibrating with a subtle tension, like a rich uncle's funeral where everybody's shamming grief and wondering who's in the will.

Finally a soldier told us to move along, so we joined the majority and wandered into town. Lock was essentially a sleepy river town like the Hannibal, Missouri of my birth: frame buildings crowding the streets that fanned out from the docks; shanties and warehouses on the mud of the bottoms with high water marks on their walls; more substantial two story shops and houses on higher ground; a handful of comfortable homes on the modest bluff to the south. The bustle of wagons and horses and passersby on the wooden sidewalks, occasioned by the steamboat's arrival, lasted all of twenty minutes. Then the town went back to sleep.

While Marina shopped for hair ribbons or some such frippery, I observed the river traffic. A spry old Chinaman was tarring a bunch of piles laid out on a pier. I tried him in my Russian and my Spanish and my Esperanto, then discovered that he had a tolerable store of English left over from years of shrimping out of New Orleans. He told me about runaway serfs who float down the Sakrametska River on logs, at night when the locks are left open, sneaking past the guards and the guns of the fort in the tule fog.

"They call them Wetbellies," he said, "They look for better wages and more opportunity in Alta California."

"Do they find them?" I asked.

"Quien sabe?" he said with a grin.

"What about you? Why don't you go South?"

He shrugged and grinned again. "Everywhere bad for

Chinese." He filled me in on life as a Chinaman in Rossland: building levees and growing rice in the island paddies of the delta, delving in the gold mines of the Sierra, laying track across the deserts. While he talked we watched the river. Around the bend came a dark, low craft trailing thick black smoke. The deck was perfectly flat, with no rail, scarcely any more freeboard than a raft. Amidships was a queer iron structure like a giant metal hatbox. It was an iron warship the like of which I had last seen in the Mississippi Delta.

I asked the Chinaman, "What is a turreted monitor doing on the Sakrametska?"

"American war surplus. Rosslanders bought from Confederates. Dons bought from Union."

"How'd they get here? They swamp and founder as soon as they hit the open ocean."

"Navy seals them with rope and tar, tow them through the Panama Canal."

"How can they operate here? They draw more than two meters."

"Many run aground, get stuck in mud."

We had a good laugh about that. I made a photograph of the gun turret after they had tied up at the lock.

I asked the Chinaman where was a good place to buy guns in town, and he directed me to the pawn shop. There I found a pair of Nagant pistols for only R425. The bluing was worn off the sights and the edges of the cylinders, but you couldn't tell that when they were in the holsters. More important, they had the cavalry butt rings and the long red leather thongs that would swing beneath one's coattails as one promenaded in the evening, looking like stylish Death on Two Legs.

Marina found me in the pawnshop, practicing my quick-draw.

"Are you crazy?" she said.

"Yes," I said with a dangerous leer, "and well-armed."

She shook her head. "In this country, you should not wear a gun unless you can use it."

"Exactly," I said, striking a pose.

She shrugged and sniffed and otherwise indicated female disapproval. I removed the guns, but asked the proprietor to wrap them up for me.

## 80. The Golden Arm

When Mark returned from his excursion downriver his good spirits had been returned to him, no doubt by Marina's kind attentions. He was his old self, cheerful, brash, looking forward to his second lecture in Sakrametska with enthusiasm. At dinner he explained his plan to wear his new pistols onstage, and draw them at the beginning when he was startled by first noticing the audience.

I asked him, "Why do you start your talk like that, ignoring the audience and then pretending to notice them suddenly? No one really believes you are caught by surprise—after all, there you are, up on the stage, obviously expecting an audience when the curtain is raised."

"I reckon I do it for the same reason you use empty space in a painting: Contrast, a little pause to focus people's attention on what I am about to say. Without the pause, half the audience wouldn't catch my first remarks. They would still be fiddling with their opera glasses and picking their teeth with their ticket stubs."

"Are you saying that you structure your speech with silence and words, the same way I might compose a painting with emptiness and form?"

"You bet. You organize the space of the canvas, I organize the time of the lecture. Within our boundaries, we can only have stuff or no stuff. Your stuff is paint, mine is words."

I shrugged. He was a smart man, no doubt. But it seemed all rather too abstract.

"I'll tell you what," he said, "I'll demonstrate what I mean tonight. I'll tell a story that depends on the length and quality of the pauses for its effect. Can you come to the lecture with Miss Marina?"

"Of course."

"Capital. I'll give her the Golden Arm. Make sure that she sits in the first five rows."

That night Marina and I were sitting in the center of row three when Twain introduced his famous Golden Arm story:

"This afternoon I was talking to a friend about how the pause is an exceedingly important feature in any kind of story, and a frequently recurring feature, too. It is a dainty thing, and delicate, and also uncertain and treacherous; for it must be exactly the right length—no more and no less—or it fails of its purpose and makes trouble. To illustrate my point, allow me to tell you the negro ghost story of the Golden Arm."

He lapsed into a thick Negro accent that I'm sure 90 percent of his audience could not interpret.

"Once 'pon a time dey wuz a monsus mean man, en he live 'way out in de prairie all 'lone by hisself, 'cep'n he had a wife.

En bimeby she died, en he tuck en toted her way out dah in de prairie en buried her. Well, she had a golden arm—all solid gold, fum de shoulder down. He wuz pow'ful mean—pow'ful; en dat night he couldn't sleep, caze he want dat golden arm so bad.

"When it come midnight he couldn't stan' it no mo'; so he git up, he did, en tuck his lantern en shoved out thoo de storm en dug her up en got de golden arm; en he bent his head down 'gin de win', en plowed en plowed en plowed thoo de snow. Den all on a sudden he stop."

Twain made a considerable pause here, looking startled and taking a listening attitude.

"En he say: 'My *lan'*, what's dat!' En he listen—en listen—en de win' jus howl."

Twain set his teeth together and did a credible imitation of the howling and hissing wind.

"En den, way back yonder whar de grave is, he hear a *voice!*—he hear a voice all mix' up in de win'—can't hardly tell 'em 'part – 'W-h-o — g-o-t — m-y — g-o-l-d-e-n — *arm?* W-h-o g-o-t m-y g-o-l-d-e-n *arm?*'"

Twain began to shiver violently.

"En he begin to shiver en shake, en say, "Oh, my! *Oh,* my lan'!" En de win' blow de lantern out, en de snow en sleet blow in his face en mos' choke him, en he start a-plowin' knee-deep toward home mos' dead, he so sk'yerd—en pooty soon he hear de voice agin, en…it 'us comin' *after* him! 'W-h-o — g-o-t — m-y — g-o-l-d-e-n — *arm?*'"

"When he git to de pasture he hear it agin—closter now, en a-*comin'!*—a-comin' back dah in de dark en de storm. When he git to de house he rush up-stairs en jump in de bed en kiver up, head and years, en lay dah shiverin' en shakin'—en den way out dah he hear it *agin!*—en a-*comin'!* En bimeby he hear…"

Again Twain paused, head tilted to the side, listening.

"Pat — pat — pat — *hit's a-comin' up-stairs!* Den he hear de latch, en he *know* it's in de room! Den pooty soon he know it's a-*stannin' by de bed!*"

He paused again. Every time he paused, Marina at my side

and any in the audience who understood him, leaned forward to catch the next words.

"Den—he know it's a-*bendin' down over him*—en he cain't skasely git his breath! Den—den—he seem to feel someth'n *c-o-l-d,* right down 'most agin his head!"

Another pause.

"Den de voice say, *right at his year*—"W-h-o — g-o-t — m-y — g-o-l-d-e-n *arm?"*

He wailed this out very plaintively and accusingly. He stared right at Marina in silence. When the pause was well-nigh unbearable, he shouted out to her:

"*You've* got it!"

Marina squealed and jumped in her seat. The audience laughed and broke into applause, many of them looking somewhat confused, but clapping their hands anyway.

Twain caught my eye and smirked, the picture of satisfaction. He had proved his point.


### 81. Posing

Henry James
Lamb House, the Willows
Rye, East Sussex
England
July 16, 1879

Dear Hank:

It seems ironic to me that you, with your wide circle of friends and voluminous correspondence, would caution me about being drawn into the sphere of Tsar Nicholai and his court. Certainly the associations I form here can only work in my favor, both while I am here, and when I return to Europe. I assure you that Nicholai has been most charming and demure, at least in public.

In private Nicholai has proved to be just as human as you or I. In fact, he is one of us, if you take my meaning. Together we have given in to certain inverse desires and indulged in certain private practices, from which I have heretofore refrained.

I can hear your voice in my mind's ear, warning me to be careful. And I am being careful, as careful as I can. But oh, it is hard (and difficult as well). I ask you, how can one say "no" to the emperor? Enough said in print.

In a safer vein, Nicholai reminds me of a character in one of your stories: at turns clever, dull, energetic, weary, vibrant, sickly, intimate, distant. He has shared with me the most incredible confidences. It is a revelation to me that this man, born of royal blood and reared from infancy to rule, has doubts about his own capacity. His high position does not protect him from fear. As you and I might fear poverty, he worries about public debt. As we fear robbers and burglars, he fears assassination. As we are jealous of lovers and spouses, he suspects his ministers of treachery.

Nicholai visits the atelier frequently when I am working there, to pose, to chat, to inspect my canvas . . . and other things. I have had much more access to him than I was led to believe, although he is no more eager to sit still for long periods than any other subject. Twain quipped the other day that I am the only one in Rossland who has the king as his subject. Mark is as fond of puns as you are not.

The illustrious Twain has been cutting a wide swath through the nightlife of Sakrametska, drinking and dancing and gambling till three or four in the morning. He and Marina go everywhere together. I hardly see her, nor get any of her time to pose for me. Of course I am too busy with the Tsar's portrait anyway, so my sketchbook and watercolors gather dust. I told Mark that when I finish with the Tsar, I would like to paint him (Mark I mean—I am so conscious of my pronouns when I write to you!) in his new buckskin jacket with his revolvers in hand, like Buffalo Bill Cody, the American circus cowboy.

The others in the atelier are jealous of the attention I receive from Nicholai, so I have not made any friends in that quarter. Minister Krepotsky continues to be helpful, however. He has got his brother Vladimir to approve a tour of the imperial gold mines for us. Apparently they discourage casual tourists in that part of the country, so V. Krepotsky's letter of authority will be invaluable, allowing us to see sights that normal visitors miss.

I enjoyed your description of the new novel. Exploring

the differences between Americans and Europeans is always interesting, and no one does it better than you. I am surprised you chose to set the story in a backwater like Washington. It seems to me that you could treat your theme just as well in a London setting, and your British readers, who certainly buy more of your books, would feel more at home. Or is it the exoticism of Washington that appeals? These questions of creating and selling are maddening. Or should I say creating *versus* selling?

Now I must go to sleep, perchance to dream of painting, as I often do. Do you ever dream that you are writing? I wish the work I do in the daytime could be as fast, as fluid, as free as what I paint in my dreams.

Your friend forever,

John

## 82. Experienced

Violet Paget
17 Rue Des Jardins
Montparnasse
Paris, France
July 16, 1879

My dear Violet:

Do you remember all the times you have called me repressed and diffident in carnal matters? All the times you have teased me about my inexperience in the ways of the flesh? Specifically the time we sat in *Café Le Chat* and you pointed out each person in the room, and asked why each was not good enough for me? And who in the world *would* be good enough?

I now have an answer: Nicholai, Tsar of the Eastern Empire of Rossland. For once I am in love, or lust, and have done something about it. I will spare you all the crude details except to say that it all seems perfectly natural, or if not natural, at least inevitable. I don't know why I have waited so long to give in.

There are some advantages to monarchy that even Mark Twain might admit, if he knew, which he must not, ever. When Nicholai wants to be alone with me, he simply orders all his attendants to withdraw, and suddenly we are in the center of a perfect bubble of solitude. Guards in all the adjoining rooms, behind thick, soundproof doors, make sure no one disturbs us. It is a curiously public privacy.

As for all my previous reservations and doubts and resolutions, they still exist. They are still on the canvas of my mind, but dim and buried under a thick glaze of infatuation. I know that time will wipe the glaze away, that my folly will become clearly visible, but not now, not today. Today I prefer not to be prudent, prefer to squint my eyes and see only the surface pleasure of the moment. I do not know what tomorrow brings. I scarcely care, as long as I can paint and pass a few moments with Nicholai. He has asked me to stay in Rossland, says he will provide me with a studio and commissions to paint and an apartment on the palace grounds. It sounds very grand, but even in my fevered state I know it may be only fond talk.

I wish I had you here to talk to, since you are the only person in the world with whom I can share my excitement, the only one who might be happy for me and with me. I think our guide and translator Marina has guessed about my stolen moments with Nicholai, but I am too shy to talk to her. At dinner last night Mark made a pun about the king being my subject, and Marina added "and perhaps object as well...of affection?" and gave me a certain look. You know that look—it is in your own arsenal of interrogation—that look that invites, nay insists, on the revelation of some choice morsel of gossip withheld in vain. It is an imperious kind of begging, the same way a goose begs: "Give me food or I shall eat you!" I resisted her entreaty, but I think she knows.

At times I think everyone knows, that everyone can see on me the mark of Cain. No, not of Cain, that would reveal a murderer. Whose mark would reveal the murder of domestic propriety? It must be in the Bible somewhere, but I shan't ask you. I know you use yours solely for pressing flowers and propping open your window in summer. How I wish I were there with you, looking out that window at Monsieur Leclerc's socks and garters on the line. By the time I see you again, it will be fall turning to winter, and the window fogged over with your cigarettes.

I have sunk into a fog of my own, a fog of pleasant nostalgia and longing for your company and conspiracy. I shall close, and remain always …

Your experienced friend,

John

### 83. A Scurvy Lot

Reprinted from the *Atlantic Weekly*, August 15, 1879

Mark Twain
Lock, Rossland

Dear Reader:

Rossland is a country of contrasts and contradictions. In the capital and principal cities they have gas light everywhere, electric lights in the palace and downtown streets, the latest steam locomotives and luxurious rail cars, automatic printing presses, precision sewing machines, exquisite timepieces, and modern weaponry to rival any European nation. However, in the country a mile out of town, life goes on much as it did in the Middle Ages.

This week I took a boat trip down the Sakrametska River and back in time four hundred years. The Rosslander serfs of the delta region are born and die on the same hundred acres of boggy turf. That the real Tsar in Mother Russia freed the serfs 18 years ago is the merest rumor to them. They plow with a board slightly shod with iron; their trifling little harrows are drawn by men and women; small windmills grind the corn, maybe ten bushels a day, and when the wind changes they hitch on some donkeys and actually turn the whole upper half of the mill around, instead of fixing the concern so that the sails could be moved instead of the mill. Oxen tread the wheat from the ear, after the fashion prevalent in the time of Methuselah. There is scarcely a wheelbarrow in the land—they carry everything on their heads, or on donkeys, or in a wicker-bodied cart, whose wheels are solid blocks of wood and whose axles turn with the wheel.

The climate is mild; they never have snow or ice, and I saw no chimneys on their hovels. The donkeys and the men, women, and children of a family all eat and sleep in the same room, and are unclean, are ravaged by vermin, and are truly happy, according to their masters, who live in town with chimneys, gas light, and all the aforementioned conveniences.

If the Russian serfs live in the Middle Ages, the Chinese live in the Stone Age. The government sends to China for coolies and farms them out to the planters at five roubles a month each, for five years, the planter to feed them and furnish them with clothing. The Tsar's agent fell into the hands of Chinese sharpers, who showed him some superb coolie samples and then loaded his ships with the scurviest lot of pirates that ever went unhung. Some of them were cripples, some were lunatics, some afflicted with incurable diseases, and nearly all were intractable, full of fight, and animated by the spirit of the very devil. However, the planters managed to tone them down, and now they like them very well. The coolies' former trade of cutting throats on the China seas has made them uncommonly handy at cutting corn stalks and mine timbers.

A Rossland coolie is as much a slave as any nigger in Alabama was thirty years ago. He works at the hardest labor, stooping knee deep in a rice paddy fourteen hours a day, carrying rails and ties across the Mohave Desert, wielding a pick on his knees a mile underground. For this he gets rags to wear and slop to eat and at the end of five years has nothing to show for it and no more prospects than the chance to be signed up for another five years or be cast aside. He cannot own land, travel freely, bear arms, or even take a wife without permission from the overseer. And yet, the Chinese manage to band together, forming squatter communities in the unused corners and margins, raising children and chickens and rabbits, taking in laundry, scratching out truck gardens on land even a Russian serf would scorn.

It proves to my mind that, color and nationality and circumstance aside, at bottom a man *is* a man. Whole ages of abuse and oppression cannot crush the manhood clear out of him. Whoever thinks any people constitutionally debased or unsuited for democracy is mistaken. There is plenty good enough material for a republic in the most degraded people that ever existed.

Your faithful correspondent,

Mark Twain

## 84. Naïve Booby

I woke Marina early and took her to the river, to catch the dawn mists off the water. I posed her in an enormous cashmere shawl I bought in the bazaar. She draped it over her head like a hood and wrapped it around her body like a toga. The wide dark brown border of the shawl and the cream colored fabric in the middle broke her body into interesting light and dark shapes, linked by the sinuous folds of drapery.

She said, "At least this is warm. For once you've got me in a costume that suits the weather."

"You sacrifice so much for me."

"If you only knew how much."

"What does that mean?"

"Never mind. Just don't make my nose so long this time."

"Nature gave you the nose, not I. Uncover your hair and turn away a little. That's good. Look down at the ground." I started another version of her, on the same sheet of paper, in front of the first figure.

"Why don't you use a fresh sheet of paper? You can afford it now."

"I want to make a line of you, a string of mysterious Marinas, walking through the mists of time. Like a classical frieze."

"If you want me to freeze, I'll have to take my clothes off."

"Ha ha. Hold still." I blocked in the second figure. I was working on a midtoned gray paper with charcoal for the darks and white chalk for the lights. I let the gray of the paper stand for the foggy background and the border of the shawl, used scumbled white chalk for her skin and the light parts of the shawl, and reserved the charcoal for her hair, facial features, and the shadows in the folds of fabric.

"Cover your head again," I said, "but this time have the dark part of the pattern around your face. Here, let me show you." I pulled the shawl off her and wrapped it around her again, so that the dark border framed her face and an edge made a diagonal across her hips.

"Hold it together here, at your bosom, and turn your head toward me." I moved her chin around, arranged the folds of fabric around her face, and tucked in a lock of her hair. She crossed her eyes and stuck out her tongue at me.

"You are such a strange man," she said. "You scarcely touch me when we dance at a ball, where we are supposed to touch, but now, in public where you should be more reserved, you handle me as a butcher handles meat. You mold me like clay."

I stepped back and started a third figure, walking in advance of the first two.

"At the ball, you were a woman. Here you are clay."

"I'm not sure that's flattering."

"I'm sorry," I said, although I knew she was merely "joshing" me again. "I don't mean to be rude. It's just that I wasn't at the ball to dance, and this morning I'm not here to be proper. In both cases, it is business for me. The dance was part of the portrait business, meeting the kind of people who need their

portraits painted. This morning I am going about the business of the imagination."

"What is the business of imagination?"

"Turning reality into art, into something more, something better, more beautiful. Making the quotidian timeless."

She sniffed and said no more. I had her turn away, rewrap the shawl. Look up, look sideways, and so on, adding poses until I had a pleasing composition of seven figures in a loose procession, moving from left to right like dancers frozen in time or notes on a staff of music.

All too soon we had to stop drawing and make for the train station. The fog was dispersing into shining pink trailers of mist. The sun was coming out, painting cadmium orange and saffron yellow highlights on the east side of everything. Marina removed the shawl and folded it. It was a fine morning.

Krepotsky met us on the platform at the train station. He gave Marina our travel passes.

He said, "Allow me to introduce Grigory Sharvsky, guide of you today." He stepped aside to reveal a short, older man in a worn black suit."

"Mr. Sharvsky is retired Public Works official. Can tell all information of gold rush, gold mines, everything."

We were a little early for the train. Mark was late. While we waited for him, Krepotsky took me aside and handed me four copies of the *Atlantic Weekly*.

"These have just arrived," he said. "I thought you would enjoy seeing your name in print." He shook hands, said goodbye and left us.

I read Mark's letters about our arrival in Petalumo, Juan Diego's mantle in the cathedral, the hearse in Gratonia, the firecrackers in Pueblo Forestal. A slow burn of shame and anger came over me. In each letter I featured as a comic character, a naïve booby, a silly, shallow young man. All the time Twain was inviting me along with him, acting friendly, he was using me. He had no more care for me as a person than I have for a tube of paint.

Marina read over my shoulder. She moaned and touched my arm. "Oh no. This is bad. This is not good."

Mark arrived then. I was too angry to even speak to him. He and Marina boarded the train and I saw Marina whispering to him and they looked back at me on the platform. As the train began moving, I stepped aboard, but I stayed outside the car, in the wind, for many miles.

### 85. Sorely Disappointed

Mary Sargent, c/o Sanderson
Apartments Genessee
10 Clarastrasse
Berne, Switzerland
July 18, 1879

Dear Mother:

I am writing on the train, so please excuse my shaky handwriting. I am returning to Nicholagrad from the Sierra gold country with Twain and Marina, although at the moment I have withdrawn to another carriage to be by myself.

Today we visited the gold country of Rossland, a scene that reminded me most distinctly of our visit last year to the marble quarries of Carrara. It is just as high, hot, and dry. Most of the trees have been cut and burned or used for mine timbers long ago. The naked bones of the planet are exposed, in granite here, as in limestone there. To the painter's eye the landscape composes itself into large, monochromatic masses—strong geometric shapes that beg for the pencil. I spent several hours sketching the rocks and the men crawling over them like ants. I enclose a tracing of one of the sketches that I think will put you strongly in mind of the stone cutters at Carrara.

The others of our party spent most of the day underground, touring the gold mines. I did not mind missing the tour—too dark, too deep, and in too close proximity to Twain. I am very

angry with him. He has betrayed me and I cannot forgive him. This morning my good friend Minister Krepotsky provided me with the first four installments of Twain's writing about our trip. In each he portrayed me as a stock character of low comedy, falsifying events to glorify himself at my expense, making himself the witty man of the world and me the butt of all jokes: *le naïf, le nouveau venu, le cancre.*

What pains me most is my own blindness that led me to so severely misjudge the man. I thought he was my friend, my peer, my fellow artist. But from the beginning he was just using me to advance his own interests. He has sorely disappointed me, and I would not paint his portrait if he were the last famous scribbler on the planet and he begged me on his knees. Henceforth I shall stick to my Tsars and Barons and leave the journalists alone.

I was sorry to hear that you will be leaving the Sandersons' apartment earlier than you thought, although it means that I can avoid an evening pretending to court *la Betsy*. Your proposed visit to the Greens in Florence seems a good plan to me. I can join you in your new *pied-à-terre* at Christmas instead. We will haunt the Uffizi, have tea on the Ponte Vecchio and watch the Arno rise in the rains.

Your loving son,

John

## 86. Objective Journalism

William Dean Howells
Atlantic Weekly
Boston, Massachusetts, USA
July 18, 1879

Dear William:

Yes, I fully realize that your esteemed publication is not my personal soapbox, but I reckon it is unkind of you to say that my last piece was entirely devoid of humor and composed solely of political diatribe. You know that beneath my comic exterior I am a social reformer (and beneath the reformer is a despairing skeptic, and beneath that a hopeless romantic, and beneath that a jaded libertine, and beneath that the very re-incarnation of Dante).

Very well. Enclosed you will find a frothy piece of comic fluff, by way of apology. It is more in the line of "Gibralter the egg mule," miles divorced from any taint of political reality. The political reality of Rossland is a mystery to me anyway. The more I study on 'em, the more tetchy the Russians seem to me. They huddle in corners and gobble Russian to each other like turkeys on Christmas Eve. They know Something is about to happen, Something Bad, but the details are unclear. From the Tsar giggling and prancing about in his palace, down to the lowliest serf picking up my cigar stubs in the gutter, they are all trying to hide in plain sight, to appear so innocuous and innocent and invisible that they each will be the last turkey left alive on Boxing Day.

The acquisition of the enclosed literary confection was not without its cost. I had to give the slip to our guide, a limp member of the body politic called Greg Sharvsky, provided us by the Tsar's mysterious jack-of-all-trades, Krepotsky. Every time I turn around in this country, I bump into one Krepotsky or another—shining my boots, holding my coat, standing behind me with a razor to my throat when I think I am shaving myself.

Here is what the American miner told me that did not fit into the frog story: The Russian's alluvial mines are all pretty much played out. The hard rock mines are all owned by the state and "leased" to various well-connected aristocrats. They kick back about 10% of the profits to the crown, above the table in taxes, and another 25% to the Tsar and his cronies under the table, bribes for renewing the lease every year. All the work is done by what amounts to slave labor: criminals serving out long sentences, serfs of the Lord of the Mine, immigrant Ukrainian peasants without estate, Chinese coolies, Indians, Yankee and Confederate deserters, etc. Scores of 'em die every year in cave-ins or from gas or flooding.

He said that the Alta California mines operate much the same. They were originally owned by individuals, but now are operated more and more by conglomerations of investors, who

hire the same type of workers and treat them no better. Along
the border the hard rock miners are all digging as fast as they
can under the boundary, so that most of the AC gold produced
there is from Russian ore, and vice versa. I plan another letter
about that, on the "grass is always greener" theme.

Krepotsky's stand-in Sharvsky was quite upset when I
returned from our unauthorized tour of Two Eagles Mine.
In fact, his language might be deemed more critical than
diplomatic. In further point of fact, he had us escorted back to
our train by soldiers, and they bivouacked out on the platform
until the train departed. Since then, an unobtrusive gent in
a gray horse coat has been loitering in the hotel lobby and
following me around town, competing with the beggars for my
cigar butts. I do not think he is working up his nerve to ask for
an autograph.

I am surrounded by critics this week. That skunk
Krepotsky has slipped John Sargent some of the early numbers
of your rag, where I write about our Californian adventures.
He feels I have portrayed him as a "naïve booby," and is
in high dudgeon as a consequence. No matter that he often
*is*, *in fact*, a naïve booby. That dog won't fight. He has no
appreciation of objective journalism. Ah well, I have often said
that there is no suffering comparable with that which a private
person feels when he is for the first time pilloried in print. As
you know, I have had this problem before—after crossing the
Atlantic together, my fellow passengers on the *Quaker City*
swore undying friendship, until the publication of *Innocents
Abroad,* when they became my lifelong enemies.

Anyway, there is no mollifying John Sargent. He will
just have to cool down over time, and I hope it happens soon,
because the sight of him sulking like a schoolgirl is mighty
tempting to me to lampoon, and that would truly put the cap on
it. I've grown fond of the boy, and must resist the temptation to
make further fun of him. Sometimes honor is a harder master
than the law.

I reckon it is the writer's doom always to be

misunderstood. Doesn't John know that objective journalism is impossible? That all writing is fiction? That writers of fact are the worst liars in Christendom? In their efforts to report to the public what the public wants to hear, they soar into flights of fancy lying that make the inventions of Munchausen seem poor and trifling in comparison.

Sorry, I have slipped into more diatribe, this time of the literary variety. I must close before I hurt your tender feelings as well.

Your cruelly misunderstood compatriot,

Mark Twain

## 87. The Golden Frog

Reprinted from the *Atlantic Weekly*, August 22, 1879

Mark Twain
Two Eagles Mine
Rossland

Dear Reader:

This tall tale I have from a Yankee miner I met yesterday, miles deep underground in the Two Eagles Imperial Gold Mine #4:

When I first come to Rossland, I were a flume dog out Placerville way. That laid it over any job I ever had, being out in the fresh air and light, letting the water do the minin', just pickin' nuggets outen the flume. But the old Baron, he finally ketched me hidin' out nuggets for my own self, so now I stay down here mostly, keepin' the tunnels up. Three more years my sentence is done en they'll let me out. If I live that long.

Every flume dog steals. You cain't help it when you see a little nubbin of gold just a-lyin there, and the guard ain't lookin'.

The problem is where to hide it? We was all livin' in tents, and every week er so the guards'd strip everbody nekkid and shake out them tents and all yer clothes and belongins. You's watched ever minute, even in the outhouse, so a feller cain't just swallow the gold and retrieve it later, if you take my meanin'.

I hit on a good notion for awhiles. One of my jobs was ketchin' frogs for the Baron's Sunday dinner. He'd spent time in France and he had him a taste for their legs. I'd ketch a frog er two ever day, in the swamp at the end of the flume, en keep 'em in a little lattice box. When I found me a gold nugget, I'd keep it in my mouf till I found a frog, then stash it in the frog's belly. Your average frog'll swaller anything that'll fit in its mouf.

Sunday afternoon they allus let us off early, en I'd take my box of frogs up the hill to the Baron's cook. He were a old Chinaman and he had to see them frogs alive, to make sure they was fresh and all. After he inspected my frogs, I'd take em out back of the chicken coop and dress em out. I hid the nuggets from my golden frogs under the bottom step of the coop stairs, which was loose. I reckoned when I had a big enough stake and the snows melted in the spring, I'd sneak out of camp one dark night, get my nuggets, and head out east over the mountains, then south into Mexican territory.

One day a guard lef' me alone for an hour when the monitor washed out a partik'ler rich seam, en I scooped up 'bout five pound of nuggets at once, and stuffed em into the onliest frog I had on hand. That were a Saturday, en Sunday I scoot up to the Baron's. But whilst the cook is inspectin' my frogs, the Baron and some of his gang come into the kitchen, drunk as lords, which they was, of course—lords, I mean.

"Here," says the Baron, "Gimme them frogs. We gonna have us a frog race."

Well, wouldn't you know it, the Baron hisself got the golden frog, and wagered a hunnerd roubles on it jumpin' furthest. They set five frogs out elbow-to-elbow, with they forepaws just even, and give 'em each a poke to the tail. Four of them frogs jump a goodly distance, but the golden frog don't budge. He jist give a heave and hysted up his shoulders so, like a Frenchman, but it weren't no use; he were planted solid as a anvil.

The old Baron, he scratch his head and look at his frog like it on trial for treason. He look at me, an' he look back at the frog, an' he say, "That frog 'pears mighty baggy," an' he grab a cleaver offen the block and *BLAM,* off come that frog's head an' out pour my nuggets.

I were lucky the baron's cleaver stuck so hard in the floor, or my head would've come off next. Well, his gang commence to laughin' an' everbody thought it were a pretty good joke, 'cept me.

I left the hapless miner pickaxing chunks of quartz out of the mountain in the darkness. I hightailed it over to Placerville and made inquiries about the Baron's chicken coop, but it had been torn down years before.

Your unlucky correspondent,

Mark Twain

## 88. Code Duelo

I was confined to my hotel room all afternoon, delivering myself of the Golden Frog letter. In the early evening Marina and I walked out to secure a dram of vodka, or rather more than a dram, but surely short of a hogshead, to be followed by a bite of supper, or rather more than a bite, but surely short of a whole hog.

We repaired to the Three Gents saloon, a favorite watering hole of mine, where the three gents were inclined to stand me drinks, thanks to a photograph I had made of them one afternoon.

There the vodka portion of our programme stretched to nearly midnight. A small band of musicians were taking requests. A party of four young sports in cavalry boots and pistols and tattersall waistcoats of questionable taste were whooping it up in the corner, requesting various Russian tunes of a patriotic nature. The band struck up one of their many national anthems, with a melody remarkable similar to a favorite of mine, the scurrilous "Mother Mabel's Muffins."

Mostly I got by in Rossland with Esperanto, hand signals, and my dear Miss Marina's translations. But occasionally, merely for the pleasure of being cruel, I put unoffending Russians on the rack with the incomprehensible jargon of their native language. While they writhed I impaled them, I peppered them, I scarified them, with their own vile verbs and nouns. By this point I had acquired a good stock of Russian words and phrases, mostly of a vulgar, scatological nature. I began singing along with the Mother Mabel number, inserting every rude Russian word I could recall, keeping to the rhythm fairly well, if not the rhyme. Marina tried to shush me, but half-heartedly, laughing the while, somewhat encumbered by drink herself. I have always admired a woman who can drink like a man, although upon reflection, that is no compliment.

The four sports were mightily offended by my improvisations, remonstrating with me in incomprehensible Russian that only inspired me to redouble my efforts, standing on my chair like a tiny stage. They pushed forward the youngest of their party and he walloped me across the jowls with a stiff leather riding glove. I fell off my chair and under the table. By the time I crawled out, they were dictating to Marina the time and place and terms of a duel at dawn. It was to be pistols at thirty paces in Red Square.

Events were proceeding a might faster than my ability to comprehend them, but I might still have extricated myself with an apology, were it not for two factors: to wit, I was wearing my gaudy pistols, which gave me a feeling of deadly prowess; and the sports called Marina *метис шлюха*, two words that had a home in my abbreviated Russian lexicon and translated to "half-breed whore." The insult made my blood boil. I swore I'd be in Red Square at dawn with my seconds, and teach them a lesson.

Red Square was so named because of all the blood spilled there. In fact, it was neither red nor square. It was more a Gray Pentagon, an irregular space down by the river, bounded by windowless warehouses, paved with slimy cobbles, a fine and private place to violate Sakrametska's official ban on dueling. I was tired and excited at the same time, and still feeling the effects of drink somewhat. These sensations combined in me to produce a state of heightened awareness in which events seemed to unfold very slowly, so that a duration of mere minutes appeared as an hour to me.

John was my second, backed by Marina, who in a pitched battle would outfight John, so fiercely was she aroused. The miserable curs from the bar pushed forward their younger member again, and we stood back to back. I for one was glad of the support and the warmth in the chill dawn air. Our pistols were inspected and furnished with one cartridge each. The instructions droned on for the longest time, although the only facts I retained from Marina's translation were "15 paces, turn and fire."

We paced off our distance resolutely, and with each step I reflected on another aspect of my life: its promise, its preciousness, its potential brevity. I turned and saw my opponent in the swirling mists, his arm already raised and pointing at me. I extended my pistol and fired as soon as the sights crossed his breast. At the same instant, I saw a yellow flower bloom from the barrel of his gun and felt a sharp pain in my head.

From that moment onward, time resumed its rapid pace. Policemen ran into the square at the far end. Marina and John grabbed my arms and dragged me away, stumbling over the slick cobbles, skidding around the corner of a warehouse and down an alley, to the strand by the river. I fell twice, and the transom to my trousers was all fetched away, the legs of them riddled to rags and ribbons.

We hid in a woodpile, under a tarp, while the coppers ran past us and their clamor receded into the distance. I mopped up blood from where the bullet had grazed my head, feeling suddenly very tired. For me, the duel had fallen short of its noble potential. Honor was satisfied, I suppose, but scarcely upheld.

### 89. A Coward and a Fraud

Twain and Marina woke me, pounding on my door and talking much too loudly for the hour of four AM in a good hotel. They were both flushed and flustered with drink.

Twain said, "John, you must help me. I have challenged a man to a duel and you must be my second."

"No, no, John," Marina said, pulling on my arm, "Don't do it. Mark must not get involved in a duel. It is too dangerous."

I said, "What is going on?"

Twain said, "I ain't afraid of nothing, let alone bullets."

Marina said, "Oh stop being silly and shut up. You are like a child. The thing that you should do is to leave town today. This minute. Only bad things can come to you in Sakrametska."

Nobody was talking to me. I said again, "What in blazes is going on?"

"Adventure, the true business of men," Twain said, reeling in place. "I must clean my guns. Get dressed in your best—put on your war paint and your tomahawk. I'll be right back."

He left for his own room. Marina explained to me what had happened. When Twain returned, we could not dissuade him. I put on my clothes, and we three set out in the dark about 5AM, arguing with Twain all the way. Marina and I were unwilling seconds, going along to talk him out of the duel, not to support him in it.

Twain looked lumpy and he clanked a bit. He could hardly walk for all the trash he had stuffed into his vest and coat: a bible, cigar cases, lucky gold pieces, copies of *Innocents* and *Tom Sawyer*, and two tin ashtrays he had stolen from the hotel.

"I am giving Providence every opportunity to stop bullets," he explained.

"Mark," I said, "This is not a story. This is real life. In real life, real people get killed."

"Listen to him," Marina said. But Twain didn't listen. He strode on, turning into Red Square just as dawn was painting a light magenta line on the horizon.

Four men were waiting in the square. Twain's opponent was a handsome brute in a camel's hair overcoat with an astrakhan collar. He took it off and handed it to his companions. They were all wearing revolvers like Twain's, tied to their holsters with scarlet leather thongs that hung down like old men's suspenders.

Twain handed me his little black camera. "When everyone is standing still, hold the shutter open for five seconds. There is not really enough light, but maybe we'll get lucky."

"You could use some luck. Are you sure you want to go through with this?"

"Damn sure."

The duelists were placed back to back. Marina translated the Russian's remarks and continued to beg Mark not to be an idiot. All the men looked on her with scorn, and even I felt she should give up her protestations and behave appropriately.

One of the other side's seconds did something with a handkerchief. Mark's opponent crossed himself. Mark placed his hand on the bible inside his coat. Everyone backed away. The duelists counted out fifteen full paces, thirty steps, taking unnaturally long strides to put the maximum distance between them. Twain's opponent turned a half step early and fired. Twain raised his gun and fell down. He later said his gun "misfired." I suppose that's what they call it when one fails entirely to pull the trigger.

At this point the police arrived and everyone ran away. We headed for the river, skidding around corners on the slick cobbles. At one point Twain stumbled in an alley and fell, bumping his head and getting a little nick on the temple. That is how he got his famous "dueling scar."

We hid under a filthy tarpaulin smelling of fish guts, until the police were long past us. Mark was complaining and whining like a baby. Marina said it would be better if we separated. She took Twain off to a barber to have his "wound" stitched. I went for a long walk across the river.

The sun was well up now, turning the east golden with touches of vermillion. I walked for a long time, enjoying the warm highlights and cool shadows, reflecting on the morning. Twain's silly duel angered me. It was dangerous, selfish, and illegal. We could have been in serious trouble if the police had caught us. I was tired of Twain using me for his own ends, first in his articles, then in the streets.

I decided that continued association with Twain would be a liability for me. He was too unpredictable, too rash, and at bottom a coward and a fraud. I resolved to distance myself from him. I would move to a different hotel and not tell him where. I would avoid his company and concentrate on finishing the Tsar's portrait. I hoped that Twain would take Marina's advice and leave Sakrametska soon. I would stay behind, looking for other commissions among the Rossland gentry.

## 90. Recriminations

After finding a sleepy barber to pull the gaping edges of my bullet wound together, Marina stashed me in the Anastasia Hotel, into a room registered to her name, so the police could not easily find me at the Imperial. I was to lay low while she booked passage on the next steamer south. It was time to leave Rossland.

"Stay here," she said, "Keep quiet, don't go out, and please, do not fight any more duels for me. I'm not worth it."

"Don't say that. I would do it all over for you."

She sighed and shook her head. "You are the most foolish wise man I ever met. You see to my heart, but you miss the very nose on my face."

"The expression is 'nose on *your* face.'"

"There," she said, "you do it again. You joke and make fancy language, and you get angry when others call a whore a whore."

"You are not a whore."

"Yes I am. My government sends me, a half-breed woman, alone, with two men, two foreigners, from town to town, in hotels, with no older woman as chaperone. I share your bed. That makes me a whore. Those men were right."

"Marry me," I said, "and make a respectable half-breed out of yourself."

"Oh, you are impossible." She slammed the door, leaving me alone in the shabby room.

I spent the morning napping and arose at noon, dry-mouthed, sick at stomach, and tremulous. My head throbbed with every beat of my tired old heart. I was feeling low as a snake's belly, the familiar queasy guilt of hangover exacerbated by shame over how I had been treating Marina. I hadn't fully realized before what an insulting assignment she had been given—accompanying two foreigners on her own, in a country that hates foreigners and hates women.

I sat at a desk with uneven legs and cheap stationery, filling the time with a miserable attempt at a letter for William at the Atlantic.

*Dear Reader:*

*Here I sit, my head bandaged on the outside and pounding on the inside. I am alone in the Anastasia Hotel, a fleabag of the Russian variety, with no heat and no hot water except for the samovar, which I am hugging like a lover. My friends have deserted me in disgust, since I dragged them into a silly and illegal duel...*

I crumpled this false start. Too confessional and not funny.

*Dear Reader:*

*When traveling in foreign climes, one must always be a good sport. One must endeavor to fit into the local society, even when its customs are different from what one learned at mother's knee. So last night, when I was challenged to a duel, I thought, "Well, it is only polite to accept a stranger's invitation."*

Another false start, but at least the tone was lighter. They say the third try takes the charm, so I soldiered on in my campaign against Memory and Reality:

*Dear Reader:*

*There is a common confusion in English between the meaning of a step and a pace, and translation from Russian only complicates matters. To me, there are two steps to a pace, and so this morning in a duel I took two steps for each of my opponent's one, which put us rather farther apart than is customary. Nevertheless, I managed to shoot my opponent's pistol out of his hand just as his bullet grazed my scalp...*

At this point, Marina banged on the door and banished all thoughts of letter writing from my mind with her first words.

"Mark, John Sargent has been arrested."

## 91. Sleeping Subjects

I did not want to return to the hotel and run the risk of encountering Twain, so I stayed on the north side of the river, walking deeper into the slums than I had gone before. In a doorway I came upon a middle-aged man asleep. He was stretched out on his back with one leg propped up on the doorpost, utterly relaxed on the filthy planks as if they were the softest bed. His clothes were dirty, but of decent quality. He could have been napping in his parlor on a sunny Sunday afternoon.

I opened my sketchbook, sat cross-legged near his feet, and made a quick study. The angle was steeply foreshortened, making his near foot appear twice the size of his far face, whereas in reality one's foot is only 1.2 times longer than one's face. While I worked the sun came out and laid a handsome highlight across his features. Sleepers fascinate me. I can study them at my leisure, far longer than when they are awake and self-conscious, always trying to twist their expression into a perfectly acceptable and conventional mask, always jabbering about rubbish when I am trying to see who they really are. In sleep our mask drops away to reveal a more open, childlike visage. In the face of a derelict old reprobate asleep, one can see the dewy innocence of his boyhood. In the artfully made-up face of a witty, sophisticated woman asleep, one can see the sentimental, naïve girl she once was. I'd slip all my subjects a dose of chloral and paint them asleep, if I could.

I still had Twain's camera, so I made an exposure of the sleeping man. I thought Twain owed me that much. I would send the camera back to him by messenger, with no note. The

sun was strengthening, getting under the sleeper's eyelids and making him start to stir. I tucked some rouble notes into his boot top and slipped away before he knew I was there.

The sketching had sweetened my sour mood. The sun was spreading buttery light across the façade of apartments and storefronts, turning the shabby buildings into a gilded Versailles. I had a fine artist's ramble, pausing here and there in a warm corner to sketch a row of bay windows, a dog, a horse, a wood pile, a fence—whatever caught my fancy.

I turned south around noon, heading back to the river in what I thought would be plenty of time for my assignation at the palace. Nicholai was to pose for me in the studio from two to two forty-five. He had taken pains to tell me that this would be a "private sitting," no courtiers or other artists around, and I was looking forward to working on his face.

I had wandered farther than I knew. The walk back took longer than I estimated, so I went straight to the palace and arrived just at two o'clock. I entered at a nondescript side door, mildly surprised that the guard's station there was empty. I took the back stairs to the atelier, through servant country. The stairways and back halls were deserted, which was also unusual—no cleaners, no chambermaids with trays, no pages rushing around with messages and papers. I was a couple of minutes late, but I wasn't worried. The chances of Nicholai being on time were extremely remote.

When I entered the atelier, I thought it deserted at first. Then I saw Tsar Nicholai reclining on a divan in the corner. He appeared to be asleep, and I tip-toed over, thinking I might try to sketch him in repose. I sat quietly in a chair and took out my sketchbook. Then I realized that the Tsar did not appear to be breathing. I cleared my throat, but he did not stir. I coughed loudly, scuffed my feet, and rattled some brushes in a pot of turps. Still no response. Hoping that he was teasing me by pretending to be asleep, I gave his foot a playful kick. Even as I kicked him, I noticed the unnatural pallor of his cheek, a waxy gray tinge to the flesh. His head to rolled to one side, and I could see that his throat had been cut wide open. The dark scarlet on his shirtfront that I had taken for a scarf was blood.

I backed slowly away from the horrible sight. Just as I was thinking that I should tell someone, that I should spread the alarm, soldiers entered the room and pushed me to the floor.

"Let me up," I cried, "the Tsar needs me."

The officer in charge shouted at his men, and they shackled my hands behind my back.

"Wait, you've got the wrong idea," I said, but no one understood English and my few words of Russian had fled my brain. They pulled me up and all but carried me out of the room.

I was marched downstairs and into a part of the palace I had never seen. They pushed me into a small room with two hard chairs. In one sat a Captain of the guard with a drawn gun. He motioned for me to sit in the other chair. The other soldiers left. Every time I spoke, the Captain put his finger to his lips to shush me.

After what seemed like hours, the Captain took me to Vladimir Krepotsky's office. I was relieved that finally I could talk to a friend, or at least the brother of a friend, someone who knew me and understood my language. My guard pushed me into a chair, hurting my hands which were still shackled behind. Vladimir rose from his desk and ordered the soldier to remove the chains.

"Minister Krepotsky," I said, "Tell these men I am innocent. Tsar Nicholai was dead when I found him."

"Be quiet," he replied. "You are in serious trouble."


## 92. Wetbellies

When Marina told me John Sargent had been arrested, I swept my wretched Atlantic letter into the wastebasket.

"Why did they arrest John?" I asked, "I'm the one who was dueling, not him."

"It has nothing to do with the duel. The Tsar has been assassinated. Apparently John was at the palace at the time, so he was arrested."

"Balderdash. John couldn't assassinate a sparrow."

"I know, but here people are arrested for balderdash all the time."

"We have to do something. Where are they holding him? Can I get in to see him?"

"No, Mark, you can't get involved." She took me by the hand. "John is still at the palace, and I have been ordered to report there. I will see what can be done. I fear that they will round up everyone connected to John, starting with you. You are in great danger."

"Pshaw and piffle."

"Stop joking, Mark." She started throwing her things into her carpet bag, shaking her head at my patent stupidity. "John is in more trouble than you know. He has become . . . intimate with the Tsar recently."

"What do you mean, intimate?"

"Lovers."

"I don't' believe it."

"It's true. I've known about John's problem for some time, but I promised not to tell."

"This does make things more complicated."

"Their involvement is an open secret at the palace. It makes John a very convenient scapegoat."

"I still find it hard to believe that about John. Are you sure? I've shared rooms with him, and he never…What should we do?"

"The best thing you can do is pack your things and be ready to leave Sakrametska at a moment's notice. You might have to leave John and me here, and get across the border while you can."

"You can't be serious. I'd never leave you here. If we're in such danger, let's light out for San Francisco together, right now."

"What about John?"

"I don't know, I'll figger something out. Maybe the American ambassador can do something. Just set down and let me think a minute."

She wouldn't wait. She was panicked in a way that I had not seen before. In five minutes she had packed all her things, erasing every hint that she been in the room.

She paused in the doorway, torn between haste and some

further secret she had neither time nor temerity to confide.

"Mark, whatever ugly things you hear about me, whatever happens next, you must believe I love you."

"Of course, I believe it with all my heart, but…"

"I have to go. I hope I can see you again."

She kissed my hand and left.


I was flummoxed. Marina gone, John taken, the authorities presumably after me. Every instinct of self-preservation and propriety urged me to flee.

"After all," my worser self whispered in my ear, "what do you really owe these chance companions of the road? Marina is a comely wench, and a warm bedfull, but is she a suitable ornament for your life back in the islands—a self-described half breed whore? And what about John Sargent? A likeable lad on first acquaintance, but secretly a damned soul full of unspeakable desires? Just imagine what deviant designs he has had on you."

I started packing, all the while moderating a debate between my worser and better selves.

"Indeed," my better self chimed in, "Marina is hardly the well-bred southern Protestant lady your mother expects as a daughter-in-law. And John, alas, has got on the wrong side of Providence, where you dasn't follow for the sake of your soul. The Christian thing, the proper thing to do, is to cut your losses while you may and make tracks south."

I have always admired how my better Christian self can contrive to put such a high gloss on the base motives of my worser animal self. But this time "I," some other, more real self, remained unconvinced. Some stubborn Mark Twain, or more likely Sam Clemens, in the middle between the better and the worse, continued to chew over the argument, refusing to swallow it.

What Marina and I had together, if not proper love, was too good to be bad. She was not perfect, and nuther was I. She was not Athena or the holy grail, but goddess and cup enough for me. What we could make of a life together I would pursue, despite my qualms, through hell itself. If our desires led us ultimately to Perdition, so be it.

I continued to pack my things, but now planning to scoot to the steamship office via the palace, to pick up Marina and convince her to run away with me.

John Sargent was a tougher nut. My natal faith condemned his sort, and my first reflex upon learning of his true nature was to recoil in shock. The shock was doubled because of his resemblance to my brother Henry—I had the two of them connected in my mind, and now my memory of Henry seemed dishonored somehow. And I felt ashamed of my own self, for a moment, because I had liked John, and what did that say about me?

But honesty prevailed—I knew both Henry and John to be sweet, good men, whom I genuinely loved and liked. How could it be that Providence, the benevolent creator, would set on the earth a man who desired congress with another of his same sex, and then condemn him for that desire? How could such a sweet, good person, so talented, so like my own brother, be doomed by a vengeful God for his perverse desires, which he most likely hadn't chosen and didn't want? As if the Great Watchmaker should design a perfect clock, wind it up, set it running, and then forbid it to tell time.

It seemed I could not have all of Faith and Propriety, and still keep my friends and my own self respect. So I chose the latter. I could not give up Marina, nor abandon John, so I determined to break John out of jail.

I carefully reviewed all the methods I knew from my wide reading of escape literature, to wit, the *Man in the Iron Mask* and *The Count of Monte Cristo*. One by one I discarded the options for which I was not equipped: I lacked the cavalry for a large mounted assault. My stock of explosives was not adequate. I had neither steel file nor culinary skills to bake it into a cake. What remained was bribery and trickery. I would have to make do with a wad of rouble notes and my native guile. I got all my money out of the Imperial Hotel safe and sharpened my wits with a dram of vodka. Just in case, I wrapped up one of my loaded pistols in a box with white paper and a red ribbon.

The palace was in turmoil. I went round to a side court overhung with trees, where the cooks and chambermaids loiter for a breath of air, playing hooky from their duties. There I found an under-butler being interviewed by two reporters from the local paper. By hanging about I found out that John had not left the palace, as far as the butler knew, and butlers know everything. John was somewhere in the suite of chambers occupied by Vladimir Krepotsky, sinister brother to the smarmy but no less sinister Gregor Krepotsky. That suited me just fine. It meant that John wasn't locked away in an iron cage yet. I approached the guards at the front entrances and said that I had an appointment with the undersecretary of literary affairs, one of Krepotsky's flunkies.

"I am presenting him with copies of my collected works," I said, holding up the gift-wrapped box.

One of the guards recognized me from the recent command performance, and passed me inside. A few roubles got me to the office of the undersecretary, who was not in, thanks to Providence. I convinced my escort to leave me in the antechamber to wait. When he left, I skedaddled down the hall and around the corner to Vladimir Krepotsky's neighborhood. If anyone was involved in a frame-up, it would be that sly weasel.

His secretary was not at his post. I heard voices from his office. I laid my ear gently against the oak panel of the door, but it was opened out from under me by two soldiers. Past them I saw Vladimir Krepotsky at his desk and John sitting in a side chair, rubbing his wrists.

"Mr. Twain," Krepotsky called out, "You are welcome. Come in, please come in."

I went in and the soldiers went out and closed the door.

Krepotsky indicated my package and said, "Is for me?"

"No, it's for John," I said. "It's his birthday." I handed John the package and he took it with a wry lift of his eyebrows. Krepotsky looked at some papers in his hand and said, "is not

Mr. Sargent's birthday. He was born January 12."

"The Tsar has been murdered," John said to me, an adroit change of subject.

"I know, I came as soon as I heard." I turned to Krepotsky. "I have made a deep study of modern police methods. I can help find the assassin. Have you ever heard of the science of finger-prints?"

"That will not be necessary. We know who killed Tsar."

"Really, who?"

He indicated John. "Mr. Sargent."

John went white, then Krepotsky laughed.

"Sorry, Mr. Sargent." he said. "I joke. But is not funny. Is serious. You are both in serious trouble."

I asked, "What are you talking about?"

"Allow me to explain." Krepotsky went to a door nearby and opened it to reveal Marina. She entered the room without a word and sat down on a spindly gilt chair. She looked grim and distant, avoiding our eyes. Krepotsky lowered himself to a chair and pulled a sheaf of papers from his desk drawer. He leaned across the desk and tossed them into my lap.

"You know these letters, yes?"

I riffled through them and my heart dropped into my boots. The letters were in Marina's handwriting, in Russian, with Bill Howells name and address at the top of each and my name at the bottom. They were Russian transcriptions of all my satiric Atlantic pieces. I glanced at Marina but she would not meet my eye. I now knew one of the ugly things she had warned me about.

I handed the letters back to Krepotsky and said, "Sorry, I don't read Russian."

"Of course. You do not. Why learn language of stupid people?"

I shrugged, at a loss for words, for once.

Krepotsky continued, laying out his points on his fingers, like the terms of an indictment: "You write lies about Rossland for USA newspaper. You sneak into Rossland to spy on quicksilver mine. You try to buy dangerous, illegal chemicals. You ask everyone questions. You hide from my man and spy on gold mines. Just today you make illegal duel. You make..." He turned to Marina and rattled off some Russian for her to translate. "You make embarrassment for me."

"It was just for fun," I said. "Nobody takes my writing seriously."

"Everything I take seriously. Tsar Nicholai is dead. He has no son. Today, army rules. Today, I am Tsar. Everything I take serious."

He turned to John. "You also spy on quicksilver mine. You make drawings of mines, docks, ships..." he looked to Marina for another word. "...fortifications."

He was frustrated with his own lack of vocabulary, although I thought he was doing quite well, considering: clear, forceful, and very damning in a certain light. He began speaking in Russian with pauses for Marina to translate.

"Mr. Twain," she said, as if she had not been rubbing my feet and buttering my biscuits for weeks, "You and Mr. Sargent are in serious trouble, for more than just dueling or writing letters. The cabal to which Minister Krepotsky belongs has seized power in the interim and is trying to prevent civil war. In their eyes, you are both spies."

"*You* have been spying on *me*," I said. "Those copies of my letters are in your handwriting."

"Quiet. I told you, everyone spies on everybody here. I was just doing my job: copying your letters, reporting all your activities." She put little quotation marks around "all" with her eyes, letting me know that not all our activities had been in her reports.

John said, "But we are just tourists. We have merely been seeing the sights and writing letters home."

"Oh John," she sighed, "You and I know that, but think how it appears to the secret police. To state security, everyone is guilty."

Krepotsky cleared his throat and said something to her in

Russian. He understood enough English to know that she was not on his topic.

She continued: "Times have changed now. With the Tsar dead, there will be a great purge of dissidents. All enemies of Rossland will be rounded up and executed, or put in prison for years, until they are too old and feeble to be a threat. They might think twice about hanging a popular foreign author, but they won't hesitate to eliminate a young painter whom nobody has heard of, who was found standing over the dead body of the Tsar. Mr. Sargent would make a convenient scapegoat for whoever really killed Nicholai, and Mr. Twain, your snooping makes you a likely accomplice."

Krepotsky chimed in with more Russian, and Marina translated his speech:

"We know you are innocent, but you have been very careless. The cabal is full of hotheads who want an immediate purge of all foreigners. If you remain in Rossland, you will be held in custody for a very long time, and might even be executed."

Krepotsky handed me a thin stack of bank notes.

"Use this money to book passage on the six o'clock steamer to Alta California, under the names Mr. Dostoevsky and Mr. Turgenev. You won't have any trouble leaving the country if you are on that boat, using those names. Remain in this room for twenty minutes, to give the minister time to clear an exit path for you. Leave by the same door Mr. Sargent used to enter this afternoon."

Krepotsky and Marina left the room. We sat in silence for a moment, then John asked me, "What was that all about?"

"The end of the vacation."

"What are you doing here?"

"I came to bust you out of jail."

"Like the Man in the Iron Mask?"

"Exackly. I can't let the Russkies nab my pardner."

"Well, thank you

"You're welcome."

I looked at my watch. It was awfully quiet in the room.

"Now why," I said, "do you reckon Krepotsky wants us sneaking out on our own? Why not just waltz us out the back door himself, and turn us loose?"

"Marina said he had to clear the way."

"I know, but something don't smell right about this situation."

"You've never trusted the brothers Krepotsky."

"Correct, and I'm not starting to trust them now."

At that moment, Marina came back into the room and threw her arms around my neck. She was breathing hard and struggled to catch her breath.

"Oh, Mark, thank God you haven't left yet. You can't leave the way Krepotsky told you. He has two sharpshooters waiting outside that door. They'll kill you the moment you leave. He'll say you were shot trying to escape, and save them the risk of a trial and the truth coming out."

"What truth is that?"

"I don't know. But if Krepotsky's involved, it's a nasty truth."

John said, "How can we get out of the palace? It's full of soldiers with guns, and we're unarmed."

"Happy birthday," I said, pointing at the package in his lap. He looked at me like I was crazy, but he unwrapped the gun.

"I never thought I'd be glad to see one of these," he said.

I said, "To get out of here, we'll have to fit in. We need to get the drop on a couple of palace guards and take their uniforms."

"No," John said. "I have a better idea."

He led us to a closet in the portrait studio where he had been working on the Tsar's Portrait. He opened the door and began pulling out uniforms, formal gowns, fancy peasant dress, and other Rosslandish finery.

"We dress up Ivan the Terrible in these when their owners can't pose in person," John said.

"Who in blazes is Ivan the Terrible?" I asked.

He pointed to a dressmaker's dummy in the corner.

I became General Gogol, with a fine brocaded coat, a red

293

sash heavy with medals, and a long gold scabbard with a broken sword in it. John put on the jodhpurs, boots, and gold-appliquéd horse coat of a cavalry commander. Marina became a Kazak princess with paste pearls and a veil.

John and I led Marina, wearing John's shackles loosely about her wrists, out the front door, bold as brass. The guards and palace functionaries we passed were all too accustomed to deferring to uniforms, and no one wanted to question high ranking officers about what they were doing with a beautiful young prisoner.

In the Grand Plaza we hailed a cab, and I sat up top with the driver to keep a lookout. As we pulled away there was a commotion on the front steps of the palace. A captain of guards ran down them and shouted to our driver to halt. I pushed the driver from his perch, grabbed the reins, and shook them out over the horse's back. We clattered out of the plaza and onto the wide boulevard leading to the bridge over the river.

I looked over my shoulder to see men and horses milling in the courtyard. All too soon a mounted pursuit was after us. We shot over the bridge, John yelling to me to "Turn left, turn left." I hauled the terrified animal around to the left and careened down the strand. After a couple of blocks John and Marina yelled to me to stop. We spilled out of the cab, and Marina grabbed the gun. She shot twice over the horse's head and it took off down the street like a scalded cat, the empty cab bouncing and jouncing behind.

John led us down a passage alongside some pilings, to the waterside between warehouses. He had us wade among the confusing piles until we emerged inside a warehouse, where we climbed up a ladder to the upper floor level.

"This is a boat loft we almost rented as a studio," John explained. "It's empty now and the owner is unlikely to come around."

We sat on nail kegs and sawhorses under some high windows and watched the day slowly dim. From time to time traffic would pass outside and we would freeze, then continue our quiet conversation.

I asked Marina, "Have you been copying all of my letters?"

"Yes, and John's as well, when I could find them." She did not seem particularly embarrassed by this. In fact, she added, "You both lie to your mothers. You should be ashamed."

"How could you spy on us?" John asked, "I thought we were friends."

"We are friends now, but when we met, you two were my job, nothing more."

"Some job," I said.

"I had no choice. If I didn't report on you to Krepotsky, he could have me arrested as a spy for the Dons. It wouldn't matter that I was a spy for him too."

"So you are a half-breed double agent, which makes you two and half people. It's a wonder you can keep it all straight."

"You are angry, of course. Anyone would be angry. But look where I am now—at your side, not back in the palace, standing with Krepotsky over your dead body. My life here was not going to be easy, but it will be much harder, now that I have sided with you. If they catch us, I will hang as surely as you."

"Then I reckon they better not find us."

"Wait a minute," John said, "Can't we let things calm down a little, then give ourselves up to the police? At a trial, we'd have a chance to tell our story and prove our innocence."

Both Marina and I laughed at that. Marina said, "We would never get to trial. The police will do what Krepotsky's ministry tells them to do. Turning ourselves in would be suicide."

"But we are just tourists."

"That is how I have been trying to paint you: both just silly tourists, with no good sense, but no political motives either. It would have been enough to keep you safe, in normal times. But you made too good a pair of scapegoats for Krepotsky and his cabal. You arrived just in time to take the blame for the assassination—a foreign journalist of known Democratic ideals, and a foreign youth from artistic circles in Paris, long known for breeding revolution. You nearly placed your own heads in the noose."

"Then what are we going to do?" John asked. "We can't just buy a ticket on a train or a boat, and it's too far to walk to Alta California.'

"We could float down the river," I said. "We could be Wetbellies."

"That's crazy," John said.

"Not at all. I did it all the time on the Mississippi when I was a boy. We'll make floats out of these nail kegs, and drift out of town in the dark of night." What do you say?"

John looked at the keg he was sitting on and sighed. "All right. You did get me this far, and you were right about not trusting Krepotsky. But I could have made something of that portrait. Some hack will finish it now, if it gets finished at all."

"So we are a couple of Wetbellies?"

"Sure." We shook hands.

"Make that three Wetbellies," Marina said. "I'm going with you all the way."

### 93. Care Cannot Assail Us

At full dark I waded after Mark and Marina into the water. The water felt warm against the cool of the evening. I had a short bench to serve as a float. Marina had a burlap sack full of cork fishing floats. Mark had a nail keg sealed with tar. Inside the keg were our watches, matches, cigars, my sketchbook, and Mark's fountain pen and revolver. We waded until the muddy bottom dropped away beneath us and we were floating down the river.

"Spread out some," Mark said. "Don't clump together. Keep your head low, and keep your float between you and the moon."

We kicked to the middle of the river. It was only about 100 meters wide in the center of town, so we could easily see figures on shore under the electric street lights. The lights reflected in the water like a scumble of pure pigment. We could even hear them talking, as the sound carried far over the water. But we were hidden in the dark. Mark said it would take a theater spotlight to illuminate us in the middle of the river. Twice we saw rowboats with lanterns, and once a big steamboat churned upstream, lit up like a carnival, making us bob up and down like corks. But nobody saw us, we three tiny specks of humanity, drifting on the waters.

Slowly we drifted into the outskirts of town, where the buildings were only one story, and increasingly far apart. The lights of Sakrametska became dimmer and fewer, until the last glimmers faded away to the north. Only the moon and the occasional dock or warehouse lantern lit the night.

We paddled closer to shore, looking for a rowboat or a raft to steal. Mark directed us to an unguarded raft of lumber, tied to trees on shore, waiting to be pushed downstream for sale in San Francisco. He found the ropes and deciphered the intricate knots in the dark, untying the raft and launching us into the current with one deft kick.

At first it was cold, being out of the warm water in the night air. We huddled together, shivering, hugging each other like orphan children. But soon our clothes dried and we became warmer. We moved apart and I was just a little sad to remove my arms from Mark and Marina's shoulders. It was lovely on the raft, floating silently south, further and further from Sakrametska and our troubles in the north, with the problem of crossing the border still many miles away to the south.

"Care cannot assail us here," Mark said. "We are beyond its jurisdiction." He had his clasp knife out, prying at the bung of the cask to liberate his precious cigars.

The raft was about five meters square, made up of thick planks of white wood bound together by a "crib" of poles pegged and wedged together. Mark said that they would make up a "string" of such rafts nine or ten units long, and push them with a stern wheel steamboat. Men with three meter sweeps would stand on the downstream raft to steer the front, communicating with the pilot in the wheelhouse by elaborate hand signals.

Mark puffed on a cigar and said, "What I can't figger is why the Tsar invited us up here in the first place, with all he had on his plate, and as much as the Rosslanders hate foreigners."

Marina answered, "You were part of the plot."

"What plot?" Mark asked, "the plot to get Nicholai a new boyfriend?"

I cringed inside, but Mark kicked my ankle, as if to say, "I know all about you, and I don't care." I felt a large weight slide off my heart.

Marina explained: "I think your command performance was part of the assassination plot. Vlad Krepotsky invited you to Fortress Ross, not the Tsar. They planned to kill Nicholai there, away from the capital, and blame it on one of you."

"But the Tsar wasn't even in Fortress Ross when we got there."

"Because the ferry was shut down. You came a day late and they couldn't keep the Tsar there. He got suspicious."

"How do you know all this?" Mark asked.

Marina sighed, "Vladimir told me, just yesterday. I swear I did not know anything about the assassination or their plans to implicate John."

Mark tilted his head. "How long have you been working for dear old Vlad, anyway?"

Marina hung her head. "Since before I met you. Sometimes I translated at government meetings in Alta California, and I would make a few pesos selling information to Rossland."

Mark threw his cigar into the river. "I thought you despised Rossland."

"Yes, but I needed their money," Marina said, "You must realize that near the border, espionage is a cottage industry. Everybody does it, who can."

"You might have told me, after we started sharing a bed and all."

"I'm sorry. Secrecy is a bad habit of mine."

"Is this one of the ugly things you warned me I might hear about you?"

"Yes, but at least it's me telling you, not some Rosslandish prosecutor."

"Good point. How many more ugly secrets are there?"

"Well, just one. Sometimes I also sold Russian secrets to the Dons."

"So whose side are you really on?"

"Mine. Yours. Ours."

The moon set about 4AM. The river was windless and still, its banks visible only as black velvet shapes against a sky blazing with stars. Tule fog rose from the dead calm water and the stars dimmed and went out. The black velvet folded over us and when Mark stubbed out the last of his cigars, I could not see him or Marina or even my own hand a foot from my face.

"It is dark as the devil's coal cellar," Mark said, never one to let anything pass unremarked. Marina chuckled a little and then we all three fell silent.

I sat on the nearly motionless raft, drifting in perfect darkness, thinking about light and its absence. It was as near to nothing as I had ever come, thrilling, and melancholy, and just a little unnerving.

Like a perfectly painted gradation, on a canvas an hour long, black night faded into gray dawn. The solid fog started to break up into twisting spectres of mist, shredding and lifting off the water. We paddled to shore and tied up to what Mark called a towhead at the foot of an island, or where a stream or slough joined the main river, it was impossible to tell.

Mark and I cut willow branches and Marina draped them over the raft to hide us. From the channel, our little craft would look like a clump of vegetation, where a section of bank has given way and slid into the water, just one more brushstroke in a jungle of green hues and values and intensities.

We sat on our raft, in the dappled shade of the willows, as the morning warmed. We were safe from discovery for the day, tiny specks in a vast reach of soggy farm land. With nothing to do until dark, we drowsed and napped and chatted, eating peaches Mark "borrowed" from a tree planted unwisely close to the bank. After all our adventures and misadventures, it was very peaceful and soothing to the soul. I sketched my companions as they napped among the cattails. Later Mark got so relaxed he became bored, and borrowed a page from my sketchbook to write a letter. For all his claims to be the laziest man alive, he was never very good at idleness.

**94. Fugitives in Repose**

William Dean Howells
Atlantic Weekly

Boston, Massachusetts, USA
July 22, 1879

Dear William:

I am writing you this letter on a long summer's afternoon, on
a page borrowed from John Sargent's sketchbook, as I take
my ease on a sandbar along the Slavyanka River. All my life
I have felt a fugitive from something, and now it has come to
pass that Providence, for it is certainly not of my own human
contrivance, has made me a fugitive in reality. Although quite
relaxed at the moment, I am in the process of fleeing for my
life, with the hounds of monarchy abaying on my trail. I have
been wounded in a duel, implicated in the Tsar's assassination,
accused of spying, and involved in an armed breakout from
jail: Altogether a busy and profitable two days, which I think
will make a rousing climax for the book.

Young Sargent and Miss Marina are with me, fellow
fugitives. We three were caught up in the net of the secret
police when Tsar Nicholai was assassinated and were lucky to
escape with our scalps intact. About that assassination, I am
sure you are by now better informed than I, and whatever we
both know as you read this, it is a pack of lies, anyway. Suffice
it that the powers around the throne were reshuffled and a face
card of high value wickedly discarded.

It did me no good to ask you to postpone the publication
of my Rossland pieces. The Russkies were reading my mail all
along, and they are not pleased with my observations of their
realm. The only disgruntled reader who exceeds the choler
of a private citizen pilloried in print is a politician accurately
satirized.

For a few hours I was quite short with Miss Marina
Turncoat. She was copying my letters for the secret police,
reporting on all my conversations and adventures, and spying
on John Sargent as well. This understandably went against my
grain. But I now believe that her affection for me was sincere,

and that she was taking advantage of her unique "double agent" status to shield me and John, to cast our guilty actions in as innocent a light as possible. In fact, I am even more impressed by her astounding skill at deception, considering how she managed to spin tales to two Krepotskys, the Dons, Sargent, and myself, and keep them all straight in the bargain. She might have got us safely away in style on a steamboat, herself included, had not los Krepotskys' cabal chosen this week to kick over the bliny cart. I gaze on her at this moment, her majestic form and stature, her imposing and statuesque profile, her noble and graceful gestures with which she essays to catch minnows and polliwogs.

This river reminds me mightily of the Mississippi, this lumber raft so like those on which I would play pirate as a child. I have even savored the sweetness of stolen fruit again. Our breakfast, our supper, and our dinner consists of borrowed peaches. I am sure my digestion will never be the same. Tonight or very early tomorrow morning we will sneak our raft across the border, along with all the other "wetbellies." I am certainly getting the most out of my riparian upbringing on this trip. If that experience proves insufficient to our survival, this letter may have to serve as my last will and literary testament. I would like the future income from my writings to be divided equally between my mother and Marina Miranova. Although, if I am not on this earth tomorrow, Marina will probably be likewise absent.

My one consolation, aside from being still among the living, is that John has admitted to me that I was right about not trusting the Russians. His meteoric rise as the *portraiteur* of the moment was due, at least in part, to Krepotsky's wish to use him, to put him close to the Tsar as a plausible scapegoat. True to their natures, the aristocrats and bureaucrats turned on him as soon as it was expedient. I am pleased to report that he now shares my opinion of monarchy and aristocracy—to wit, they should all be drowned in a butt of Malmsey wine like George, Duke of Clarence.

I must close, not because I would short you of my wit, but because I draw near the end of my only sheet of paper. I hope to see you again.

Fondly,

Mark

## 95. Turreted Monitor

Mark and Marina and I pushed our raft into the river as soon as it was dark. There was a sliver of moon in the center of the sky, but the night was dim, all color leached away, and Mark said that the moon would set before dawn. At about one in the morning a misty fog arose from the river and all but erased the sense of sight.

By two AM we were near the border. We began to hear and occasionally see patrol boats—dark, sleek launches that sped past with a hiss and chuff of steam. We slid into the water with our makeshift floats, and tried to keep the raft between us and the patrol boats. The first time the beam of a searchlight, dimmed by fog, swept over the raft, I thought we were discovered. But apparently the soldiers on the boat never saw us, because the light swept past us and did not return.

The sound of the patrol boats took on an echoing quality, and Mark said we had entered the narrow channel of the locks.

"There are about forty cannon pointed at us now," he whispered, "If they could only see us." He was next to me in the water, holding onto the raft, and I could just see his teeth flash in a grin. Marina chuckled from somewhere behind him.

At that moment, another beam of light caught us and stayed on the raft, not moving away. We heard voices calling in Russian to each other, and the sickening sound of an engine growing louder as the boat churned toward us. We pushed away from the raft and paddled as fast as we could on our clumsy floats, out of the misty circle of light.

The fog swallowed the raft in a glowing bubble of mist. We could hear the soldiers on the boat talking, clear as if they floated among us, but we could see nothing.

Marina whispered, "They are going to tow the raft out of the locks. It is a hazard to navigation."

"Another crime to add to our indictment," Mark said.

"Shush."

We paddled to the side of the lock, a shear iron wall like a cliff, and it seemed to stream past us like a train headed north. The current was swifter here, confined by the lock walls, but I felt as if I were motionless and the wall were moving. I could judge its speed by the iron mooring rings and ladders inset into the wall every few meters, which would appear out of the mist, slide past us, and disappear in seconds.

A deep *thrumming* sound began to echo off the iron. A larger ship was coming up the river, fighting the current.

"Dad blame it," Twain said, "It's one of those dad blamed monitors." He pushed Marina and me up the iron rungs of a passing ladder. He passed up the keg containing our valuables, then scrambled up himself, just in time. Out of the mist came a dark shape, the low rail of a turreted monitor. The flat iron deck was only about a meter above the surface of the water, but Mark barely got his feet clear before the gap between the ship's sheer side and the lock wall narrowed to inches. Had we remained in the water, we might have been crushed like bugs between two bricks. As it was, I heard something splinter in the crack between the ship and the lock—the bench I had been floating on.

Just as the giant cheese box of the turret came opposite us, the slowing ship came to a halt, the engines turning just enough to hold it still against the current. Gears clashed and the huge iron cylinder of the turret began turning. I heard a crack and a fierce sizzle as an enormous spotlight came to life, blasting through the fog like a fire hose through tissue paper. The arc light seemed to pin us against the night like stunned moths. Marina pulled us behind a huge bollard, where we hid in a pool of shadow not quite large enough to contain three people.

"I hope they're not going to tie up," Mark said, pulling his revolver from the keg. But he hoped in vain. A sailor emerged from a hatch with a rope over his shoulder, and started to climb the ladder below us.

"Wait here," Marina whispered, peeking around the bollard. As the sailor reached the top of the ladder, she dashed out and butted him like a billy goat, square in the stomach. He pitched over backwards, arms wind-milling, falling back to the deck of the ship with a meaty thump. Russian voices rang out from the turret, and a shot was fired. I heard it "zing" off the top of the bollard above my head. Marina dashed back behind the bollard.

Mark stuck his gun around the corner and fired three shots, to no apparent effect.

Marina grabbed the gun from his hand.

"Marky, I love you, but you're a terrible shot." She lay down on the wooden surface of the dock, squirmed over so she could see the turret, aimed carefully at the spotlight, and seemed to take forever to fire the gun. The light remained on.

"Only one bullet left," Mark said.

"Shut up, please."

She squeezed off her last shot and the light went out, darkness flooding the lock to the delightful sound of tinkling glass.

"Let's go," Marina said, sprinting for the ladder. We piled over the edge after her, no questions asked.

At the bottom of the ladder she jumped onto the deck of the ship, just as the stunned sailor was painfully getting to his feet. She butted him again in his tender parts and he sat down suddenly. More gunshots came from the turret, but no brave Russian sailors came to their comrade's aid. I think they were more afraid of Marina than of Mark's empty pistol.

She ran to the stern of the ship and we followed. Gears clashed and the turret started rotating again.

"Jump, jump," Mark shouted. Marina jumped off the stern, then me, then Mark. As Mark hit the water, I heard a tremendous roar, and a gout of flame passed overhead. The cannon in the turret had fired as soon as it was pointed down-river, away from the lock wall.

The cannon's recoil pushed the ship away from us, and the water surging from its propellers combined with the current to push us away from the ship. In moments the monitor's running lights were swallowed up in the fog and we were invisible again.

We were all panting, treading water, paddling weakly downstream. When I had caught my breath, I asked Mark, "Will they come after us?"

"No, not the monitor. It's too big. We'll be over the border in ten minutes. I think we are fine now."

"You call this fine," Marina said, spluttering as she dog-paddled. "Don't you know Indians can't swim?"

"I reckon you better be a Russian tonight. They swim like ducks."

"Quack, quack."

"Could you translate that, please?"

He was in high spirits, and his silliness was infectious. We were laughing like loons as we floated across the border into Alta California. The fog lifted, the sun came up, and we made landfall at a customs dock, where we were promptly arrested.

### 96. Safe With Saint Frank

Reprinted from the *Atlantic Weekly*, August 1, 1879
Mark Twain
San Francisco
Republic of Alta California

Dear Reader:

Contrary to recent reports, neither I nor my friend John Sargent assassinated the late Tsar Nicholai of Rossland. On the contrary, I rather liked the gent, he being the most civilized savage in a land of savages. That his civility caused him to be removed early from history's stage is sad enough; that I and my friend should be blamed for it is tragic.

Likewise, the fact that we escaped Rossland across the nearest border into Alta California is not to be construed as evidence that we are spies for either country. I would not take the job, not if I were broke and starving, not if I could work for both countries at once and draw double wages, which I understand is the most common arrangement. I would rather shovel coal for Beelzebub. Had I the endurance or a river going the right direction, I would have preferred to swim all the way home to Honolulu, or East across the deserts to America, rather than rely on the hospitality of either the Russians or the Californians.

After a decade of striving, Columbus reached the New World sailing on the Nina, the Pinta, and the Santa Maria. My companions and I reached San Francisco, with no lesser effort, aboard the Cask, the Bench, and the Sack o' Cork, floating down the Slavyanka River, with a Russian monitor dogging our wake all the way.

We arrived in San Francisco as wet and dispirited as drowned rats. The freedom-loving republicans of AC spent sixteen hours debating whether they should throw us back to the Russians or shoot us on the spot. We were so beset by Alta Californian customs agents, border guards, and secret police for our illegal entry, you would think we had not only assassinated the Tsar, but also had designs on the lives of General Vallejo and the Pope. We were almost sent back to Rossland several times, and I lost my last fondness for the Republic. Providence deliver me from bureaucrats, and allow me to live out my days alone on some Polynesian atoll under the benign and enlightened governance of volcanoes and typhoons.

Nevertheless, we are finally safe and enjoying the simple, primitive pleasures of San Francisco. The other day the bureaucrats allowed us out of our hotel for a guided tour of local sites of religious interest, yet another form of institutionalized cruelty. I took my camera and amused myself by photographing the Catholic Church's real estate. The original chapel flung up by Padre Serra was a modest affair, compared to the official papal residence on the cliffs overlooking the Pacific, fondly referred to by the locals as Vatican West.

Our guide explained that San Francisco, this foggy, noisy, rollicking fleshpot, is named for that most amiable denizen of the Catholic pantheon, the venerable Saint Frank. His portrait is on the bank notes and coins, which all say *Esperamos en Dios,* "In God We Trust," a fine motto that would not sound any better if it were true. Saint Frank is always pictured with a dove on each shoulder and sometimes a squirrel or a snake or a donkey in his pocket. Somehow the patron saint of dumb animals makes an appropriate mascot for San Francisco, where his values are honored more in the breach than in the observance, as Pliny or some other dead Greek said.

One feature of San Francisco that I cannot satirize is The Bay, a vast body of water teeming with shipping. In San Francisco Bay, the Californians have materialized the vision and realized the dream of centuries of enthusiasts of the Old World. They have found the true Northwest Passage—they have found the true and only direct route to the bursting coffers of "Ormus and of Ind"—to the enchanted land whose mere drippings, in the ages that are gone, enriched and aggrandized ancient Venice, first, then Portugal, Holland, and in our own time, England. Each in succession they longed and sought for the fountainhead of this vast Oriental wealth, and sought in vain. The path was hidden to them, but the Dons have found it over the waves of the Pacific.

Now if they could but stretch those riches far enough to supply their hotel rooms with soap. I was obliged last night to sally forth with no hat and my nightshirt tucked into my pantaloons, in search of a bar of soap for my toilette.

I beg to remain your respectful, affectionate…and admirably clean correspondent,


Mark Twain

## 97. House Arrest

Violet Paget
17 Rue Des Jardins
Montparnasse
Paris, France
August 1, 1879

My dear Violet:

I hesitate to describe to you the way I arrived here from
Rossland. When I look back, it seems like some outlandish
adventure in one of those cheap novels hawked by train boys.
Suffice it to say that Mark Twain and I *swam* across the border
without benefit of boat or passport. That is outrageous enough,
and enough said. Thankfully, the local newspapers have not
got hold of our story. That would be *tres embarassante.*

We are fairly comfortable in a second-rate hotel—guests of
the government, if you ask the government; under house arrest,
if you ask Mark. Fortunately they have let me have paints and
canvas. I have finally prevailed upon Mark to pose for his
portrait. I am painting him in his disreputable tan duster, but
I have made it red as blood, a sort of raffish dressing gown.
His treasured pistols figure prominently, although I had to
pose him using only one, the other being irretrievably lost in
Rossland. He mourns for the separated twin. I think the effect
of the painting will be *outré* enough to appeal to the masses
of viewers at next year's *Salon,* while the composition and the
celebrity of the subject are *de la mode* enough to satisfy the
judges. Or so is my hope.

I am experimenting with a radical *a la premiere coup*
technique, hacking and slashing at the canvas like a berserker
with a sword, even in the quieter areas of the composition
where I have previously preferred a smooth surface. By
carefully modulating the values, I can achieve a deep
background shadow, for instance, that *looks* smooth and quiet,

but *feels* active and full of energy, like a dark pit of writhing snakes (that sounds very melodramatic in print—you will have to see it in person to understand).

If Twain's portrait hangs in the *Salon*, it will sport a red *"vendu"* dot. Mark has offered to buy it as soon as he receives his advance for his next book. What he doesn't know is that I plan to give it to him, as a wedding present. Marina tells me that Mark is about to propose, although I do not think he knows it himself yet. It is like a scene out of one of Hank James' novels around here.

For such virtuous and important *personae*, we are rather *non gratae* in San Francisco. The Adjudicate General's office has finally made a recommendation to our keepers. After sixteen days of house arrest, they have decided not to hold us in hard labor or extradite us back to Rossland. We will be allowed to leave next week on a steamer to Honolulu.

I have employed the time well. In addition to painting, I have renewed my acquaintance with Francisco Goya. His letter of introduction to Minister Krepotsky was the beginning of our troubles. I now realize, with some tutoring from my suspicious and pessimistic friends Mark and Marina, that Francisco was using me for his own purposes. As near as we can reckon, he was passing some kind of message from the royalist faction here in AC to their foreign supporters in Rossland, bringing me to the attention of dangerous and unscrupulous men. I don't know if the local bureaucrats would think that Francisco's misdeeds rise to the level of treason, and frankly, I don't care. In return for my silence about his part in our adventures, he has been most helpful in securing identity and travel papers for Marina.

I also have from Goya one of his grandfather's paintings, a very rough study that Goya the younger pressed on me as a souvenir of our acquaintance. It is really a bribe for my silence, but I am taking it anyway. I have removed from the canvas my earlier attempts to "restore" it, as being too near forgery or some such fraud, and not the kind of thing I am interested in anymore. I will put it up for sale as it is, and let future agents improve it as they will.

Sadly, the voyage to Honolulu will be my final adventure with Mark and Marina. But we have promised to write often and stay in touch in future. We have become the best of friends, and I have extracted Mark's promise to paint their wedding portrait. He has confided in me that he plans to ask for her hand as soon as he feels she is ready to entertain the notion. He says he needs the steadying influence of a wife and family, while she needs a focus for her energies that is safer than meddling in affairs of state. Their romance is more entertaining than a four act play.

I realize now, more than ever, and Mark agrees, that one can only count on friends in this world, not kings or the People with a capital P.

Hoping to see you soon, perhaps next month, I remain,


Your true friend,


John

## 98. Painter's Revenge

I came out from behind my canvas and said to Mark, "There's something wrong with my drawing. You look like a wax works dummy."

"I *am* a dummy, for having my picture painted."

"No, no, I can fix it. I just need to study the underlying musculature. Strip off your clothes for a minute."

"You jest, sir."

"I never joke about art, you know that. I have to see your bones and muscles."

"Tarnation. The last person saw me undressed was my mother, when I was six, and ever since then she ain't been right in the head."

"I can endure it if she can. Come on, Mark, this is business and I'm a professional. This is how we do it." He grumbled and groused, but he slowly pulled off his boots and shirt and trousers.

"The underclothes too," I said, "I have to see how the gluteus inserts into the maximus."

"I'll maximize you, you unnatural deviant, if'n you ever tell anybody about this."

"Please, Mr. Clemens, just relax. You ain't my type, anyways." I turned away and fussed with my brushes to hide my wicked smile. I turned back and soberly appraised his pale, stringy frame.

"Just as I thought," I said. "Your trapezium muscles are uncommonly small and they make your shoulders hunch forward. You stoop over like a charwoman."

He pulled his shoulders back and pushed his narrow chest out, blushing all over in constellations of freckles.

I shook my head, as if it were a hopeless problem. "Taking off your shirt has messed up your hair as well. Go give it a brush-up."

"You can see my damn hair any time. Let's get on with it."

"Everything's connected to everything else. Just fix the damn hair, if you please."

He stomped off to the washroom and slammed the door. I knew I could count on his vanity about his hair.

I shouted, "Wash that ring from around your neck, while you're in there. It's distracting."

All the while, I was gathering up his clothes, cigars, and room key. I slipped out the door and hung on the doorknob the pasteboard placard with the words "Please Make Up My Room." The maids were around the corner, working on the room next to mine. I had previously removed every stitch of my own clothing from my room, so Mark was left with nothing but sheets to wear.

Marina opened her door across the hall.

"Did he fall for it?"

"Oh yes, he's nekkid as a jaybird." I slipped into her room and we watched the hallway through a crack in the door.

It went better than we could have hoped. Two young Spanish maids opened the door with their passkey. Over their shoulders we could see the celebrated Mark Twain, bright pink in his birthday suit.

*"Lo siento, lo siento,"* the maids gabbled, backing out and slamming the door. They retreated down the hallway, giggling loudly. Through the door we heard a muffled "Tarnation."

We left him in there a good half hour. Twice he came into the hall draped in sheets like a Roman senator, and banged on Marina's door. We kept quiet, rolling on the bed with our hands clamped over our mouths to stifle our laughter. When we finally relented and went back into my room, Mark was wearing a counterpane like a toga, trying to roll cigarettes from hotel stationery and stubs from the ashtray.

"Sorry folks," he said, "You'll have to leave. You're overdressed for this party."

## 99. Fond Farewell

Reprinted from the *Atlantic Weekly*, September 5, 1879
Mark Twain
San Francisco
Republic of Alta California

Dear Reader:

As my trip to the Russian and Spanish New Worlds draws to a close, I confess a growing reluctance to pick up my pen and share my thoughts with you. This is a normal and commonplace occurence, that a travel journal so voluminously begun should come to so sparse, lame, and impotent a conclusion. That is the nature of travel writing, whether professional or amateur. On the first night of any voyage, ink and paper are at a premium and the saloon bar is full of passengers scribbling page after page in their journals. Everything is fresh and novel and fascinating and must be minutely dissected in print.

But on the final leg of any protracted voyage, the inkwells have crusted over, the stack of ship's stationery in the purser's cabin is foxy with coal dust and damp, and nothing seems worthy of note. If the heavens should open and the Archangel Michael appear in the sky above the ship, sounding his trump astride a fiery meteor, no one would deem it worth the trouble and time it would take to exhume his journal from the bottom of his valise, where it molders under dirty laundry and forgotten tidbits of exotic food stuffs. Oh, the most verbose and indefatigable old lady diarist might jot down, "seas v. rough, trifle again for dessert, M. in sky." But that is all.

I have contracted a curious malady, a sort of omnibus affliction of the various humors that combines the symptoms of the influenza, the flux, the grippe, and the fantods. This is also commonplace among travelers: those who do not get sick the first week will certainly succumb by the last. But all is for the best. The enforced idleness of illness has afforded me the luxury of protracted meditations and prayerful cogitations on the State of Man, mostly while enthroned in the water closet.

I must have a prodigious quantity of mind; it can take me as much as two weeks to make it up. I have come to the same conclusion as Saint Paul, that it is better for man to wed than to burn; or for that matter to drip, to wheeze, to evacuate, to cough, to sneeze, or to freeze with the chills. During my illness I have experienced all or most of these options, and have been nursed back into health by the most excellent attentions of my beloved Marina. She has impressed upon me the fact, obvious lo these many years to everyone around me, starting with my mother, that I need a helpmate and a keeper. I assured her that I have held the position open so long, only in hopes of finding the perfect applicant, and that I am pleased to report that she fits the bill in every particular.

In short, I have decided to wed and the woman for once agrees with me. And that now colors my every waking moment. In the glow of restored health and anticipation of domestic bliss to come, I float through the days without a care. I scarcely notice the insufferable idiocies of Alta California's tribunals as they tangle and confuse my affairs. When my court-appointed lawyer shows up late and drunk and dribbles snuff down his coat and asks me the same questions for the fifth time, I just smile.

And so as my faith in democracy and common sense sinks slowly in the West, and my suspicion of monarchs and bureaucrats rises fierce and fiery as ever in the East, and my native negativity and pessimism rest dormant in the North, and my newfound hope for the future basks in the sunny South, I bid fond farewell to both empires of the left hand coast. May they enjoy the passage of arms to which they have so frequently invited each other; may they revel in every discordant note of the symphony of war about to be played; and may they devour a minimum of their people in the process.

Your matrimonial correspondent,

Mark Twain

### 100. Betrothed at Last

Mary Clemens
17 Thatcher Street
Davis, Missouri
U.S.A.
August 23, 1879

Dear Mother:

How are you? I hope this finds you well and in good spirits. I am fine and dandy: clear eyed and sober, cheerful of outlook, digestion regular as grandfather's clock.

I cannot thank you enough for the copy of Reverend Iskey's sermon. I found it very inspiring and enlightening, especially the parts about filial piety and the relation between the Father and the Son.

Once again it has been too long since I wrote you. I have no excuse but the press of business, which has been extremely burdensome recently. My letters to the Atlantic have stirred up a power of interest, and created some unforeseen demands on my time that have robbed me of many precious hours that I would rather devote to domestic correspondence.

Please do not be alarmed if any news has reached you about my recent departure from Rossland. I was in Sakrametska, the capital, when the Tsar was assassinated. The local papers gleefully covered all foreigners' normal travel arrangements as if they were fleeing the country. It's true my Atlantic pieces have been somewhat critical of the regime and that they were not sad to see me go, but at no time was I in any danger or even inconvenience.

I was more than ready to leave Rossland, anyway. My only fond memory of that country is that I met my fiancée there. Yes, it is true—I am finally to be married! Her name is Marina Miranova, of the Fortress Ross Miranovas. Marina comes from a long line of Californians and Russians with connections on both sides of the border. However, she is an only child, and her parents have both passed away, so she is most willing to return to the Islands to set up housekeeping there with me.

That is our plan. We shall be married in Honolulu, by Bishop Staines, if he has gotten over the jokes I published about him last fall. I deeply wish you could be present for our nuptials, but am painfully aware of the many impediments: the vast distance, the need on our part for haste due to some jurisdictional and diplomatic complications, your vow after our dear Henry's accident never to set foot on a steamboat, and so on. We shall have to visit you in Missouri very soon, perhaps in spring. I can just see you and Marina sipping tea, nibbling on lady fingers, passing summary judgment on the affairs of the day, and parsing gossip in your parlor.

I wish my friend John Sargent would be my best man, but

he must return to France, where he plans to enter his portrait of me in the *Salon de Paris*. It's a stunner, and I plan to pay him well for it out of the advance for my next book. I have made a photograph of the painting and will send it to you when I can develop the plate. You will have to imagine the colors, though.

Life is full and exciting for me, the most fortunate of men: soon to be married; enjoying good health, a loving mother, close friends; looking forward to getting home and working on my next book.

Your loving son,

Sam

### 101. A Tramp Abroad?

William Dean Howells
Atlantic Weekly
Boston, Massachusetts, USA
August 8, 1879

Dear William:

I have at last granted to John Sargent the boon of painting my portrait, with the understanding that it will not be one of those constipated European funerary markers that paper the walls of Italian museums and English manor houses. I shall miss John when we must go our separate ways; he is a talented youngster and a man of unusual parts whom I am proud to call a friend and fellow artist, and who I predict will go far. I am almost sorry for making fun of him in print. He's painting me with my trusty *pistola*, in my favorite cavalry coat, but he has got the color all wrong. Before we leave, I hope to get Jaime Roldolfo to make an engraving of the painting, for you to use in the newspaper some day, and for the frontispiece in the new book.

What do you think of the title, *A Tramp Abroad*? It seems a likely consequence to *Innocents Abroad*. On the voyage back home I will get busy on the connective material needed for the book version of my dispatches. I know already that I will remove many references to the mere getting from one place to another, especially by boat. One reviewer said of *Innocents Abroad* that it was "full of brawn and marrow." But I now disagree. When the Lord finished the world, he pronounced it good. That is what I said about my first work, too. But Time, I tell you, Time takes the confidence out of these incautious opinions. It is more than likely that God thinks about the world, now, pretty much as I think about *Innocents Abroad*: there is a trifle too much water in both.

I will be glad to get shut of Alta California. They are too litigious and concerned with the letter of the law, especially as it applies to yours truly. On top of my illegal entry difficulties, Hilario Amado has brought suit against me for canceling some lectures, appropriating some trifling sums to cover my expenses, and for incurring advertising and hall rental expenses in his name—expenses that were properly his by contract. I was forced to hire a lawyer, who blandly advises a counter suit for breach of contract and to recover other cash expenses out of pocket. When the dust settles I predict that this whole trip will have made no money for Twain, no money for Amado, and considerable money for two lawyers.

While John has been daubing at my portrait, I have been blackmailing his royalist friend, Goya the Younger. He is an old rascal, but he put me in touch with the best forger in San Francisco, who created for Marina a credible passport and visa that will get her safely back to the Sandwich Islands. There we will be married, conferring American citizenship and allowing her to acquire bona fide papers. Would have done it here, were there advantage to it; but AC does not believe in citizenship conferred by marriage, so there is no use marrying hastily. I have promised her a big church wedding with the bishop of Honolulu presiding. I still hold his marker from a poker game, so I can deliver on that promise.

She has become my Muse. Her dilemma of double agentry has put me in a mind to write about twins. Her mixed parentage and feelings of not belonging have made me think about a book concerning someone drastically out of place and time. After that, maybe something about fugitives on a raft.

Knowing that this letter incriminates my fiancée, I shall entrust it to her tender hands to deliver to the Post Office without detours to any quaint olde spy shop on the way. We sail day after tomorrow, so the next time you hear from yours truly, he will be writing under a palm tree with his bare feet in the sand. Please do not allow me to take another of these trips, not ever.


Your weary friend,


Mark


## 102. Homeward Bound


Mary Sargent, c/o Sanderson
Apartments Genessee
10 Clarastrasse
Berne, Switzerland
August 8, 1879


Dear Mother:

Thank you for the money you sent. It was waiting for me in San Francisco at the Western Union office, just as you said it would be. I was delighted to receive it, you may believe me.

Our travel arrangements from Sakrametska to San Francisco were terribly difficult, with missed connections and lost luggage. Having your funds to draw on was very helpful.

At last I am ready for the next *Salon*. I sail for the canal on the day after tomorrow, and I shall reach Paris by the 16th. I have retrieved the canvases I had in storage here, and a carpenter made up a large crate for them. Tomorrow I will pack them away in feathers and pine shavings. At this point, I intend to enter two canvases into consideration for the *Salon* —the Twain Portrait and the Clam Gatherers I painted in Tomales Bay. I think there is a good chance that both will be accepted. The Twain portrait has everything the judges look for in style and execution, including a subject sufficiently *outré* to attract the *gazettieres*, and sufficiently famous to show that *Beaux Arts* can still produce commercially successful *portraiteurs*. The Clam Gatherers should appeal to the new Democrats, and if not, the handling of light combined with the realism of the drawing will make it stand out in the *Salon de Refusés* exhibition.

Alta California and Rossland have opened my eyes to the several ways society may be organized, and the wide variety of lives that people may live, rich and poor, powerful and weak, sophisticated and simple. I have had an interesting time, but I am ready to return to safe and predictable Europe, where we can count on the military might of Switzerland to keep the peace.

Please give my fondest regards to Papa and the rest of the family. I expect to have settled my affairs in Paris by mid-October, and look forward to an extended holiday with you all in Italy.


Your loving son,


John

## 103. The Portrait

Marina and I stopped by John's room to say goodbye to him and to my portrait. It was leaning against an enormous wooden crate in the center of a room awash in feathers and shavings. John was running his fingertips over the surface with his eyes closed.

"It is barely dry enough," he said. "I used as much turpentine as I dared and painted it leaner than I should, but the surface is still awfully tender."

"I reckon I should have told dryer jokes while you were painting it," I said, admiring my own form on the canvas. I liked how the light glinted off my eyeballs and gun barrels.

Marina rubbed my cheek. "His skin is often damp, and very tender," she said, "so you have captured his essence."

"Oh posh," I said.

John stepped back from the painting. "Yes, I think there is something about the eyes, the shifty way they droop and don't quite focus, that suggests a very tender, sensitive feeling."

They went on in this vein for some time, but they could not provoke me.

"What say you, Mark?" John asked, "Have I expressed your essence? Have I frozen your most characteristic expression in time and revealed your true feelings?"

"It vexes me," I replied soberly, "to hear people talk so glibly of 'feeling,' and 'expression' in conversations concerning pictures. Those are easily acquired and inexpensive terms that mean nothing."

John glanced at Marina and raised his eyebrow. I knew they were laughing at me, but I didn't care. I was in good spirits and forged ahead anyhow:     "There is not one man in five thousand that can tell what a pictured face is intended to express."

"Nonsense," Marina said, "I can easily tell what you are thinking in this picture. You are challenging the viewer to a duel."

"No, no," John said, "He is trying to remember where he put

his bullets."

They were both unlearnable, but I persevered in making my point: "What's more, there is not one man in five hundred that can go into a court-room and be sure that he will not mistake some harmless innocent of a juryman for the black-hearted assassin on trial. Yet such people talk of 'character' and presume to interpret 'expression' in pictures."

Marina started tickling me and said, "Oh Marky, save it for the rubes. You know you look like a literary lion and a black-hearted assassin, and a fine figure of a man. John has done you proud and you should just admit it."

"Never," I said. "It doesn't do to encourage us artist types. It only makes us stuck up and swell-headed. We get so far above ourselves our feet don't reach the ground anymore."

John said to Marina, "Be careful how much fun you have at Mark's expense. Remember that you are not only to be a wife, but also a thinly disguised character in some future *roman a clef.*"

That earned him a swift poke in the shoulder from Marina. I shook hands with John and bade him farewell. "Good luck in Paris," I told him, "you've got what it takes to go far, if they don't hang you first. Watch out for the Philistines and the prigs, and if you find yourself a woman half so fine as my Marina, latch onto her and don't let her go."

"That's right," she said as she hugged him, "A wife is good cover for a man of unusual parts."

We all embraced and I left the room before everything could degenerate into tears and flapdoodle.

**THE END**

## Alternative History Timeline

Events as they occurred in our ordinary universe are in regular type.
**Events as they occurred in the alternate universe of Infidels Abroad are
in bold type.**

1519-1522
Cortes conquers Aztecs, Zapotecs, Mixtecs, etc.

1524
Friars arrive. Cortes asked for mendicant orders such as Franciscans instead
of corrupt secular clergy. He wanted to incorporate Indians into the new
society, not annihilate or enslave them. Allowed himself to be publicly
scourged by monks for his sins to impress the Aztecs with the preeminence
and seriousness of Catholicism.

1531
Apparition of the dark Virgin of Guadalupe to Juan Diego, denied and
resisted by local Bishop Zumarraga. **Confirmed as a full miracle by
Zumarraga. Founding event of the Western Church.**

1540-47
Cortes' lieutenants warp his original vision and begin to massacre and
subjugate Indians.

1547
Cortes dies. **Cortes lives three more years and purges the most vicious
of his lieutenants.**

1550-1750
200 years of gradual expansion and ruin of Indians. New Spain struggles
along as old Spain declines as a world power. Many greedy and corrupt
viceroys rule.

**1550-1750**
**New Spain becomes a haven for free thinkers, religious dissidents,
Spanish *conversos* Jews and Moors fleeing the Inquisition. The Western
Spanish Church fights constantly with Rome, refusing to institute
many practices of the Spanish Inquisition.**
1578
Russian Cossacks attack the Tartars and begin expanding to the east toward
Siberia.

**1600**
**Spanish playwright Félix Lope de Vega y Carpio arrives in Monterrey for the premiere of his play *La Hermosurea de Angelica.* Stays to become the father of Alta California Theater.**

1742
Russian Cossack expansion reaches Kamchatka and fur traders start exploring islands in the Bering Sea.

1750
Junipero Serra, age 37, arrives in Mexico City. Teaches and works among Indians there for the next 17 years. **Has a St. Paul experience, departs for upper California 12 years earlier. Becomes Pope Innocent I of the Western Church in a schism from the Roman papacy. As Pope, he is dedicated to the spiritual and political sovereignty of the indigenous people.**

1767
Jesuits expelled from Mexico. **Some sneak north to join Serra, providing the Franciscans with the political and economic savvy they need to prepare for independence from Spain and autonomy from Mexico City. Painter Francisco Goya immigrates to San Francisco to paint portraits of the prosperous upper classes.**

1769
Portola and Serra sent to upper California to colonize it and keep it out of the hands of the Russians and English.

1776
American Revolution. Reform efforts in Mexico fail to break the *gachupin* (settlers born in Spain) monopoly on land ownership. Time is ripe for Mexico to break with Spain. **While Mexico is occupied with becoming independent from Spain, Serra institutes land reform in Alta California, breaking up vast ranchos and redistributing property to a middle class of merchants, farmers, miners, and Indians. Alta California secedes from Mexico.**

1784
Serra dies at age 71. **Succeeded by Innocent II.**
Russian fur traders reach Alaska and start probing south along the coast.

1799
Russians found New Archangel on the site of modern day Sitka.
**They move more quickly south, establishing colonies in present day Washington and Oregon, building Fortress Ross in California in 1802 rather than 1812.**

1803
U. S. president Jefferson sends James Monroe to Paris to buy the port of New Orleans from Napoleon. Monroe negotiates the $15 million Louisiana Purchase, essentially the entire Mississippi watershed.
**Under pressure from eastern seaboard senators who want to limit the number of potential new states in the union, Monroe buys only the port for $4 million. Napoleon peddles the rest to Spain and Russia, who want a large buffer between their west coast settlements and the USA.**

**1810-1823**
Mexico's war of independence from Spain. Mexican leaders were Hidalgo, then Morales, then Iturbide. Morales wrote a republican constitution and convened a fairly representative congress, but Iturbide defeated him, weakened the constitution and the congress, declared himself emperor, was overthrown within a year, and fled to Europe.
**Morales and Iturbide establish a representative, republican form of government. Morales, the Mexican George Washington, is elected by a large middle class as the first civilian president of Mexico in 1819. He is succeeded by Iturbide in 1825.**

**1820**
Sea otter population on the north Pacific coast depleted, Russian fur trade and colonies begin to decline. Foggy, gopher-ridden coastal land around Fortress Ross cannot support the colony of fur hunters turned reluctant farmers.
**Commander Kushov of Fortress Ross moves most of his people to a colony on good arable land in the Sacramento Valley, recruits local Indians as agricultural serfs, and sends many untrainable Kodiak Islanders home.**

**1828**
Russian American Company bankrupt.

1830
**Kushov declares himself Tsar of Rossland, stretching from the Russian River in California north to Vancouver Island. Assassinated by Tsarist agents in 1833. Tsar sends his son Alexander with 1,000 troops to**

**establish a traditional government.**

**1834**

After 11 years of confusion and strife, Santa Anna takes over as military dictator of Mexico.

**Mexicans and Alta Californians no longer need to own land to vote. True land reform breaks up the last of the ranchos. Friars in the north create false birth certificates so that many Indians and mestizos can claim homesteads and exercise their franchise. In the north, United States citizens are expelled unless they renounce the USA and become citizens of the Republic of Alta California. Poor immigrant Yankees become the lowest class, below the peons, below the Indians.**

**1836**

Battle of the Alamo. Texas wins independence from Mexico and is recognized by the USA, England, France, and Belgium as a sovereign nation.

**Texas remains part of Alta California, governed by Santa Anna, who becomes an enemy of USA slavery and sets up an underground railroad for escaped slaves through Louisiana. Many work their way north to Alta Californian provinces of New Mexico, Arizona, & Nevada.**

**1845**

Texas admitted as a state to the USA.

**1846**

USA declares war on Mexico. Doniphan conquers New Mexico and Zachary Taylor captures Monterrey.

**USA never declares war because Mexico and Alta California are too strong. Washington is more isolationist, less expansionist. Manifest Destiny fizzles.**

**1847**

Kearny takes California, Winfield Scott takes Vera Cruz and advances to Mexico City, becomes military governor of Mexico.

**1848**

In the treaty of Guadalupe Hidalgo, Mexico cedes New Mexico, Arizona and California to the USA, gets $15 million, keeps Baja California.

**1849**

Gold discovered by Americans at Sutter's Mill.

1854
**Gold discovered by Californians under General Vallejo in Grass Valley.**

1855
**Gold discovered by Russians on the middle fork of the Sacramento near Buck's Lake. Alta Californians and Russians divide the gold fields at the Yuba River. Since the Gold Rush occurs in a more densely settled and law-abiding area, it is more orderly. Miners are Russian, Indian, Mexican, and Chinese, with very few Americans crossing the Mississippi, the Rockies, and sneaking over the Sierras to take part.**

**1855**
Santa Anna ousted, flees abroad.

**1857**
Juarez becomes president of Mexico, first civilian to rule. Civil war begins in USA. European armies invade Mexico. French take Mexico City in 1863 and install Maximilian Hapsburg as Emperor. Juarez flees to New Orleans and organizes resistance.
**France sends an expeditionary force to Vera Cruz that is soundly trounced by the Mexicans.**

**1865**
USA civil war ends.
**USA civil war drags on until 1871, with guerilla skirmishes and economic collapse. Alta California enters a golden age of building, invention, statesmanship, learning, scholarship, etc. Rossland likewise enjoys gold-funded prosperity, although the wealth is concentrated in the upper classes and the serfs don't see much trickling down.**

**1866**
Mark Twain tours California and Nevada lecturing on life in the Sandwich Islands.
**Twain tours New York and Massachusetts lecturing on the Sandwich Islands.**

**1867**
Maximilian executed. Juarez regains power, resumes democratic reform efforts.
Mark Twain contracts to write 50 letters at $20 each for the *Alta California.* His letters become his first book-length work, *"The Innocents Abroad."*
**Twain writes letters for the Atlantic Weekly, William Dean Howells' newspaper in Boston.**

**1871**
Mark Twain settles in Hartford and takes up the literary life.
**Twain returns to Sandwich Islands to escape war-torn and
economically depressed USA.**

**1872**
Juarez dies. Porforio Diaz overthrows his legally elected successor and
becomes dictator in 1876.

1876
**In a close and fraudulent election, Ulysses S. Grant secures a second
term as president of the USA. Reconstruction flounders in the south,
inflation and stock panics plague the economy, and several western
states are under martial law.**

**1879**
Mark Twain, age 44 and newly married, is living on royalties from *Tom
Sawyer*, touring and lecturing, working on *A Tramp Abroad.*
John Singer Sargent, age 23, has just finished his studies at the Beaux Arts
school in Paris, and has exhibited *Oyster Gatherers* to great acclaim at the
Paris Salon. Tours Spain and Italy looking for fresh subject matter for salon
paintings, aiming to build his reputation and attract portrait commissions.
**USA recovers economically from civil war. William Dean Howells,
editor of the *Atlantic Weekly*, contacts his friend Mark Twain in the
Sandwich Islands, where he has been living, unmarried, to escape the
war. Twain has been invited to lecture on the islands and his European
travels in Alta California, and Howells commissions him to extend his
tour to include Rossland to the north, so that he can contribute a series
of letters to the *Weekly* describing the Mexican and Russian coastal
empires.**

      **John Singer Sargent is taking an around-the-world trip,
sketching and painting, looking for exotic subjects to exhibit in Paris
and London. He meets Twain on the ship from the Sandwich Islands
to San Francisco. They agree to travel together for a while, Singer
wanting to paint Twain's portrait and Twain wanting to use singer as a
tenderfoot character to write about in his *Atlantic Weekly* letters.**

**Photographs**

**Chapter**

## About the Author

Patrick Fanning is a writer and painter living in Sonoma County, California. For years he has painted plein air watercolors and oils of the local landscape, amusing himself by making up a fantasy version of the county's history.

This novel explores that fantasy landscape in the personas of his favorite writer, Mark Twain, and his favorite painter, John Singer Sargent. You can see full color versions of the watercolors and oil paintings illustrating this book at www. fanningartworks.com